BEVERLY LEWIS

SummerHill Secrets · 1

BEVERLY LEWIS

SummerHill Secrets · 1

SummerHill Secrets: Volume 1
Copyright © 1995, 1996, 2007
Beverly Lewis

Cover design by Eric Walljasper
Cover landscape photography © 2006 Ed Heaton

Previously published in five separate volumes:
Whispers Down the Lane © 1995 Beverly Lewis
Secret in the Willows © 1995 Beverly Lewis
Catch a Falling Star © 1995 Beverly Lewis
Night of the Fireflies © 1995 Beverly Lewis
A Cry in the Dark © 1996 Beverly Lewis

Published by Bethany House Publishers
11400 Hampshire Avenue South
Bloomington, Minnesota 55438

Bethany House Publishers is a division of
Baker Publishing Group, Grand Rapids, Michigan.

Printed in the United States of America by Bethany Press International, Bloomington, MN
November 2009, 16th printing

Library of Congress Cataloging-in-Publication Data

Lewis, Beverly.
    SummerHill secrets 1. / Beverly Lewis.
       p. cm.
    Summary: Fifteen-year-old Merry Hanson, living amongst the Amish in rural Lancaster County, Pennsylvania, relies on her Christian faith to guide her through such challenging situations as the physical abuse of her schoolmate, an arson investigation, a car accident, and an abandoned baby.
    Contents: v. 1. Whispers down the lane — Secret in the willows — Catch a falling star — Night of the fireflies — A cry in the dark
    Notes: "Previously published in five separate volumes"—Copyright p.
  ISBN-13: 978-0-7642-0445-6 (pbk.)
  ISBN-10: 0-7642-0445-9 (pbk.)
    1. Country life—Pennsylvania—Lancaster County—Juvenile fiction. 2. Country life—Pennsylvania—Lancaster County—Fiction. 3. Amish—Fiction. 4. Christian life—Fiction. 5. Conduct of life—Fiction. 6. Lancaster County (Pa.)—Fiction. I. Title
  PZ7.L58464 Sum   2007
  [Fic]—dc22

2007028932

About the Author

BEVERLY LEWIS, born in the heart of Pennsylvania Dutch country, fondly recalls her growing-up years. A keen interest in her mother's Plain family heritage has inspired Beverly to set many of her popular stories in Amish county, beginning with her inaugural novel, *The Shunning*.

A former schoolteacher and accomplished pianist, Beverly has written over eighty books for adults and children. Five of her block-buster novels have received the Gold Book Award for sales over 500,000 copies, and *The Brethren* won a 2007 Christy Award.

Beverly and her husband, David, make their home in Colorado, where they enjoy hiking, biking, reading, writing, making music, and spending time with their three grandchildren.

Books by Beverly Lewis

GIRLS ONLY (GO!)*
Youth Fiction

Girls Only! Volume One
Girls Only! Volume Two

SUMMERHILL SECRETS†
Youth Fiction

SummerHill Secrets Volume One
SummerHill Secrets Volume Two

HOLLY'S HEART
Youth Fiction

Holly's Heart Collection One†
Holly's Heart Collection Two†
*Holly's Heart Collection Three**

www.BeverlyLewis.com

*4 books in each volume   † 5 books in each volume

Whispers Down the Lane

To
my aunt Ada Reba,
who held my little hand
long ago ...
and whispered a prayer.

Happy is the house that shelters a friend.

—RALPH WALDO EMERSON

A cry rang out in the stillness.

"Merry Hanson!"

I jerked into consciousness, tense and trembling. Sitting up, I peered out at my moonlit bedroom through sleep-filled eyes, listening. The gentle, steady purr of kittens filled the peaceful quiet. Their soft, warm bodies snuggled close on top of the comforter as I moved my feet.

Must be a dream. I leaned back onto my pillow, my body stiff from the rude awakening.

Then in the silence, I heard it again. A determined voice, quivering with desperation. "Merry, please wake up!"

Stumbling from the bed, I dashed to the window and looked out. Shadows played beneath the white light of a full November moon. One shadow stood out from the others and moved slowly toward the house.

I bumped my nose against the cold window as I stared down at a fragile-looking figure. Light from the moon had turned her wheat-colored hair almost white. I drew in a quick breath. *Lissa Vyner!*

Straining, I lifted the storm window and poked my head out into the frosty Pennsylvania night. Squinting down from the second story of our hundred-year-old farmhouse, I tried to brush the sleep away. My school friend was crouched near the old maple.

"Lissa, what are you doing out there?" I called to her in a hushed voice. Shivers danced up and down my arms.

She pulled her jacket against her body. "C-can I sp-spend the n-n-night?" she pleaded, tears in her voice.

"Meet me around back." I closed the window and scrambled for my fleece-lined slippers and robe. Shadrach and Meshach, my two golden-haired kittens, were curled up on it. "Sorry, little boys," I whispered, pulling it out from under their drowsy heads. "Where's Abednego?" *That ornery cat is always missing,* I thought.

Silently, I slipped down the hallway and past my older brother's room to the stairs. I didn't dare let Skip in on this thing with Lissa, especially since he was in charge while Mom and Dad were overseas on a mission trip.

I stopped in my tracks as I came within a few feet of the kitchen. Shafts of light streamed into the hallway. It meant only one thing. My know-it-all brother was still up—the last person I wanted to bump into on a night like this!

Tiptoeing closer, I peeked around the door. He was stuffing his face with the leftovers from supper. This could be tricky—smuggling Lissa into the house without Skip knowing.

He glanced up. "Hey, feline freak. Can't ya sleep?"

I ignored him, heading for the back door.

"Sleepwalking, Mer?" he persisted.

"What?" I muttered, pulling the curtains to one side and peering out. Skip smacked disgustingly on a meat loaf sandwich while I devised a way to distract him.

"You should be in bed," he demanded.

I whirled around. "*You're* still up!"

"Don't get smart, cat breath." Skip gulped down half a glass of milk in one swallow.

In a flash, I remembered Abednego, my wayward kitten. Genius! I turned the doorknob and stepped outside.

"Hey, close that door!" Skip yelled.

"Lost my cat," I said, pulling the door shut. Casting a fleeting glance over my shoulder, I went in search of Lissa. Around the side of the house, near a stack of firewood, I found her.

"I s-saw the l-light in the k-kitchen," she stammered. "D-Didn't want t-to—"

"C'mon, it's awful cold." I led her around to the long front porch. "Wait here—I'll go through the house and open the door."

Meow!

I leaned over and spotted two shining eyes under the porch.

Then I heard Skip calling, "Merry, get your cat tail in here!"

My heart pounded as I scooped Abednego into my arms. Lifting his black furry body to my face, I darted around the house and into the kitchen.

"That's one fat cat," Skip said, casting a scornful look my way. "Too bad you found him."

I shot him a fake smile. No time to argue; Lissa was waiting, half frozen to death on the front porch.

Cuddling Abednego, I spoke in my best baby talk. "Hello, my pwecious little boy."

Skip groaned. "Are there any strays that *don't* live here?"

"Good night," I snapped, turning to go. When I was safely out of Skip's sight, I dashed for the front door with Abednego still in my arms.

Lissa moaned softly as I let her in.

"Follow me," I whispered.

We sneaked up the stairs to my room. This wasn't going to be a typical sleepover. Lissa's eyes were swollen from crying, her bottom lip cracked and bleeding. And she was limping!

Two Whispers Down the Lane

Back inside my bedroom, I put Abednego down and locked the door. Lissa sat on my bed while I turned on the lamp. "I'll get something for your lip," I said, hurrying to the bathroom adjoining my room.

Lissa was pulling off her jacket and scarf when I returned with damp tissues. Her tennies were stiff from the cold.

"Here, this'll help." I gave her the wet tissues. "Careful. Don't press too hard."

She nodded as if to thank me, holding the crumpled wad on her bottom lip. Tentatively, she glanced around the room, taking note of the wall nearest her. It was covered with framed photography—some of my very best. Lissa was shaking, so I turned up the controls on the electric blanket.

"You'll warm up fast in here," I said, pulling back the blanket and the blue hand-quilted comforter, the latter a gift from my Amish neighbors down the lane.

Lissa crawled into bed, jeans and all.

I searched in the closet for my sleeping bag and rolled it out on the floor next to the bed. "If we're quiet, Skip'll never know you're here."

Lissa looked at me sadly through the slits in her puffy eyelids. She dabbed her lip gently.

I sat on top of my sleeping bag, worried for my friend. "You're really hurt, aren't you?"

She squeaked, "Uh-huh," in an uncontrollable voice. Tears filled her eyes.

"What happened tonight?"

Her shoulders heaved under the blankets as she buried her head in my pillow. The wad of wet tissues rolled out of her hand and onto the floor.

"Talk to me, Liss," I said, kneeling up, stroking her back. I hoped her answer wasn't something truly horrible.

Minutes passed. Except for an occasional sob, the room was silent. At last, she looked at me with tearful blue eyes. "My dad got mad."

A lump caught in my throat just as Abednego jumped onto the bed. I moved the cat trio one by one on top of the little lumps made by Lissa's feet.

She eased back against the pillow. "I freak out, Merry. I freak when my dad's drunk." She wiped the tears. "I can't go home anymore."

Pulling the covers up around her chin, I tucked her in like she was a helpless little child. "Don't worry, Lissa, I'll think of something. Maybe we can talk to the school counselor tomorrow."

"I can't go to school," she blurted. "People will be looking for me."

"Which people?" I sat on the edge of the bed.

"Maybe the cops," she whispered. "I'm a runaway, aren't I?" She watched the kittens congregate at her feet.

"What about your mom? She'll be worried."

"I told her I'd leave someday." Lissa stopped.

"What about the history test? You can't skip out on *that*. Mr. Wilson's make-up tests are hideous." I was groping at thin air. Anything to talk sense into her.

She sighed. "I need your help, Merry."

"What can I do?" I whispered.

"Keep me safe." She touched me. "Please?"

I looked down at her hand on my arm. "Don't you have any relatives in Lancaster?" It was a long shot.

She shook her head.

I pulled my left earring out, glanced at it, and put it right back in. "What about your grandma?" I asked.

"She lives in Philadelphia now," Lissa said.

I pushed my hair back, taking a deep breath. Lissa was asking a lot, especially with my parents gone. I started to speak, to set her straight about what I should and shouldn't do, but tears began to flow unchecked down her cheeks.

"Okay, Liss," I said, "but only for tonight." I clicked off the blue-and-white striped lamp on the table beside the bed, hoping I was doing the right thing.

In the darkness, my friend pleaded, "Promise to keep my secret?"

I shuddered at what it meant. If Mom and Dad were back from their mission trip, they'd know exactly what to do. I pushed my fingers through the length of my hair and crawled into my sleeping bag. A moonbeam played hide-and-seek as a cloud drifted by.

Lissa reached her hand out to me. "Merry . . . please?"

A feeling of determination flooded me as I took her cold hand in both of mine. "Don't worry. You can count on me."

I stared at a small photo on the far wall. Small but distinct, the picture was a close-up of a gravestone covered with yellow daisies. The gravestone reminded me of another place, another time. A time when I could've helped but didn't.

I hardly slept the rest of the night. I'd given my word to hide Lissa and keep her secret. A secret bigger than us both.

I awakened the next morning to pounding. "Get up, Merry! You're going to be late!" Skip hollered through the door. "Don't you know people die in bed?"

I groaned, then bolted upright, glancing up from my sleeping bag. Lissa was still asleep. Thank goodness for locked bedroom doors!

"Last call, cat breath," my big brother called. "Or you're history!"

History—Mr. Wilson's test! I dragged my limp legs from the sleeping bag as the events of last night came rushing back. I hurried into the bathroom adjoining my room and turned on the shower. Reaching for a clean washcloth and a bar of soap, I lathered up, remembering the first day I'd met Lissa Vyner.

It was eighth grade. Last year. I'd taken first place in the photography contest at Mifflin Junior High School. Felt pretty smug about it, too. It was a high that set me sailing into second semester. That's when the new girl showed up in my class—a pretty girl—with hair the color of wheat at harvest. As for her broken arm, she'd blamed it on being accident prone.

Lissa was also quite forgetful when it came to necessary things, which I discovered after our first P.E. class together. The teacher had insisted on everyone hitting the showers, sweaty or not. But Lissa had forgotten her soap. And a hairbrush!

The next day, I came to her rescue again. This time it was a matter of life and death. She'd misplaced her red pen, and red pens were essential equipment in Miss Cassavant's math class. *"If you aren't prepared to grade your classmate's homework, you aren't prepared for life,"* the flamboyant Miss Cassavant would say.

Soon Lissa and I became good friends. Occasionally, she confided in me about her family. She felt lonely at home and hated being the only child. Lissa hated something else, too. The way her dad drank. The way it changed him. Now all of it made sense: her frequent black eyes, her broken arm . . .

A knock on the bathroom door startled me. "Thought you'd left," Lissa whispered as she crept in.

I peeked around the steamed-up shower door. "Sleep okay?"

"I think so," she said. "Mind if I use your brush?" She leaned close to the mirror, untying her yellow hair ribbon before brushing her wavy, shoulder-length hair. "It feels good being here, Mer. It's as if I have a real sister."

Grabbing my towel, I sighed and wrapped it around me. I didn't want to think about sisters. Real or not. "I've come up with a solution," I said, changing the subject.

Lissa kept brushing her hair.

"First of all, help yourself to anything you'd like to wear in my closet while I get something for us to eat. And . . . could you just hang out in my room today?"

Lissa nodded, holding my brush in midair.

"Now, be sure to keep the bedroom door locked just in case," I continued, reaching for my bathrobe. "We'll talk more after school, okay?" It was the best I could do on such short notice—a rather boring scheme, not the creative kind I was known for—but at least she'd be well hidden.

"What about your brother?" she asked.

I wrapped my hair in a towel. "Don't worry. Skip has intramurals on Tuesdays, so we're set."

Lissa wandered out of the bathroom over to my white corner bookcase and reached for a poetry book.

"Help yourself," I said, spying the book she held. "That one's pure genius."

"I thought only bleeding hearts read poetry."

"*I* read it," I said. "And I'm far less anguished than you think." A few strands of hair escaped, tickling my shoulders with water drops. I pushed them into the towel and investigated my wardrobe.

"Remember, don't tell anyone at school where I am, or I'm doomed!" There was desperation in Lissa's voice.

"Count on it," I said, choosing my favorite sweater, a delicious coral color. It made my chestnut brown hair and eyes look even darker. Aunt Teri had knit it for my fifteenth birthday, September 22—almost two months ago. Confidence exuded from the sweater. Some clothes were like that. Maybe it was because Aunt Teri, creative and lovely, was so confident herself, despite being completely deaf. Anyway, I needed this sweater today for more than one reason.

Lissa sat on my bed, paging through the poetry book. Just then Abednego raised his sleepy head and made a beeline for my friend. "Hey," she said, giggling, "look at you, big guy." She patted his head.

"He's super picky about his friends." I watched in amazement as Abednego let her hold him.

"I know just what you need," she said, carrying him into the bathroom. When they came out, Abednego was wearing Lissa's yellow hair ribbon around his chubby neck.

"You look very handsome," Lissa cooed into his ear. Then she put him down, headed back into the bathroom, and closed the door.

"Boy cats don't wear hair ribbons," I muttered, quite puzzled at Abednego's obvious interest in Lissa.

The phone rang and I hurried down the hallway to Skip's room.

"How's every little thing today?" came the scratchy voice as I answered the phone. The voice belonged to Miss Spindler, our neighbor around the corner. Mom had asked her to check on us while she and Dad were gone. And check up, she did. In fact, the last few days she'd been calling nonstop, even showing up nearly every evening with some rich, exotic dessert.

"We're fine, thanks," I reassured her.

"Anything you need?" came the next question.

I thought of Lissa. I'd be crazy to let Miss Spindler in on our secret. "I think we're set here, but thanks," I said, discouraging her from coming over today.

"Well, just give a holler if you think of anything you need."

"Okay, I will . . . if we need anything." I hung up the phone, heading back to the bedroom. "I need my hair dryer, Lissa," I called through a crack in the bathroom door.

No answer. I paused, waiting for her reply.

"Lissa, you okay?" I knocked and waited a moment, then lightly touched the door. Slowly, it opened to reveal ugly welts and bruises on Lissa's right thigh. I cringed in horror.

Startled, she tried to cover up her leg.

"I-I'm sorry," I said.

Silence hung between us, and then she started to cry. Deep, heart-wrenching sobs.

I ached for Lissa. "How did this happen?" I asked, squelching my shock.

"You'll never believe it." She kept her head down.

"Try me, Liss."

"I fell down the steps."

Anger swelled inside me. Not toward her, but toward whoever had done this. "Now, how about the truth," I whispered.

Wincing, she stood up. "It's a long, long story."

"I should call our family doctor." I leaned on the doorknob, hurting for my friend.

"Right, and I'll end up in some lousy foster home. No thanks, I've already been *that* route."

The impact of her words sent my mind reeling. "A foster home?"

"Two years ago." She said it through clenched teeth.

"What happened?"

"What do you think?" She sighed. "Now things are even worse with my dad at the police department. He's got every one of those cops fooled."

I didn't know what to say. Lissa's father was a policeman, too, so he was supposed to be one of the good guys.

Lissa's words interrupted my thoughts. "If caseworkers get involved," she added, "they'll eventually send me back home, and he'll beat me up again."

My throat turned to cotton.

"I hate my dad." Tears spilled down her cheek. "And Mom, too, for not making it stop."

I wanted to wave a wand and make things better for my friend. "I'm so sorry," I said, determined more than ever to take care of her.

Abruptly, Lissa stood up, reaching for the shower door. "He'll never hit me again." By the cold stiffness in her voice, I knew the conversation was over.

Four Whispers Down the Lane

Frustrated and terribly worried, I mentioned breakfast. Lissa needed something nourishing, but I had only enough time to grab some juice and sticky buns.

While in the kitchen, I filled the cats' dishes with their favorite tuna food. They crowded around, nosing their way into the breakfast delight.

I washed my hands before putting three sticky buns—two for Lissa, one for me—and two glasses of orange juice on a tray. Then I headed up the back stairs.

Lissa was sitting on the bed admiring my wall gallery when I came into the room. "When did you start taking pictures?" She studied a tall picture of a willow tree in the springtime.

I set the tray down on the bed. "I won a cheap camera for selling the most Girl Scout cookies in first grade," I explained. "Taking pictures started out as a hobby, but somehow it's become an obsession."

"Your shots are great," she said, reaching for a glass of juice.

I gathered up my books and found my digital camera, one of three cameras in my collection, lying on the desk near the window.

"Taking more pictures today?" she asked.

"I like to have a camera handy at all times. You never know when a picture might present itself."

A pensive smile crossed Lissa's face.

"Let's pray before I catch the bus," I suggested.

Lissa seemed surprised. "Why?"

"Because I care about you. And God does, too."

She smiled weakly, then nodded her consent.

After the prayer, Lissa wiped her eyes. "That was sweet, Merry. My grandmother talks to God, too. I wish I could be more like her . . . and you."

"I don't always do the right thing." *After all, how smart is harboring a runaway?* "Don't forget to lock this door when I leave." I grabbed the sticky bun and bit into the sugary bread. Then I washed it down with a long drink of orange juice. My mother would worry if she knew I hadn't had a full breakfast today. Oh well, what was one day?

I glanced in the mirror again. "Maybe we should call your grandmother after school. Someone in your family ought to know you're safe."

"I guess I should call," Lissa agreed. "But I don't want Grandma to know where I am."

I thought of the years of abuse Lissa must have endured and nodded my consent.

"You're a true friend, Merry." She sat on my bed like a wistful statue as I turned to go.

———

The school bus was crowded and noisy as usual. I slid in beside Chelsea Davis, another friend from school. She glanced up momentarily, said, "Hey, Mer," then resumed her frantic cramming.

Her thick auburn hair hung halfway down her back. It nearly covered her face on the side facing me. I pulled back the curtain of her shining tresses. "Wilson's test?" I asked, smiling.

"You got it." She didn't look up.

Kids jostled against the seats and the doors swooshed shut. Ignoring the clamor, I centered my thoughts on Lissa's hideous bruises. Why hadn't she told me before that her father could be abusive? I shivered, thinking about the horrible scenes at Lissa's house, surely multiplied many times over. Outraged, I was determined to protect Lissa. Or to somehow get her linked up with her Philadelphia grandmother, the one who talked to God.

Staring out the window, I watched the familiar landmarks on SummerHill Lane. Thick rows of graceful willows separated our property from the Zooks', our Amish neighbors. Acres of rich farmland stretched away from the dirt road. A white fence surrounded their pasture. Near Abe Zook's brick farmhouse, one of his horses, Apple, was being hitched up to a gray buggy.

We zipped past a field of drying brown cornstalks. The oldest Zook boys, Curly John and Levi, were working the field, harvesting the remaining stalks with a mule-drawn corn picker.

I snapped out of my daze when I saw Levi. Tall and just sixteen, Levi was the cutest Amish boy around. I'd saved his life once. He'd nearly drowned in the pond out behind our houses when his foot got caught in some willow roots. It happened the year after my own personal tragedy, when I was eight and Levi was nine. But in my mind, it was as clear as yesterday.

"*I'll get myself hitched up with you someday, Merry Hanson,*" Levi Zook had said. I figured he had beans for brains, since the Amish church forbids baptized Amish from marrying "English," as they called us non-Amish folk.

I leaned toward the window, accidentally bumping Chelsea. She glanced up, half snorting when she spied Levi. "I guess you wanna hand sew all your clothes and survive without electricity for the rest of your life."

"Not me," I said, backing away from the window.

Farther down the lane, we passed the old cemetery, where gravestones lay scattered across a tree-lined meadow. *Stark and lonely.* A lump sprang up in my throat, but I forced it down, purposely looking away.

As we neared the end of the lane, a group of Amish kids, two on scooters and all carrying lunch boxes, waited at the intersection. One boy caught my eye and smiled a toothless grin under the shadow of his black felt hat. It was Aaron Zook, Levi's little brother. I waved.

The bus came to a grinding stop, and the Amish kids crossed, heading for the one-room schoolhouse a half mile away. The older girls held hands with little brothers and sisters as our school bus waited. It set my thoughts spinning back to Lissa. She had no big sister or brother to look after her. Being an only child had to be tough, especially in an abusive family. Waves of worry rushed over me.

At school, I scurried to my locker, wondering how I could concentrate on Mr. Wilson's test with Lissa in such a mess.

Unloading my things, I spied Jonathan Klein coming toward me, wearing a heart-stopping grin. A perpetual honor student, Jonathan always snagged top grades in Mr. Wilson's class. He looked confident enough.

"Merry, mistress of mirth. Ready for Mr. Wilson's wonderful world of terrible, tough, terminal tests?"

I scanned the history outline one last time. "Tearfully trying," I replied, playing our little game.

"Good going." He laughed. "Can you beat this one? Every eventful historical example ends up on Mr. Wilson's engaging exams." The Alliteration Wizard was two jumps ahead of me. His brown eyes sparkled. Looked like he'd had a full night's sleep. No runaways in his closet.

I accompanied him to his locker and tried to conjure up a clever response. Then it spilled out. "Each enormous expanse of energy excites brain cells—" I caught my breath.

Way at the end of the hallway, a police officer—Lissa's father—was marching through the crowd of students. Heading straight for me!

"Jon, quick! Stand in front of me," I said, squeezing into his open locker.

"What're you doing?" His eyes filled with questions.

"Fake it!" I whispered through clenched teeth. "Pretend you're hanging up your jacket." My heart thumped so loudly I just knew the noise would lead Mr. Vyner straight to his target. Me!

Five *Whispers Down the Lane*

I held my breath as seconds sauntered by. At last, I peered around Jonathan's jacket. "The coast is clear."

He looked puzzled. "What was that all about?"

"Say it with all *p*'s," I said, hurrying to first-period history class.

He slammed his locker door. "Hey, not so fast!"

I brushed my hair back and rushed through the hall, cautiously looking in all directions.

Is Mr. Vyner gone? I wondered.

Sneaking around the corner, I made a detour to survey the school office. Yee-ikes! There sat Lissa's father, waiting for the principal.

I could see it now. Mr. Vyner would ask the principal for the names of her best friends, maybe even call them out of class. *"Merry Hanson, please come to the school office. . . ."*

Pins and needles pricked my conscience, and I spent the rest of the day on the verge of hysteria, waiting to hear my name over the intercom.

───

After school, I scrambled onto the school bus. Sliding in beside Chelsea, I tried to avoid Jon by scooting down in my seat. When he boarded the bus, I lowered my head.

"Hiding from someone?" Chelsea whispered, giggling.

"Sh-h!"

"He's coming," she teased.

Jon planted himself in front of us, leaning his arm on the back of the seat. His light brown hair was cropped short, and a cream-colored shirt peeked out of his open jacket. "You can't ignore me all day," he said.

I sat up and pulled a snack-size bag of chips out of my schoolbag. I shot glances at Jon while Chelsea smirked knowingly.

Persistence, a fine trait in a fine guy. And fine was putting it mildly. "That was some history test," I said.

"You're changing the subject," Jon replied.

"What?"

Chelsea pretended to choke. I poked her in the ribs as my handsome interrogator grinned, waiting for an answer.

I sighed. "Things are blurry, bleary, blue. Sorry, I can't share 'em with you."

Jon's brown eyes grew serious. "Coming to the church hayride tonight? Everyone will be there."

Our eyes locked. "I can't." It was a hayride not to be missed. Full moon. Good times. Too bad Jon thought of me only as a friend.

His smile warmed my heart. "The hay wagon's coming right down SummerHill Lane, past your house," he persisted. "We could stop and pick you up."

"I'm sorry, really." I hoped he'd let it drop.

The bus slowed to a crawl as we came up on a horse and buggy. The Amishman sat in the front seat on the right, holding the reins. His wife sat on the left. Two cherub-faced girls stared over the backseat from beneath black bonnets.

"It's the Yoders," Chelsea said, shoving her knees up against the rear of the seat. "My mom drives Mr. Yoder and his business partner to town every day."

The kids behind us jumped up for a better look. "Why don't they just buy a car?" one boy taunted. "Those old buggies are tearing up the roads."

"Relax," Jon told the boy, who was new to the Lancaster area. "They'll be turning off soon." And in a few minutes they did.

The bus sped down the lane past the Amish farms, to my house, one of the few non-Amish residences on the three-mile stretch. The bus groaned to a halt, sending a cloud of dust swirling as I hopped out.

Eager to get back to Lissa, I made a quick stop at the mailbox. Its contents almost spilled out with tons of important-looking mail. A letter from Aunt Teri and Uncle Pete caught my eye.

Dashing into the house, I dumped Dad's mail on the hall table. Checking for any early signs of Skip, I raced upstairs.

"Lissa, I'm home," I called, digging into my jeans pocket for the key to my bedroom.

Inside, I discovered Lissa asleep on my unmade bed, the book of poems open on the floor. The cat trio bounded into the bedroom, nosing their way into my hands as I sat on the floor watching my sleeping friend. I rubbed Abednego's black neck. His gentle purring rose to a rumble. I smiled at the yellow ribbon on his neck, the one Lissa had tied there this morning.

"You look beautiful, little boy," I whispered, hugging him. As usual, Shadrach and Meshach fought for equal time. Once they were settled, I leaned back and pulled my baby album out of the rack on my desk. Opening to the beginning, I found the pages I loved most—the first seven birthdays of my life. I smiled at the photos, fingering the shoulder strap on my camera still in the schoolbag beside me.

The phone's jangling made me jump. I closed the album and pushed the cats out of my lap. Running down the hall to Skip's room, I hoped the phone wouldn't awaken Lissa. It was probably Miss Spindler calling to check on "every little thing."

I picked up the phone. "Hanson residence."

"Is this Merry Hanson . . . on SummerHill Lane?"

My hands perspired. The man's voice sounded familiar. "Who's calling, please?" I asked without revealing my identity, the way my parents had instructed.

"This is Lissa Vyner's father. I wonder if you might be able to help me."

My fingers squeezed the receiver. My lips and throat turned to cotton. Swallowing, I prayed silently, *Lord, guide me!* Then I took a deep breath. "What can I do?" I said, scared he'd hear the quiver in my voice.

He continued, "Lissa is missing and her mother and I are gathering information from her friends. Have you seen her by any chance?"

I hesitated. What would happen if I said the wrong thing and gave away Lissa's secret?

My heart began a fierce pounding, but I spoke slowly. "Yes, I've seen Lissa."

"Where? When?" the frantic questions came.

"Yesterday at school," I replied. It was the truth, at least part of it. Still, I felt guilty.

"Did she say anything to you about running away?"

"No, sir." Again, the truth. But my deceitful words haunted me.

"Well, if you happen to see or hear from her again, I'd appreciate it very much if you'd give me a call. Thank you, Merry. Good-bye."

Confused, I hung up the phone. Lissa's father had always treated me cordially the few times I'd visited there. Now he sounded concerned, almost panic-stricken. Not like a child beater.

I hurried down the hall to my bedroom. Lissa was stretching her arms and yawning as I came in. She sat up, her eyes still puffy and her bottom lip slightly swollen.

"How'd you sleep?" I plopped down on a shaggy rug near the bed.

"I dreamed my dad was out looking for me."

"He is looking for you."

She gasped. "At school?"

I nodded.

"Merry, you didn't talk to him, you didn't—"

"I promised, remember? But . . ."

"But what? Tell me!" Her cheeks were flushed and she leaned forward as if her whole world dangled on a thread.

"Everything's fine, trust me," I began. "But your father just called here a few minutes ago. He sounds very worried."

Lissa pounded her fist into my comforter. "He knows how to do that. Don't you see, Merry? He changes. He fools people!"

The desperate feeling returned. This time it was a jerking, twisting knot deep in the pit of my stomach.

I studied my friend. "Please, Lissa, let's talk to a professional—"

"You don't know what you're saying," she interrupted. "No one can help my dad!" Her eyes glistened. "We've been through all this before."

"Why didn't you tell me?"

Lissa's lips were set. "It's not that easy to talk about."

"And it's hard for me to relate," I whispered. "I'm sorry." Glancing at my blue-striped wall clock, I thought of the long-distance call she needed to make. "It's almost four. We've got about an hour before Skip shows up. Why don't you call your grandmother now?"

Lissa looked at me, tears coming fast.

"Stay here. I'll get the portable phone." I ran downstairs to my dad's study. Poor Lissa. Things just had to work out for her.

Back upstairs, I offered to leave while she made her call. "You could use some privacy," I said.

"No, I can be alone any old time," she replied, punching the numbers on the receiver. "It feels good having you here."

Seconds passed. Then she spoke. "Hi, Grandma, it's Lissa. I miss you like crazy." She sounded sugary sweet. I couldn't help noticing the change in her countenance. It was obvious Lissa loved her grandmother. Trusted her, too.

I sat at my desk, studying Aunt Teri's unopened letter. The words *The Hanson Family* jumped out at me, so I tore open the envelope.

Then without warning, Lissa was sobbing. "I want you to come get me, Grandma," she pleaded. "I can't go back home."

There was a long pause. Her grandmother was probably trying to comfort her. Maybe arranging transportation.

Then I heard, "No, they don't know where I am. Can't you please come?"

I held the letter in my hand, waiting breathlessly for the response. But there was only more pleading from Lissa. My heart throbbed with worry. What if Lissa's grandmother couldn't help?

"It's no use," Lissa cried into the receiver. "Dad's a cop; the police department only sees his good side. They'll never believe me, Grandma. You've got to help me!"

It didn't sound like Lissa's grandmother was going to budge. Now I knew for sure I was in over my head.

Silently, I prayed, *Dear Lord, please help Lissa out of this mess. And help me, too. I want to do the right thing.*

While Lissa continued to talk through her tears, I began to read Aunt Teri's letter. My eyes stopped on the second sentence. I shook my head. "Just what we don't need," I muttered.

Aunt Teri and Uncle Pete were coming to Lancaster on Wednesday night—tomorrow!

I looked up to see Lissa turning off the phone as she scooted off the bed. "Grandma's got her own ideas," she complained. "I guess she doesn't want to get involved this time."

Exasperated, I slipped the letter back into the envelope. "So she's helped you out before?"

"Yeah, but this time she told me to call my mom."

"Sounds like a winner," I replied.

Lissa turned to me, looking horror-stricken. "How can you say that? After everything?"

I stood up, hands on my hips. "I want you to tell me everything, Lissa, starting with last night. Tell me exactly what happened."

She glared at me. "So now you think it's *my* fault." Two giant tears spilled down her cheeks.

"I never said it was your fault, Lissa. I just want you to level with me."

"You won't believe me anyway," she scoffed.

"Whoa, wait a minute. I don't deserve that and you know it," I shot back. "Your grandmother believes you, and she thinks you should call your mother. I happen to agree with her. Rethink what your grandmother said."

"Oh no, you don't. I'm not calling my mom and that's final." Defiance laced her words.

"Your mom deserves to know you're safe, Liss. *I'll* call her."

Lissa shook her head. "You can't do that. We have caller ID."

I groaned. "What about the abuse hotline on TV? You can call them without giving your name."

"They can trace calls from the hotline," she said. "Besides, my dad goes on duty pretty soon. I can't take any chances."

I wished my parents were here. "So much for that idea," I mumbled, thinking about my mother. *What would she do if she were me?*

To begin with, Mom wouldn't have promised Lissa she'd keep her secret. She was smart that way—didn't let people push her into a corner. I missed her now more than ever.

Lissa leaned back against the pillows on my bed, looking thin and frail. She scarcely filled out my clothes. "There's something you don't know," she began. The tone of her voice had gone deep and sad. "It's about my mother."

I shivered, not sure I wanted to know more.

"My dad hits her, too," she said softly. The truth hung heavily between us. "Mom knows all about abuse. But if she can't help herself, how can she help me?"

Her words cut through me. I sighed. "I know someone who can help."

Lissa leaned up on her elbow, an eager look in her eyes.

"My dad's a doctor." I sat on the bed. "He's good friends with this lawyer who goes to our church. My parents'll be home on Thursday—if I can hide you out till then, I guarantee they'll help us."

"That's only two days away," she said, looking more hopeful.

"But there's a problem. My aunt and uncle are coming tomorrow on their way to Pittsburgh."

Lissa looked as frantic as her father sounded on the phone. "What'll we do?"

"Don't worry, I have an idea." I slipped my hair behind my ear, thinking about a plan to hide her. "But there's something we should talk about first."

"What?"

I pulled my camera out of my schoolbag. "This."

"I don't get it." She looked totally confused. "What's the camera for?"

"Your bruises might start fading before my dad gets back," I said. "He'll need documented proof."

Lissa groaned.

"It won't be so bad," I assured her as she exposed the bruise on her thigh. "Now hold still." I took several good close-up shots of her leg, then her swollen lip.

When the cap on the lens was secure, Lissa limped over to my walk-in closet. She opened the door and hobbled inside. "I could hide in here, easy," she announced with a face full of sunshine.

She's desperate, I decided. The closet was spacious, but hardly big enough to set up housekeeping. "It won't work. My aunt and uncle always stay in this room when they come."

A disappointed look replaced her sunny countenance. "What about your parents' room?"

Out of the question. "It's just too risky, but don't worry. I think I know what we can do. C'mon, let's grab a snack. You're hungry, right?"

I helped Lissa down the stairs. She moved slowly, one step at a time. "What's your plan?" she asked.

"I have to work some things out first," I said, holding out my hand to her at the bottom of the staircase.

When we arrived in the kitchen, she stared at the wallpaper. "Your mom must like strawberries." She traced the outline of leaves on the wall.

I laughed, glancing at the strawberry clock and cookie jar to match. "We don't live on the corner of Strawberry Lane and SummerHill for nothing!"

She looked at me. "Merry, merry strawberry," Lissa rhymed.

"Hey, I like that." I got sandwich fixings out of the fridge. "Did I ever tell you how I got my name?"

Lissa shook her head, leaning her elbows on the oval table.

"My parents said I didn't cry when I was born. I laughed!" I spread mayonnaise over two pieces of bread.

She chuckled. "Brain damage?"

"Probably. Mom says they named me just right because I'm a happy person."

Lissa's face turned solemn. "Then I must've bawled my eyes out when I was born, because I've been crying ever since."

"Ham and cheese sandwich comin' up," I announced, ignoring her morbid comment.

She pulled the bread apart and peered inside. "Where're the pickles?"

"Who's boss around here, anyway?"

Her face lit up. "You're wonderful, Merry," she said. "Wouldn't it be fun if we could be sisters somehow?" She bit into her sandwich while I poured a glass of milk for each of us.

So *that's* what Lissa wanted. Not to run away from a family, but to belong to one. Really and truly belong.

I slid the pickle jar out of the fridge. "I had a sister once. A twin sister."

A frown appeared on Lissa's face.

"Faithie died of leukemia when we were seven. It seems so long ago, it's hard to know if my memories of her come from pictures and what my parents say, or if they're my own." I cut a pickle lengthwise.

"Did she look like you?" Lissa asked.

"We weren't identical twins, if that's what you mean, but everyone said we had the same eyes." I paused, handing her the pickle slices. "I miss her. Every day of my life."

Suddenly, a knock came at the back door. Lissa leaped off her chair, almost falling. Panic shot through her eyes like those of an animal caught in a deadly trap. "Remember—you haven't seen me!" And she limped off toward the hall closet.

When Lissa was safely out of sight, I went to the back door and pushed the curtain back. Outside, a friendly face smiled at me. It was Rachel Zook. She held a basket of fresh eggs in her gloved hands.

I opened the door. "Hi, Rachel."

She smiled. "Hello, Merry. Fresh eggs for my English cousin."

I brightened at her warm greeting. Rachel thought of me as a close friend because our family trees branched back to the same ancestors. She called me "English" because I wasn't Amish.

"Thanks to Skip's giant omelets, we're all out of eggs." I took the basket from her. "He uses up twice the eggs Mom does." And with that, I went to find the egg money in the utensil drawer.

Rachel twinkled a smile. "Come on over for Curly John's wedding on Thursday, *jah?*"

"Wouldn't miss it," I said, feeling rude about not inviting her inside.

"Curly John wants all of you to come," Rachel said. She adjusted the black woolen shawl draped over her shoulders. It was fastened in front with a safety pin.

Curly John was Rachel's nineteen-year-old brother—two years older than Skip. I couldn't imagine *my* brother getting married, tending a farm, and raising a family at that age.

"Mother and Daddy won't be home till Thursday night, but Skip and I can come for sure."

Rachel pushed a strand of light brown hair back under her black winter bonnet. "Such good fun, weddings." She turned to go.

"Thanks for the invitation," I called after her.

She waved. "*Wilkom*, Merry."

I watched as Rachel hurried past the white gazebo in our backyard. The deep purple skirt whipped against her ankles, covered with black cotton stockings. "Please don't misunderstand, dear friend," I whispered, leaning against the door, wishing I'd taken a chance and invited her in.

Remembering Lissa, I dashed to the hall closet and opened the door. "Come finish your sandwich."

"Who was that?" Lissa asked, moving out from behind the vacuum cleaner.

"Rachel Zook, my Amish friend."

Lissa eased herself into a kitchen chair. "Do I know her?"

"She lives down the lane." I pointed in the direction, still hoping I hadn't offended Rachel. "She went to the one-room Amish school."

Lissa drank some milk. "Went?"

"Eighth grade was her last year."

Lissa's eyebrows shot up. "She dropped out?"

"Amish go only eight grades. After that, they get ready to settle down and marry."

"At fifteen?"

"Right now Rachel's helping out her mom, learning everything an Amishwoman needs to know. At sixteen, she'll start running around, as they call it, hanging out with friends like we do. Except Amish teens get together on Sunday nights at singings. It's where guys meet girls."

"While they're singing?" Lissa's eyes were as big as windows.

"They sit around a long table with boys on one side and girls on the other. And . . . guess what else?"

Lissa snickered. "Can't wait to hear this."

"Adults aren't allowed."

"So what?" Lissa stared at me. "Doesn't sound like much fun anyway."

I got up and looked out the window. "They pick out fast hymns and sing for a couple hours. Sometimes it turns into a square dance, but it's not supposed to."

"How come?"

"The older Amish don't want their teens dancing." I peeked out the back window again, watching for Skip's return. "Sometimes they have secret dances and disobey the *Ordnung* anyhow."

Lissa frowned hard. "What's Ordnung?"

"All the agreed-upon rules for the Amish community."

"How do you know all this Amish stuff?"

"You won't believe it," I said. "Rachel and I traced our ancestry back to Switzerland to the original Amish immigrants. They sailed on *The Charming Nancy* in 1737."

"What a cool name for a ship."

"Cool, but slow," I told her. "It took eighty-three days to finally dock in Philadelphia."

"So why aren't you Amish?" Lissa asked before taking the last bite of sandwich.

"One of my great-great-grandfathers pulled away from the Amish faith." I glanced at the strawberry clock on the wall, keeping track of time before Skip's arrival. I went to the sink, which was still piled with dishes from his marathon midnight snack. Slowly, I opened the dishwasher.

Lissa took another sip of milk, then set the glass down firmly. "Somehow I can't picture you being friends with a girl like Rachel Zook."

She sounded jealous, but I let it go. I'd heard that sometimes abused kids are insecure. Lissa was probably suffering from a lot of things like that. As her friend, it was my job to protect her, not judge her.

After scraping the dishes, I loaded the dishwasher. "I really think you'd like Rachel if you got to know her."

"You see beauty in everything, Merry. Maybe it's the photographer in you." She looked depressed again. "What's wrong with *me?*"

I turned the dial on the dishwasher. "Nothing's wrong, Lissa."

She sat up. "I love the guitar. I had one before we moved here, but my dad sold it out from under my nose." She paused for a moment, as though reliving a sad moment. Then she asked, "Ever make up a melody?"

I breathed deeply. "No, but Jonathan Klein has."

"Your boyfriend, right?"

I wiped the crumbs off the counter. "Oh, he's nice enough."

"C'mon, Merry, I know you like him!" She leaned back in her chair and squinted at me. "But I still can't believe a guy would propose to a girl based on her singing."

"Let's face it, Liss, if you were Amish, you'd be livin' for Sunday nights."

We burst into giggles.

Just then I heard the front door open. I grabbed Lissa's arm and whispered, "Quick! Upstairs!"

It was slow going for Lissa, but we managed to get up the back steps. Like frightened mice, we scurried to my room.

"In there," I whispered, pointing to my walk-in closet.

Lissa pulled me inside with her. "For how long?"

"What?"

"C'mon, Mer, you say 'what' when you don't know what else to say."

"Hardly ever," I huffed.

Lissa sat cross-legged in the middle of the closet floor, straightening a row of shoe boxes. "Did you know you have six of these?" It was obvious she didn't want me to leave yet.

"Take a peek." I motioned to the shoe boxes.

Hesitantly, she opened the first one and discovered a plastic bag brimful of granola. Sliding the lid off the second shoe box, Lissa stared in amazement at a variety of fruit leather.

"What's your favorite flavor?" I asked, hoping to dispel her dismal mood.

She looked puzzled. "What's fruit leather doing in a shoe box?"

"It's shoe leather replacement." I laughed. "Let me introduce you to my snack pantry." I popped the lid off the third shoe box, revealing a plastic container of powdery Kool-Aid. "Care for a lick?"

Lissa smiled. "You're crazy."

"I always get hungry when I do homework, so I stash food in my closet," I said, offering her a strip of apple fruit leather. "You can snack till I smuggle dinner up."

Her face lit up. "How can I ever thank you?" she said. I knew it had little to do with the fruit leather.

"Hm-m, let's see," I said. "How about that new down-filled jacket of yours? Think you could loan it?"

"No problem."

I studied Lissa, helpless and forlorn, sitting there on the floor of my closet. "You'd really let me?"

She nodded. "Except it's at my house."

I pretended to be disappointed. "Oh, phooey."

Lissa brightened. "I have an idea. You could sneak into my house and get it tomorrow afternoon."

"What?"

"Mom works Wednesdays all day, and Daddy, well, he'll be asleep. Or—" She sighed.

"Or what?" I asked.

Lissa gave a piercing look. "Drunk," she said slowly. "He'll be drunk." Tears spilled down her cheeks, and I couldn't help but put my arm around her, even though I felt sad inside, too. But I needed to be merry and strong. For Lissa.

"You okay?" I asked.

She shook her head, and I tried to picture her situation at home. Coming from a background with loving parents, it wasn't easy. I stood up. "I'll be right back, okay?"

"Promise?" She looked at me with pleading eyes.

"Count on it," I said.

⌒

Downstairs, I hurried into the kitchen. Skip was moving things around in the freezer, obviously searching for just the right casserole. He must've sensed I was observing him, because he straightened up and, with a grand flourish, whipped out one of the frozen casseroles Mom had prepared in advance. "Tah-dah!" he shouted.

I giggled. "What's for supper?"

"Wouldn't *you* like to know?"

"C'mon, I'm starved," I said, settling down into one of the kitchen chairs. I watched him set the oven and loosen the aluminum foil on the casserole dish.

"How was your history test?" he asked.

Mr. Wilson's terrible, terminal test, as Jon had described it, seemed so far away now. I took a deep breath. "It was . . . well, I guess I should've studied more," I admitted.

Skip cast a hard look at me. "It might help if you studied instead of chasing orphan cats all night."

"Don't exaggerate," I said, tossing Aunt Teri's letter on the table. "Guess who's coming to visit?"

Skip's shoulders drooped. "Don't people know Mom and Dad are overseas?" He took a quick look at the letter, then a smile spread across his face. "Hey, this could be a blessing in disguise."

A blessing for him, I thought, wondering how to make my scheme to hide Lissa work.

"Aunt Teri cooks like nobody's business," he said.

"Food—is that all you ever think about?"

He poured milk into a tall glass. "You'd better get your room ready." He lifted the glass to his lips and gulped down half the contents.

"Yeah, yeah." I reached for the tablet of instruction notes Mom had left on top of the fridge.

Playfully, Skip grabbed the notebook from me and scanned the list of events, holding it higher and higher, playing keep-away. "Hey, we're in luck," he said. "The cleaning lady comes first thing tomorrow."

I jumped up and grabbed the tablet out of his hands. "Let me see that."

Skip muttered something about sisters with cat breath. I stared at the list, making a mental note to tell Lissa about the housekeeper.

My brother nosed around in the refrigerator. He spotted the fresh eggs from Zooks' farm. "Looks like Rachel was here."

"Which reminds me," I said. "Don't forget, we're going to Curly John's wedding on Thursday."

"An Amish wedding feast? I'll be there!" He pulled the basket of eggs out of the fridge. "Hey, Mer, how about one of my omelet specials?"

"Oh, ick. I'd eat Mom's casseroles rock hard before—"

"That does it!" Skip grabbed a tea towel and flipped it around, winding it up for a good cracking.

I dodged the flicks of his towel. "I love your omelets, Skip. Honest!"

"Say it louder," he demanded as a mischievous grin slid across his face.

I ran behind the table, away from my power-crazed brother. "I wish Mom and Dad could see you now," I shouted. "Then they'd never leave me alone with you!" He chased me around the kitchen, and when I passed the window, I noticed a police car pulling into our driveway.

"Skip, look! Police!"

"I never fall for that trick," he said, coming after me. But when I didn't move, he stopped in front of the window and we both stared out at a white patrol car. "What's this about?" he said.

My heart pounded *Lissa, Lissa, Lissa* at ninety miles an hour.

"Wow, I hope this isn't about Mom and Dad!" Skip said as the doorbell rang. He went to answer it while I dashed up the back steps, my heart in my throat.

I tore into my bedroom. "Lissa!" I opened the closet door and looked around. She was nowhere in sight. "Lissa?"

Silence.

"C'mon, Liss, where are you?" I turned around, closing the closet door behind me. I thought back to my last conversation with her. "What have I done?" I said out loud. *I should've known better than to leave her alone, crying.*

I scrambled to my desk, looking for a note. *Anything.* Glancing out the window, I saw another policeman standing like a guard out front.

Maybe it was a stakeout. And maybe I was a suspect. I cringed, wondering how I'd gotten myself into such a horrible mess. What if the police had a search warrant?

And what about poor Lissa? Visions of foster homes or maybe more parental abuse crisscrossed my mind. Where was she now? Had she run away—again?

"Merry!" Skip called from downstairs. "Come here a minute."

"Lord, help me," I whispered, making my way down the long staircase, holding the railing for dear life.

Skip stood in the entryway talking to a tall, heavyset policeman. They turned to face me as I reached the bottom of the steps.

"Merry, this is Officer Rhodes," Skip said. "Did you know Lissa Vyner is missing?"

I held my breath to keep from saying the wrong thing as the policeman waved his identification under my nose. "I'd like to talk with you, Merry, if that's all right."

I nodded and Skip led the way into the living room. It bugged me how my big brother seemed so eager to accept this unwelcome guest. I took Mother's overstuffed chair across from Officer Rhodes. It was as comforting as her arms might have been, if only she were here. Abednego leaped up, searching for a cozy spot on my lap.

"I'm sorry to bother you like this, Merry, with your parents gone and all," he said in a voice as stiff as the way he sat on the edge of our green paisley sofa. Looking puzzled, Skip perched himself on the matching ottoman.

I felt the policeman's eyes studying me, so I managed to say, "Is everything okay?" My voice seemed to spell out g-u-i-l-t-y.

"We certainly hope so," the policeman said. "But it appears that Lissa Vyner has run away, and since you're one of her friends, her parents thought you might be able to help."

I looked him in the eyes, stroking my cat's neck to beat the band, wondering how he'd react if he discovered Lissa hiding upstairs. His gray eyes looked kind enough. And his chin was firm and strong, but it was a chin that meant business, and from the way Skip leaned forward, I knew they were both waiting for an answer.

"Has Lissa called you? Have you talked to her?" Officer Rhodes asked.

I gave him the most innocent look I had and hoped it was good enough. Steady, unblinking eyes are supposed to make a person look trustworthy. I'd read that somewhere.

I was determined not to lie, unless . . .

"Merry!" Skip urged. "Tell him if you know something."

"Well, yes, sir," I admitted.

"Has Lissa called here?" the officer asked.

"Well, no, not called, really . . ."

Skip was beside himself. "Out with it, Mer. Did she call or didn't she?"

I wanted to hide from Skip's accusing eyes. It was one thing to see questions in the policeman's eyes, but quite another to see them in my brother's.

I thought of Lissa. She certainly wasn't anywhere to be seen last time I looked upstairs. It wouldn't be a lie to say I didn't know where she was—at least not at the moment.

"Lissa's dad beat her up," I said glumly.

"So you have heard from her?" Officer Rhodes asked.

His eagerness made me even more jumpy. I nodded.

"Do you know where she is?"

"No." I shook my head. *Not anymore,* I thought.

The sound of static, followed by a muffled voice, came over Officer Rhodes' pager. Abruptly, he stood to his feet, answering it as he did. He seemed taller than before, and I kept shooting my most innocent look up at him while I wore out Abednego's neck with rubbing.

Seconds passed, uncomfortable seconds. How much longer?

Finally, he hooked the pager back onto his belt. "Thanks for your time, young lady." His gaze dropped to my cat.

"You're welcome, sir." I watched his face as he stared at Abednego. Gently, I lifted my black cat down. That's when I put two and two together. I swallowed hard as Officer Rhodes studied the yellow hair ribbon tied around Abednego's neck. It was Lissa's!

Without another word, the policeman headed for the front door with Skip on his heels. I stayed frozen to my mother's chair while Skip showed the man out. I didn't care to hear what else he said to my brother, but after he left, Skip marched back in.

"I don't figure you, Mer." He sat down. For the first time in ages, his face had a stern coolness to it, not like the half-mischievous looks I usually got. The ones he could turn on and off whenever he pleased.

I was silent.

Skip stood up. "Well, if you happen to see Lissa or hear from her again, be sure to call this number." He flicked the officer's card at me. "If her dad did beat her, she needs help."

I picked it up, feeling horribly guilty about my deceit. It was time for the truth, whether Lissa liked it or not. But first, I had to find her.

Upstairs, I locked my bedroom door and sat down, wondering how Lissa could've made the slip. She was nowhere in this room.

Then, out of the stillness, I heard a soft giggle. I flung the closet door wide and listened. "Lissa?"

Another giggle drifted out from the hanging clothes on the left side of my closet. Whirling around, I stared. "Lissa, you in here?"

"Inside your winter coat."

I stared in disbelief. A pair of fashion boots was sticking out of my long red coat. "What are you doing? Didn't you hear me calling you?"

Her face poked out, flushed from the warmth of my coat. "I heard the doorbell. What's going on downstairs?"

"I think your dad's on to us."

Lissa gasped. "Help me out of here."

"The police are looking for you," I said. "They were just here."

Wide-eyed and breathing fast, she grabbed my arm. "Do they know you're hiding me?"

I told her everything, except the part about the hair ribbon on Abednego's neck. I didn't have the heart to upset her more than she already was.

Her face drooped. "Now what?"

"Sh-h, we better keep our voices down," I whispered. "I have to get you out of here—fast!"

She sulked, her hair brushing the side of her face as she leaned forward. "Where to?"

I sat on the floor, still shaking from Officer Rhodes' visit. "You need to do exactly what I say, no questions asked." I leaned forward, my gaze boring into hers. "It's total obedience from here on out. Just like the Amish."

Lissa's eyes almost popped. "I'll do anything to keep from going home," she said, "if that's what you mean. But what's this about the Amish?"

I felt tense as I looked into Lissa's questioning face. *This has to work,* I thought.

Ten Whispers Down the Lane

Downstairs, I ate Mom's delicious Hungarian goulash. And I did some fast talking to get Skip to let me stay home from the hayride.

"Pete's sake, Merry," he said. "Can't you leave your dumb cats home alone for once?"

"It's not the cats."

His fork hung in midair. "Oh, I get it. You think you might hear from Lissa again?" He paused. "Maybe you're right, Mer. Maybe you should stay home."

I couldn't believe how easy that was. The second he pulled out of the driveway, I raced to the fridge, slapped leftovers onto a plate, and tossed them in the microwave. Poor Lissa. Not only was she beat up, she was probably dying of hunger, too. By the time I got upstairs with a plateful of hot goulash, she was gobbling granola like crazy.

I sashayed across the room, singing a silly song. "Are you lookin'? It's home-style cookin'!" I waved the plate in front of her nose.

"I can't wait," she said, reaching for the fork.

Just as she opened her mouth, I stopped her. "You oughta thank God first."

"But I'm starving!"

"Still, you can be thankful."

"Will *you* pray?" she asked.

"Sure." I took a deep breath. "Dear Lord, please bless Lissa's supper. And I need your help tonight, Lord. I know some of what I've done may not make you very happy . . . especially the deceitful part. Please forgive me for that. Amen."

Lissa studied me before digging in to her supper. "It seems like you really know Jesus, Merry. The way you talk to Him, I mean."

"You can know Him that way, too," I said. "He's always there for you. Like a best friend, or . . . like a big brother. And you can always count on Him."

The tears came again and she brushed them away as she began to eat.

I hated to leave so abruptly, but time was wasting. "I have a quick errand to run now, but if you stay in my room, you'll be safe," I assured her. "I'll be back in no time."

"Where are you going?"

"If things work out, I'll tell you all about it when I get back." I felt prickles pop out on my neck.

Her eyebrows knit together into a hard frown.

"Oh, before I forget, our cleaning lady comes tomorrow," I said.

"For how long?" Lissa asked, scraping her plate clean.

"She's thorough," I said. "It'll take her till around lunchtime. Especially when I tell her we're having company."

Lissa groaned. "Will I have to stand in your coat all day?"

"Trust me, you won't."

Lissa's shoulders straightened a bit. "Anything's better than going home."

I grabbed my jacket and locked up the house before I left.

———

Outside, a red moon wore a shawl of lacy clouds over its shoulders. Woodsmoke hung in the air as I hurried down SummerHill Lane. I turned off at the willow grove, making every step count. Pushing my way over the hard ground, I found the shortcut between Rachel Zook's house and mine.

A chill wind whipped through the willows, and I pushed their swaying branches away from my face. Two crows flew high in the November sky, *caw-caw-caw*ing back and forth.

Over the crest of an embankment at the edge of the willow grove, Zooks' pond sparkled in the moon-drenched light. I'd saved Levi from drowning in that pond. Hurrying, I came to a white picket fence and climbed over, then scurried across the meadow, dodging a few cow pies. I pinched my nose shut.

Like the fence, all the outer buildings on the Zooks' farm were a bright, clean white. The woodshed, the milk house—even the old outhouse. The fresh paint meant a wedding was coming.

The light up ahead in the Zooks' kitchen looked warm and inviting. At the front of the house, small kerosene lanterns twinkled in the living room. It was a large house, built by Rachel's grandfather years ago. Large enough to hold 250 or more wedding guests.

A long porch framed the front of the house. As I ran up the steps, I heard someone tooting out "Oh, Susannah" on the harmonica. Anxious to talk to Rachel, I knocked on the door.

"Wilkom, Merry," Abe Zook said as he opened the door wide. His bushy beard, beginning to gray in spots, spread from ear to ear, and tan suspenders held up his black trousers. "Look who has come," he called as Rachel came in from the kitchen to greet me. The smell of brewed coffee wafted through the house.

"*Mam* has shoofly pie," Rachel said, leading the way through the living room and dining room, where brightly colored china decorated the shelves.

Amish life revolved around the home and the kitchen, especially in winter. I felt the heat pouring from the large stove in the center of the kitchen. With no central heating, the stove provided enough heat for this room and the bedroom above it.

I couldn't remember visiting Rachel's family and not being offered more food than I could hold. This time was no different. An enormous pie and some sliced bologna and cheese graced the long wooden table in their spacious kitchen.

Rachel's father wandered back to his straight-backed rocking chair near the gas lamp in the corner. A German Bible, its pages brown with use, lay open on the reading table near his pie plate. But it was the pie he reached for. *"Des gut."* He licked his lips.

Levi and his little brother, Aaron, played marbles near the stove. Levi glanced up at me, but I quickly looked away.

Nancy, Ella Mae, and little Susie, Rachel's younger sisters, played checkers on a table in the ring of light near their father's reading lamp. Their rosy-cheeked faces shone when they looked up to greet me.

Only Curly John was missing. I didn't have to ask where he was. With just two days before his and Sarah's wedding, they were probably out under the moon, riding in his open-topped courting buggy.

Rachel's mother stopped braiding a rug to dish up a hefty serving of pie. "What do you hear from your parents?" she asked.

"They've called several times," I said, wishing they were here now. "They're excited about bringing suitcases filled with study Bibles into China."

She placed the pie in front of me.

"Thank you," I said, sitting at the table beside Rachel. I felt guilty being here, enjoying the peaceful Amish evening and the delicious after-dinner treats while Lissa was locked away in my room, waiting for my return.

And there was Skip. What if he decided to come home early after the hayride? I glanced at my watch, wishing I could arrange to talk with Rachel in private.

When I finished the gooey molasses pie, I wiped my sticky lips with a napkin. "Can you show me the pillow you're making for Curly John and Sarah?" I asked Rachel. It was the only way to get her alone.

"We must go upstairs a bit, *Dat,*" she told her father as we slid out from behind the wooden table.

"Do not delay," he answered, and I knew it meant Rachel must not go off for long with her English cousin, excluding the other members of the family. Evenings were together times, and individualism was frowned upon.

Rachel carried a small kerosene lantern in one hand and held up her purple dress in the other as we climbed the stairs. I trailed close behind. When we got to the bedroom she shared with twelve-year-old Nancy, I closed the door. She placed the lantern on her antique maple dresser.

The room was scantily furnished with only a double bed, a small bedside table, the dresser, and a long wooden chest—Rachel's hope chest. None of the furniture pieces matched. She opened her dresser drawer and pulled out a green-and-pink hand-stitched square pillow.

"It's beautiful," I said, admiring it closely.

"I can make one for you, Merry," she said, smiling.

"That's sweet of you, but you don't have to."

"Maybe I want to," she answered cheerfully. "For your hope chest."

I touched the ruffled edging. "Okay," I said, ignoring the fact that I didn't even own a hope chest. Right now, I was more concerned about hiding Lissa. "I have to talk to you, Rachel. Friend to friend."

Rachel's smile faded. "What is it?"

"I need your help," I whispered. "We're having company tomorrow night and I need a place for a friend of mine to stay. Just until Thursday, after Curly John's wedding. But we must keep it a secret."

Rachel hesitated. "From Dat and Mam?"

"Yes, even from your parents." I watched her face, desperately hoping that she'd consent.

"I cannot lie about anything," she said. "I must always tell the truth."

"You won't have to lie." I felt bad about putting her in such an awkward position.

Rachel adjusted the waist of her long black apron. "I know Dat and Mam will say your friend is our friend, too." She paused for a moment. "Please—I *must* tell them."

Lissa's secret was serious business. I couldn't take any chances with her safety. Rachel simply couldn't tell her parents or anyone else. She'd have to hide Lissa, just the way I'd been hiding her.

Then it hit me—the Amish had very little contact with the outside world. Maybe it wasn't such a big deal for Rachel to tell her parents. I studied her, half holding my breath. "Okay, Rachel, you may tell them. Just please don't spread it around."

Rachel nodded. "Jah, good. Your friend can stay in the *Grossdawdy Haus*." She was referring to the large addition to the main house where her grandparents lived. "*Grossmutter* and Grossdawdy have a spare bedroom. Jah, that will be good."

"What about Curly John's wedding? Can my friend come along, too?" I asked, feeling more and more confident that I'd made the right choice.

Rachel's cheeks were pink in the dim light. "Jah, your friend must come. With you and Skip."

My eyes caught the wooden clothes rack on the wall. Rachel's clothing—for work and "for good"—was hanging there. The Amish had certain clothes they wore only for doing farm chores, and the good clothes were worn on Sundays or other dress-up occasions like weddings and singings. "My friend should come Plain to the wedding," I said, overjoyed with this perfect solution to Lissa's problem.

"English don't dress Plain," Rachel argued.

"This is *very* important. I promise to tell you everything later," I assured her.

Thanks to our family connection, Rachel and her family considered me a close friend, even though it wasn't too common for the Amish to associate closely with outsiders. Once Rachel entered her *Rumschpringe*, the Zooks would allow their oldest daughter much more freedom in her choice of friends. Later, she would be baptized into the Amish church if she decided to follow the teachings of the

Ordnung. After that, her association with English friends would be more limited.

"Is there trouble, Merry?" she asked.

"No trouble." *Better not be trouble.* I remembered the way Officer Rhodes had stared at Lissa's yellow hair ribbon on Abednego's neck.

"Good, then," Rachel said.

"Is it all right if I borrow your dress for my friend?" I asked.

Rachel reached for the green dress and a black apron and bonnet hanging on the wooden pegs, her eyes searching mine. "I can help you, cousin." And by the way she said it, I knew she still suspected something.

I folded the handmade garments carefully, zipping them into my jacket for safekeeping. "When can I bring my friend to the Grossdawdy Haus?"

"The door is always unlocked. Come on over any time," she said.

"Thank you very much, Rachel," I said, relieved. "We'll probably be over first thing tomorrow."

She reached for the heavy black shawl hanging on the farthest peg. Her innocent face glowed in the lantern's golden light. "*Da Herr sei mit du*—the Lord be with you," she said, handing me the wool wrap.

<hr />

I chose the shortcut home. Hurrying over the picket fence, I could see ripples of wind making swirls on the pond in the distance. Up ahead, the willows cast eerie shadows as I slipped through the grove. Pressing my jacket against my chest, I hurried onto the dirt lane toward my house. The Amish clothes were safe inside my jacket, and I smiled at the success of the evening.

In the distance, I heard the sound of singing. I recognized Skip's strong baritone over the other voices. Peering down the lane under the light of a winter moon, I spotted a large wagon on the crest of the hill. It was scattered with several bales of hay. Streams of light bounced around as the kids swung their flashlights.

They'd be passing my house in a few minutes. Yee-ikes! If my brother spotted me, he might get suspicious. I couldn't let that happen!

I began to run. Faster . . . faster. If I could keep up this pace, I might make it home without being seen. My leg muscles ached. *I can't slow down*, I told myself.

Sucking in short breaths of air, I pushed forward, harder and faster. The edge of our front yard was within reach. I forced my legs to keep moving, ignoring the throbbing pain in my thighs.

The singing was clear and strong now. My feet pounded the dirt road. No willows to hide me now.

The songs grew louder as the clip-clop of horses and the rattle of the hay wagon rang in my ears. Glancing over my shoulder, I judged the distance without stopping. Then my eyes caught something across the street. Someone—a dark, menacing shadow—crouched behind the bushes!

My heart pounded. Fear stuck in my throat. But a surge of energy propelled me across the side yard toward the gazebo behind our house. I made a dive under it, hiding there till the laughter and the songs slowly died away.

Meow!

I jumped as Abednego nuzzled my face in the dark space under the gazebo. "Oh, it's you, little boy," I said, still panting hard. I crawled out quickly and brushed the dirt off my jeans. Relieved but out of breath, I fished for the house key in my pocket.

Suddenly, I heard footsteps coming up the side yard toward me. My hand went stiff in my jeans pocket. I tried to pull the key out, but my fingers stuck clumsily in the fabric. Gasping for air, I panicked, only a few yards from the safety of my home.

Eleven *Whispers Down the Lane*

"Help!" I shouted.

"Mistress Merry, you'll wake the dead!"

I spun around. "Jonathan Klein, you scared me silly!" I almost hugged him, I was so relieved. "Where'd *you* come from? Why'd you hide in the bushes like that?"

He shoved his hands into the pockets of his blue winter jacket, looking confused. "Questions, questions," he said. "What are you doing out here?"

I ignored his question. "Are you saying you weren't hiding out front just now?"

"You know me better than that."

"But I saw someone hiding . . . I thought it was you!"

"I would never try to scare you like that, Merry. I saw you running toward your house, that's all—just jumped off to say hi."

I looked around him, worried about whoever—whatever—it was I'd seen out front. "He's probably still out there."

"Who's out *where?*"

I pulled the house key out of my pocket. "Quick, we have to get inside! Someone's out front, hiding in the bushes."

"You're not making sense, Merry," he said. "I didn't see anyone."

"C'mon." I unlocked the back door. "I'll prove it to you." Without another word, I dashed to the dark living room and peered through the window curtains. I scanned the bushes with my eyes. Nothing!

"He was just there," I said, pointing.

Jon crept up behind me. "Are you sure it wasn't a moon shadow or something?"

"You don't believe me?" I shot back. "I know I saw someone over there."

"Sure, show me the shady, shaggy stranger," he said, starting up his alliteration routine.

"It's not funny," I retorted.

"Say that with all *f*'s."

"I'm not playing your game, Jon. I mean it."

Slowly, he turned and headed for the kitchen. I followed him and flicked on the tiny stove light. "I'm glad you're here." I felt Rachel's clothes still hidden inside my jacket.

"I can't stay," he reminded me. "I have to catch up with the hay-ride. The group was going to stop down the lane for a quick hike." He stopped talking and smiled like some terrific idea had struck. "Hey, why don't you come along?"

"I would, but—" I couldn't leave Lissa with some stranger lurking around.

Jon leaned closer. "But what?" I smelled a slight hint of his peppermint gum.

"Please stay here till Skip gets back."

"I'll have to walk all the way into town if I don't catch up with the group," he insisted, heading for the back door.

"I'll get Skip to drive you," I offered.

He suddenly seemed shy. "I shouldn't be here anyway."

"Skip'll understand when he comes home. I'll tell him what I saw."

"Really, Merry, I think you'll be fine. Just keep the doors locked." He smiled, running his long fingers though his hair. "Guess I'll see you later."

It was no use. Jonathan didn't understand. And I couldn't explain my real fear—that maybe the tall shadow out there was Lissa's father. With a quick wave good-bye, Jon opened the back door and left.

Alone again, I groped my way through the dark hallway to the front door, shivering with fright. I didn't dare turn on the lights.

I remembered what Rachel said about the Amish always keeping their doors open as I gripped the lock, double checking it. Satisfied it was secure, I peeked out once again. Maybe Jon was right. Maybe the moon had played a trick on me.

Feeling better, I headed upstairs, pulling Rachel's Amish clothes out of my jacket. I found Lissa staring at one of the pictures on my wall gallery. When I came in the room, she turned away, reacting as though she'd been caught. "I . . . uh, didn't mean to—"

"Go ahead, it's okay," I said.

She moved back to look at the photo of the flower-strewn gravestone. Leaning closer, she read the words, " 'Faith Hanson, precious daughter and dear sister, in heaven with our Lord.' " Lissa stood silent for a moment. "Was your sister sick long?"

"Not long." I kept the Amish clothes hidden behind my back.

She turned away from the wall to look at me. "How'd you handle it when you knew your twin was dying?"

A lump grew in my throat, but I forced it down. "It was hard for all of us. Really hard."

"Did you cry a lot?" Her gaze penetrated me.

Uncomfortable, I looked away. "Mother cried enough for all of us," I said, avoiding the question. The truth was I'd never let myself cry about Faithie.

Lissa limped past the picture of the gravestone to more of my photography—Amish windmills, water pumps, and landscapes. There was even a picture of the playground at the Amish school, without the children. I'd always respected their wishes by not photographing the Amish, unlike some tourists who had been known to stalk young Plain children, bribing them for a snapshot.

I was relieved that Lissa didn't say anything more about crying for Faithie. Glancing out my window, I peeked through the side of the curtain. Slowly, I surveyed the area below. That's when I saw the tall gray shadow emerge from the bushes. It was a policeman, and he was motioning to someone.

Quickly, another policeman appeared, coming around the corner and across Strawberry Lane toward the house.

"Lissa!" I called.

Startled, she jerked her head. "What?"

"Quick! Kill the lights." I waved her to the window. "Two policemen!"

Terror filled her eyes as she scrambled to the lamp beside my bed. In the darkened room, we stared through the curtains, scarcely breathing.

Lissa gasped. "That's my dad! I know it is . . . and his partner, Officer Rhodes, he's the other one . . . the big guy."

I could hardly breathe, let alone think. "That's the cop who questioned me this afternoon," I muttered. "Why's he back?"

Then I remembered the strange way he'd looked at Lissa's yellow ribbon on Abednego's neck. What if Mr. Vyner had described what he'd last seen his daughter wearing?

Lissa grabbed my arm. "What'll we do? They're going to take me back home!"

I pulled her into the closet, the Amish clothes still draped over my arm. "I'm going to help you escape." I flicked on the light. "See this?" I held up the green dress and long black apron. "It's your way out of here."

She reached to touch the dress, then her hand sprang back. "Ee-ew! It's disgusting."

I began to unfasten the Velcro on the front. "You'll get used to it."

She shot a weak smile through her tears. Then the doorbell rang. Lissa grabbed the dress. "I'll wear it, disgusting or not." And she began to undress.

Br-ring!

I opened the closet door to answer the phone, but Lissa pulled me back. "You can't!"

"It could be my parents," I said. "They'll worry if no one answers."

"And it could be a trick." Lissa's white, fearful face said it all.

The phone rang a second time. Lissa struggled with the Velcro on the dress as I counted the rings under my breath. Finally, I couldn't take it any longer. "What if Skip's calling?"

"Let it ring," Lissa insisted. She held up the black apron. "Which way does this thing go?"

"Here," I said, positioning it against her as she slipped her arms through the openings. My fingers trembled as I attached the apron with pins. "You're almost ready. I'll fix your hair." I hurried to my dresser in the darkness.

"It doesn't matter what my hair looks like," she wailed.

Back inside the closet, I parted Lissa's hair down the middle and pushed it into a quick bun, securing it with three hair clips. "Now you're Plain."

The phone kept ringing.

I was dying to answer it. "How do we know it's the police?" I said. "Besides, if it's my parents, they could help us!"

Lissa's mouth pinched up like she was disgusted. "You couldn't say anything on the phone anyway. The phone lines might already be tapped."

Maybe she was right. But right or not, the ringing phone made me feel uneasy. And very homesick to talk to my parents!

Suddenly, I heard Skip's voice. "Merry! Are you home?"

I flung open the closet door and ran across the bedroom to the locked outer door. "I'm up here," I called down the steps, never so delighted to hear his voice.

"Will you *please* answer the phone?" he asked. "We've got company again."

I knew he meant he was talking to the cops. Scurrying to the hall phone, I picked it up. "Hello?"

"Hello, Merry. I thought you'd never answer." It was Miss Spindler.

"Uh, we're sort of busy right now," I said. Miss Spindler's nickname was Old Hawk Eyes. She made it her duty to keep close tabs on things in the neighborhood. Seemed to me she had it down to a near science!

I could hear Officer Rhodes' voice downstairs. There was another voice, too. I clenched my teeth, remembering the voice from the phone call this afternoon. Lissa's father! He was right here—inside my house!

Old Hawk Eyes' scratchy voice continued, "I see police cars parked around the side of your house, Merry."

"You do?"

"Oh dear, it looks like—"

"What?" I interrupted. "What do you see?"

"More police," she moaned. "Oh, horse feathers! They're surrounding your house!"

"How many?"

"Well . . ." She hesitated, as though counting. "I saw at least two at your front door a while ago, but now there are two more behind your house. What in this wide world is going on?"

"Thanks for calling, Miss Spindler," I said abruptly. "Thank you *very* much."

"But, Merry—"

"I'm sorry, Miss Spindler, I have to go now." I hung up. Thank the Lord for nosy neighbors!

There was no time to waste.

Twelve *Whispers Down the Lane*

Downstairs, the muffled voices grew louder. Then, unexpectedly, I heard my name mentioned. If a search warrant was involved, the police would be checking the upstairs room any second!

I flew down the hall to the bedroom and tore into the closet. Cramming the black Amish bonnet down on Lissa's head, I noticed with relief that her bottom lip was nearly back to normal. "Follow me and don't make a sound," I whispered.

Lissa's lips quivered as she nodded.

"You'll need this heavy wool shawl." I snatched it up as we left the room.

"Where are you taking me?"

I pressed my finger to my lips as a wide-eyed Lissa tiptoed slowly behind me toward the back steps.

"Merry!" It was Skip again. "Get down here."

I cast a silent warning signal to Lissa as we descended the back stairs leading to the dark kitchen. With my hand gripping her tiny wrist, I peered through the window in the back door.

Two policemen were standing across the yard near the gazebo, probably waiting in case Lissa came running out.

One glance at my friend's tear-filled eyes gave me the courage I needed.

"Here's what you do," I whispered. "Head for the Zooks' farm. Walk slowly—try not to limp, and no matter what, keep your bonnet on. If anyone questions you, look down, act shy." I hugged her quickly.

She clung to me. "Aren't you coming?"

"Wait for me in the willow grove. You can't miss it," I said. "You'll be well hidden there."

She clasped her hands tightly. "Merry, I'm scared to death."

"Remember what I said." I felt the tension, the stubbornness in my jaw. I was determined to take care of her, to rescue her from the abuse. If I could just get her to the safety of my Amish neighbors until my parents returned!

I took a deep breath and casually opened the back door. "See you tomorrow!" I called, pretending she was Rachel Zook.

Lissa waved back, cooperating with my little scheme.

Slowly, I closed the door, silently praying for her safety. And for forgiveness, too, for this deceitful play-acting.

I heard voices down the hall. My heart pounded as I hurried to the living room.

"What took so long, Mer?" Skip asked when I came in.

I sat beside him. "Miss Spindler's worried silly about us. She saw the squad cars. That's why she called." I looked at the policemen sitting on the love seat.

Officer Rhodes studied me with his piercing gray eyes. "Heard anything more from Lissa?"

"She hasn't called here," I said without lying.

I noticed the other policeman, Lissa's father. His face looked grim, though his lips were framed by a bushy mustache. His bloodshot eyes, small and pouched, reminded me of a sick bullfrog's. I saw a ripple in his nose. How had it been busted? In a drunken brawl?

Officer Rhodes introduced him, but instead of offering to shake hands like a gentleman, Lissa's father rubbed his thick hands together. If I hadn't known better, I'd have thought *he* was the one on trial here.

"I believe we've met," he said, nodding his froggy head. He squeezed his sausage fingers into tight fists, like he was itching to get them on his daughter. No telling what he'd do if he found her!

Officer Rhodes seemed preoccupied, brushing cat hair off the cushion. "By the way, may we see your cat again, Merry?"

Skip looked puzzled, then he chuckled. "Merry's got three cats."

Lissa's father leaned forward suddenly. "Let's have a look at them," he demanded, not in the polite way he'd spoken to me earlier on the phone.

I swallowed hard. They were on to something. Probably the yellow ribbon. Why hadn't I gotten rid of it before, when I had the chance? "I'll call the cats," I said, excusing myself.

Quickly, I ran into the kitchen. It was a good excuse to check up on Lissa's whereabouts. I hurried to the side window, so the police in the yard couldn't see. "Here, kitty, kitty," I called, pretending to search. I kept my eyes peeled for Lissa as I continued calling for the cats.

Way down the lane, I spotted a thin shadow in the moonlight, walking with a slight limp, as demurely as a real Amish girl.

Good! Lissa had made it past the cops!

Two of my cats came bounding across the kitchen floor, sliding on the rug as they came to a stop. I picked up Shadrach and Meshach and nuzzled them against my face.

Where was Abednego? And what could I dream up about that yellow ribbon without telling a lie?

My heart in my throat, I called to my wayward cat. "Abednego, where are you?" Carrying Shadrach and Meshach into the living room, I felt the hairs on the back of my neck prickle.

Officer Rhodes glared first at one cat, then the other. He frowned, obviously puzzled.

"Abednego's missing again," I explained, directing my comment to Skip.

"That cat's *always* missing," my brother said, getting up to find him.

I wished Skip would sit still. Abednego needed to stay hidden!

Staring down at the golden cats in my lap, I wondered what to do or say next. My heart throbbed.

"Abednego. Isn't that a biblical name?" said Officer Vyner, obviously trying to sound more cordial.

"Yes, sir. Abednego is the name of one of the three Hebrew children who were thrown into the king's fiery furnace." I felt a bit hot myself.

Shadrach broke the silence by coughing up a hairball. I snickered quietly as the two men tried to keep from grossing out.

Soon, Skip came in the room, carrying Abednego by the nape of his yellow-ribboned neck. "Here's the rascal."

"Be careful," I said, reaching out to rescue my pet.

Skip plopped him down on top of the other cats in my lap. "You've heard of three blind mice," he said, showing off for the police. "Well, here we have three dumb cats."

I wished there was a way to get rid of that yellow ribbon before . . .

Instantly, Officer Rhodes stood up. Towering over my lapful of cats, he reached down to touch Abednego.

Pph-ht! The cat hissed and sprang his claws out in defense. Officer Rhodes jumped back.

"Sorry, sir. He's real funny about strangers," I said. But the policeman approached Abednego again and the black cat leaped off my lap, scurrying out of the living room, meowing angrily.

"Why, that little—" Officer Rhodes boomed.

Frightened by the thunderous remark, Shadrach and Meshach jumped off my lap, too, racing after big brother.

"Uh, I'll be right back," I said, joining the chase.

Skip ran after me, following a trail of cats into Dad's study.

"I'll check upstairs," I said, running for dear life up the long flight of steps. "Here, kitty, kitty." I searched everywhere. In the bathroom, even Skip's room. But Abednego had vanished. My heart pounded. I had to find him before Skip did!

Shouting and hooting came from downstairs. What was going on? I listened again. It sounded like—could it be? Were our visitors actually chasing my cats around the house? It wasn't funny, but for a microsecond, I couldn't keep from smiling.

Turning back to the problem at hand, I frantically checked all of Abednego's favorite hiding places. No cat. While in my room, I opened my dresser drawer and found my own yellow hair ribbon. I wouldn't have to lie about the ribbon—if only I could switch it with the one on Abednego's neck.

"Dear Lord," I murmured, "this is urgent stuff. I have to be the one to find Abednego. Can you please help me?" It was a desperate plea, one that needed immediate heavenly attention!

I kept searching, hoping Abednego had outsmarted his pursuers. Frustrated and thinking of Lissa, I sat on the edge of my bed. "Where are you, kitty?" I sang softly.

Whish, swish.

I looked down. A long black tail flicked against my ankle. Slowly kneeling beside the bed, I pulled the comforter up and peeked under. "Come here, little boy," I pleaded.

Cautiously, timidly, Abednego came.

"Good boy," I whispered, untying the hair ribbon with shaking fingers. Quickly, I replaced it with my own yellow one, an exact match, except for one thing: My initials had been cross-stitched on one end of the ribbon.

Before taking Abednego downstairs for further questioning, I tossed the old ribbon in the fruit leather shoe box in my closet. And pushed the lid down hard.

"Hold him still!" Mr. Vyner commanded.

Gently, but firmly, I held my whining, hissing kitty as Officer Vyner's fingers carelessly untied the yellow ribbon. I remembered the way Abednego had warmed up to Lissa. He was smart that way. He knew the difference between kind and cruel.

Roughly, Lissa's father pulled the ribbon off my cat's neck. A determined scowl swept across his face and stayed there. "It's hers all right," he growled, handing over the evidence to his partner. "Where is she, young lady?"

I held my breath, terrified.

"Hold on a minute, Vyner." Officer Rhodes stared at the ribbon, turning it over. "These aren't Lissa's initials. Take another look."

I sighed a deep, trembly sigh, waiting . . .

Lissa's father grabbed the ribbon from Officer Rhodes, then tossed it gruffly onto the coffee table. "We're wasting our time here," he grumbled and marched out of the room.

Officer Rhodes stayed behind a few minutes, boring his stern eyes into mine. "We suspect Lissa may try to contact you again, Merry."

I could read between the lines. It wasn't so much what he said, but the way he said it.

"Yes, sir," I managed to say.

Officer Rhodes excused himself, apologizing for taking up so much of our evening. Skip got up and showed him out. When Skip returned, he collapsed in a chair. "Man, this better be the last time. I can't take all this excitement."

He can't? What about me!

As soon as Skip settled down in front of the TV, I hurried into the kitchen and grabbed a handful of cookies. I put them in a sandwich bag for later, still thinking about the police encounter. These guys meant business! And I knew it wouldn't be long till they were back. In the meantime, they'd probably be watching the place like hawks.

Another thought disturbed me: Mr. Vyner had seemed more angry than anxious over Lissa's disappearance. Shivers flew up and down my spine.

I waited till the squad cars left before going upstairs. Quickly, I packed my gym bag full of clothes—non-Amish ones—for Lissa. Along with the clothes, I squeezed in a few books. Some poetry, and my Bible. Then I crept downstairs, put on my jacket, and stood in the hallway hoping Skip wouldn't notice I was leaving.

Suddenly, a news announcer's voice came on the television, stopping me cold. "We interrupt our regularly scheduled programming for this bulletin: Fourteen-year-old Lissa Vyner of Lancaster county has been reported missing as of this evening," the news reporter said. "If you or anyone you know has seen or heard from Lissa, please call the number on the screen immediately. Authorities are standing by."

"Did you hear that, Mer?" Skip yelled from the living room.

I bit my lip, hoping he wouldn't wander out here. "I heard," I called back to him. "Sounds real serious."

"Yeah, you're not kidding," he hollered.

I waited a few more minutes to make sure he wasn't going to continue talking. When I felt it was safe to leave, I slipped out the back door.

Lissa was huddled against a tree deep in the willow grove when I finally got to her. She looked around as if she was still afraid of being seen out in the open. "I thought one of the cops was going to stop me at first," she whispered. "But I remembered what you said and kept my head down. I guess they thought I really was Amish."

"Wow, was that ever close!" I glanced around beneath the willow branches.

She tugged on her woolen shawl. "What happened? What did my dad say?"

"You'll never believe it." I told her everything, even about switching hair ribbons on the cat.

"You did that?" she asked, her eyes wide.

"Lucky for us I had one the same color, but with my initials stitched on it."

"Good thinking," she said, looking positively Amish in the moonlight.

A nervous giggle burst out of me.

"What's so funny?" she asked, reaching up to touch her bonnet.

"You look like a regular Amish girl, that's all."

We approached the picket fence. "You saved my life, Merry Hanson," she said solemnly. "That's what you did."

I helped her climb over the fence in her long dress. "I did my best," I said, wishing I could say the same about Faithie. I hadn't done a thing to save her.

Lissa winced as she limped across the meadow. I reached out to steady her, thankful to have been given a second chance. This time I would not fail another human being. I would do whatever it took to protect my friend.

"Where are we going?" she asked.

I glanced at her, feeling the urgency sweep over me. Still a bit unnerved and worried about the police showing up in the neighborhood, I summoned the courage I needed for Lissa's flight to safety. "To the Grossdawdy Haus." I pointed to the large addition on the north side of Rachel's house where her grandparents lived. "We're all set," I said as confidently as I could. "Rachel says you can stay with her grandparents till after Curly John's wedding."

"By myself?"

"Don't worry," I said, offering her a couple of cookies. "You won't be alone."

We quickened our pace through the cow pasture, toward the Zooks' house. "I think you'll be very safe here, Lissa," I said, guiding her around through the backyard. Slowly, we approached the sun porch of the grandparents' addition to the main house. "You shouldn't have to worry about your dad or Officer Rhodes coming around here."

"Hope not," Lissa said in a hushed voice.

I tapped on the door.

"Wilkom, Merry," Rachel's grandfather greeted me. He smiled, nodding politely to Lissa as we walked inside.

A gas lamp hung over the kitchen table to the right of the living room. It was set up much like a smaller version of the main house where Rachel and her large family lived. A pair of wrinkled faces smiled as I introduced Lissa to Rachel's grandparents.

"Let me show you where you will sleep." The stout Amish grandmother wore a long gray dress with a black apron attached and a white head covering. She led the way through the living room with a large kerosene lantern just like Rachel's.

The spacious spare bedroom was sparsely furnished with a double bed, a dresser, and a cane-back chair. I noticed a hand mirror on the dresser on top of a white crocheted doily.

"We hope you will be comfortable here," the white-haired woman said cheerfully. And by that I knew Rachel had filled her grandparents in on our conversation.

"Thank you," Lissa said. "Thank you *very* much!"

After the woman left, Lissa slipped off the Amish bonnet and looked around cautiously. "You're sure it's okay for me to be here?"

"Rachel said so, and she never lies." I wished I could say the same thing about myself. Up until this situation with Lissa, I'd been a totally honest person.

"They sure don't have much furniture," Lissa commented, heading for the bed with its solid maple headboard. Gingerly, she sat down.

I took off my jacket and dropped my gym bag on the floor, sitting beside her. "The Amish live super simple lives. Look at this," I said, reaching for the thick handmade afghan at the bottom of the bed. I traced the intricate patterns as Lissa commented about the hardwood floor.

Then she spotted a paper mobile hanging in the corner. "What's that?"

"Looks like something one of the Zook kids made at school." I got up to investigate the mobile, lifting it off its hook. "Could be Ella Mae's."

Lissa studied it, holding it close to the lantern on the dresser. "Who's Ella Mae?"

"Rachel's eight-year-old sister."

Lissa started reading the words on the mobile. "Be cooperative, be honest, be kind, be orderly." She stopped. "Yeah, I need *that* one." She pointed to the word *orderly*. "You should see my room sometimes."

"Believe me, I have." We chuckled in the semi-darkness.

Lissa leaned closer. "What does the rest say?"

"Be willing, be respectful," I said.

Lissa touched the mobile again. "It sounds like something the Girl Scouts would pledge."

"Except that the Amish teach their kids to turn these words into action—it's part of growing up Plain."

Lissa was silent for a moment. The moon cast a lovely glow over her slight frame as she stared at the mobile. "These are hard words to live up to."

I understood what she meant. "I guess it doesn't seem quite as hard for the Amish. Maybe because their world is so different from ours. Insulated, in a way." I glanced around the room. No framed pictures of family or painted scenes graced the walls. In fact, there were no decorations at all. But somehow the simplicity felt calm and comforting.

I hung the mobile on its hook and returned to the window, where Lissa stood motionless. "You okay?" I put my arm around her thin shoulders.

"Look out there," she said, gazing at the large white birdhouse standing on a tall wooden pole in the yard. "How many bird families live in there at once?"

"About twenty purple martins," I said of the four-sided birdhouse with the green gabled roof. "Martins are like the Amish—they stick together. And they return here every spring to raise a new family."

"That's what I need," she said softly. "A new family."

I peered sideways at her. "Maybe you're ready for God's family."

She glanced at me quickly. "How do you know God wants me in His family?"

"Because He sent Jesus to earth, that's how. And you can be adopted into the family just by asking. Then you'll have a big brother, too. One who died so you can live with Him in heaven someday." *Where Faithie is,* I thought.

Silently, we watched wispy clouds loop over the moon like butterfly nets. I could feel Lissa's shoulders stiffen, and I knew she wasn't ready.

Fourteen *Whispers Down the Lane*

Lissa gripped my arm. "Stay here with me overnight. Please?"

"I would, but Skip'll freak out if he discovers I'm missing. Besides, we can't risk his getting suspicious again."

Her eyes flashed fear.

"You'll be safe with the Zooks," I said, hoping I was right.

Someone knocked at the door and I went to answer it, expecting to see the grandmother again.

Rachel stood in the doorway, dressed in a long white cotton nightgown and robe. Her light brown hair hung down her back in a single braid. In the golden glow of the lantern's light, she looked like an angel.

"It's good to see you again, Merry," she said, appearing surprised. "Is this your friend?"

"This is Lissa," I said, purposely leaving off her last name. Just in case.

"We are ready for evening prayers." She smiled as always. Still, I could tell she was probably wondering why Lissa was dressed Plain and here in their house so soon.

We followed Rachel through the kitchen, down the short hallway connecting the grandparents' side of the house to the main house. Three generations of Zooks met silently in the large kitchen, where only a few hours earlier I had snacked on shoofly pie.

Abe Zook sat in the corner of the kitchen, near the gas lamp, still dressed in his white shirt, suspenders, and black trousers. His wife, Esther, sat to his left with all the children gathered around them in a semicircle. All but Levi, who sat a short distance away from the rest.

The grandparents sat at the kitchen table across from Lissa and me, each with their own sets of grunts and groans as they got situated.

Abe Zook picked up his German Bible and began to read, first in German, then in English, probably for Lissa's and my sake. "Romans twelve, two," he began. " 'Do not conform any longer to the pattern of this world, but be transformed by the renewing of your mind. Then you will be able to test and approve what God's will is—His good, pleasing, and perfect will.' "

After a short prayer of thanksgiving for the Bible and its final authority, for the blessings that come from total obedience to its words, and for the work and toil of the day, Abe Zook said, "Amen. We'll have lights-out by nine."

Lissa looked surprised. "Why so early?" she whispered as we followed the grandparents down the connecting hall to their part of the house.

"Five o'clock comes fast," I answered. "You're going to find out firsthand exactly what it's like being Amish."

"I am?" she said as we headed for her bedroom.

"Well, to start with, tomorrow's the day before Curly John's wedding. I'm sure Rachel will invite you to help with preparations for the wedding feast and all the festivities. Don't be bashful about it, okay? It's the Amish way of including you—extending their welcome."

"I can't wait to wear *real* clothes again," she said, eyeing the gym bag. "These clothes aren't my style."

I helped unfasten the waist of her long apron, then watched as Lissa carefully folded it, placing it over the back of a wooden chair. "I can't imagine wearing a dress like this all the time," she said.

"Amishwomen don't seem to mind."

Lissa sat on the edge of the bed, gently rubbing her right thigh. "Guess you better get back before Skip wonders where you are," she said, looking more confident.

I nodded. "I'll see you as soon as I can after school tomorrow, okay?"

She wiggled her fingers in a tiny wave.

"Oh, you should probably wear your Amish clothes tomorrow so you fit in around here. Just in case." I threw her a quick kiss and left.

When I arrived back home, I could hear the TV still blaring. I hurried up the back steps to my room, nearly falling over my cat trio. "Hello, little boys." Abednego followed me into my closet. "It's nice to see you hanging around here for a change."

He responded with a cheerful *meow.*

I undressed and brushed my teeth, wondering if Lissa had tucked herself in for the night. Before crawling into my own bed, I thanked the Lord for providing a safe place for her.

Slipping into bed, I thought back to my efforts to protect Lissa from her abusive father. Now that she was hidden in the Amish community, I ought to feel relieved, but a veil of guilt hung heavily around me. I tried to pray it away.

Then I reasoned with God. "I don't have a choice. I *have* to take care of Lissa. She's a helpless victim."

Exhausted, I gave up the struggle and fell into a deep sleep.

In the midst of my aimless dreaming, someone called my name. It was a familiar voice. I tried to sit up, but my head seemed too heavy to lift off the pillow.

"*Merry!*" A child's voice rang out.

I forced my eyes open, overwhelmed with an intense desire to see my twin again. "Faithie?" Even as I said the words, my heart beat with anticipation.

In confusion, I watched Faithie's voice take on first one shape, then another. It was as though I was observing a passage of time, from the dreadful diagnosis to the very day she died three short seasons later. Like flashing lights, the eerie forms sprang up one after another until all that was left was a frail little girl beneath hospital sheets, her cheeks sunken and eyes lifeless.

I squeezed my eyes shut, waiting, longing for tears—the tears locked away in my heart. I tried, but I could not cry, even as I saw Faithie dying before me again.

"I'm here to help you," her voice called.

"Where are you, Faithie? I can't see you." I tried to shake off the sleepy haze paralyzing me. "Please let me see you again." I longed to touch her, to tell her how much I missed her. To ask her to forgive me.

A hush fell over the room. And then I heard her voice again. *"Will you cry for me?"* The question hung like snowflakes suspended in midair, building intensity in the silence.

I struggled to speak, but the words dried up in my throat. Thrusting my hands out of the covers, I reached for her with my trembling fingertips, aching to touch her.

"Please cry for me," she said again, this time more softly.

"I want to, Faithie," I shouted. "I want to with all of my heart."

Thud!

A door slammed and I heard Skip's voice. "Merry, wake up! You're having a nightmare," he said, inches from my face as I opened my eyes.

Startled, I looked around. Disappointed.

He touched my forehead the way Mom did when she suspected a fever. "You feel hot," he said. "We better check your temperature."

"I'll be fine," I said, lying back on my pillow. "If I'm still hot in the morning, I'll check it then."

A thin golden light from the hallway allowed me to see the concern in his face. "You sure, cat breath?"

I forced a smile at his lousy nickname. "Don't worry about me."

"Okay, if you're sure." He glanced up at my wall clock. "It's almost four-thirty. Get some sleep."

I heard the click of his door as he headed back to bed. Seconds passed as I waited, listening to the deathlike silence. "Faithie?" I whispered, certain that Skip was wrong. It was not a dream. It couldn't be. It—she—seemed so real! The wall clock ticked away uncaringly as I lay in bed, holding my breath for Faithie's return.

It was nearly five o'clock when I gave up trying to go back to sleep. I heard the muffled sounds of horses and buggies *clip-clop*ping down SummerHill, heading for market.

Emotionally exhausted, I went to my closet, searching for one of my scrapbooks. I found it on the shelf above my hanging sweaters and shirts. Powder blue with a silver lining around the cover edges, this scrapbook held some of my best early photography.

I turned on the lamp beside my bed, propped up my pillows, and prepared for a quiet visit into the past.

Besides being a photography enthusiast, I was a scrapbook freak. I'd always been partial to pictures. For me they were better than words.

I opened to the first page. Four photos, all scenes from my childhood, greeted me. I preferred settings and things over pictures of people.

I studied the first picture—our gazebo. White and latticed, its frame was surrounded by our tall backyard maples. Flaming reds and fiery oranges told an autumn story. A sad, hopeless story—the season we were told about Faithie's cancer.

The picture had been captured by the cheap camera I'd won in first grade. Even so, the fall colors stood out as a brilliant backdrop to the stark gazebo.

I studied the second picture—a winter scene. Again, the gazebo was center stage, but it seemed nearly lost in the white fury of snow and ice. Just as our hopes had been dashed as the cancer took its toll on Faithie.

Skipping to the third picture, I remembered the spring. Mom had placed flowering plants around the gazebo, making the outdoor room especially pretty for Faithie's afternoon visits. The empty chaise, surrounded by spring flowers, described the emptiness I felt as my sister's illness worsened.

Then came summer. The most heart-wrenching season. The fourth photo displayed a sun-drenched gazebo, minus the chaise lounge. Dad had removed it promptly when Faithie died. But along the white railing, small brown pigeons with pointed tails perched and twittered in the hot sun. Seven mourning doves—one for each year my sister had lived and laughed—had chosen to summer in our gazebo.

The mourning doves called and called during those long, scorching months. They continued for days at a time. Dad said they were calling for rain. It was bone dry, after all.

I stared at the sad scene, reliving the emotions. The mourning doves never did call down enough rain, at least not enough for the farmers around us. A fierce drought had come that year. And like the rain, my tears were dried up.

Closing the scrapbook, I placed it gently on the lamp table beside me. I turned the problem over in my mind. *How do I unlock my heart? Allow my tears to fall?*

I thought back to a long-ago morning recess when Faithie had first told me her head ached. I'd thought it was no big deal. She'd gone to the school nurse, rested for a while, and felt better. Several weeks later, the same thing happened. Faithie never told anyone at home and I thought nothing more of it.

When the final diagnosis came, months later, the cancer had already become too advanced for effective treatment. I blamed myself.

I closed my eyes, drifting into a troubled sleep. Morning came all too soon.

Skip knocked on my door more calmly than usual. "Merry, how're you feeling? Still hot?"

I felt my forehead. "Can't tell," I said. But I thought of Lissa suddenly and realized how much better it might be if I stayed home from school today.

"I'll get the thermometer."

"Okay," I said, hoping for the chance to stay home. I sat up as he knocked again, feeling dizzy from lack of sleep. "Come in," I called, and the cats scampered out of the room as the door opened.

Skip came in sporting a thermometer in one hand and rubbing alcohol in the other. "Stick this under your tongue." He placed the thermometer on my lower lip and slid it into my mouth as if I were a child. "Keep your lips tight." I nodded and he stepped back to survey the situation. "You look wiped out, Mer."

It turned out I didn't have a fever according to the thermometer, but Skip decided I should stay home anyway. He said I looked pale. Probably from a lousy night's sleep. Without arguing, I slid back under the covers.

"Don't forget, Mrs. Gibson comes to clean today," he said before closing the door, and without much effort, I fell back to sleep.

Around nine o'clock, I woke again. I could hear vacuuming downstairs. Feeling renewed after the extra sleep, I headed for the bathroom to shower. It didn't take long to dress and grab a bowl of cereal and some juice. I was all set to dash out the back door when Mrs. Gibson came into the kitchen. Her hair was wrapped in a blue kerchief, but her eyes were bright and alert.

Now, here's a morning person, I thought.

"I hope you're feeling much better," she said. "Your brother left a note about you." I thought she was going to touch my forehead at first, but she stroked my hair instead. "If you're not planning to go back to bed, I'll clean your room now. I understand you're having company tonight."

"My aunt and uncle are coming," I said, reaching for the newspaper. I nearly choked when I saw Lissa's school picture plastered on the front page.

Br-ring! I scooted the kitchen chair back to answer the phone. "Hanson residence."

"Oh, Merry, it's you," Miss Spindler said. "I wondered who that was wandering around with Mrs. Gibson in your kitchen. Are you ill?"

"I felt a little sick this morning, so Skip said I should stay home," I explained, wondering how she could see things so far away. "I feel much better now."

"Oh, that's good." She cackled a bit. "Then you'll be able to enjoy the apple pie I baked first thing this morning."

I grimaced at the thought of her coming over. I wanted to get going to see Lissa. "Uh, could you bring it over around lunchtime?" I asked.

"Well, I suppose I could do that, dear."

"Okay, thanks. I'll see you then."

"Have you heard anything more from your parents?" she persisted.

"Everything must be fine with them, thanks," I said, eager to hang up.

"Well, that's good to know." She paused as if she was dying to discuss something else. "Merry, dear, how did everything turn out with those policemen last night?"

She would bring *that* up.

"It was, uh . . . I think everything's been cleared up." It bugged me that I couldn't articulate clearly when I felt cornered.

"That's good," she said. "And I was meaning to ask you about Rachel Zook. What's happened to her leg?"

I froze. Had Miss Spindler been watching the kitchen last night? Did she know about Lissa's Amish disguise? I cleared my throat. "Uh . . . did you say Rachel?"

"Yes, dear. I saw her limping down the lane last night after that parade of policemen arrived."

What could I say? Was Miss Spindler on to something?

She sighed into the phone. "What do you suppose Miss Rachel was doing standing out there in the willow grove half the night? My, oh my, she looked cold . . . and quite alone, I must say."

Yee-ikes! I stretched the phone cord all the way across the kitchen and looked out the back door. Miss Spindler's house was about a half acre away, set on a gentle slope that made it possible to survey things quite nicely from her second-floor bedroom window. And if I guessed correctly, the nosy old lady probably had some assistance—like some high-powered binoculars.

"Well, you know Rachel's almost at the running-around stage the Amish let their teens go through," I said, trying to steer her away from all the questions. "But I don't think you have to worry about her, Miss Spindler."

"Well, I certainly hope every little thing is just fine at the Zooks' house," she said. "I don't want to see fishy goings-on over there."

I swallowed hard. *What does she mean?*

At that moment, I couldn't decide which was worse. Two policemen by night or a snoopy old neighbor by day.

In my ultra-polite voice, I said, "Thank you so much for calling, Miss Spindler. I hope you have a wonderful day, and I'll look forward to that pie of yours at lunch."

"There's a dear," she said and hung up.

In one gulp, I swallowed the rest of my juice and left the kitchen, safely out of view.

Who knows what Old Hawk Eyes would think if she saw me leave for the Zooks' farm. This was truly horrible. Here I was, stuck at home with no possible way of getting to Lissa.

Sixteen *Whispers Down the Lane*

I hurried upstairs to Skip's room. One of his windows faced north, overlooking the Zooks' farm. Quickly, I looked out, past the willow grove to the strip of dirt leading to Rachel's house.

More than thirty gray buggies were parked outside. The Amish farm bustled with activity as men and women hurried here and there, doing assigned chores—helping Rachel's parents prepare for their oldest son's wedding.

A group of bearded men worked an assembly line, unloading two wagons filled with wooden benches used for seating at the Sunday house services and weddings. They unfolded the bench legs before carrying them inside the house, all part of the Amish tradition.

By the looks of this large crew of helpers, the Zooks were expecting a big crowd tomorrow. I wondered what chore Rachel had invited Lissa to do.

I remembered when my first invitation had come. It was last year. Rachel and her younger sister, Nancy, had been assigned to bake molasses cookies for her cousin's wedding, three houses down the lane. It took us almost all afternoon, but when we finally finished, eleven dozen cookies graced the table. For weeks after that, I nearly choked whenever someone so much as mentioned the word molasses.

The wedding preparations made me miss Lissa. She was probably caught up in the middle of things by now. Rachel would see to that. I just hoped that Lissa was being careful not to give herself away. It was important for her to blend into the Amish community until my dad got home tomorrow night. As for the police, they'd never think of looking for Lissa at an Amish wedding!

Dashing to my bedroom, I started pulling the sheets off my bed. In short order, Mrs. Gibson and I had the room ready for company. While she cleaned the bathroom, I sat on my bed, dreaming up a new scheme and deciding what role our housekeeper might play.

I needed a way to distract Old Hawk Eyes while I made a run for next door. *What if I get Mrs. Gibson to pay her a little visit?* I waited till she was gathering up her things and saying good-bye before I sprang it on her. "I wonder if you could do me a favor?" I said, following her to the front door.

"Of course, Merry. What is it?"

"Could you go around the corner to Miss Spindler's house and tell her everything's fine over here? She's been calling a lot lately. I think she's worried about Skip and me." I went on to tell her briefly about the visit from the police, playing it down as best I could.

"Well, of course, I'd be happy to." She tucked a loose strand of dark hair into her bandana. "Tell your mother I'll be back next week, same time. And if there's anything I can do before then, just give me a call."

"Okay, thanks," I said, waving as she headed for her car. I ran to the kitchen and hid behind the back door curtains, watching old Miss Spindler's place. In a few minutes, Mrs. Gibson's car pulled into the driveway. She got out and walked to the front door—my cue to hightail it out of here.

Past the gazebo, down the lane, and through the shortcut I ran. By the time I leaped over the last picket fence, I was out of breath. Walking up to the back porch, I hid behind the ivy trellis, trying to see in the window. Suddenly, a familiar face greeted mine. Lissa was washing windows with Rachel!

"We could use another pair of hands," Rachel said as I entered the back door.

I sniffed a familiar scent. Glancing around the kitchen, I noticed two Amishwomen working over the hot cookstove, baking doughnuts and . . . molasses cookies! I tried to keep from pinching my nose shut, and held my breath instead.

"What are you doing, ditching school?" Lissa whispered, wearing one of Rachel's work dresses.

"Skip said I was too sick to go."

"You look fine to me," Rachel teased.

"I feel fine," I said, holding the bucket of water for the window washers. "Must've been that strange dream I had last night."

"A dream made you sick?" Lissa asked.

"I got too hot, I guess," I said, hoping to move on. I backed away from the woodstove, noticing how crowded the house was with all the helpers. "Looks like everything's going well here."

Lissa nodded, seeming more relaxed than she had in a long time. "Rachel showed me how to milk a cow today," she whispered. "It felt . . ." She stopped, looking up at the ceiling, then scrunched up her face. "Let's just say it was real different."

I sucked in my breath and bit my lip, worried about Lissa blowing her cover.

Rachel must've seen my concern. "Don't worry, Merry. Everything's *Plain* good."

I smiled. It was like a secret code. Her way of saying no one suspected a thing. So far.

After two more windows, we took a break. Rachel led us upstairs to her room. She showed Lissa the cross-stitched pillow she'd made for her brother's wedding gift. When Rachel's mother called, she responded quickly, leaving me alone with Lissa at last.

"How's everything going today?" I asked, eager for more details.

Lissa grinned. "You were right, I do like Rachel," she said, obviously not catching my concern. "I love it here, Merry. I really do."

I forced the air through my lips. "Please be careful about getting too friendly with the other young women. If you talk too much, they might suspect something. For one thing, your accent's a little off."

"Jah?" Lissa answered, smiling. "How's that?"

I motioned her away from the door. "You can't take any chances," I warned, filling her in on the phone calls from Old Hawk Eyes. "I'm worried about what Miss Spindler might do. She knows lots of Amish people around here. I mean *lots* of them."

Lissa frowned. "What do you think she'll do?"

I sighed. "Miss Spindler suspects something. I know she does. I'm not sure how far she'll take it."

Terror returned to Lissa's face. "You mean I'm not safe here, either?"

"We can't be too careful." I turned away from Lissa's piercing eyes and picked up the hand mirror on Rachel's dresser. "Have you seen yourself lately?" I held the mirror up to her.

Lissa backed away, her lips set. "Plain women never admire themselves."

I laughed. This remark, coming from her, seemed weird. "What are you talking about?"

"Their religion teaches against making an image of themselves to save or admire. It's part of not being proud," Lissa explained as though I didn't already know.

"I know all that stuff, but what do you care?"

She smiled knowingly. "I thought if I was going to pretend to be Amish, I'd better act it."

"Well, it's a good thing *I'm* not Amish," I announced. "Life could be mighty tough without a camera."

"Maybe you could learn to make quilt designs or something else," she suggested as a tiny smile crept across her face.

I got up and went to the curtainless window. Dark Amish-green shades were rolled all the way up to allow the morning sun to heat the room. "I haven't seen Mrs. Gibson's car drive down the lane yet," I said absentmindedly, "but I'm sure as soon as it does, Old Hawk Eyes will take up her post again."

"Well, I guess we'd better let God worry about her," Lissa said out of the blue.

"What did you say?"

Lissa ignored my question. "Did you know there's stuff about birds in the Bible?" She reached for the German Bible on the dresser. "I found a verse last night." She flipped back and forth between the pages. "I can't find it in German," she said, "but I know it's in the Bible you loaned me. Something about not one little bird will fall to the ground unless God lets it happen." A look of excitement crossed her face as she stood up, slowly making her way to the window.

I watched her stare at the birdhouse outside. There was a thoughtful, faraway look in her eyes. Lissa's voice was soft. "Birdhouses never have doors."

And without a word of explanation, I knew exactly what she was thinking.

I hated to spoil the moment, but I wanted to impress on Lissa one last time to be careful. "Please remember, you're being watched," I warned. "Even though Miss Spindler may have thought you were Rachel Zook last night, she *did* see the limp. The police are telling Lancaster residents to be on the lookout for certain details. Specific things."

Lissa's eyes expressed fear.

"It's everywhere, Lissa. All over the media—TV, newspapers. Like it or not, you made the front page of the morning paper today!"

"It's a good thing the Amish don't have newspapers or TVs," she said, sounding relieved. "Don't worry, Merry. I won't do anything dumb, I promise."

"We have to keep you hidden till my dad gets home. It won't be long now." I glanced at my watch. "Oh no, it's almost noon!"

Grabbing my jacket, I flung it on, muttering brainlessly to Lissa about being late for Miss Spindler's apple pie. I hurried toward Rachel's bedroom door, vowing to return later.

"Don't forget to tell Skip you're spending the night over here," Lissa reminded me.

"Good thinking." I waved good-bye.

Halfway home, I stopped walking and turned to look at the Zooks' farm through the willows. Why hadn't I told Rachel about

Miss Spindler's snooping? More than anything I wanted to go back and warn her, too, just in case. But it was getting late. Old Hawk Eyes herself would be arriving at my house any minute.

Eventually, the apple pie was delivered. Miss Spindler—her hair a puff of gray-blue—brought it over. As usual, her tongue was flapping to beat the band.

"What a frightful thing it was last night. All those police officers surrounding your house!"

I tried to comfort her. "Don't worry, everything's fine now, Miss Hawk . . . er . . . Spindler." I nearly choked! But she kept chattering on and on, never even noticing my slipup.

Finally, she left, and I sat down to some lunch, topping it off with two slices of pie for dessert. Before I cut into it, I went upstairs to get my digital camera. I had to take a picture of the lightly browned, fork-dotted crust. I don't know why, I just did.

Click!

I ate the scrumptious dessert, enjoying the moist, delicious fruit and the crispy homemade crust. When I was finished, I aimed my camera and took another shot.

Click!

The before-and-after thing was something I'd picked up at the photography contest last year. Several kids had used the approach, and when I thought about it, I realized I'd been doing it, too. Mostly since Faithie's death.

Long before Skip arrived home from school, I called Chelsea Davis to get my homework assignments.

"Feeling better?" she asked.

"Lots."

"So I'll see you on the bus tomorrow?"

"Only in the morning," I explained. "My brother and I are going to an Amish wedding around noon, so I won't see you after school."

"Well, have fun with Levi," she said, chuckling. "He'll be there, right?"

"It's his brother's wedding, silly."

"Oh yeah," she said, playing dumb. "Well, maybe you'll rack up some extra credit for your social studies grade."

"Maybe. Except I'm only going to witness the marriage vows. The rest of the wedding ceremony starts at eight o'clock and goes till about noon."

"Why so long?" she asked.

"For one thing, there are two preachers. One tells Bible stories from Creation to the Great Flood, and the other preacher finishes with love stories like how Isaac married Rebecca. And, of course, there's the Amish favorite: the great love story of Ruth and Boaz."

"Ruth and who?" Chelsea asked. "I never heard of a Bozo in the Bible."

I giggled. "I'll tell you about it sometime."

After we said good-bye, I headed downstairs to set the table. I wasn't sure when Aunt Teri and Uncle Pete would arrive, but I set places for them anyway.

Halfway through Skip's supper of overcooked cheese omelet, our relatives arrived. I dashed to the back door and flung it wide.

"Merry, Merry," Uncle Pete said, greeting me. He *always* said my name twice.

I hugged and kissed Aunt Teri as she followed her husband's fat stomach into our kitchen. She spied the omelet morsels left on our plates and promptly began signing to Uncle Pete. Something about stirring up a decent meal for these poor orphans, to which Skip mouthed a hearty, "Amen!"

We sat down, except Aunt Teri, who moved around the kitchen with the ease of a ballerina. We were talking ninety miles an hour, probably because we hadn't seen Mom's sister or her husband since last summer. But with the talk flying so fast, we caught up quickly, especially on family matters.

The biggest news was that Aunt Teri was pregnant!

"How soon?" I asked.

Uncle Pete sat up tall and proud in his chair. "Next summer—and it's twins," he boasted, turning to sign so Aunt Teri wouldn't be excluded from the conversation.

I almost swallowed my tonsils. Thank goodness Uncle Pete started yakking his head off, otherwise it might've been obvious that I suddenly clammed up.

"Mom's gonna be so-o surprised," Skip was saying. But I tuned them out, and in a few minutes excused myself to do my homework.

As for Skip letting me sleep over at the Zooks', it was no problem. Uncle Pete, however, threw a royal fit when he heard I was going to the neighbors' so he and Teri could have my room.

"Everything's cool," I assured him. "You'll see me in time for breakfast tomorrow." No one in her right mind skipped out on Aunt Teri's mouth-watering waffles!

Skip waited to take me to Rachel's until after dessert—Miss Spindler's apple pie certainly had come in handy.

Thick clouds covered the moon as I followed my brother out to the car. The clouds were a heaven-sent blessing. Old Hawk Eyes would have a troublesome time focusing on the comings and goings of Merry Hanson on a night like this!

Skip drove me the short distance to the Zooks', even though I could've walked. Rachel and I always ran back and forth, even at night. After all, SummerHill Lane wasn't a superhighway or anything. The most traffic we ever had was the scurry of Amish buggies heading for house church or the market. I'd taken Skip up on his offer only because I didn't want to cause trouble between us. No need to stir up new suspicions about Lissa's whereabouts.

Loaded down with my overnight case in one hand and schoolbag in the other, I hopped out of the car near the wagon wheel mailbox on Zooks' private lane. I waved to Skip as he backed up and headed home. I felt good about outsmarting Old Hawk Eyes once again!

Feelings of excitement grew with each step. I thought back to my plan to disguise Lissa as an Amish girl. Sure it was risky, but it worked. Mom and Dad would be proud of how I'd handled things.

Protecting Lissa from her horrible father. Sharing God's Word with her. Encouraging her . . .

Suddenly, I saw headlights coming over the crest of the hill. The car came fast, spitting dust out beneath its tires.

Was it a squad car? Had the police returned? Uneasy about what to do, I stood frozen in the middle of Zooks' private lane.

The moon slipped out behind the clouds and I could see more clearly. The car kept coming closer. . . . Anybody could see it was definitely *not* a squad car.

Concerned that the driver was out of control, I stepped back, away from the main road. The car swerved to the far left, coming straight for me. Just when I thought it would jump the ditch and ram the mailbox, the car squealed into Zooks' lane and stopped in a cloud of dust.

Instantly, I thought of Lissa's father. My mind filled in the blanks easily enough. This must be one of his wild and drunken joy-rides. . . . He'd seen me walking alone at night. Yee-ikes! I was about to become a statistic!

Eighteen *Whispers Down the Lane*

Just when I was close to totally freaking out, I realized the car was a snazzy red sports car—Miss Spindler's! In a split second, the dark-tinted window on the passenger's side glided down automatically.

"Hello there, Merry," she called to me, leaning over in spite of the shoulder harness. "Is every little thing all right?"

Her favorite expression, I thought, not amused by her dreadful timing. Or the way her driving had triggered my imagination.

"Thanks for asking," I said, trying not to exhibit my fright. "I'm just spending the night at Rachel's." I nodded my head in the direction of the house. "You probably heard my aunt and uncle are staying at our house, in *my* room."

Now maybe the questions would stop. I hoped so.

She fluffed up her blue-gray kink of hair. "Oh yes . . . that's right, I do remember that dear cleaning lady of yours saying something about it." Miss Spindler stared curiously at my schoolbag, which was gaping open, revealing my camera. "It was awfully kind of her to stop by for a chat and a cup of hot coffee." Her eyes were still glued to my camera. I could almost hear the wheels spinning in her nosy blue-gray head.

"Well, I'll see you later." I took two steps away from her red wheels, hoping the conversation was over.

"How was the pie?" she continued.

I turned quickly. "Oh, we finished it off at supper. Thanks very much," I said, squelching the desire to ignore her.

"I'm so glad to hear it," she said and put the spiffy car in reverse, grinding the gears as she backed down the lane behind me.

"Close call," I muttered, but I kept walking, refusing to look back. No way did I want her snooping around here with Lissa hanging out with the Zooks!

When I got to the Grossdawdy Haus, I peeked in the living room window. Lissa was sitting in one of the rocking chairs, beside Rachel's grandmother. I tapped on the door, and Grandfather Zook let me in. Quickly I explained why I'd come.

"Oh, please make yourself at home. There's always room for one more around here," the grandfather said, smiling and tapping his pipe in his hand.

Lissa seemed pleased to see me, but I knew something else was on her mind when she pulled me into her bedroom.

"Hey, you're not limping that much," I remarked as she closed the door. "It's good we got photos of your bruises for my dad."

She nodded, but by the eager look in her eyes I knew the subject at hand wasn't her recent abuse. "Remember how you told me you didn't cry when you were born?" she began. "And how I said I cry all the time?"

"Uh-huh." What was she getting at?

"Well, I was reading your Bible again, and I found the coolest verse." She stopped talking and I saw her eyes glisten. "Oh, Merry, I used to be so ashamed of my tears, until now."

"Show me the verse," I said, moving the lantern closer.

Placing her hand over her heart for a moment, she appeared to gather courage. Then she turned to Psalms, and I peered over her shoulder as she read. " 'You have collected all my tears and preserved them in your bottle. You have recorded every one in your book.' "

Lissa looked up. "You know what that means, don't you? Our tears are precious to God—so precious He keeps them." She was obviously amazed at this news.

I was silent as she took the lantern from me, placing it back on the dresser. "Thanks for bringing me to this peaceful place," she said. "I will never forget this day as long as I live."

"I'm glad you trusted me to help you," I said, still grasping the significance of Psalm 56:8.

We undressed for bed, and when Lissa put on a long cotton nightgown, I giggled. "You're turning into a real Amish girl, Liss."

"It's kinda fun while it lasts," she said, a sad quiver in her voice.

"What's wrong?"

"I'm nervous about what happens next. You know, tomorrow when your dad comes home and talks to his lawyer friend."

"Don't worry, Liss. My dad'll take care of everything. You'll see."

That seemed to calm her down a bit, but it was my bedtime prayer that made a bigger difference. Before slipping into the creaky bed, she looked at me wide-eyed. "I'm so glad you're here."

"You can count on me, Liss, you know that." I reached for my camera. "You look so cute in that Amish nightgown," I said, taking the cap off the lens. "Mind if I take a quick shot?"

She posed comically as I aimed my camera.

Click!

"Now hop in bed," I said. "And cover up with the pretty Amish quilt."

Click!

Another one of my before-and-after sequences was complete.

Later in the moonlight, we lay side by side in the double bed. Lissa was silent except for her breathing. Soon it became steady and slower, and I knew she was asleep. The five-o'clock milking experience had taken its toll.

I, on the other hand, tossed and turned, struggling for sleep. I couldn't stop thinking about Lissa's amazing discovery. *God saves our tears?* Who would've thought the Bible contained such a strange verse! The fact that it did had a peculiar effect on me.

At last, I slept.

Long before dawn the next day, Rachel's grandmother knocked on our bedroom door. "Rise and shine, girls," she called. "It's weddin' day!"

Lissa groaned. "I'd never make it as an Amish girl," she said. "Starting with this five-o'clock cow-milking thing."

I crawled out of my side of the toasty-warm bed. Swinging my legs over a mountain of quilts, I tested the floor with my big toe. "Ee-e-ek!" I squealed as my bare skin touched the cold floor.

"*That's* another big problem," Lissa said, referring to the icy floor. "Hurry, let's get dressed before we change our minds!" She laughed out loud.

I noticed a tranquil look on Lissa's face. Something was different.

She avoided my eyes, looking down at the hardwood floor. "It's not polite to stare."

"I'm sorry, Liss, it's just that you seem so . . . settled, so happy. It's a nice change," I said, touching her shoulder.

She went to the dresser and lit the lantern, holding it close to her face. "Is this the face of a lost soul?"

"Huh?" I frowned. *What is she doing?*

"Well, is it?" she persisted. "Look closely. What do you see?"

I inched my way across the cold floor, studying her hard.

With a confident thud, she set the lantern down on the dresser. "Remember what you said about the family of God?" She smiled. "Well, I'm a member."

"When did this happen?"

Her face shone. "In the middle of the night."

"*This* is the middle of the night," I teased.

A giggle escaped her lips. "I talked to God last night—by myself—just Him and me. I'm so-o happy, Merry, and it's all because of you." She hugged me close. "Thanks for showing me the way to my heavenly Father."

I was speechless. Life sure was full of surprises!

Lissa put on one of Rachel's brown work dresses, and we hurried outside to the barn. I helped by pouring fresh milk into the aluminum container and rolling it into the milk house. Tough stuff for a modern girl.

Levi offered to help on the next trip to the milk house. When I thanked him, a smile spread across his face. "Comin' to the wedding?"

I felt my face grow warm. "Skip and I'll be there."

He looked quite pleased as he straightened to his full height and marched off toward the house. I wondered what was going through his Amish head. Surely he knew better than to flirt with an English girl like me.

I turned my attention to Lissa, who was washing down the next cow. When she touched the cow's udder, I had to look away. Ee-ew!

Lissa got down and got dirty right along with Rachel and her brothers. It said a lot. Lissa was willing to do anything to fit in with this family. Willing to do whatever she had to, to keep from going back to her dreadful family situation.

Just then Curly John ran outside looking *ferhoodled,* as the Amish say—running around like a chicken with its head cut off—looking for his suspenders. Levi and Aaron slinked around the side of the house looking awfully guilty.

Tomorrow the real pranks would come. I'd heard of newly married Amish couples trying to do the family laundry only to discover that parts of their washing machine had been removed!

By the time we finished milking, wedding helpers, cooks and waiters, thirty in all, began arriving in horse-drawn buggies. Curly John, dressed in his new black Sunday suit, hurried to hitch Apple to the family buggy.

"He seems nervous," Rachel said as we watched. "He's off to Sarah's place, to get his bride."

I glanced at Sarah's mother, who was already checking off a long list of chores as Amish friends and relatives filed into the Zooks' farmhouse. Usually Amish weddings were held at the bride's home, but this time the groom's house was bigger, and every inch of space from living room to kitchen would be needed for the guests.

I could almost smell Aunt Teri's waffles, so I said good-bye to Rachel and Lissa. "I'll be back around noon," I said. "In time to see Curly John and Sarah become husband and wife."

We giggled. Amish or not, weddings were a blend of excitement and hope. Hope that someday each of us would be getting married, too.

Levi tipped his black felt hat flirtatiously as I left the barn. When I peered back at Lissa, I caught her eyes on us and she grinned.

All the way home, through the willow grove and down the lane, I remembered that grin. How thankful I was for the truly peaceful way about her. Best of all, Lissa was a child of God. I could hardly wait to tell my parents. Tonight!

Aunt Teri's waffles tasted the best ever, even though I had to wash the last bites down with a glass of milk. I hurried upstairs to shower away the disgusting smell of cow manure. There were better ways to influence friends . . . and teachers.

Soon Skip was calling for me. "Hurry, Mer! You'll be late for the bus."

In a whirlwind of books and winter clothes, I managed to race downstairs, kiss my aunt and uncle, and remind Skip to pick me up by eleven-thirty. "Don't be late!" I dashed down the steps in time for the bus.

Chelsea slid over to the window when she saw me. "How ya feelin'?" She gave me a wide grin.

"Not bad for a very short night," I said, but caught myself before saying where I'd slept.

Jon was waiting at my locker when the bus dumped us out. "Lookin' light and lovely, Merry, mistress of mirth."

"Thanks. Feeling fine and fancy." I thought of Lissa, dressing Plain and not-so-fancy these days.

"Still seeing moon shadows?" he asked.

Yeah, right, I thought. Wouldn't he be surprised to know about those moon-shadow police?

Jon leaned his tall frame against the wall, waiting for me to collect my books. "You should've been here yesterday." His voice rose with excitement. "This place was crawling with cops—they nabbed anyone who even remotely claimed to know Lissa Vyner."

"What?" I managed to say, in spite of my cottony throat. What would he think of me, his Christian friend, hiding Lissa from the authorities?

Jon promptly filled me in on the whole scenario.

"Anything new on the case?" I finally asked, feeling lousy asking such a question.

"Only that they've planted informants all over Lancaster County." He shuffled his books. "Ready for class?"

I nodded, stacking up an armload of books, wondering what it would be like to have Jon carrying them. Maybe someday . . .

Halfway through history, I tuned out Mr. Wilson's droning voice. What if the cops had planted one of their informants in the Amish community? Right now, someone dressed as an Amish farmer—or maybe his wife—was riding in a buggy, going to Curly John's wedding.

I sat up like I'd been hit by lightning. In the process, my note-book flew off my desk, clattering to the floor. I stretched to retrieve it, counting the minutes till the end of first hour.

Jon's concerned smile warmed my heart. He mouthed, "Are you all right?" from across the aisle.

I nodded, feeling foolish for reacting so strongly to my latest fears. Yet deep in my heart, I wondered. Was Lissa truly safe?

Twenty *Whispers Down the Lane*

By the time Skip and I arrived at the Zooks' farmhouse, there were gray-topped carriages lined up all over the side yard. Several black open buggies, called courting buggies, were parked here and there. So were a few cars and vans belonging to non-Amish neighbors and friends.

Skip and I headed in the back way, since the service had already begun. I looked for Lissa immediately and noticed a few empty spaces on the wooden benches in the kitchen. Mostly mothers of infants, and some of the bride's aunts and cousins helping with food, sat out here. That way they wouldn't disturb the ceremony when they checked on food simmering in the summer kitchen.

Amishmen always sat in one part of the house, while the women sat in the opposite end, facing one another the way they did for church. It didn't matter where English friends like Skip and I sat, though. We took the nearest seats available, holding the long wedding gift on our laps—a white blanket I'd found in Mom's "gift" drawer this morning. Aunt Teri had wrapped it beautifully while we were at school.

I spotted Lissa out of the corner of my eye. She was sitting near the wall, wearing Rachel's green dress and black apron. She turned slightly when she heard us come in. Wisely, she turned away.

Whew, close call! Skip would recognize her profile in a second.

Curiously, I watched as Curly John and Sarah stood before the bearded Amish bishop. Sarah looked shy and demure in her long cotton wedding dress of pale blue. Her white cape and apron matched her attendants', who sat in straight, cane-backed chairs in the front row. Curly John stood tall and proud in his black suit. I wondered if he'd found his suspenders in time for the wedding.

I leaned up to see him take Sarah's hand. They seemed too young for marriage, but I could see the glow of love in their eyes.

The old bishop asked Curly John a question. "Are you willing to enter wedlock together as God ordained and commanded in the beginning?"

The groom answered, "Yes."

Again, the question came. This time for Sarah, who answered, "Yes," softly.

More serious questions were asked. Then came Curly John's promises to his bride, and hers to him. At last, the bishop pronounced the couple husband and wife. Many people wiped away tears. I thought of the Lord saving our tears—the happy and sad ones. By the looks on the faces here, the tears were sober ones; the Amish understood that marriage continues until death.

No rice was thrown, no cheers were shouted, and no rings were exchanged. The mood was very serious.

My brother, however, wasn't the least bit serious. "Chow time," he whispered in my ear. And I remembered the main reason for his being here. After all, the Amish wedding feast was the most lavish part of the wedding festivities.

Complete with chicken and duck roasted in pounds of butter, and veal with rich gravy and stuffing, a kid could eat on and on into oblivion! I could almost taste the creamed celery and fresh applesauce. And washtubs full of mashed potatoes and platters piled with sausage, along with fresh bread, cheeses, and many kinds of candies. Not to mention thirty cherry pies and four hundred doughnuts!

The young people were dismissed, followed by the bridal party. The boys went outside while the girls and the bridal party went upstairs to the bedrooms, making room for dinner preparations below.

I heard the men setting up tables downstairs as I searched for Rachel and Lissa upstairs. I found them talking with the bride and groom in one of the bedrooms.

When Rachel and Lissa stepped back to let other girls visit with the bride, I went to stand beside them. "Hi, you two," I said, careful not to call too much attention to Lissa. "Everything still *Plain* good?"

Rachel nodded and Lissa smiled.

I took a deep breath. "We may have a slight problem," I said, filling Rachel in on Skip's being here. "He'd recognize Lissa in a flash."

"Jah, he would," Lissa said softly.

Rachel's eyes flashed concern. She probably wondered why Skip shouldn't know Lissa was here. Especially since I'd told her Lissa was *our* company! But she remained silent.

I whispered in her ear, "Remember, I promised to tell you everything?"

She nodded.

"You have my word."

Rachel brightened a bit, glancing toward the stairs. "Maybe if it works out, Skip might end up eating with some of the boys during the second shift," she said.

"No chance," I said. "He's got his mind on food, and nothing this side of the Susquehanna River is gonna change that."

Rachel adjusted her apron, smiling sweetly. "I know about menfolk. Curly John and Levi are the same way."

Just then, I heard the familiar grinding of gears. "No, it can't be." I raced to the window. Sure enough, my suspicions were confirmed. Miss Spindler had just arrived!

Lissa frowned when she spotted her from the window. Old Hawk Eyes touched up her blue-gray puff and strutted to the back entrance.

"Was *she* invited?" I whispered to Rachel.

"All neighbors were invited for the wedding dinner," Rachel informed us. "It's *unserer Weg*—our way." I knew what she meant. The Amish were the very best when it came to making guests feel welcome, English or not, especially at weddings.

"What'll we do?" Lissa's eyes looked serious.

"Don't worry," I said. "I'll think of something."

It was time to go down for dinner. The bridal party had already gone. "Stay here till I can see where Miss Spindler's going to sit," I told Lissa. I knew that Rachel would sit with her brothers and sisters near the bride and groom, so Lissa and I were on our own.

When Rachel and all the girls had filed down the long staircase, I tiptoed down partway and surveyed the situation. In a separate room, off the side of the kitchen, I saw Skip sitting with several male cousins of the groom. With that problem settled, I searched for Miss Spindler.

She was nowhere to be seen.

Quickly, I went back upstairs. Lissa was staring out the window when I found her. "Look, we're in luck. I think Miss Spindler's going to eat with the second shift," she said.

Sure enough, Old Hawk Eyes was standing out near the barn talking to a group of women. Since there wasn't enough space for everyone to sit together, the Amish had scheduled the dinner in shifts.

"C'mon, Liss, now's our chance," I said, and we hurried downstairs and found two places in the far corner of the kitchen.

When every table was full, the bishop gave the signal for silent grace. Soon, everyone was eating and talking while waiters and helpers scurried around like worker bees, serving tables. Lissa seemed perfectly relaxed with the setup, in spite of possible threats to her security lurking outside . . . and in the next room.

I constantly checked the window, hoping Miss Spindler would stay put at least till we finished eating.

After the final dessert came another silent prayer. Then the first shift of guests were to leave the house and go outside while the next group came in. Nervously, I steered Lissa away from the kitchen door, walking in front of her all the way to the front door, trying to avoid a direct encounter with Skip.

Once outside, the first shift of guests went around inspecting the farm. Abe Zook passed out candy bars, visiting and joking with old friends and neighbors. Fortunately, it was a mild day for November—cloudy, but mild—so a light jacket was all I needed. Lissa wore a wool shawl like the other women.

We tried to stay in the middle of the group of guests touring the farm, dodging Skip by hiding behind the barn door once. Later, we maneuvered our way past him again by climbing the ladder to the hayloft.

"I'm gonna schedule a nervous breakdown when this is over," I said, falling back into the hay.

Lissa tucked her Amish dress under her legs and pulled her shawl close as the dust settled. "What a day. I'm too stuffed to be scared!" She rubbed her stomach. "Have you ever seen so much food in your life?"

I groaned, holding my middle as I sat up in the soft hay. As I did, I spied Miss Spindler standing in line to go into the house. She happened to glance our way through the open barn door. I felt uneasy staring back at her, but then, unexpectedly, she pulled something out of her purse. Binoculars!

"Duck down," I whispered.

Lissa obeyed.

I sat there, straight as the barn rafters above us, as Old Hawk Eyes gawked at me through her powerful glasses. "She's up to no good," I said like a ventriloquist through a fakey smile.

"What's she doing now?" Lissa asked from her bed of hay.

I watched as the old woman stuffed the binoculars into her purse and marched off to her car. "I think we're set. Looks like she's leaving!"

"Really?" Lissa sat up like she'd popped out of a cannon.

I pushed her back down. "Not so fast."

But it was too late. Old Hawk Eyes had glanced back just then and spotted her. Opening her car door, the old sneak leaned down, casting a leery look back at us. *Now* what was she doing?

I zeroed in on her hands, clocking her every move. That's when I saw the cellular phone. "Oh no! This is so-o bad!" I wailed.

Lissa sat up again. "What is?"

"We're finished!" I groaned.

Old Hawk Eyes peered over her shoulder as she talked on her phone.

"She must be an informant," I cried, watching her in disbelief as she pointed triumphantly at the barn—at us!

"How do you know?" Lissa asked.

"Can't you see—she's calling the cops!"

Twenty-one *Whispers Down the Lane*

I grabbed Lissa's arm, pulling her out of Miss Spindler's line of vision. "C'mon, let's make a run for it. We have time!"

Lissa's arm stiffened. "Wait!"

"There's no time to wait. Let's go to the Grossdawdy Haus. I'll hide you there!"

"No," Lissa shouted.

I whirled around, staring at her incredulously. "What did you say?"

"I can't keep running, Merry. It's time to tell the truth." Her face had a look of peaceful determination. I wanted to throw my arms around her, to take care of her, to talk sense to her. But her words rang out. "I'm going to do the right thing. When the police come, I wanna tell them about my dad. I have the courage to do it now." She put her hand on her heart as she spoke. "And," she added softly, "we have proof—remember the pictures you took?"

"Are you sure about this?" Something in me still wanted to keep her from going through with it.

"It's the right thing," Lissa insisted, studying me. "I can almost tell what you're thinking, Merry, but please stop worrying. I'll be fine. I'm a member now." Her face lit up with a rainbow smile.

Police sirens began to squeal, soft at first, then louder as they sped their way up SummerHill Lane.

Lissa's tears threatened to spill at any moment. "You're a good friend," she said. "You're my sister, too, don't forget. We're part of the same family now."

I hugged her close. "I want you to be safe, Lissa. Forever and always."

The slamming of squad car doors and the thud of footsteps signaled the end of our time together. A crowd of bearded men gathered near the barn. Their Amish wives and children scurried to the safety of the house.

Miss Spindler's scratchy voice could be heard over the chatter of German as Amish husbands and fathers hurried to form a human barrier around the barn. The Amish were peace-loving people who would not allow outsiders to take away one of their own, especially an innocent young girl like Lissa.

"In the hayloft!" Miss Spindler shouted.

I watched as Officer Rhodes and several other policemen approached Abe Zook and two Amish bishops. They showed their badges, but Abe shook his head slowly, standing his ground as he blocked the open barn door with the others. The police persisted, and I strained to hear, but they kept their voices low and calm, trying to strike a bargain, no doubt.

I turned to my friend. "Quick! Take off your bonnet," I said. "Show them your short hair! The Amish will know you aren't one of them."

Lissa followed my suggestion and removed her bonnet. Her shoulder-length hair fell around her neck. Gasps and shouts rose up from the crowd, and Officer Rhodes moved through the barricade as the Amish parted, astonished.

Before Lissa left the hayloft, I took her hand in both of mine. "You okay?"

She nodded. "What about you?" Her blue eyes cut to the quick of me. "Remember your tears, Merry. They're precious to God." And with that, she scooted through the hay toward the loft ladder.

"I'm praying for you," I whispered.

Officer Rhodes, with his piercing eyes and that businesslike chin, waited for Lissa to climb down the ladder. Just as she reached the bottom, a woman came running through the crowd—Lissa's mother! Her cries of joy rang out as she held out her arms to her daughter.

I stayed in the hayloft long after things settled down. Lissa told her story—all of it—to the police. Her mother seemed to verify the occasions of abuse. She even said that Lissa's running away had had its merits. It had startled her into taking a hard look at the abuse she and her daughter had suffered, and four days without Lissa had given her the strength to arrange a confrontation with her husband. Best of all, Mr. Vyner had consented to treatment and extensive counseling. It was safe for Lissa to go home!

Lissa and her mother walked arm in arm to a waiting squad car. The line of police cars stirred up a trail of dust on Zooks' lane as they made their way to the main road. The Amishmen milled around, whispering and shaking their heads.

I knelt in the hayloft, watching till the last car turned onto SummerHill. Lissa's words echoed in my mind. *"Remember your tears. They're precious to God."*

I scurried down the ladder to the Grossdawdy Haus. It was time for a date with my camera. An overwhelming desire spurred me on as I hurried to the room where Lissa and I had slept. Locating the camera, I ran out the back door. A lump caught in my throat as I passed the martin birdhouse in the side yard. I paused to look up at its many-sided refuge. *"Not one little bird will fall to the ground unless God lets it happen,"* Lissa had said.

I swallowed hard and for the first time in a long time felt the sting of tears. Heading for the main road, I held the tears in check until I could be alone with them. And with Faithie.

At last, I stumbled into the small cemetery where my twin sister was buried. The gentle hills surrounding the white gravestones had been alive with wild flowers eight summers before. There, I'd placed yellow daisies on her grave under a peaceful sky, setting up the shot for that long-ago special picture.

Now as I stood here, camera in hand, it was as though I'd never cried in my life. My soul was bursting, needing an outlet—wanting to make up for all the years of pain. The pain of blaming myself for Faithie's death.

I knelt in front of her gravestone, leaning my head on my arm as I sobbed. "I miss you, Faithie. I miss you . . . with all my heart."

The tears, locked away for so long, began to cleanse me. I cried the pain away, forgiving myself for the years of false blame while a November wind wrapped its gentle whispers around me.

I don't know how long I knelt there, but slowly I began to pray. "Thank you, Lord, for loving me enough to care about the tears I cry." I wiped my cheeks. "And thanks for Lissa . . . for helping her show me the way to peace."

Looking down, I noticed a clear puddle on the ledge of my sister's gravestone. My tears. Thoughtfully, I reached for my camera, adjusting it for shadows and dim light. Then carefully I aimed, creating a focal point: my fallen tears, with Faithie's gravestone as a backdrop.

Click! My before-and-after gallery was complete.

The sun poured through the clouds, creating a brilliant light. I squinted into its brightness, slipping the camera over my shoulder, and headed for home.

Secret in the Willows

To Charette,
With thanks for many things.
Best of all—
friendship.

We cannot tell the precise moment when friendship is formed. As in filling a vessel drop by drop, there is at last a drop which makes it run over; so in a series of kindnesses there is at last one which makes the heart run over.

—SAMUEL JOHNSON

It was one of those soggy springtime mornings when nothing goes right. First off, I slept through my alarm, which led to another problem: my hair.

Flat and fine, my shoulder-length locks only looked good freshly washed and blown dry. To give the illusion of more body, I always added a leave-in conditioner. Today there was no time for that ritual.

"Ugh!" I moaned.

My brother, Skip, poked his head into my room. "What's the problem? Lose a cat?" He cast an older-brother sneer at me and snapped up his high school letter jacket.

"Like you really care." I pulled at my limp hair and glared.

Skip laughed. "Maybe you oughta call that friend of yours, uh, Chelsea Davis, the girl with all the great hair."

"And why don't you just disappear," I retorted. But instead of leaving, Skip inched farther into my room.

"Mom!" I yelled.

Skip mumbled some unintelligible comment about my room smelling like kitty litter. Just then, Shadrach, Meshach, and Abednego, my three courageous cats, bounded off the bed toward him. Skip spun around and raced down the hall with a trail of hissing felines at his heels.

Served him right.

At last, Mom arrived on the scene. She surveyed my stringy hair with an audible sigh. Reaching for a yellow hair wrap, Mom began to pull my hair back. "How about a ponytail today, Merry?"

"Mom, please," I whined. "I'm going to school."

"You're absolutely right," she said, still holding my hair. "But I have a wonderful idea."

"Like what?" I glanced at my watch. "We really don't have time for a total remake here, Mom. The bus comes in exactly eighteen and a half minutes."

She marched into my bathroom, expecting me to follow. Reluctantly, I did. She grabbed a bottle of reviving mist and began spritzing it on my limp hair.

I groaned.

"Trust me, Merry Hanson," and the way she said it sounded exactly like me. I leaned down while she flipped my hair over my face. Next, she turned on the blow dryer, high heat. "This'll help seal in the shine," she said over the noise.

I had an instant vision of Marcia Brady from *The Brady Bunch*, wearing her linear locks center parted and slightly greasy. "Uh . . . Mom . . . not too shiny, okay?"

When my hair was completely dry, I flipped it back over my head. Mom wanted to help brush it out, but she'd done enough. I moved closer to the mirror. "Not bad," I said. "Thanks, Mom."

Downstairs at breakfast, Skip pretended not to notice my new look. Mom's strong kitchen presence always helped bring on spurts of Skip's most civilized behavior. She gave me a piece of toast to go with my scrambled eggs and piled it high with homemade strawberry jam from the Zooks, our Amish neighbors down the lane.

Before leaving the house, I rechecked my hair—still holding. That done, I set off down SummerHill Lane to wait for the school bus near the willow grove. Abednego and his feline brothers scampered after me.

Wild strawberry vines, glistening with April morning dew, graced the grassy slopes on either side of the dirt road. It was a misty Pennsylvania morning, complete with thunder. I almost went back to the house for an umbrella, but I could see the bus topping the hill in the distance.

In the opposite direction, I spotted Rachel Zook, my Amish friend, walking barefoot with her younger sisters, Nancy, Susie, and Ella Mae. Aaron, that rascal brother of theirs, ran ahead as if daring one of them to catch him. They were headed for the one-room school her younger siblings and other Amish kids attended in this part of Lancaster County.

Rachel stopped, turning to wave as her long green dress and black apron billowed out softly in the warm spring breeze. "Good morning, Merry!" she called.

I was too far away to see the permanent twinkle in her blue eyes, but I was sure it was there.

"Come on over later today, *jah*?" she called again.

Something was wrong. The cheerful ring was missing from Rachel's voice. Maybe she was on some kind of special errand this morning.

"Everything okay?" I asked, hurrying to catch up with her. She cast a cautious eye on the younger kids and shook her head.

"What is it, Rachel?" I asked. "What's wrong?"

She raised a finger to her lips. Her eyes looked suddenly gray. "Not now," she whispered fearfully. "I mustn't talk now."

I touched her arm. "I'll be right over after school, okay?"

She nodded, avoiding my eyes just then, and I knew something was dreadfully wrong.

Rachel ran ahead to catch up with her brother and three sisters without offering her usual good-bye wave. I turned back toward the willow grove to wait for the bus, worried.

Thunder gave way to pelting rain, and the Zook children scurried down the lane, splashing their bare feet against the muddy road. Rachel and little Susie opened their umbrellas and Aaron balanced his lunch box on top of his straw hat. My cats scampered home to safety as another thunderbolt boomed overhead. As for keeping my hair dry, I tried to protect it with my schoolbag. So much for maintaining my hairdo.

I thought about Rachel's Plain Amish hairstyle while I waited for the slowpoke bus. She never had to fuss with things like blow dryers or hair spray. Her long hair, like that of all other Amishwomen, was simply parted down the middle, pulled into a bun at the back of her head, and never cut. Since there was no electricity in Amish homes, it was the easy way.

Just when the cloudburst had nearly destroyed my entire look, the bus showed up. I climbed onto the noisy school bus, searching for Chelsea Davis. My friend was nowhere to be seen, so I scooted into the nearest available seat.

The bus lurched forward, and I could see the Zook kids up ahead. Rachel was still trudging along, head down. I leaned against the window, watching until I could see her no longer. Rachel's dark mood made my heart pound. She was usually so cheerful.

What could be wrong?

Secret in the Willows Two

By the time I arrived at Mifflin Junior High, my hair had begun to dry out. At least *some* things were improving.

I pit-stopped at my locker on my race to art class. Students were slamming locker doors and shouting at one another in the hallway while I scrounged through the junk in my locker, searching for my sketch pad.

That's when it happened.

In the midst of the noisy scrambling, a strange sensation began at the back of my neck. Like someone was staring at me. Really staring. Tingles crawled up my scalp, but I kept facing the locker, determined not to turn around.

Someone's eyes were boring a hole in the back of my head. And I was pretty sure who it was.

Jonathan Klein.

Tall with light brown hair and brown eyes that matched mine, Jon was the one guy at school I secretly had a thing for. In reality, Jon Klein was the one and only guy on the planet that I could even begin to think of in terms of the M word.

Only one question remained: When would he come to his senses and notice I was girlfriend material? Jon and I did have one thing going for us—the Alliteration Game. It was a word game he had initiated months ago, and I'd surprised him by meeting the challenge. Anyway, it was a private, very special thing between us. At least from my point of view.

Say it with all p*'s,* Jon would say, each time choosing a specific letter of the alphabet. And we'd go off doing our word thing, the Alliteration Wizard and I.

Today, however, Jon was silent behind me. I stuffed my sketch pad into my schoolbag and grabbed my books for morning classes. The uneasy feeling continued. Why wasn't he making his usual crazy comments?

I waited another second, scarcely breathing. What would it be like for him to carry my books? Was he going to ask me today?

A brilliant idea flashed through my brain. Quickly, I reached for my camera. Taking pictures, good pictures, was my main hobby in life. My camera accompanied me everywhere and always.

Swallowing a giggle, I took the lens cap off, keeping the camera close to my body until just the right moment. Wouldn't Jon be surprised when I took a candid shot of him?

Like right . . . about . . .

Now! I spun around. *Click!*

Light exploded, surprising my subject. His hands flew to his face, shielding his eyes. I lowered the camera and gasped as I realized my mistake. Across the hall from me, Elton Keel, a special-needs student, stood dazed.

This is truly horrible, I thought as I left my locker and hurried over to him. His arms still covered his face as I sputtered out my apologies. His hair was short and blond, the color of sweet corn, and he wore a blue-and-red plaid backpack.

"I . . . I'm really sorry," I said again, waiting for his boyish face to emerge out of hiding. Slowly, he lowered his arms, letting them hang at his sides. They seemed too long for the rest of his body.

"You okay?" I asked.

Elton nodded his head emphatically again and again. Then he stopped abruptly and looked down at his shirt pocket, pulling on it. With a little grunt, he grasped the tip of a blue ink pen and brought it up out of his pocket, displaying it proudly.

I still felt lousy about startling him with my flash. "Really, I thought you were someone else."

He didn't answer and I didn't expect him to. Everyone knew Elton Keel didn't speak; at least no one had heard him say anything since he transferred here.

He started clicking his ballpoint pen fast. On and off. Over and over, like the monotonous ticking of a clock. I'd heard about Elton's quirks and rituals. But this . . .

"Hey, Merry!"

I turned to see Chelsea. Her sea-green eyes sparkled as she flew down the hall. Her auburn hair floated like a curtain around her.

"Hi," I said, taking a step back from Elton. "Did ya miss the bus?"

"Mom drove me. She had a bunch of errands." Chelsea looked at my still-damp hair. "Get caught in the rain, Mer?" Before I could answer she pulled a tan corduroy newsboy cap out of her schoolbag. "Here, try this."

She plopped it on my head.

"Thanks," I said.

She grinned. "Stunning." And just like that she was off, without so much as a glance at Elton.

I looked at my watch and at Elton, still standing there. "It's time for first hour. You coming?"

He leaned his head down as if he wanted to listen to my watch. I held my arm out. "It doesn't make sounds," I said, feeling slightly awkward about having Elton's head so close. But the embarrassment didn't last. He stood up and started clicking his pen again. I turned back to my locker to put my camera away.

Without warning, Elton began grunting in a sort of high-pitched way. I turned to investigate and saw that he had jerked his backpack around and was pulling out his sketch pad, holding it high.

"Oh, you think you're gonna be late for art?" I said. "Well, so am I. Let's go!"

We made our way through the chaotic maze of students together. It felt a little strange walking with Elton to class, but I ignored the weird looks from other students as they dodged first him and then me.

Weird looks aside, it was impossible to miss the rude stares as we entered art class. Several guys whooped and hollered as Elton held the door for me. I glanced over my shoulder, wondering how much of the ridicule Elton had absorbed. Even without the smile he was cherub faced, though his eyes looked dull and almost lifeless. Kids like Elton experienced the same emotions as everyone else, I'd been told. Their emotions just didn't register in the eyes. I knew this from hearing my dad talk about several of his hospital patients.

A quick look around Mrs. Hawkins' art room told me she hadn't arrived yet. So I made a big deal about thanking Elton, staring especially hard at Cody Gower, one of the roughest kids in school.

"Hey, looks like Merry's got herself a new man," Cody taunted. A bunch of guys joined him with whistles and laughter. I felt truly sorry for Elton, but he didn't seem to mind.

The bell rang and Mrs. Hawkins showed up wearing her usual array of colorful bangles and beads. Before sitting down, she glanced at her seating chart. She made no comment about Elton's choice of seating—the empty desk directly across from mine.

I got right to work refining my charcoal sketch. Unlike some students who'd elected art as a sluff course, I enjoyed the class. Besides that, I valued Mrs. Hawkins' expert input.

Someone else was an expert in the class: Cody Gower. His expertise had nothing to do with art, though. Cody was a natural at stirring up trouble.

I concentrated on my project, taking time to shade in my charcoal sketch of an old covered bridge—Hunsecker's Mill Bridge— which I'd photographed many times. The 180-foot bridge crossed the Conestoga River not far from my house. I knew it was really old, built in 1848. Rachel Zook called it the Kissing Bridge because it was where her oldest brother, Curly John, had stolen his first kiss from Sarah—now his bride.

I stopped working long enough to blow some fine gray dust off my paper. As I did, Cody got up and stood in the aisle beside Elton's desk. Definitely up to no good.

Where was Mrs. Hawkins? I leaned up out of my seat and scanned the classroom. She was gone—again! Probably called out while I was deep in thought, working on my project.

"Cody! Leave him alone," I demanded, suddenly attracting the attention of the whole class.

Cody ignored me and picked up Elton's sketch, inspecting it. "Is this your work?" he asked in a friendly yet mocking tone.

Elton nodded, wearing a vacant stare. A rush of whispers and giggles rose from the room, mixed with the unmistakable sound of "retard" as he kept on nodding.

I sucked in a breath and held it till I nearly burst. Elton, on the other hand, seemed calm enough. Poor guy. I had to find a way to help.

Cody leaned down, studying Elton. "Mind if I show the others?" he asked, casting a repulsive smirk at the class, like a fly fisherman throwing out his line.

"Yeah, let's see the retard's masterpiece!" shouted one boy. That was all it took to lead the pack of shouting maniacs.

I leaped out of my seat. "Give me that!" I yelled, lunging for Elton's art.

"Stay out of this," Cody sneered, but I grabbed the sketch out of his hand anyway.

"No, you sit down, Cody Gower. You don't wanna mess up your grade in here, do you?" It was a threat, but I couldn't help it. Everyone knew why Cody had signed up for this class—an easy A.

"C'mon, Merry. Show us the picture!" called one of Cody's friends.

I ignored the pleas to exhibit Elton's work. Still standing, I deliberately placed his sketch facedown on my desk. As for Cody, he had no choice but to comply with my demand, because at that moment, Mrs. Hawkins waltzed into the room.

I sat down and handed Elton's drawing back to him. He started working on it as if nothing had happened.

The girl behind me tapped my shoulder. "Good going, Merry," she whispered.

I made a thumbs-up gesture without turning around. Mrs. Hawkins, meanwhile, started moving from one desk to another. She didn't get far, though, because the bell rang.

I stayed at my desk until everyone had left. Elton sat, too, off in another world, oblivious to the bell and the noisy mass exodus. I leaned forward to get his attention, pointing to his drawing. "Is it okay with you if I take a look?"

He began his nodding ritual.

Curiously, I studied the picture on his desk. It was a near-perfect ink-drawn sketch of a girl. I glanced over at his ballpoint pen dangling between two fingers. Whoever heard of doing sketches with a pen! No second chances like with pencil, yet in Elton's case it appeared that no erasures were needed. "It's genius," I whispered. "How'd you do this?"

Elton stared blankly at the drawing, and for an instant I thought I saw the corners of his mouth twitch. Clutching his pen, he began to nod again. He clicked his pen on and off and stopped. Was he trying to communicate with me? It was then that I noticed a faint brightness in his normally empty eyes.

I gazed at his sketch again. What lines—what style!

Suddenly, with an uncontrolled, jerking motion, he wrote *4 U* at the bottom and handed the picture to me.

"I can't take your work, Elton. You'll be getting a grade for this— a terrific grade!" I traced my finger around the soft curve of the girl's shoulder-length hair, noticing the bright, expressive eyes.

Then it hit me—the girl he'd drawn wasn't just any girl.

Elton Keel's art project was a sketch of me!

"I've never seen anything like it," I told Chelsea as we waited for the bus after school. "Elton Keel sketches with a ballpoint pen."

"So?"

"He gets it right the first time," I insisted. "Nobody does that." I went on to tell her about the drawing he'd made of me.

She pulled her hair back over one shoulder, smiling. "Where's the drawing now?"

"I gave it back to him."

"Oh, that's just great," she said. "He's probably depressed. Don't you know anything about retards?"

My blood boiled. "Don't say that!"

"What's *your* problem?"

"You're wrong," I heard myself saying. "He's not that . . . that word you said. Elton's a person. A very special and totally gifted person!"

Chelsea didn't say anything. She simply looked at me. And when the bus came, we climbed on in silence.

"God created each of us with unique gifts," I said, settling into our regular spot close to the front. "You make straight A's consistently, and I see beauty in nature and photograph it, and Elton . . . well, you know . . ."

Chelsea frowned, scooting back and pushing her knees up against the seat in front of us. "You're not going to launch off on one of your Bible stories now, are you?"

It's no use, I thought, glancing over my shoulder at Lissa Vyner, another one of my school friends. She was sitting and laughing in the back of the bus with Ashley Horton, our new pastor's daughter, and several other kids from my church, including Jon Klein. I watched Lissa for a moment. She seemed so much more settled—happier, too, since her dad was in therapy. Lissa and her mom had even started coming to church nearly every Sunday.

I sighed. *Why can't Chelsea be more like Lissa? Why does she fight me every time I talk about God?*

Chelsea poked my arm. "Hello-o?" she taunted. "Wanna go back and sit with the Christians?" She nodded her head in the direction of Lissa, Jon, and friends.

"Please, Chelsea," I said, "don't do this."

She slapped her hand down hard on her history book. "Well, then, don't preach."

I wanted to tell her to stop hiding her head in the sand, to open her eyes to God. But I knew better than to push things.

———

At home, I dropped off my books, eager to see Rachel Zook. I ran down SummerHill Lane, turned, and took the shortcut through the willow grove to the Amish farmhouse. The house was set back off the main road with a white picket fence circling the pasture area. There were empty fruit jars turned upside down all along the fence for storage, a sure proof that Rachel and her mother expected an abundant crop of garden vegetables. All around me, rich and moist Lancaster County soil was ready for spring planting.

I noticed Abe Zook and Levi, his sixteen-year-old son, out on the front porch repairing a shattered window. Abe stopped working and straightened up. Levi's eyes lit up when he saw me. Silly boy.

When would he learn that it made no sense to flirt with a modern girl like me?

Levi's father smiled a greeting and stroked his long, untrimmed beard as I came up the front porch. I hated to think what would happen if Abe Zook knew that Levi had taken a more-than-friendly interest in me. Amish were supposed to date among themselves. Even casual dating of English—the term they used for non-Amish—was not allowed. It was a fearful thing to be reprimanded by the bishop, though far worse if one was baptized and continued in rebellion. A shunning was sure to follow.

Levi carefully removed a shard of glass that still clung to the window frame. When his father wasn't looking, he tipped his hat at me.

"What on earth happened here?" I asked.

Levi started to explain, but Abe touched his son's shoulder, shaking his head solemnly. It was clear enough to me that someone had thrown a brick or something else through the Zooks' living room window. But since the Amish were peace-loving folk, the police would never know about it.

"Merry!" Rachel called to me from inside the house. "Come on in. I've been waiting for you."

My friend wasn't exactly sitting around twiddling her thumbs. She was helping her mother with spring cleaning. And by the looks of things, it was a day to scour the tinware—loaf pans, cookie sheets, and pie pans. The Zooks definitely liked to have things sparkling and clean.

Rachel went to wash her hands at the sink before joining me. "Come on out to the barn," she said, drying her hands on a corner of her black apron. There was a look of apprehension in her eyes.

I followed her through the large kitchen. The gray-painted walls looked bare without pictures; not a single border of wallpaper or a lacy white curtain graced the monotonous walls. A tan oilcloth covered the table with a royal blue place mat at its center. On it, a square glass dish held rooster and hen salt and pepper shakers and a white sugar bowl. Plain though it was, the Zook home was always one of my favorite places.

Outside, Rachel's younger sisters stirred up a cloud of dust as they swept the back steps and sidewalk. I stopped to talk to Nancy and Ella Mae, but Rachel ignored the girls and made a beeline around the barn.

The Zooks' barn was called a "bank barn" because an earthen ramp had been built on one side, leading to the doors on the second floor. The dirt ramp made it possible to store additional farm equipment on the upper level.

Rachel stood at the top of the ramp, motioning for me to hurry. "I can't be long. *Dat* and Levi need help with the milking."

I knew the Zooks started afternoon milking around four, so I ran to catch up with my friend.

"Someone is trying to hurt us," she said softly, her eyes more serious than I'd ever seen them. She leaned against the wide barn door.

"Are you talking about the broken window?"

She nodded solemnly, much the way her father had. "Someone is mighty angry." She paused, peering into the barn where the second story was divided into sections of feed bins, haymows, and two threshing floors. Then her voice became a whisper. "Very bad things are going on around here, Merry."

I stared at Rachel. "What else?"

"Tuesday a hate letter came in the mail, and yesterday someone let Apple out of the barn."

"Did you find your horse?"

"Dat and Levi found her near the Conestoga River. They looked all around everywhere outside and never did find out who let her out." She tucked a strand of light brown hair into the bun at the back of her neck. "You know what I think? I think one of Jake Fisher's boys is mad at us."

Now I was really curious. "Old Jake has six boys."

"But only one of them caught trouble with the Lancaster bishops." She studied me hard. "If you promise you won't tell anyone, I'll say what happened."

"I'll keep it quiet. I promise."

Rachel stepped close to me, eager to divulge her secret about the Amish boy down the lane.

"I think Ben Fisher's the one causing trouble," Rachel whispered. "Dat caught him out joyriding with a carload of Englischer girls. Even after being baptized and all, Ben made no bones about it. Didn't even say he was sorry."

"Your father saw him for sure?"

"Jah." Rachel nodded. "Worse than that, Dat found out Ben Fisher owns that car!" Cars were strictly forbidden among the Old Order Amish.

Just last fall Ben had made a vow to follow the rules of the *Ordnung*—the community's agreed-on rules for Amish life. At his baptism, he would have been told it was far better to never make his vow than to make it and break it later.

Rachel continued. "My father told our deacon about it, and the church members had a meeting with the bishops. From what I heard, Ben didn't go along with a kneeling confession for driving a car. And he wasn't just a little huffy when he stormed out of the meeting."

"Do you think Ben will confess?"

"The bishops gave him six weeks to do it, but the time's already half up." Rachel's eyes were bright with sudden tears. "Oh, Merry, he's one of Levi's best friends, and he's in danger of the *Meidung*—the shunning!"

I put my arm around Rachel. "You okay?"

"I'm afraid for him," she cried. "The shunning is awful!" Rachel leaned her head against mine. "None of us can talk to him or eat with him if he's shunned, and it can last for a lifetime unless—"

"Don't worry," I said, comforting her. "Maybe he'll come back and repent."

She wiped her eyes. "If only Levi could talk sense into Ben . . . before he does something real terrible."

Shunning was something I didn't fully understand, but I knew it meant being cut off from the people you knew and loved. Like being disowned.

I followed Rachel through the hayloft and climbed down the ladder to the lower level. Cows shuffled into the barn, some mooing loudly as they slapped their tails, swishing flies away. Like clockwork, the herd headed for the milking stalls, twenty-four strong.

I wondered how strong an influence Levi might be on Ben Fisher. If Ben didn't repent and sell his car, Levi could lose his friend forever. "Does your father think Ben's the one who threw the brick?" I asked.

Rachel raised a finger to her lips and wiped her eyes, shielding them as her father entered the barn. He set down clanking milk buckets in preparation for the afternoon milking. "No one in the house talks about it, and neither must you," she said, reminding me of my promise.

"You can count on me," I replied firmly.

———

The next day was Friday and the school cafeteria was bustling with noise. Everyone seemed wired for the weekend. And the closer to summer we got, the harder it was to concentrate on school.

I was settled in at a table, leaning back in my chair while I ate a tuna sandwich. Chelsea and Lissa sat with me, having hot lunch. Elton Keel sat three tables behind us. He was holding a hamburger in one hand and, with the other, clicking his pen to beat the band.

Chelsea noticed me watching him. "I wonder if I could check out that supposedly incredible picture of you," she said. "The one Elton Keel, that uniquely gifted person, drew in pen."

"Don't make fun," I said, chomping down on my words.

Chelsea's voice rose against the swell of the lunchroom sounds. "I'm just saying it like it is," she said, reminding me of my "lecture" on the bus yesterday.

I took a sip of soda. Chelsea had no right to throw things back in my face like this. But I decided not to make a big deal of it and kept eating.

Chelsea persisted. "What do ya think? Does Elton still have that sketch he did of you?"

"He might," I said. "He carries his artwork around with him everywhere."

Chelsea laughed. "In that plaid little-boy backpack of his?"

Lissa intervened, changing the subject. "I saw him yesterday on Hunsecker Road at the covered bridge," she said. "Looked like he was sketching it."

Was Elton drawing the same thing I was? Too weird. "There's an old millhouse near that bridge, built back in the 1700s, I think. Maybe that's what he's sketching."

Chelsea grinned. "Bridges, millhouses, and silly girls," she teased. "What an amazing portfolio."

I kept quiet. Chelsea was really pushing things and it bugged me.

Someone yelled my name. "Hey, Merry!"

I turned to see Cody Gower sauntering around with a trayful of food. His usual entourage of male trouble followed.

"Where's the new man in your life?" He shot a grin toward Elton's table.

"Pick on someone else," I said as he passed within punching distance.

"Hey, whatever the retard lover says." He hurled his words back at me as he and his friends spread out, taking up the entire table across from us.

"Hey, dork brain," Chelsea blurted out. "Get a life."

I pushed my tray back. "Oh, so now you're on my side."

Chelsea ignored my comment, staring at Cody. "What a total jerk."

Suddenly, Cody's table shook with fierce pounding. The noise caught the attention of everyone in the room. Cody leaped out of his seat. Then he blasted, "This is for *yo-o-ou*, Elton Ke-e-e-el. One, two, three, hit it!"

On cue, the guys at his table—Cody included—began clicking their ballpoint pens, held high for everyone to see. The cafeteria rocked with laughter. And my brain nearly exploded.

Elton watched the commotion with a deadpan expression. Who could tell what perceptions flitted around inside his mind?

I wanted to get up and give Cody and his cohorts a taste of my anger. That's when Jon Klein showed up at our table.

Chelsea excused herself almost immediately while Lissa and I filled Jon in on what he'd missed. "It was truly horrible," I said, describing the humiliating act.

Lissa nodded.

"We should do something," I said.

"Like what?" Lissa responded.

"Let's pour soda down Cody's back." I leaped out of my seat, ready for justice.

"No, Merry!" Jon grabbed my arm. "That won't solve anything."

I knew he was right. I slumped down in my seat, simmering. "Say that with all *t*'s," I muttered.

Jon grinned. "C'mon, Mer. Let's help Elton instead."

"How?"

Jon picked up his fork. "What about—"

"I know!" I surprised myself with a sudden outburst. "Why don't you invite Elton to our youth service? Remember, we're having that young artist-evangelist from Vermont tomorrow night?"

"Sounds cool enough," Jon said.

"Yeah, he does really great chalk drawings," I said. And since Elton understood the language of pictures . . .

It was pure genius!

The chaos at the next table began to die down. Even though Cody was trying desperately to worm some sort of response out of me, I deliberately refused to react. Sigh. What if I acted upon everything in my heart? What if everyone did? The world would grind quickly to a horrible end.

"Please, pardon me, pals," Jon said, getting up. He proceeded to walk right up to the table where Elton was still eating . . . and clicking his pen.

Lissa smiled at me, her blue eyes shining. "You really like Jon, don't you?"

"What?"

"Don't ask what, Merry. You know what."

I looked away from her curious smile. "Jon's a good guy."

"And?"

"And we're good friends."

"But?"

"But nothing—that's it." I watched Elton nod his head again and again. "Good! Looks like he wants to come."

"Really?" Lissa turned around to check it out.

I happened to look over at Cody's table just then. They were nodding their heads—every single last one of them.

"I hate this," I muttered. "Cody Gower has no heart." I pointed to the rowdy ringleader and his table of followers imitating Elton.

Lissa shook her head. "Guess we oughta invite Cody to the youth meeting, too," she said innocently.

"What?" I said, horrified.

"You know," Lissa said, "seems like Cody could use a good dose of church, or something."

"Something is right," I said under my breath.

I have to admit I wasn't thinking in terms of God or church at that moment. My thoughts were on the seat portion of Cody's blue jeans—as in a powerful, swift kick!

Secret in the Willows **Five**

By last period, everyone in school had heard the news. Elton Keel had been caught starting a fire in a trash can outside the school. Suspended for three days!

Chelsea, Lissa, and I closed in around Jon's locker, eager for more news. Since Jon worked in the office during last hour, he was the logical person to interrogate.

"Did Elton really do it?" I asked.

"Yeah, did you hear anything?" Lissa probed.

"All I know is I saw Elton come into the principal's office for questioning today."

"When did the fire happen?" I asked.

"Yesterday," Jon said. "Sometime before lunch."

"Did the cops show up?" Lissa's eyes grew wide. "Was my dad one of them?"

"Your dad and his partner were there all right. It was some sad scene," Jon replied. "And Elton confessed to the charge. Well, he never really said he did it—just kept nodding."

Chelsea flung her schoolbag over her shoulder. "C'mon, guys, we've got a bus to catch," she said, dashing for her locker.

Cody Gower and his friends passed us in the hall. "Hey, Merry, what do ya say? Looks like you've got yourself a real live firebug!" he taunted.

Jon spun around. Anger shot from his eyes. "Gower!" he yelled. "Leave Merry out of this."

Cody laughed and elbowed his friends, slinking down the hallway.

I felt sick about Elton. This had to be some kind of mistake!

I wasn't much good for either Lissa or Chelsea on the bus ride home. I played with my camera case, snapping and unsnapping it, reliving my encounter with Elton the previous day.

Mom had a ton of chores lined up for me when I got home. "If you hurry, you'll be done before supper."

"But it's Friday," I whined as she waved her list in my face.

"It's also a very messy Friday," she said with a frown.

Mom was right. My room was messy. I just didn't feel like doing anything about it. Not today.

I curled up on the bed with my wonderful cats—two golden-haired ones and a sleek black one. "Tell me, what do you think of Jonathan?" I asked Abednego, my favorite. He seemed more interested in licking his dark coat clean than hearing me moon over some boy.

I couldn't get Jon out of my mind. He had, after all, stuck up for me—to Cody Gower of all people.

At times like this, I wished Faithie, my twin sister, were still alive. She wouldn't have minded listening to my triumphs. Or to my tragedies. I thought of Jon's words. *"Leave Merry out of this."* I thought of poor Elton. Playing with fire? Suspended?

I slipped away from my cats' cozy nest on my bed and went to my dresser. Picking up a gold-framed photograph, I stared into the past. Before the world of guys and junior high. Before the days of blow dryers and hair products. To the first real tragedy of my life.

Sitting cross-legged on the rug beside my bed, I cradled the picture in my hands. We were seven then. Our last birthday to-gether . . .

I stared at the image, remembering the dazzling white pony. Faithie sat behind me in the peppermint-striped saddle, wearing a pink lace dress like mine. She had slipped her arms around my waist, holding on for dear life until the photographer finally succeeded in getting her to smile.

Posing for pictures at that age gets awfully tiresome. But now, as I held the enchanting photo in my hands, I was glad we'd done it. Glad, too, for all the special times we'd had together. And for the many firsts we'd shared. We'd been inseparable friends, Faithie and I. Until the cancer came and took her away.

Mom wandered into my room, and by the look on her face, I knew she wasn't exactly thrilled. "Merry, your room still looks—"

I glanced up. "Oh . . . I'm sorry."

She spied the picture in my hands. "Honey . . . are you all right?" She came and knelt beside me on the floor.

I nodded, tears falling fast.

She swept the hair off my brow, pulling me gently against her. "Oh, Merry, why didn't you say you needed some space?"

"Please, Mom. I'm okay, really." It felt strange hearing her go on like this.

"You know, Mer, this room has looked a hundred percent worse many, many times before this," she said. "It can certainly look like this for one more day."

"I'll clean it up."

"No, no. It's not necessary. Not today. You just go outside and have a nice long bike ride or do whatever you'd like for a while."

I sat up and looked at her. Smile lines sat on each corner of her mouth; worry lines furrowed her brow. There was a teeny touch of gray every so often in her hair. But love shone out of her deep-set brown eyes. "Thanks for understanding, Mom."

"Any old time." She laughed as she pulled herself up off the floor.

When she was gone, I returned the photograph to my dresser. Stepping back, I glimpsed myself in the mirror. How much I had changed!

Merry, the little girl, had disappeared. In her place stood a young woman. I stared long and hard. How had my twin's death changed me? How had it changed the entire course of my life?

I leaned closer, shifting my gaze to the picture and focusing on Faithie's arms wrapped around me. It seemed I'd always been the strong one. Especially with Faithie. And now even with some of my closest friends.

At that moment, I thought of Elton. It startled me that I should think of him in terms of friendship. I felt truly sorry for him. Pure and simple.

Reaching for my backpack, I stuffed my trusty Polaroid camera, sketch pad, and several charcoal pencils inside. Mom was absolutely right. I needed some space, and a long bike ride to Hunsecker's Mill Bridge was just the thing. Quickly, I changed into my grungiest pair of jeans.

I flew down SummerHill Lane on my bike, past the willow grove where Faithie and I had played. Once, we hid buried treasures there. Mom wasn't too wild to discover part of that treasure included the wedding band she had innocently removed while washing dishes. After a whole day of digging, I retrieved it in time to avoid major disciplinary action.

Farther down the lane, Zooks' farm was hopping with Amish folk. Looked like a quilting bee. I scanned the women milling around on the front porch, probably having a lemonade break—the real stuff, freshly squeezed, of course. I looked for Rachel but didn't see her.

In the field beyond the Zook farmhouse, Levi and Aaron were tilling the soil, preparing for corn planting. With a little help from their mules.

Soon, the cemetery came into view. We'd buried Faithie there nearly nine years ago. A warm breeze rippled through my hair as I stood up, pedaling hard. Standing on tiptoes, I could see the top of her gravestone peeking over a small rise in the graveyard. A feeling of uncontrollable joy filled me as I flew down the lane. Faithie's soul, her true self, wasn't stuck away in that old grave. She was alive. And someday in heaven I would see her again.

The joyful feeling turned to one of quiet resolve and I sat down on the seat of my bike, letting my legs rest as I coasted toward Hunsecker Road.

At the intersection, I looked both ways before heading down the road to the covered bridge. As I made the last turn before the bridge, I heard the loose boards clatter under the weight of a car as it drove across the one-laner. The sound lingered in my mind until the car honked and I saw Miss Spindler, our neighbor, waving. I waved back, wondering what Old Hawk Eyes was doing out here. Probably spying—her favorite hobby.

She turned the corner in her snazzy red car, grinding the gears as usual. I waited till she was gone before parking my bike on the narrow shoulder near the bridge. Then I ran through the high grass along the bank of the Conestoga River.

Finding just the right vantage point, I sat under two large oaks that leaned together overhead, as though locking arms in friendship. I took two shots of the bridge with my Polaroid, then sat down and began to sketch while the pictures developed.

Insects buzzed around me. Martins swept down to the river's edge, searching for an insect supper as the cool, sweet smell of April filled my senses. Taking all the time in the world, I referred back to the Polaroid pictures, now very clear. Sometimes photographs called attention to things missed in real life.

I put the finishing touches on my sketch, confident that Mrs. Hawkins would be truly pleased with the finished project.

The sound of a horse and buggy caught my attention. When I looked up, I saw an Amish couple in an open courting buggy make the sharp turn before heading into the covered bridge. Rachel had said covered bridges were made for kissing. Maybe a kiss was on the way....

I had the strongest urge to sneak up on the couple, and I probably would have if I hadn't noticed a blond-haired boy sitting high in the twin oaks above me. Squinting up into the afternoon sun, I shielded my eyes. "Elton, is that you?"

He began nodding.

"What are you doing up there?"

He held his sketch pad high, his eyes shining.

"That's good." I felt awkward. I wanted to ask why he'd taken my idea and sketched this bridge, but the more I thought of it, the more I decided it was a compliment, not a threat. "Are you okay up there?"

He nodded repeatedly.

"How far along is your sketch?"

Without warning, Elton scrambled down from the tree. He leaned over to show off his drawing.

"Wow! It's genius!" I raved, still sitting on the grassy bank. How could a sensitive kid like Elton draw a picture like this, start a fire, and get suspended all in one week?

Elton stood there with a blank-eyed look on his face. Was he waiting for me to show my drawing of the bridge? More awkward seconds passed.

"Oh no, you don't," I said, laughing, realizing I was right about what Elton wanted. "My sketch needs major help compared to yours."

I stood up, noticing a bike parked beside mine near the bridge. Probably his. Brushing off my jeans, I loaded my backpack. "Here, pick one," I said, holding up the Polaroid pictures. "They're great for reference."

He studied them carefully before choosing.

"I take pictures here all the time. Everywhere, really," I said more to myself than to him. And with camera in hand, I headed up the riverbank. "I have to leave now."

Elton stared almost sadly as I waved good-bye. I wondered how on earth he'd arrived here without my noticing.

By the time I reached my bike, the Amish buggy was emerging very slowly from the bridge. I grinned at the couple as they rode out. Time for more than one kiss, I thought, as the horse picked up speed and pranced down the road.

Saturday morning, bright and early . . . well, really more like around nine-thirty, I got up and tore into my messy room. The cleaning lady was coming in a couple days, but Mom always liked the house picked up for the occasion. I never could figure out why we had to scour the house for the cleaning lady's arrival. Seemed like a waste of money. And energy.

After brunch I headed to Rachel's. She wanted to make a patchwork pillow for my hope chest and said I should choose the colors. When I arrived, she was helping her mother bake bread for tomorrow's noon meal. It was the Zooks' turn to have church at their house, and since the Amish always shared a meal after the service, it was essential that food preparations were completed before sundown Saturday.

"What are you serving tomorrow?" I peered over Rachel's shoulder.

"The usual," she said, showing me cold cuts, red beets, pickles, and cheese already cooling in the refrigerator run on twelve-volt batteries.

Rachel's face grew serious. "Something else happened yesterday." She motioned me to the corner of the kitchen, out of her mother's hearing range. "Our chickens all died," she said quietly. "Someone poisoned them."

"That's horrible!"

I must've spoken too loudly because Rachel's mother looked startled as she set two loaves of bread out to cool on the sideboard. "Ach, Rachel! Hold your tongue."

That was the end of that. Rachel clammed right up, obeying her mother. Even after she took me to her bedroom to choose squares of various colors for my pillow, she refused to discuss it.

I did not like this Ben Fisher person. Anyone who could kill off innocent chickens—it was the most hideous thing I'd ever heard. What would he do next?

On the way home I was so deep in thought, fussing and fuming about Ben, I nearly walked right over Elton Keel sitting in the thickest part of the willow grove.

Willow branches draped around us, forming a canopy so dense that the sun only filtered through it, casting whispers of light here and there. It was a very secret place.

"Elton, what are you doing here?"

He pulled his legs up next to his chest and rested his chin on his knees, squinting up at me. That's when I saw his plaid backpack and the sketch pad lying on the grass beside him.

"Oh, you're sketching again."

He started nodding.

"May I see?"

Elton reached for his sketch pad. He pointed to the Zooks' barn in the distance and then to his pad. The drawing was an exact replica of the huge white barn, complete with silo. I stared in awe at the pen sketch. Flawless artistry.

"Oo-oh, Elton. This is so-o good."

He clicked his pen without stopping. The clicking seemed to provide a sense of security.

Suddenly, I had a great idea. "Want to borrow my Polaroid for a while? You can sketch from the photos at home. Sometimes it helps catch details you might've missed."

Elton didn't move his head, but his eyes said yes.

"Are you coming to the youth service?" I closed the sketch pad and handed it back to him.

He stopped clicking his pen and began to nod.

"I'll bring the camera tonight, okay?"

His nodding continued.

I was dying to ask him about the fire at school: Why he'd started it. What had really happened. But almost before I finished thinking that thought, Elton turned abruptly and reached for his backpack.

"Are you leaving?" I asked.

His attention seemed focused on whatever he was searching for in his backpack. Then slowly, and with a high-pitched grunt, he pulled out a folded paper. Its edges were charred black and flaking off. Elton handed the paper to me.

I took the fragile paper from his hand. "Is this for me?"

He nodded only once.

His reaction startled me. In the short time I'd known Elton, he'd never, ever nodded only once.

Carefully, I unfolded the charred paper. My breath caught in my throat as I recognized the sketch. It was the drawing of me—the one I'd returned to Elton.

I squinted at the fair-faced boy. With a totally blank look, Elton stared back. It occurred to me that if I observed him long enough, carefully enough, I might find my answers in his eyes.

A sudden breeze made the willows whisper above us and the drawing tremble in my hand. Between alternating intervals of shade and sun, flickers of light played on Elton's face. "You want to tell me something, don't you?"

Again he nodded one time.

"Do you want to tell me why you started the fire at school?"

He nodded. This time more quickly.

"Okay," I said. "Here's what we'll do. I ask the questions and you give the answers. One nod means yes, and nothing means no. Okay?"

He nodded. This was incredible!

"Did you start the fire by burning my picture—this picture?" I held up the charred drawing, tapping it lightly.

He nodded.

"Were you mad at Cody Gower?"

Not a single eyelash fluttered.

"Were you mad at the others who teased you?"

Nothing.

"Were you—" I paused. What other reason could there be?

Elton waited for me to finish, his blond hair dazzling white, halolike as the sun danced on it.

I inspected the sketch again. The *4 U* jumped out at me. Then I remembered Chelsea's comment yesterday. *"He's probably depressed."* That's exactly what she'd said! Elton would be depressed if I gave the sketch back. Maybe, for once, Chelsea was right.

I held up the drawing, charred edges and all. "Were you upset because I didn't keep this?"

He paused almost thoughtfully, then began nodding.

I felt lousy about the part I'd played in his wanting to burn the picture. "I'm really sorry if I upset you, Elton. I only wanted you to get a good grade," I explained. "Well, I better get going. I have homework to do before youth service."

Elton picked up his sketch pad and began to draw as I headed down the narrow dirt path toward the road. I called, waving the charred picture in my hand, "Good-bye—and thanks." But Elton was already preoccupied with his work.

I kicked at the stones along the side of the road. Bottom line: I was partly responsible for the trash-can fire. Elton had been offended by my returning his sketch. And I was sorry.

Almost home, I heard a buggy speeding down the lane behind me. I knew it was Levi Zook just by the way he handled his spirited horse. Everyone in SummerHill knew he was a hot-roddin' buggy driver. He yanked on the reins as I turned around, pulling the buggy off the road.

"It's a good thing they don't let you drive a car," I teased, hiding Elton's drawing behind my back.

Levi stood up in his open buggy, tipping his wide-brimmed straw hat. "Going my way?"

"Better watch it, Levi. You don't want the bishops to find out, do you?"

He grinned. "Find out what? That you're goin' riding with me?"

I shrugged my shoulders, feeling the warmth creep into my face. "Says who?"

"*You* could say it if you wanted to, Merry Hanson." Levi was flirting like crazy. It was a good thing he was in his *Rumschpringe*, the Amish term for the running-around years before baptism into the church. During that time, Amish teens were allowed to experience the outside world and decide whether or not to return to their roots. Most of them did.

Levi put his foot up on the rim of the buggy and leaned on his leg. He was still smiling. "How about tonight? Jah?"

"I'm sorry, Levi. I don't think it's such a good idea."

He flashed a smile. "Why not?"

I looked down at my feet. Why was my heart beating like this?

"Merry?" His voice was mellow and sweet. And gently persistent.

Without looking up, I found myself saying something like, "Well, maybe . . . sometime."

You would've thought he'd gotten a yes, because in a split second, Levi sat down, slapped the reins across his beautiful Morgan horse, and took off, racing.

The wild way he drove that buggy called for a good nickname. That's when I thought of Zap 'em Zook.

Wouldn't the Alliteration Wizard be proud?

When I arrived home, I called Lissa to invite her to spend the night. She agreed to bring her things to youth service and ride home with Skip and me afterward.

"Thanks for asking," she said on the phone. "Besides, I really need to talk to you."

"About what?"

"Something personal."

I felt nervous. "Is everything still okay at home?"

"I'm fine, Merry. It's not that."

"Then what?"

"It's nothing to worry about. It's just—" She stopped.

"What?"

Lissa hesitated before saying softly, "Okay, it's about Jon Klein and—"

Skip yelled, "Supper!" in my ear.

I covered the receiver, glaring at him. "Can't you see I'm on the phone?"

He shrugged uncaringly. "Mom said to get yourself to the table fast; we're running late."

I tried to shoo him away, but he kept hanging around, acting like a real dope. Finally, I turned back to the phone. "Sorry, Liss.

Guess we'll have to talk later, when we can talk in private," I said loudly for Skip's benefit.

Lissa said good-bye and we hung up. I raced Skip to the kitchen, wondering what sort of personal thing Lissa had to tell me about Jon.

Later, when Skip and I showed up at church, it was crowded. I spotted Jon and Elton in the lobby. Jon looked wonderful as always, tall and with an air of confidence. Elton seemed nervous, though. His eyes darted back and forth, and I wondered if he'd ever been inside a church building before.

Since two other local youth groups had joined us for the service, seating was limited. I hurried to claim the empty chair beside Lissa, placing my Polaroid camera under my seat. If we'd arrived sooner, I might've asked her what was so important about Jon, right then and there.

Soon Jon, with Elton following close behind, found seats at the far end of our row. Jon leaned over and smiled at us, but Elton sat straight and rigid, staring at the platform where the musicians were warming up. I decided to wait till later to hand over my camera.

After the second praise chorus, Lissa whispered, "Do you think Elton's into this at all?"

"You might be surprised."

There were the usual announcements about social events going on during April, but I was most interested in the upcoming Spring Spree, one week from today. It was an annual thing at our church. Girls could invite the boy of their choice to the church-sponsored dinner, which raised money for a Christian hunger-relief organization. Because it was for a good cause, most guys paid their own way, but some girls opted to cover the cost of both tickets.

Was it possible that what Lissa wanted to tell me about Jon had something to do with the Spring Spree? Maybe she'd heard that Jon wanted me to ask him! *That* kind of talk would be sweet music to my ears.

I hadn't gone last year, because at fourteen, my parents had considered me too young to go. This year, however, I hoped to get up the nerve to ask someone.

While the youth pastor plugged the spree, Lissa looked at me curiously. "You going?"

I shrugged. No sense telling her till I knew if Jon agreed.

After several songs, the offering, and a couple of numbers by a local Christian band, the special speaker was introduced. "I am happy to have a very talented artist, Anthony Fritchey, with us tonight . . . all the way from Vermont." The youth pastor grinned and sat down.

Everyone clapped, welcoming Anthony to our church.

A tripod with a green chalkboard stood ready. Anthony picked up a piece of chalk and quickly drew a giant ant, then made a plus sign. Next to that came a two-thousand weight, another plus sign, and a quick sketch of a human knee. "What's my name?" he called, pointing to each of the three symbols.

"Ant-ton-knee," we all shouted. The service was off to a great start. I crossed my legs and settled back in my seat, eager to watch the work of this artist-evangelist. I'd heard of people using their talents for the Lord, but I'd never seen an artist do chalk drawings to inspirational music.

Beginning with a choral piece, "God So Loved the World," as a backdrop, Anthony created a detailed sketch before our eyes. His hand movements were quick, yet graceful, as he portrayed God saying good-bye to His only Son as Jesus prepared to leave heaven.

Deftly, Anthony drew one scene after another, telling the story of Jesus' short life on planet earth. When it came time for the picture of Jesus hanging on the cross, most of the kids were leaning forward on their seats, spellbound. It was so moving the way Anthony portrayed the pain, the agony, in Jesus' face.

God's Son was dying for us!

I happened to look over at Elton. To my surprise, big tears rolled unchecked down his face. Forcing my gaze away from him, I prayed silently, tears coming to my own eyes as I tried to focus my attention on the grand resurrection scene coming up. The "Hallelujah Chorus" set the stage for the triumphal moment, and I wanted to cheer as the artist finished his incredible work.

Unprepared for Elton's initial reaction, I was even more surprised when he stood up and began clapping slowly and somewhat awkwardly. In a moment, all of us were on our feet applauding, not so much for the unique evangelist, but because of the truth he'd so creatively conveyed.

My heart was warmed by Elton's response. Was this the first time he'd heard the Gospel? I honestly didn't know. Anyway, lots of kids greeted Elton after the service, encouraging him to come back.

Lissa and I went over to say hi. When I gave Elton my Polaroid camera and showed him how to use it, I watched his eyes. Even though his face was expressionless, I was sure I saw the beginnings of a twinkle in his eyes. The windows to his soul.

Lissa got started talking about Elton on the way home. Skip didn't act a bit interested. He was too "cool." Some older brothers were like that.

"Why'd you give him your instant camera?" Lissa asked.

"It's a good way to record the things you're sketching," I explained in spite of Skip's rude looks. "I use it all the time for that."

"Aren't you afraid he'll lose it or something?" she asked.

"Not if it's in his backpack. He wears it everywhere."

Lissa was silent for a moment. Then she asked, "What do you think is wrong with Elton?"

"I think he's lots smarter than people give him credit for," I said, turning around to face Lissa in the backseat. I didn't tell her about the "conversation" I'd had with Elton in the willow grove earlier. Skip would never let me live it down. I was surprised he hadn't overreacted about the camera by now.

"Does anyone know why he can't talk?" she asked.

Skip turned on the radio. "Ever hear of autism?" he said, as if he knew what he was talking about. "Maybe that's his problem."

"It seems as if he's always daydreaming," Lissa said. "Do you think he's out of touch with reality?"

"No!" I said, surprised at my outburst.

Skip gave me a sideways look. "My little Merry sounds pretty sure of herself tonight," he taunted.

"Don't call me your little anything," I said.

"Yeah, yeah," Skip muttered, turning up the volume on the radio. "Bet you'll be mighty ticked when he wrecks your precious Polaroid." There. Skip hadn't disappointed me after all.

I turned around, looking at Lissa again. "See what you're missing out on by being an only child?"

Lissa gave me a half smile. Her biggest wish was to have a sister or brother. She'd often said how lonely it was being the only kid in a house where both parents worked. At least now her father was sober. And going to therapy every week.

Skip checked both ways before turning off Hunsecker Road. One thing for sure, my brother was a careful driver. Nothing like Zap 'em Zook.

We passed acres of pastureland and Amish farmhouses. I stared as we came up on the Fishers' place. Was Ben at home or out causing more trouble?

Skip looked at me. "Sounds like Ben Fisher really had a run-in with the Amish bishops."

"I heard about it."

"He's only got two weeks before his probation's up and they kick him out of the Amish church," Skip said.

Then unexpectedly, just ahead, something blocked the road. "Watch out!" I shouted.

Skip slammed on the brakes. Our brights were shining on a herd of . . .

"Cows! Abe Zook's milk cows are out!" Skip hollered, leaping out of the car.

I unsnapped my seat belt and hopped out with Skip. "How on earth did they get loose?"

"One guess," Skip said sarcastically. I knew he was thinking of Ben. "You better run and alert the Zooks." He got in the car and backed it up slowly, turning off the headlights.

"Looks like everyone's in bed already," I said, motioning for Lissa to come with me.

Skip turned off the ignition. "They'll be glad you got them up. Hurry, Mer." And he headed off to start rounding up the cattle.

My heart pounded ninety miles an hour as Lissa and I hurried up the Zooks' lane. Twenty-four dairy cows roaming loose was nothing to sneeze at. Those cows were the lifeblood of our neighbors' income. With every step, I became more furious with Ben Fisher. Or whoever had done this horrible thing.

It was almost midnight by the time we got the cows in the barn. Levi volunteered to sleep outside to keep watch. It struck me as very noble. My thoughts spun a web of admiration for my longtime friend.

The second oldest son of Abe Zook was, and always had been, a friend to the end. True, he was flirtatious, but when it came right down to it, there was no way on this wide earth I'd ever be hearing about Levi being hauled off to the Amish bishop!

Abe thanked us for our help and offered to give us money as we left.

"We've been your neighbors all these years," Skip said, waving his hand. "No need to start acting like strangers now."

Abe slapped Skip on the back, grinning. Skip was right, of course. And for the first time in ages, I felt proud to be called his little Merry.

Once we got home, Lissa and I were wiped out, too exhausted to have our private talk. Whatever she had to say about Jon Klein would have to wait till morning.

The familiar sound of clip-clopping seemed to come and go as it mingled with my early morning dreams. Had it not been Sunday, I would've been content simply to sleep away the exhaustion of the night before. But Sundays were the Lord's day at our house, and no matter how late we'd gotten to bed the night before, Sunday mornings meant early rising.

It wasn't just difficult to wake up Lissa, it was next to impossible. She had burrowed herself into my blue-striped comforter. I piled my sleepy cat trio, Shadrach, Meshach, and Abednego, on top of her. A moan drifted out of the blankets. Abednego took it as a signal to play. He pawed at the covers, leaping on the mound that was Lissa's head.

"Rise and shine!" Dad's deep voice resonated through the hallway.

"Lissa," I said, shaking her. "Better wake up, or we won't have time to talk."

While I waited for her to respond, I stared at my collection of framed photography on the far wall—my gallery. It was a display area for my best work. Everything from scenes of trees in autumn and Amish windmills to Faithie's gravestone adorned the wall.

"C'mon, Lissa. Wake up!" I jostled her some more.

"I'm tired" came her sleepy voice. "Can't you shower first?"

"Only if you promise you'll be up when I'm finished."

She giggled under the covers. "You sound like a drill sergeant."

"Well, I am, and you'd better get up or—"

"Merry," Mom called through the door. "I need you downstairs as soon as possible."

"Okay," I said, feeling cheated. Now when would I get to hear what Lissa had on her mind?

On my way to the closet, I passed my bulletin board. Elton's charred sketch of me hung in the middle of it. I studied the drawing for a moment, once again amazed at his talent.

By the time I was out of the shower, Lissa was dancing around, anxious to claim some privacy in the bathroom. Quickly, I dressed and towel-dried my hair in my room, waiting for her to come back out and get her clothes before her shower. But she was taking forever and soon Mom was calling again. Frustrated, I left my room and hurried downstairs.

"Looks as if the Zooks are having church today," Dad said as he stood at the sink, gazing out the window. "Good thing they got those milk cows back in the barn last night."

"Sure would like to know who'd do such a thing," I said, setting the table. "Cows don't get out by themselves, you know."

He turned around, wearing a serious look on his unshaven face. "I think it's time the police heard about Ben Fisher, don't you, hon?"

Mom grabbed the skillet out of the pantry. "It's hard to know what to say or do," she said, pouring a cup of pancake mix into a bowl. "The Amish have their own way of dealing with things like this."

I spoke up. "But Dad's right. Something should be done, before someone gets hurt." I hesitated to say more. Rachel would be upset if I told my parents everything that had been happening.

Dad kept talking. The more he talked, the more I realized he already knew about everything: the hate mail, the broken window, the poisoned chickens . . . everything.

"I think I'll go over and have a neighborly chat with Abe," Dad said, stroking his prickly chin.

Since the Amish Sunday meeting usually meant sitting around and visiting long after the noon meal, Abe Zook would be busy with his friends and relatives till afternoon milking. I reminded Dad of that.

"That's true," he said. "And we'll be getting home too late from our evening service for me to go over then." The Amish always went to bed with the chickens, around nine or so—whether they had any or not.

"Should I tell Rachel you're coming tomorrow?" I asked.

Mom spun around, her hand steadying the mixing bowl. "That's not such a good idea," she said. "I don't want you getting involved with this, Merry. It sounds a bit dangerous to me."

"But Rachel's my friend!"

She nodded. "The Zooks are good neighbors and fine people, but they don't meddle in our affairs." She sighed, casting a look at

Dad that I interpreted to be a plea for unity. "My vote is we let them work things out according to their traditions."

Dad pulled out a chair and sat down, opening the Bible and leaning it against his empty plate. His eyebrows danced as he turned a deaf ear to Mom's chatter. Dad, being a medical doctor, focused his life on helping people. That's probably where I got my strong inclination to do the same.

Anyway, out of nowhere, Elton Keel popped into my mind. Maybe it was because he was always silent. Dad, on the other hand, was only trying to be silent at the moment. I resolved with more determination than ever to help Elton fit into our school, and possibly our church.

Lissa showed up for devotions at the same time Skip did. My brother appeared dressed and ready to walk out the door for church, but Lissa still wore her bathrobe. I could tell by his sideways glance that he thought Lissa was totally uncool coming that way to breakfast.

Maybe he'd forgotten Lissa's background. Her father had had an abusive streak and nearly every time he'd gotten drunk, Lissa and her mom had suffered beatings. The cycle of abuse had gone on most of her life, until last November when Mr. Vyner turned himself in and started getting help. Lissa told me once she couldn't remember ever sitting down with her parents and sharing a family breakfast. Maybe that's why she liked it here so much.

As Dad read the morning devotional, I wished there was something I could do to get Skip to be polite to my friend. I thought of kicking him under the table, but that seemed a bit childish. Besides, I was sure Skip had only one thing on his mind at the moment: food!

After a breakfast of pancakes and scrambled eggs, I hurried around the kitchen, assisting Mom by clearing the table and loading the dishwasher. Lissa excused herself and went upstairs to dress. Skip stuck his head in the refrigerator, searching for more food.

Mom ignored the Bottomless Pit. "Thanks for your help, Merry," she said as I finished up.

"Any time." I dried my hands on her strawberry towel. Mom had no idea why I was hurrying around. The truth was, if I finished up fast in the kitchen, Lissa and I would have time for our talk. But I was wrong.

Halfway up the back stairs, I heard someone pounding at the kitchen door. I waited, listening, as Skip flew past me with two pieces of jellied bread. "You're gonna be late, cat breath," he said.

"Go away," I muttered, listening for some clues from the kitchen.

Soon Mom called, "Merry, it's Rachel."

My throat went dry. What on earth was Rachel doing here with church going on at her house?

I sensed trouble. Big trouble.

Nine *Secret in the Willows*

Rachel was waiting for me in the kitchen wearing a Sunday dress of bright purple and a black apron.

I greeted her. "Hi, Rachel. You okay?"

She nodded, but I knew better. Rachel wasn't her cheery self. When people grow up together, it's easy to know things like that.

Mom left the room to get ready, and probably to give us some privacy. When she was out of sight, Rachel spoke softly, "Can you come over this afternoon?"

"What's up?"

She touched the strings on her *Kapp*—the white prayer bonnet—on her head. "There's a culprit that needs to be caught," she whispered.

I didn't have to be told whom she was referring to. Evidently, the Zooks wanted proof that Ben Fisher was the one causing trouble for them.

"So your parents want me to help, is that it?" I asked, a little surprised.

Rachel shook her head. "No, no. *Mam* and Dat don't know a thing about this, and we must keep it that way. My brother and I want you to help us do some spying." She took a deep breath. "To help our family."

"Levi and you?"

She nodded. "I'll tell you later what we've got planned. Jah?"

I walked with her to the door. "Are you saying you're taking things into your own hands?"

Her eyes brightened. "You may call it what you wish, dear cousin." Rachel liked to call me cousin, even though we were only distant ones. Our family trees branched back to the same Anabaptist ancestors. She gave me a long hug, then hurried out the door and down the steps.

I waved as she passed the white gazebo in our backyard. "You can always count on me," I called. Grinning, Rachel returned my wave.

I closed the back door and made some tracks of my own for my room. When Dad wanted to walk out the door on Sundays, the family had better be ready. It was the one day of the week he showed little patience for stragglers.

Briskly, I flipped on the blow dryer and brushed my hair, wondering about Lissa. Had it been my imagination, or was she avoiding me today?

Quickly, I applied some makeup, leaning close to the mirror as I brushed on some blush and a smidgen of lipstick. Mom didn't care if I wore makeup, as long as it was in good taste. Her approach made me feel sorry for some of the church girls my age who weren't allowed to wear much of anything on their faces.

I skipped the mascara. Instead, I spent the last few minutes fixing my hair, all the while a nagging thought threatening my peace of mind. Had Lissa changed her mind about having our personal talk? She'd gone downstairs to call her mom about something. Was it a stall tactic?

I was snatching up my purse and digital camera and saying good-bye to my cats when Lissa burst into the room. "I can't hold it in any longer, Merry."

I stared at her. "Hold what in?"

"Do you like Jon Klein or not?"

I looked at my bulletin board and Elton's burnt drawing, avoiding her stare. "How many times do you have to ask?" I said.

"Well, do you?"

"He's just a friend." I didn't even say a good friend. I didn't want anyone to know how I really felt about the Alliteration Wizard. It wasn't like Lissa was my best friend or anything. In fact, I hadn't really had a best friend since Faithie died.

Slowly, I turned around. Lissa sat on the edge of my bed, looking up at me like she had something earthshaking to say.

I inched toward her. "What is it, Liss?"

Quickly, she looked down, playing with her tiny gold bracelet. "I guess you could say . . . I kinda like Jon."

My heart stopped. "You mean you like Jon, uh, as in boyfriend?"

She nodded, her blue eyes wistful. "I think I sorta do, Merry. I mean . . . oh, I don't know if I can do this."

"Do what?" I could tell she was having a whammy of a time.

"I really wanted to have this talk with you."

"So, what's the point? We're talking, aren't we?"

She sighed. "Well, that Spring Spree thing is next weekend, and I just thought . . ." She stopped.

I wanted her to speed it up, spit it out.

Her eyes shone. "I think I want to ask Jon to go with me next Saturday." She stood up quickly, like she'd said something she was sorry for. "Oh, Merry, you're not mad, are you?"

My heart had stopped beating, but I managed to say, "Mad? Why should I be mad?"

She came over and hugged me, blubbering something about being awfully grateful.

I probably would've freaked out right in my own bedroom if Dad hadn't called up the stairs just then. And I must admit I don't even remember the ride to church. Frustration had taken on a life of its own. And that was putting it mildly.

We strolled into Sunday school together, Lissa and I. But I felt like a walking prayer request. If someone had taken my up-to-the-minute spiritual temperature, I might've passed for a corpse, thanks to that private talk with Lissa. Worse yet, I noticed Jon sitting with our new pastor's daughter, the beautiful Ashley Horton.

Lissa leaned over. "When should I ask him?" she whispered.

I toyed with telling her to go over right now, in front of the competition, but being a Christian friend was more important than any sarcastic comment I could've made. Besides, I had led Lissa to the Lord five months ago. She certainly didn't need her "older" sister in Christ acting like a jerk.

"Wait till after class," I suggested as calmly as possible.

Our teacher, Mrs. Simms, arrived dressed in a rose-colored challis shirtdress; her blond hair in its usual free-fall style hung down past her shoulders. I wasn't surprised when she started in by giving us girls a pep talk. "Don't be shy about inviting someone to the Spring Spree," she said, smiling. "This is your moment, ladies. A terrific cause, and maybe the opportunity you've been waiting for." She pushed her long hair behind one ear. "And, guys, make things easy for the girls, okay? Be gentlemen."

I happened to notice Jon's face brighten at that remark. Only there was a problem: He was looking at Ashley!

I glanced at Lissa. She'd noticed, too.

Just then, Elton Keel came in sporting tan dress slacks and a brown short-sleeved shirt. He was wearing his red-and-blue plaid backpack. From where I sat, it looked like my Polaroid might've found a home inside.

Mrs. Simms stopped everything to welcome him to class. He spied me and, with a childish wave, headed toward my row of chairs. Lissa and I slid over to make room for him, and although some kids might've felt uneasy sitting next to a special-ed guy with a firebug label, it didn't bother me one bit. I knew the truth.

Seeing him here made my day. Maybe I wasn't such a spiritual zombie after all. I offered to share my Bible, even though it was next to impossible to keep my thoughts focused on Mrs. Simms and the Sunday school lesson. Besides replaying Lissa's earlier conversation with me, I had to endure Jon sitting next to Ashley, probably the prettiest girl in church. Ashley was not only pretty, she was also the epitome of goodness—which smashed the preachers'-kids-are-rotten theory to pieces. I could only hope that Ashley Horton had no brains. That, and that alone, might give me an edge with the Alliteration Wizard.

In order to take my mind off this truly stressful situation, I tried to decide on my favorite month of the year. Sometimes a mental exercise can mean the difference between surviving and not.

The best month of all was a toss-up between September, my birthday month, and October, the last days before winter's power punch. I loved the sound of October leaves under my feet—like walking on a field of Rice Krispies.

In the midst of my deciding, I observed my friend Lissa. She seemed intent on the lesson. Or was her concentration on Jon?

Elton, on the other hand, seemed content just being here. He held his beloved pen in his left hand without clicking it. I wondered about that. Was it a gauge, a way to determine how attentive he really was?

Silence is golden, my dad always said. But in Elton's case, silence was much more than that. Silence spoke of childlike wonder and a secluded world inside his head. Elton's world was a place where things like seeing a chalk drawing of Jesus dying on a cross brought shameless tears. A world where discovering an oak tree near a covered bridge and settling down for an afternoon of sketching brought peace.

I was sure I was beginning to know Elton. Really know him. He was letting me in, allowing me to see inside. In Elton's world, things like the Spring Spree and a preacher's daughter with good looks didn't matter. I smiled at him and turned my attention back to the lesson.

Honestly, if Elton hadn't come today, I'd probably have had a nervous breakdown.

After class, I waited while Lissa went to talk to Jon. I watched her approach him, realizing none of this would be happening if I had asked him weeks ago. Of course, it was anybody's guess what his answer might've been. Maybe if I had asked him with all *w*'s . . .

Elton remained seated next to me. I turned to face him. "Did you like the class?"

He nodded.

"I'm glad you came today."

Again, he nodded.

"Are you staying for church?"

He tapped on my Bible, then pointed to me.

I laughed. "Sure, I'm staying, and you can borrow my Bible if you want to."

He shook his head no.

I was stunned. I didn't know Elton could do that. "Are you saying you don't want to use my Bible?"

He shook his head no emphatically.

"What, then? What do you mean?" I was feeling totally inadequate here.

He pointed to me again. Then, very precisely, he pointed to himself.

"Oh, I get it," I said, relieved. "You want to sit with me in church and share my Bible?"

He nodded and forced a half smile.

I could hardly contain my joy. Elton was changing, growing before my eyes! I explained to him that my parents thought being together as a family in church on Sunday mornings was somehow important to God. "So . . . if you don't mind sitting with all of us, we're set."

Elton nodded and when he did, I saw a hint of a smile in his eyes.

Lissa came over and stood beside me. One glance told me Jon had turned her down.

"Guess who beat me to it." She pointed discreetly to the door.

Elton stayed in the room while Lissa pushed me into the hall. "Ashley's taking Jon to Spring Spree," she moaned.

My stomach rumbled. Conflict made me hungry. "Come with me," I said.

"Where are we going?" Lissa asked, following me as I rushed toward the classroom down the hall from ours. The smell of freshly brewed coffee and sweet doughnuts drew me inside. Adults stood around, doing whatever it was they did every Sunday with coffee in hand. My dad spotted me and waved between bites of pastry.

"Here, eat this," I said, handing Lissa a jelly-filled doughnut.

Her eyes grew wide. "What's *your* problem?" She sounded like she was going to cry.

I shrugged, chewing quickly.

"What should I do about Spring Spree?"

I had to be careful what I said. After all, she had absolutely no idea how I felt about Jon. Most likely the thing with Ashley Horton was only temporary. Once Jon found out she was basically illiterate, he'd turn back to the Word Woman—me.

Meanwhile, I needed a way to distract Lissa, to get her mind off Jon. "Have you thought of asking someone else?"

"Like who?"

I wiped my mouth. "Hey, it's not the end of the world, is it? I mean, getting beat out by Ashley Horton?" I was trying to play it down. For her sake, and mine. "There are plenty more guys to pick from."

"Look, maybe you don't know it, but I saw Ashley's Sunday school lesson book," Lissa said, lowering her voice.

"So? What's that got to do with anything?"

"She thinks she's pretty cool—I mean, she's got her initials written all over everywhere. A.H. this, and A.H. that."

I smiled. "Very clever. AH-H-H never would've guessed."

Lissa and I burst out laughing. That's when I realized we were the only ones left in the room.

"Listen," I said, touching Lissa's elbow. "Sounds like the opening music has started. We'd better skedaddle."

I wiped the sticky off the corners of my mouth and hurried into the hall. Elton was waiting near the stairs. "Ready for church?" I asked.

He nodded.

"C'mon, Lissa," I said. "By the way, Elton's sitting with us today."

She looked like she hadn't heard me right, but I threatened her with a frown. She kept her mouth shut and followed me up the stairs, behind Elton.

During the part of the service when people greet one another, I introduced Elton to my parents and my brother. Dad and Mom were ultra-polite as usual, but Skip didn't exhibit the kind of enthusiasm I'd hoped for. In fact, he was downright rude. I shouldn't have been surprised. What can you expect from an eighteen-year-old sibling who hates stray cats—stray anything! Right about now, I was sure Skip was thinking about Elton as my latest stray, er . . . project.

When we settled into the pew again, I sent a serious scowl Skip's way.

He pretended not to notice. Then out of the corner of his mouth came this: "Don't be such a child, Merry."

Fortunately for my obnoxious brother, church services were designed to discourage fighting, whether verbal or a solid punch to the nose. In my opinion, Skip truly deserved the latter.

Anyway, God must've been looking out for me, because the minute our pastor announced his text, I recognized the verse—Matthew 18:3. And Skip, being the snooty high school senior he was, tried to act totally cool when the pastor's words rang out from the pulpit. "I tell you the truth, unless you change and become like little children, you will never enter the kingdom of heaven."

Not only was the verse fair reward for Skip's snide remark, it spoke an even deeper, more powerful message to me. I thought of Elton's childlike ways—often misunderstood by his peers. His simple approach to life was probably a very refreshing change to God. It must be much easier for the Lord to work in an uncomplicated life.

Finding the chapter and verse in my Bible was a snap, but sharing God's Word with Elton like this, holding my end of the Bible while he held his end, seemed almost symbolic. Rachel Zook would probably say it was providential—that God had led Elton to me so that I could lead him to Jesus. She was always talking about things like that. Simply put, it meant she believed that whatever happened to her and her family had been permitted by God. That's why the Zooks wouldn't press charges against Ben Fisher. Even if we caught him.

Rachel and I had discussed it many times, but I still struggled with the whole thing of trusting God one hundred percent, amen. It was especially hard for me since I liked to take care of things myself.

I listened to the pastor talk about the kind of faith a little child exhibits when he or she comes to God. But my mental image of Elton and the tears rolling down his cheeks last night spoke louder than any sermon.

Staring at the floor under the pew in front of me, I noticed Elton's backpack. I'd seen the contents on more than one occasion. Pens, paper, sketch pad, and my Polaroid. Something was missing, though. Elton needed a Bible, and one way or another, I was going to make sure he got one.

When the congregation stood up for the benediction, I noticed Jon Klein sitting with his two older sisters. Quickly, I bowed my head during prayer. I'd have to do some heavy praying myself to get through the next weekend. Not going to Spring Spree was nothing. But finding out my one secret crush hadn't waited for me—that hurt!

As for Lissa, I guess she'd never know why I had needed a doughnut fix this morning. She was in a big hurry to leave now anyway. "Thanks for having me over," she said, waving and dashing down the side aisle.

Interesting, I thought. Maybe Lissa had someone else in mind for Spring Spree. . . .

Instead of following my parents into the main aisle, I stood in the pew beside Elton. Actually, I was glad we were alone. "Elton, do you own a Bible?" I asked.

He shook his head no.

I thought for a minute. How could I pull this off without making him feel like a charity case? I thought of the wonderful drawing he'd made of me. The one he'd nearly burned up.

"You gave me a gift," I said. "And I want to give you one. It won't be a loan like the camera. It's something you can keep forever."

His eyes started to blink as I told him my plan to purchase him a Bible. I didn't say it would take most of the money I'd planned to spend on the Spring Spree. Elton didn't need to know about that.

After he left, I headed down the main aisle to catch up with my family. Seconds later, I heard Jon calling, "Merry, mistress of mirth."

My heart jumped as I turned around. "Hi," I managed to say.

"Hey, Mer." He was smiling. "My silly sis says if Skip's free for Spring Spree she's slappin' happy."

Some alliteration! I knew he expected me to come back with a strong reply, but I wasn't in the mood for word games. "Why don't you just have your sister call him?"

Jon leaned against a pew. "What's wrong?" His eyes grew sober.

"It's nothing." I noticed Ashley inching her way closer. "I better go now," I said, forcing a smile.

"But, Merry?"

"Uh . . . later." I turned on my heels, leaving him in the dust. Served him right. He should've waited for the Word Woman.

At dinner, I mentioned Jon's sister to Skip. Between mouthfuls, he said Lissa Vyner had already asked him.

I howled. "You're going to the spree with a ninth grader?"

Dad frowned. "Age means little when it comes to love." I waited for his frown to fade. This was a joke, right?

Mom grinned, but Skip nearly choked.

Dad looked over his plate at me. "And what terrific guy will have the honor of our daughter's company this year?"

"Yeah," Skip said, jumping right in. "Who's the lucky guy?"

"Haven't decided," I said. But that was a cop-out. Everyone was going to Spring Spree. Everyone but me.

After dinner, Dad helped Mom with dishes. I was free to leave and track down Rachel next door.

Zap 'em Zook was playing volleyball with several other barefoot Amish teens when I showed up. The net stretched high across the side yard, secured between two gray buggies. I hurried past them, hoping to avoid Levi.

"Rachel's in the house," Levi shouted, leaping up to punch the ball. I hurried past his open buggy, toward the back door and into the kitchen.

Rachel looked up from a sinkful of dishes and smiled. "*Wilkom*, Merry," she greeted me. "I'll be done here in no time."

Rachel's mother and several other women were wiping the long tables and gathering up trash. To speed things up, I took a cotton towel from the wall hook and dried dishes. I could tell by the mischievous look in Rachel's eye that she couldn't wait to have our secret detective meeting.

It didn't take long for Rachel to get Levi's attention after her chores were finished. She stood at the back door and whistled. I'd forgotten that Rachel had such a powerful pucker. In seconds, Levi dashed over to meet us.

"It's time," Rachel said, glancing mysteriously at me, then at her brother.

Levi smiled in his usual flirtatious way, but his grin faded quickly when he noticed Rachel watching him. "Let's go on up in the loft, jah?" he said, pointing to the barn. "It's as good a place as any."

Rachel, also barefoot, followed her brother. I hurried to keep up with them, glancing over my shoulder to see if we were noticed. By the looks of things, the volleyball game was back in full swing—even several adults had found their way into the game.

The closer I got to the earthen ramp leading to the upper level and the hayloft, the more I felt the excitement. Just walking up the ramp with the smell of soil and cow manure in the air made something warm and tingly drift through my body. Zooks' farm, especially the hayloft, held sweet exhilaration for me.

The smell of dried hay kissed my nose as the three of us entered the secret world. Haylofts were like tree houses—nearly sacred, secluded from the world of grown-ups, and close to heaven.

I sat in the soft hay, leaning back on my hands and feeling the dry, warm ridges push against them. The smells and the atmosphere of this place gave me confidence.

Levi sat cross-legged in the hay. Removing his wide-brimmed straw hat, he wiped his forehead as if he was going to say something important. His white, long-sleeved Sunday shirt with black trousers and white suspenders looked the same as the clothes he wore around the farm.

Rachel's white prayer bonnet had slipped cockeyed, and she fooled with it while Levi spelled out the game plan.

"I think it's safe to say that Ben Fisher won't be comin' around here tonight," he said. "There's a singing in our barn till late. Some of the crowds will be coming out for it."

By "crowds," I knew Levi was talking about several different groups of Amish teens in the Lancaster area. Some were rowdier than others.

Rachel's voice sounded pinched. "So you think Ben won't show up tonight?"

Levi picked up a long piece of straw and stuck it in his mouth. "He'd be real dumb if he did."

From behind a cube of hay, a white kitten darted toward us, followed by six or seven more.

"C'mon over, little boy," I said, coaxing the white one.

Rachel laughed. "That one's a girl."

I reached for the tiny barn cat. "What's her name?"

Levi laughed. "We don't name mouse catchers."

"Well, have a good supper, little one," I whispered to the kitten, secretly deciding to name her Lily White. Looking around, I hoped her mousey supper wasn't too close by.

Rachel was eager to get on with things. Probably because afternoon milking would be starting soon. "Should we meet right here tomorrow?"

Levi nodded, making a piece of straw dance between his teeth. "Each one of us can have a lookout post." He pointed to the three spots in the hayloft. "Merry can have the one facing SummerHill Lane away from the house. I'll take the post overlooking the house and yard, and Rachel's spot will be over there." He pointed to the one facing the field. It was the least exciting of the three, but Rachel didn't protest. Following orders made by male family members came naturally to her.

"What'll we do if someone comes prowling around, like, uh, Ben?" I asked.

Rachel whistled softly. "Can you do that?"

I nodded.

"That will be our signal, then," she said.

"Okay, we're set with a signal, but what about getting help?" I asked.

Rachel smiled. "Levi has all that planned."

"Did ya ever see a man get himself caught up in a lasso?" Levi said.

"Oh no," I said, shaking my head. They weren't kidding, these Zook kids. They had thought of everything, right down to the smallest detail.

Levi stood up. "We'll meet here at dusk tomorrow." Since the Amish didn't wear wristwatches and only went by standard time (even when the rest of us switched to daylight savings), living by landmarks of time, such as dusk, worked well for them.

I glanced at my watch. "When exactly is dusk?"

"You'll know," Rachel said sweetly. "It's when the sun starts going to bed for the night."

Why hadn't I thought of that?

Monday started out fine, except Lissa freaked out on the bus going to school. She must've been having a bad day. "I can't believe this mess," she said. "I asked Skip to go to Spring Spree and he said yes." She sounded horrified.

"What?"

"You heard me, Merry," she said. "Your brother's a senior!"

"I thought you knew that." She was unraveling before my eyes.

"Well, if it hadn't been for one of Jon's older sisters telling her girl friend, and that girl telling her mom, who told my mom," she gasped for air, "things might be cool. But this second, even as we speak, my mom's having a fit about it. I might not get to go."

"Why? Because Skip's almost three years older than you?"

"You should've seen her. I tell you, Merry, my mom's super upset about this."

"Well, what do you want me to do?"

She dive-bombed me, nearly hugging me to death. "Oh, thanks, Mer. Would you really?"

"Excuse me?"

She began to plead with me. "If you just talk to my mom, I know it'll change everything."

Honestly, I'd never seen Lissa so wired.

"You're kidding. You think your mom's gonna listen to me? C'mon, Lissa. I'm Skip's sister, for pete's sake!"

"But she worships you," Lissa insisted.

"Look, Lissa." I lowered my voice and put my head up close to hers. "You have to settle down here." I glanced around. In the front of the bus, Chelsea Davis looked like her eyes were about to pop.

Lissa leaned against the back of the seat. She took a deep breath and closed her eyes.

"You okay?" I whispered in her ear.

"I'm fine."

"Good, I'll be right back." With that, I dashed to the seat beside Chelsea.

"What's she moaning about?" Chelsea asked. Sounded like she was having a bad day, too. These things seemed to come in waves.

"It's nothing," I replied.

She poked through her pile of books. "Did you ever find out what happened to that drawing of Elton's?"

"It's mine now," I said. "Elton gave it back to me the other day." I almost said he'd nearly burned it up, but I wanted to save that news for the principal. Which is where I was headed first thing, the minute I got off this bus.

"When can I see it?" she asked.

"What for?"

"Just curious." I had no idea what she was getting at. I turned around to check on Lissa, who was staring out the window now, calm and collected.

Chelsea cracked her chewing gum. "Did anyone ever tell you that you overdo it, Merry?"

I turned to face her. "Like how?"

"Like truly this and truly that. Don't you ever get sick of dramatizing everything?" She was acting really weird. "Well, do you?" She was in my face. The strong smell of her cinnamon gum offended my nose.

"I really don't know what's bothering you." I excused myself and stumbled back down the bus aisle to Lissa.

As soon as I got things squared away at my locker, I rushed to the principal's office to make an emergency appointment. When Mr. Lowry was finally available, I began to talk sense to him about why Elton Keel, gentleman and docile human being, would never want to purposely get himself suspended.

"Elton's not a firebug," I insisted. "He merely took his frustrations out on this picture." I pulled it out of my notebook. "See this? It's truly a masterpiece. How could an insensitive firebug create something so wonderful?"

Mr. Lowry surveyed the charred drawing.

"I only wish I hadn't been so insensitive," I continued. "If I had held on to this in the first place, none of this with Elton would've happened. Don't you see, sir, it's a self-esteem problem. Plain and simple. It's mostly my fault that he's not in school today."

Mr. Lowry's crinkly eyes narrowed into slits as he steered his gaze away from the drawing and back to me. "You are absolutely right about this young man's talents, Merry. And I'd be delighted to offer leniency in this matter, but rules are rules, and your friend will have to wait out his suspension." His eyes popped open. He stood up and leaned on his desk. "I'm very sorry."

Reluctantly, I stood up, waiting for him to return the sketch. Hoping he'd catch the hint, I stared at the hand that held the drawing. Finally, I just plain asked him for it. "Uh, if you don't mind, I'd like to have that back."

Someone behind me snickered. I spun around. It was Cody Gower, sporting a sly grin. My throat turned to cotton. How long had he been standing there?

"That's a reasonable request," Mr. Lowry spouted, motioning Cody in while he dangled Elton's drawing between his thumb and pointer finger. Like it was contaminated or something. "On second thought, I think I'll keep this in Elton's file for the time being."

My heart sank.

The purpose of visiting the principal today was to try to help Elton. But by the solemn look on Mr. Lowry's face, it appeared that I may have made things worse.

———

By third-period class, everyone in school had heard the rumor. Merry Hanson was in love with a retard.

"Is it true?" Lissa asked as I deposited my books at my locker.

"What?"

She gave me a penetrating look. "You have been awfully nice to Elton lately, loaning him your camera and—"

"Christians are supposed to be nice," I said.

I noticed Lissa's eyes. They were disapproving, and when she spoke again her voice sounded breathy and nervous. "You can tell me anything, Mer. We're friends, right?"

I shrugged. "Sure."

"Well?"

"What's the point?" I punctuated my words with the slam of my locker. "Spreading rumors of this magnitude is a very nasty guy thing to do."

"Oh, so you're saying it's not true."

"Bingo!" And with that realization, Lissa's face burst into a bubble-gum smile. She scampered off to class looking downright relieved.

Even Chelsea cornered me after school. Rumors get moldy with age. As far as I was concerned, the comments floating around school weren't worth repeating, and I told her so.

"Just drop it," I said, feeling a deeper emotion than simple anger as I stood watching her peer into her locker mirror. I was worried for Elton. Really worried.

There had to be a way to stop this nonsense before Thursday. I couldn't stand the thought of him returning to school, only to experience Cody Gower's pathetic jokes.

Outside the building, I waited for the bus, ignoring whispers and the catty looks of several girls. Important things were on my mind. More important than dealing with so-called friends and their rumor-laden second-guessing. Tonight at dusk I would turn detective. Spending the evening spying with my Amish friends would be a refreshing change from this ridiculous day. Whether or not we caught Ben Fisher at his tricks didn't matter. I needed a break from the modern world!

Thirteen *Secret in the Willows*

The bus dropped me off at the willow grove. Standard procedure. Only today, something was different. Elton's bike was parked a short distance off the road.

The bus lurched forward, spewing exhaust fumes in my face. I held my breath till the fumes dissipated, and then I let my eyes comb the trees in search of Elton.

It wasn't long till I spotted him, down in a hollowed-out place nearly hidden from the road. The spot had been one of Faithie's and my favorites.

Elton was holding my Polaroid, aiming at the Zooks' barn. Watching him use the camera made me feel good about my decision to loan it out. As I watched him from afar, the frustration of the day began to seep away. Elton was making good use of his time away from school, making the best of an unfortunate situation.

I admired him for that.

Slowly, I headed into the grove toward the thickest part, delighted that Elton had returned. What a truly beautiful way to spend the afternoon—with a camera and sketch pad.

Not wanting to startle him, I stood back a few feet from where he sat in the grassy hollow.

Click. He took a picture and let the camera rest beside him.

"Hi," I said as he turned around. "Looks like you're hard at work."

Elton's eyes twinkled.

"Doing another drawing of Zooks' barn?"

A faint blush of color crept into his face. He shook his head no.

"What, then?" I asked. "Your first picture of the barn was incredible. There's no way you can improve on it."

He put his hand on his heart, as if to thank me. Then he picked up the instant picture and handed it to me.

"Oh, you're drawing cows today?"

He nodded.

"That's something I've never tried." I handed the picture back, wondering if I should tell him about my encounter with the principal today.

Then the sound of bare feet pounding the earth broke the stillness. I whirled around to see Rachel coming toward me. She was out of breath. "Merry, come quick!"

"What is it?"

She grabbed my arm. "Levi wants us to meet in the hayloft before Dat and Mam get back from the bishop's."

"Why, what's happened?"

"Ach, nothing to worry much about," she said.

"Well, it must be something," I persisted.

I could tell that Rachel was bashful about talking in front of Elton.

"I'm sorry," I said to him. "This is Rachel Zook, my friend, and I have to go with her for a little bit. I'll see you later, okay?"

The corner of his mouth began to twitch, and he put his right hand up in front of him, as though he wanted to wave.

I ran with Rachel out of the willows and toward the pasture, glancing back as we crawled over the picket fence. Elton was still fooling with my camera the last I saw him.

Rachel started talking. "Mam and Dat went to some doings at the bishop's. Levi says it's about Ben Fisher, but we can't be sure.

Anyhow, Levi wants us to go over our spying plans one more time before tonight, while no one's home."

"Good idea." I matched my stride to hers. "Maybe Ben'll repent at the meeting and you won't have to worry."

"For his sake, I hope so." She cast a furtive glance my way; her lower lip trembled. "Shunning's the last thing a body wants."

By the time we ran up the barn ramp and into the hayloft, I was gasping for air. I dove into the sweet, sweet hay, my heart pounding in my ears.

"We probably don't have more than an hour before everyone gets back home," Levi explained. He closed and latched the heavy double doors, making the loft darker and more secretive. Then he began rehearsing our plans from yesterday. "Maybe we should practice hiding at our lookouts."

"Yes, let's!" Rachel shouted with glee as though this were a game.

Levi tweaked a piece of straw and put it in his mouth. "Okay, we'll have a practice. Everyone pretend it's dusk. Now . . . sneak into the barn and take your post quietly." He lowered his voice. "Tonight when we all meet, Mam and Dat, *Grossdawdy* and *Grossmutter* will be in the house. They mustn't know we are out here."

At that moment, the tiny white kitten crept out of hiding, coming over to me. "How will you and Rachel be able to sneak out without your parents suspecting something?" I asked, picking up Lily White.

"We'll think of a way," Levi said. It struck me that he must've done some late-night sneaking before.

"Where's the lasso?"

Levi smiled. "I have it all ready." I knew better than to ask where. Amish boys were taught to model their fathers. And in Levi's case, it was obvious that he'd picked up the influential, take-charge voice of Abe Zook.

"Don't forget to whistle." Rachel leaned back in the hay, resting her head on her hands.

"Can we practice now?" I asked.

"If you want to," Levi said. "Just don't whistle too loud."

I puckered up my lips and forced the air gently through. Easy enough.

"Shhh!" Rachel cocked her head. "I hear something."

Levi's eyes were saucers. "Ach! What do ya hear?"

"I'm not sure. Sounds like a car."

Levi shook his head. He was crouched in the middle of the hayloft. "No cars."

"Listen!" Rachel insisted. I wondered who on earth would be driving a car onto Zooks' property.

Levi dashed to the window in the gabled end of the upper level. It was across from the hayloft on the opposite side of the barn. Levi's courting buggy and farm equipment were kept there. He leaped up on his buggy, gazing out the window.

"See anything?" Rachel asked.

Levi shook his head. "Nothing's out there. But we're gonna be ready if Ben—or whoever it is—shows up come dusk."

"Shouldn't we have a signal besides a whistle?" I asked. "I mean, what if we see someone and freak out, and we're too scared to pucker?"

Levi jumped off the buggy and ran alongside the wall as he made his way back to the hayloft. "If I see something, I'll whistle. Then you distract him, Rachel, with your horse sounds."

Rachel agreed, but this horse stuff was news to me. I'd never known Rachel to make horse sounds. Ever.

That's the thing about friendship: someone's always changing.

The spying rehearsal began. Rachel climbed up on a feed bin filled with loose hay—her post overlooking the field. Levi marched back to his window view of the house and yard. I settled down at my perch on a bale of hay, snuggling Lily White as I watched for intruders. The moment was soft and peaceful, and I took advantage of it by breathing in the pleasant aroma of horses and barn.

After a few minutes, Levi called to us. "Okay, time's up. Good enough for now."

He was jumping off his precious buggy when one of the horses below us began to whinny. Another horse, and another, joined in the chorus and the neighing grew to a terrifying pitch. I heard the unmistakable sound of horses kicking at the stalls, trying to escape. Lily White arched her back and let out an ear-piercing *meow*!

"What do ya hear, little lady?" I said as she leaped off my lap. Worried, I glanced around at the shadowy hayloft. Who was scaring the horses?

Levi whistled softly and I looked at him. For one eternal second our eyes locked in powerful recognition. This was no longer a practice run. This was the real thing!

Levi grabbed the rope and made a running leap. I knew what he was up to. He suspected someone was on the ground level irritating the livestock. Maybe Ben Fisher!

Clinging to the rope, Levi swung out past the loft, into the open area between the loft and the gabled end.

"See anything?" I peered over the edge.

Levi's face turned white.

"Smell that?" Rachel whispered.

I sniffed the air. Gasoline fumes!

My stomach wrenched into a cold knot.

Levi came flying back on the rope. "Get out of the barn! Fast!"

Then he did a frightful thing. Taking a running leap, Levi swung out over the second floor opening again and let go of the rope, disappearing below.

A half second later, he was shouting, "Fire! Fire! The barn is burning!"

I grabbed Rachel's hand and ran toward the closed double barn doors. Halfway across the loft, Rachel stumbled and fell. "Hurry! Get up!" I pulled on her hand.

A ball of fire shot through a small opening in the loft floor. I screamed as the flames licked at her bare foot. Stunned, Rachel's face turned beet red as she clutched her right foot. With my help, she managed to hop one-legged across the loft. We came to the locked double doors and I struggled with the latch.

Smoke from smoldering bales of hay burned my eyes. Frantically, I shoved on the heavy wooden latch.

Stuck!

I tried again and again, fear pulsing through me. Billowing smoke filled the barn as the fire spread.

I leaned hard against the latch. Finally, it popped opened. With one giant heave, I shoved the barn doors wide. "Thank you, Lord!" I shouted, helping Rachel down the dirt ramp leading to the open field below. She hobbled on one leg, leaning hard against me. At last, we were safe—away from the burning barn.

Levi emerged out of the smoky ground level at the other end of the barn, sputtering and coughing as he led the mules out. Six beautiful horses followed. Working quickly, Levi secured the animals a safe distance away. By now the barn was sending up a spiral of raging black smoke.

"Rachel's hurt!" I called, and Levi came running to inspect her blistered foot.

"It's burnt but not too badly," he said. "Get some cold water on it right away." He patted her shoulder. Then with a hopeless glance at his father's barn, he shook his head, wiping his sooty face. "I'll go get help."

"It's useless," Rachel said, still holding her red foot as she hobbled toward the outside pump well. "The ole barn'll be gone in minutes."

Levi ignored her comment and ran to the house.

"Where's he going?" I asked.

"To ring the bell on the back porch," she said. "It will bring help."

I helped Rachel to the pump, then looked back at the blazing fire, thankful to be alive. That's when I spotted the white kitten perched high on the barn's window ledge.

Lily White!

Without a second thought, I left Rachel and ran toward the bank of earth leading to the barn's second story.

"No, Merry! Come back!" Rachel called. "It's not safe!"

Peering inside, I could see the kitten. For some reason she'd chosen my lookout post. "Here, kitty, kitty," I coaxed her with my best kitty-lovin' voice. I had to get her out of there. Fast!

"Merry!" Rachel was hysterical. "Forget about the cat. Come back!"

For a split second I thought of leaving the kitten behind, but through the haze of smoke, I saw her tremble. I couldn't do it. I just couldn't leave her to die a fiery death.

I eyeballed the distance between Lily White and myself, calcu-
lating the amount of time it would take. I could make it. I was sure
of it . . . if I hurried.

"Merry!" Rachel wailed from the yard below. "Please don't!"

Taking a deep breath, I darted into the loft. The air around me
penetrated the pores of my skin like an instant sunburn as I made
my way to the window. I thought my cheeks would melt as I climbed
the bales of hay, stretching . . . reaching for the darling kitten.

Just when I thought my lungs would burst, I exhaled and took
in a quick breath. Smoke! It burned my lungs and made me cough
uncontrollably. My eyes teared up.

Zooks' bell began to toll.

In a flash, I snatched the white furball off the ledge and slipped
her into my button-down shirt. A spray of crackling fire exploded
below as I crept around the wall side of the loft. At the opposite end,
Levi's courting buggy writhed and twisted in the blazing inferno.
And for one second, I regretted never having taken a ride in it.

The heat made my scalp burn, but I kept going, making my way
toward the open double doors. Lily White meowed and trembled
inside my shirt. She dug her razor-claws through the T-shirt un-
derneath and into my chest. The pain took my breath away, and I
sucked in more dangerous smoke.

Suddenly, a wall of fire, like a volcanic eruption, spewed out of
the opening below. I screamed as it rolled toward me, blocking my
way of escape. I reeled back in terror.

My brain clouded up. I couldn't decide which way to go. The
heat . . . the fear paralyzed me.

Precious seconds ticked away.

Ding-a-dong! Ding-a-dong! Ding-a—

Zooks' bell continued its dreadful tolling.

Was I going to die?

In one last desperate move, I yanked a tarp off a rusty old push
mower and covered myself. The insulation made a difference, and
I began to grope my way to the door.

Then something knocked me off balance. A white light went off in my head and I fell backward into the hay.

Lily White shook hard and I held her close. She was safe . . . riding in a courting buggy . . . Lily White . . . dressed in a white fur coat . . . on a hot day . . . too hot . . .

Fighting the haze in my mind, I heard a voice. Harsh. Grating. High-pitched. It mingled with the sound of a distant bell.

"Merr-ry-y!"

The voice rang out again. Like the Zooks' bell, it tolled its message.

"Merr-ry-y!"

Like the monotonous ticking of a clock.

"Merr-ry-y!"

Part of me tried to step away from the blackness and survey the situation. And as if in a dream, that part of me recognized the voice.

It was his voice. The voice no one had ever heard. And it was coming closer!

I tried to rouse myself to answer his call. Afraid that I might never answer it. Ever again. Then, with every fiber of my being, I listened . . .

And heard nothing.

Secret in the Willows **Fifteen**

I was vaguely aware of someone carrying me away from the heat. My arms dangled, legs flopped. The tarp slipped to the ground.

Welcome fresh air rushed over me. I coughed, almost choking. Seconds passed and I became aware of strong arms lifting me down to the ground. The cool blades of grass under my shirt made me shiver. I felt my eyelids flutter. Slowly, I opened them.

A cherubic face looked down at mine. An innocent face, with eyes full of pain.

"Elton?" I heard myself say.

He nodded and didn't stop. Not until I reached up and touched his face. Most of his hair was gone. His beautiful blond hair had been singed off by the fire's fury. In its place were burns and blisters. At that moment, even in spite of my terrible confusion, it all made sense. Elton had saved my life.

"Thank you," I whispered. "Thank you."

Before he could respond, two men in white rushed over and had him lie down. In the midst of my fog, I heard them calling for two stretchers.

"He doesn't talk," I said softly as gentle hands inspected my body. But my words were too soft for anyone to hear, and there was no energy left in me to repeat them.

For the first time, I was aware of the crowd. I turned my head to see fire engines, police cars, and an ambulance. Huge plumes of black smoke billowed out over the area. Two paramedics placed me on a stretcher, and I felt myself being wafted through space toward an ambulance.

"Merry!" It was Levi's voice. He was running alongside the stretcher, looking down at me, his straw hat gone. "What happened? I thought you were safe at the pump . . . with Rachel."

"Don't excite her," one of the paramedics said. "She's in shock."

"Where's Lily?" I muttered. But before Levi could answer, I was lifted into the ambulance. The doors closed and the shrill siren settled into the mosaic of patterns and sounds in my mind.

Questions came, but I was too weary, too dizzy, to ask them. I let my body relax as we sped away.

When I awoke, shadows played tricks with my vision. Where was I? The smell of antiseptic tickled my nose.

"Honeybunch?" It was Dad's voice.

I opened my eyes again. Mom and Dad were leaning over my hospital bed. Dad held my hand. "Hello, baby," he said.

I yawned, still wiped out from the ordeal.

"Feeling better?" Mom asked.

"I guess." The words tiptoed out.

She smiled. "This isn't an ideal way to get out of going to school, you know."

Skip poked his head between them. "Welcome back, Mer. Heard you saved a cat." He held up the white kitten for me to see.

"Lily," I whispered, reaching for her.

Skip held her in his cupped hand. "She lost some hair, but she'll be fine."

Maybe it was the mention of hair, but suddenly I remembered. "Is Elton okay?"

Dad squeezed my hand. "He's being treated for smoke inhalation and second-degree burns. He'll be spending the night here, too." He glanced at Skip. "Your brother told us more about your new friend."

Even in spite of the haze in my brain, I knew that I could trust whatever Skip had said about Elton.

"He saved our baby's life," Mom cooed.

"Where is Elton?" I asked, trying to sit up.

"Two rooms down," Dad said.

Skip piped up. "Yeah, and if you're a good little Merry, tomorrow I'll wheel you over to visit him."

"Tomorrow?" I said, leaning back on the pillow. "What's tomorrow?"

Mom smoothed my hair gently. "Tomorrow is Tuesday, pumpkin. The docs say you'll be coming home then."

I drifted in and out, hearing them, yet not hearing them . . . so much talk of the amazing thing Elton had done. Risking his life for me. Burns . . . guardian angels . . . a miraculous escape.

Their muffled voices rose and fell, then completely disappeared. And I fell into a deep sleep.

———

Elton was sitting up in bed having breakfast the next day when Skip and I went to visit. I hadn't needed a wheelchair like Skip suggested. I walked down the hall on my own just fine.

Elton wore a porous white bandage on his head. I could tell by the way he sat, straight and stiff, that he was in pain. Tears blurred my vision as I looked at his hands and forearms. They, too, had been wrapped with sterile nonstick dressings to protect his burns and keep the air out.

A plump, older woman stood over him, holding a cup of apple juice to his lips. "Hello there." Her face broke into a wide smile as I came in.

Who is she? Then I noticed the striking resemblance between her and my friend.

"How's Elton doing?" I asked.

"Oh, he's doing just fine." She tucked a handkerchief under the waistband of her gathered skirt. "I'm Winnie Keel, Elton's grandma. And you must be Merry." She extended her hand to shake mine. "Call me Grandma Winnie."

I turned to introduce Skip. "This is my brother, Skip."

"How do you do, young man," Grandma Winnie said cheerfully.

I inched closer to Elton's hospital bed, which was cranked up too high. If I could just see his eyes . . .

"I . . . I'd like to talk to Elton," I said hesitantly. "Is that okay?"

"Oh, no bother," she said, lowering the bed a bit. Then, pulling her hankie out of its hiding place, she waved it, grinning from ear to ear.

When she and Skip had gone, Elton struggled to pick up his pen from the breakfast tray. He held it in midair, staring at it as though he wished he could click it.

"Here," I said, reaching over and taking the pen. "Your hands are too hurt for that." And I began clicking away.

On and off.

On . . . off.

I didn't feel one bit silly about clicking Elton's pen for him. In fact, I clicked it for about two minutes before I stopped. "I can't remember if I thanked you last night," I said.

He nodded.

"Everything's so blurry from yesterday. Maybe you feel the same way."

He seemed to understand as he nodded.

I thought about the fire and the way he'd called my name over and over. "I . . . I heard you, Elton. I heard your voice."

He pursed his lips, forming what looked like the beginning of an M. He tried again—this time his face turned red with the effort. But there was no sound in him.

"It's all right," I whispered.

He stared down at his breakfast tray, motionless. I looked at his head, wrapped in sterile bandages, and held my breath to keep from sobbing. Here sat a true friend. Elton had done a heroic deed for only one reason. Friendship. A powerful word for a kid who couldn't say it. And even more special for a kid who'd never experienced it. Until now.

A light tapping came at the door. I expected to see Skip, or maybe Elton's grandma, but it was a nurse leading two policemen into the room.

What are they doing here? I thought.

"You'll have to excuse us," one of the cops said. "We have a few questions to ask Mister Elton Keel." I didn't like the way he leaned on the word "mister."

Worried, but not protesting, I said good-bye to Elton, and the nurse escorted me out of the room. "Be sure and tell them he can't talk," I pleaded with the nurse. "Please?"

She smiled, assuring me that she would.

In a few minutes, Skip showed up sporting a sub sandwich. I begged him to stand outside Elton's room and listen in on the conversation with the cops.

"What for?" He bit into his sandwich.

"Please, just do it?" Miraculously, he went without an argument.

In a few minutes, Skip returned looking totally surprised. He sat down in the gray vinyl chair next to my bed.

"What did you hear?" I propped myself up with two pillows.

"You don't wanna know."

I gasped. "What are you saying?"

He leaned forward, resting his arms on his legs, studying me. "This might upset you, Mer."

"What? I can handle it. Just tell me."

He took a deep breath. "The cops think Elton had something to do with the barn fire."

"How can they say that?"

Skip stared at his feet. "Two of the cops remembered Elton from the fire at your school."

"Elton's not a firebug!" I swung my feet over the side of the bed, as though scooting to that position would make what I had to say more powerful. "You have to make them understand, Skip. You have to!"

Skip stood up. "I barely know this Elton person."

"He's not 'this Elton person,'" I shot back. "You sound like you hate him or something."

"You've got it all wrong, Mer. I think you better get ready to check out of the hospital. Dad and Mom'll be here any second." He looked at his wristwatch.

"That's just great! Change the subject, why don't you."

Skip turned and left the room in a huff.

I muttered to myself. "Dad's a doctor; maybe he can talk sense to those crazy cops."

Suddenly, Skip poked his head back into my room. "You're not thinking clearly, Mer. The police have no other suspects, and they do have reason to think that Elton was involved . . . so why shouldn't they question him?"

"How on earth do they expect to get answers out of him when he doesn't talk?" The whole thing was so ridiculous.

Skip tossed his sandwich wrapper in the trash.

"Hey, what about Ben Fisher?" I asked. "Where was he when the Zooks' barn burned?"

"I don't think you can pin this on Ben. Besides, no one saw him anywhere near the Zooks' place yesterday. But Elton Keel, well . . . he was right there."

I fought back the tears. "Elton wouldn't go to all the trouble to start a fire and then rescue me from it," I said. "He's not totally ignorant, like you think."

"C'mon, Merry. That's not fair." And with that, Skip left the room for good.

If the nurse hadn't come in, I might've cut loose and bawled. She changed the dressings on my arms, reapplying the soothing cream to my burns. "You'll want to keep these areas as dry as possible for several days," she said. "Be sure to put this cream on and change the dressings daily."

"Thanks," I said, but my mind was on Skip's words. *The police have no other suspects.*

I gathered up my things, waiting for the doctor to check me out. Actually, I was too sick to go anywhere, and it wasn't from the lousy arm burns. How could the police go and charge Elton with something he hadn't done? Had they forgotten what he had done?

How many people would risk their lives—charge into a burning barn—to save another human being?

Elton was innocent. One hundred and ten percent, amen. And I was going to clear his name!

Sixteen *Secret in the Willows*

That afternoon, instead of going home with Grandma Winnie, Elton was hauled off to Maple Springs, a juvenile detention center. He would stay there until his hearing came up in a few days.

"The Zooks haven't pressed charges," Dad explained at supper.

"Then why's Elton in jail?" I wailed.

"It's not jail," Dad said. "Not even close."

"I'm sure it feels like it," I muttered. "He doesn't belong there." Visions of Elton sitting high in the old oak tree near Hunsecker's Mill Bridge haunted me. He needed to be outdoors, in touch with nature, not in some dark holding place for delinquents.

"The district attorney pressed charges, Merry," Mom said, offering me some more noodles. "Arson is very serious business."

"But Elton didn't do it!"

Dad cut into his meatloaf, taking a bite and swallowing before he spoke again. "Remember the fire at your school, Merry? You told me yourself why Elton started it."

"He was just mad . . . uh, hurt, really."

"And why was that?"

"Because I rejected his picture. But this isn't like that. Elton's not a firebug!"

Dad looked over at Mom and back at me. "Elton set fire to his picture of you, only to retrieve it before it burned." He took a deep breath. "I think there may be a parallel here, honey."

"You can't possibly believe that he torched the barn so he could save me." It made no sense.

Dad was silent.

"C'mon, Dad, can't you at least talk to the police about his good side? I mean, what about the fact that he saved my life? Doesn't that count for anything?"

"I'm very certain the police are aware of that," he said in his most professional voice. "I think we should take a few steps back from this thing emotionally"—and here he stared at me hard—"and let the legal system do its work."

I stared at the kitchen wallpaper, tracing the strawberry vines with my eyes. Dad was beginning to sound like a shrink or something. Whose side was he on, anyway?

After supper, I fed my cats. Four of them. Lily White seemed to fit right in with the three Hebrew children. Abednego was the only one who'd exhibited the least bit of jealousy. Shadrach and Meshach actually seemed to like her.

Lily White's singed fur conjured up thoughts of Nebuchadnezzar's fiery furnace in the book of Daniel. The white color of her coat reminded me of the angel of the Lord who had walked with the three boys in the king's furnace. I smiled as I watched Lily White eat her tuna delight. An angel must've been with Elton and me during the barn fire. Only we didn't get to see it like King Nebuchadnezzar had. Maybe it was just as well.

I went to my room and threw myself on the bed, staring at the ceiling. Mom and Dad didn't understand, and it was truly horrible. The very people who you'd think would help at a time like this . . . and all they could do was talk about the legal system.

Several hours later, Mom knocked on my door, asking to come in. I wasn't in the mood for company, so she left me alone, which is exactly what I needed.

I rolled over and turned the radio on. Sometimes music helped when I was like this. That, and talking to God. But today I was too angry to pray. Pulling the pillows out from under my head, I went over the events of the week, thinking through the days since last Thursday when I'd accidentally taken Elton's picture at school.

Tons of things had happened in five days. That thing with Cody Gower in art. The lunchroom scene. Elton's suspension from school. The Zooks' fire. And now this.

I stared at the wall where my finest photography hung on display. Not a single picture was of a person. I didn't take shots of people. Places and things had always interested me more.

The moment in the hall last Thursday had come as a big surprise for Elton. I could still see his arms going up over his face, cowering away from the flash. But the encounter with Elton—bumping into his life the way I had—that had come as a bigger surprise to me.

It seemed strange to think that there was actually a picture of a human being on my digital camera, waiting to be printed. I smiled thinking about it. Most definitely a first. Maybe, by God's providence, it hadn't been an accident after all.

I sat up, looking at my arms. How much more might've they been burned—or worse—if Elton hadn't come when he did? It made me wonder where his picture fit in my gallery of photos. In my gallery of life . . .

It was late when I asked Mom to help me change the dressings on my arms. I didn't really need her help, but she probably needed to know I wanted it.

I didn't go to school on Wednesday. Mom wanted me to stay home. And it was a good thing, too. The extra day would give me plenty of time to go and visit Miss Spindler—Old Hawk Eyes. She made it her duty to keep close tabs on things in the neighborhood. People thought she had a high-powered telescope or something. How else did she know about everything and everyone?

Miss Spindler was still wearing a terrycloth bathrobe and slippers when she answered the door. "Well, my dear, how's every little thing?" She eyed the bandages on my arms.

"Well, you probably know about the Zooks' fire," I said, "and how I got out alive. So I won't bore you with all that."

"Oh my, dearie, 'tis not a bore." She cackled as if she couldn't wait to hear my version.

I began to tell her about Elton and how he'd risked his life for mine. Pausing, I took a deep breath before asking the question burning inside me. "Miss Spindler, is there any chance you saw someone prowling around on Zooks' farm Monday afternoon . . . around three?"

She cocked her head. "Uh, what time did you say?"

"Three o'clock," I repeated.

A smile burst across her wrinkled face. "Well, my dear, I must tell you that between three and four each and every weekday, the world comes to a screechin' halt."

I had no idea what she was referring to. "Why's that?" I asked.

She pointed a long, bony finger at her television. "That's the reason I didn't see nobody on Zooks' farm, dearie."

"Oh, you have a favorite show or something?"

"You heard right."

I stood up to go, disappointed by this lack of news. "It's just too bad about Elton," I said under my breath.

She leaped up suddenly. "Now, what is this wide world coming to!" she exclaimed, nearly scaring me to death. "Oddballs like that Elton fella oughta be put away for good."

"Excuse me?" I couldn't believe my ears.

"That's right," she said, waving her hands through the air. "I've heard about people like him. You just can't be too careful."

"He saved my life!"

"That's all well and good, but the thing is, the boy's trouble. Powerful big trouble." She sighed. "Why else would the police go and lock him up?"

"I'm sorry, Miss Spindler, but I have to go now." I marched straight to the front door, and just like that, I left. People like Old Hawk Eyes should have to spend one hour with someone as sensitive and kind as Elton Keel. Then they'd know exactly what this wide world is coming to!

On the way back to my house, I noticed a bunch of buggies parked at the Zooks'. Amish friends and neighbors were clearing away debris from the barn fire. Tomorrow, the foundation would be laid for a new one. That's the way it was with the Amish. Instead of buying insurance, everyone worked together to rebuild. In the Plain community, that's all the insurance they needed.

After lunch, the mail came. There was a card for me from Jonathan Klein. He'd written the verse himself.

Get well, won'tcha? Mistress Merry of mirth must make
monumental effort to match wits with the Word Wizard.
 Can't compete without clever company, comprende?
Just Jon

I smiled and read it again. The Alliteration Wizard had come through with a cool get-well card, and Spring Spree or not, I couldn't imagine him sharing our private game with anyone else. Especially not Ashley Horton!

Later that afternoon, Mom announced that she had a few errands to run. "Need anything, Mer?"

"Will you pick out a Bible for Elton at the Christian bookstore?" I asked.

Mom agreed, and I ran upstairs to get some money.

"Now, be sure to rest while the house is quiet." She blew a kiss as she left.

A nap would feel good. But before lying down, I got the brilliant idea to call Lissa's father. Since he was one of the cops at the school the day of the trash-can fire, and because I was a friend of his daughter, maybe I could get him to see the light about Elton.

Lily White followed me into Dad's study. She was fast becoming my shadow. After dialing the police department, I waited for the dispatcher to connect me with Officer Vyner. Several recordings later, he came on the line.

"Hello, this is Merry Hanson, Lissa's friend."

"Yes, Merry, how can I help?"

I explained the reasoning behind my view that Elton was innocent. "He should be set free," I insisted. "He didn't start the fire."

"I understand how you must feel," Lissa's father said, "but Elton is a very unstable person. He is autistic."

There was that word again. Autistic. Skip had used it offhand to describe Elton last week.

"But that doesn't mean he's destructive," I said. "Elton is a very sensitive person. I wish you could get to know him."

"I'm sure you've seen a side of Elton that the police force hasn't," he said kindly, "but unless you can provide something more substantial than your feelings, I'm afraid Elton will have to be tried for arson."

"What about Ben Fisher? He's been causing all sorts of trouble at the Zooks'. Have you talked to him?" I felt bad about breaking my promise to Rachel, but I had to help Elton now.

"We've heard some stories flying around, but nothing we can confirm, Merry. You know the Amish won't implicate one of their own." I heard his beeper going off like crazy in the background. "Substantial evidence is what we need."

"Thanks for your time, sir," I said, and hung up.

I needed proof to clear Elton—something to get him off the hook. It sounded so easy. Maybe a bike ride past Ben Fisher's place was the answer. Maybe I'd even get brave and talk to Ben myself.

Seventeen *Secret in the Willows*

The bike ride turned up absolutely nothing. I even went up to the Fishers' farmhouse and asked Ben's mother if I could talk to him.

Anything to get Elton off.

It turned out that Ben was in Ohio, visiting some Mennonite relatives. I didn't think to ask her how long he'd been gone. I was too depressed to think straight.

Finally, I went to my room to rest like Mom wanted. But I never fell asleep. My mind raced ninety miles an hour. The idea that Ben might've been in Ohio on Monday troubled me. Where did that leave Elton?

Lying on my bed, I played with the straps on my camera case. Soon, my cats joined me. They snuggled in as waves of depression poured over me. At long last, I was ready to pray. Sobbing, I told all my fears and concerns to God, asking for His help.

Later, when Mom got home, she came right up to my room. Her hair was windblown, smelling fresh like spring. She ran her fingers through the top of it before opening her shopping bag. She reached inside and pulled out a black leather Bible.

"It's beautiful," I said, stroking the binding.

"When do you plan to give this to Elton?" she asked, looking quite pleased.

"Tomorrow, I think." I wondered if Elton's grandma might agree to meet me at the detention center. "Thanks for getting it, Mom."

She smiled, adjusting the collar on her light blue shirtwaist dress. "It's a wonderful gift, Merry," she commented. "I'm glad you're so willing to give to others. And if you need to borrow money for Spring Spree, just ask your father."

"Oh, that," I groaned as she walked toward the door. I wanted to forget about Spring Spree.

"What, honey?" She turned around.

"Nothing."

Nothing was right.

Mom came over and sat on my bed. Lily White sniffed her hand, checking her out. "Hey, Miss Lily, I've been around here much longer than you have!" Mom said, grinning.

We laughed together. And the lighthearted moment brought welcome relief to the tension of my crazy, mixed-up life.

⌐——⌐

That evening, Rachel's sisters came pulling her in a red wagon. She smiled at me from her padded perch, lined with a bright-colored quilt. The girls giggled, their eyes bright and cheeks rosy as they called to me. "Hello, Merry! Are you better?"

I held out my bandaged arms for Nancy, Ella Mae, and little Susie as they gathered close to see. "It still hurts a bit, but not too much," I said.

Nancy and Ella Mae held up Rachel's bandaged foot. I leaned over to inspect it. "Can you put weight on it yet?"

Rachel shrugged her shoulders. "Some."

I stood up, noticing several gray buggies parked in the Zooks' lane. "Got company?"

Rachel turned to look. "Jah. Jacob Esh and his boys are over deciding things about the new barn with Dat. Jacob is the master carpenter." She turned to look at me. "You hafta come to the barn raising. It's Friday, you know."

"I don't know if I should miss school for it, but I'll ask."

Little Susie jumped up and down. "You hafta, Merry. It's so-o much fun!"

Nancy nodded. "Ach, there's more food than you've ever seen."

"Like what?" I asked, responding to the eager looks on the girls' faces.

"Like fried ham and gravy, and English walnut pie, that's what!" said Ella Mae.

"Mm-m, sounds good," I said, playing along with the younger girls, rubbing my stomach like Susie.

"Well, we better get going home," Rachel said, and her team of sisters pushed and pulled her down the lane.

"Good-bye!" I called.

"Seven sharp," Susie shouted back.

———

When I arrived at Mifflin Junior High Thursday, everyone carried on about the fire . . . and me. Even Jon hung around my locker longer than usual. I noticed Ashley Horton get tired of waiting for him and head off to first hour by herself.

At lunch, Chelsea practically hovered. "Let's see what second-degree burns look like," she said. "Is it all blistery and yucky under there?"

Lissa frowned at her across the table. "Don't be gross." She pleaded with me not to take off the bandages.

"Don't worry," I said, glancing at the table where Elton usually sat. It seemed strange that I should notice. After all, I hadn't known him that long. One week today.

Chelsea and Lissa chattered on and on about how they would've died if something horrible had happened to me.

"Did you see your life pass before you?" Lissa said softly. "That happens to people sometimes."

Chelsea snickered. "You did that for a barn cat?"

I nodded, smiling. "You sound just like my brother."

Lissa sighed. "All I can say is, God must've been watching out for you, Mer."

I waited for Chelsea to freak out about Lissa mentioning God like that. She set her glass of soda down slowly, holding on to it, then looked at me. "Well, someone sure was."

I rejoiced silently. It was a minor breakthrough for a self-declared atheist.

After school, I sat with Grandma Winnie in the visiting area of Maple Springs. Goose prickles popped out on my neck as I thought about Elton being stuck there.

"How's Elton today?" I asked his grandma, next to me on the sofa.

"Oh, you know him," she said, waving her hand. "Elton takes things in his stride. I guess you could say he lives his life in his head, so it's hard to take much away from him."

I breathed deeply before asking my next question. "Do you think Elton started the barn fire?"

"He's mighty different, that boy, but setting a barn on fire, well, that's another story."

"So, then, you think he's innocent."

"Oh indeed, I do. But it looks as though our hands are tied," she said, her voice drifting off as a counselor led Elton into the room.

Grunting, she pulled herself up off the sofa and shuffled over to Elton. "It's so good to see you, honey-boy." She wrapped her jolly arms around her grandson.

Elton was motionless. And by the blank look on his pale face, I could see he'd regressed quite a bit.

I clenched my teeth, coming to grips with reality. Isolating Elton here, away from the people who loved him, had been a big mistake.

I struggled with my good memories of him—those few times we'd spent in the willow grove and at the covered bridge. Elton had begun to grow, to change. And now . . .

I couldn't bear to see him like this.

Grandma Winnie led him to a chair, and he nearly collapsed into it, weak and dejected. I swallowed hard to keep from crying. This special kid, the boy who'd saved my life, needed help.

Elton's grandma stroked his back. "Look who's come to pay you a visit."

I stood up and walked over to him, wishing there was some way I could communicate the important things—how I'd tried desperately to clear his name. I wanted him to know. But the timing didn't seem quite right, especially with Elton's grandma right there—and the counselor breathing down our necks.

"I brought you something." I pulled the gift bag off so he could see the Bible.

He kept staring into space and rocking back and forth, his arms and hands bandaged and limp in his lap.

I thought my heart would break. This was not the same boy who'd sat in church with me, sharing my Bible. And the night he'd stood and clapped at our youth meeting—where was *that* Elton?

His grandma started to talk about the fire, but the counselor intervened. That subject was obviously off limits, and I could see why. Zooks' fire had changed everything.

That night, after supper, Dad and I had a long talk in his study. He did his best to explain Elton's problem to me. "Autism is a mental disorder that occurs in one out of every one hundred fifty live births," he said. "It's found more often in boys than girls." He continued to describe some of the behaviors of autistic people. Elton had nearly all of them.

Everything seemed so complicated, but it was good to know Dad wanted to take time to explain. "There's something else I want to say, Merry," he continued.

"What, Dad?"

"This has to do with your views concerning Elton's innocence." He paused for a moment, scratching his head. "I want you to know I respect your opinion about your friend, and I hope the best for him." He smiled.

"Oh, thank you!" I said, rushing into his arms. Things were so much better now. Finally, Dad was sounding less like the resident shrink, and more like my father.

With little fuss, my parents agreed to let me go to the Zooks' barn raising. "As long as you get your homework assignments finished before tomorrow," Mom said.

"And please be careful with your arms," Dad said, glancing at the bandages still there.

So it was set. I was looking forward to a frolicking good time, as Susie Zook would say. Frolicking good had its limitations, of course. Tomorrow wouldn't be half as much fun with Elton locked up.

Setting my alarm for six o'clock, I climbed into bed early, wishing and praying that Elton were free. And struggling with what to do to make it happen.

When the alarm sounded the next morning, I was in a deep sleep, dreaming that I was dragging my camera collection through a field. Things were hazy and I tried my best not to stop dreaming, but the alarm clock had done its work. The dream faded away.

Later, I stood in my closet trying to decide what to wear. That's when I remembered my Polaroid camera. I'd loaned it to Elton. Had it burned in the fire? Frustrated about not knowing, I pulled on a lightweight shirt, careful not to disturb the new, clean bandages on my arms. There was really no way to ask Elton about anything these days.

It was full light when I hopped onto my bike and rode over to the Zooks'. I didn't want to offend my Amish friends by carrying a camera in plain view, so I wrapped it in a paper bag, securing it in my bike basket.

The Old Order Amish didn't allow photographs of themselves. The scriptures about not making any graven images were taken literally.

Abe and Levi were in the field welcoming friends and directing buggy traffic when I arrived. More and more horses and buggies pulled into the yard and parked, lining up all the way to the wagon wheel mailbox at the end of the private lane. Minutes later, a bus came bouncing down SummerHill, packed with Amishmen from Strasburg and surrounding areas. They were wearing their work clothes.

By seven sharp, everyone was present—about three hundred Amish folk. Even the Zook grandparents settled into their rocking chairs to sit and watch and visit with the others their age.

Rachel waved when she saw me. "Come on inside, Merry!" She hobbled around on a single homemade crutch.

I parked my bike near the back door and went into the kitchen. Rachel and her mother were arranging homemade pies and cakes baked by the women whose husbands would build the barn.

Soon the women began stewing chickens for the noon meal. Rachel and I helped fry potato chips with several other women until her mother caught our attention. "Rachel! Merry!" she called. "You girls go and get off your feet now for a while." She shooed us out of the kitchen like flies. Then, turning to her Amish friends, she said, "Ach, that fire was such a terrible fright."

Terrible was putting it mildly, and I thought of Elton again as Nancy and Ella Mae showed up with their wagon for their big sister. I smoothed out the wrinkles in the quilt and helped Rachel get situated.

"Ask Mam if we can take some angel food cake and cookies with us," Rachel told her sisters.

The girls scampered into the house, letting the screen door slap against the frame. I watched Susie play a game of chase with a friend in the backyard near the old pump. Aaron Zook was hauling tools with a wheelbarrow, helping his dad.

I could hear the joking going on among the men as they divided into groups to begin erecting the main timbers and frame. It would take sixteen strong men to lift one beam into place.

Nancy and Ella Mae came running with two large pieces of angel food cake and six peanut butter cookies. Nancy handed the plates wrapped with clear plastic to Rachel, who sat like a princess in the wagon.

"That's a very good after-breakfast snack," Rachel said. "Can you bring us some lemonade later on?"

Ella Mae smiled broadly, showing her missing front tooth. "Where are you two going now?"

Rachel looked up at me and I leaned down to pick up the wagon handle. "Merry, where do you want to sit and watch the barn go up?" she asked.

"How about the secret place—in the willow grove?" I suggested. "You girls can come later if you bring us some lemonade," I teased Nancy and Ella Mae.

They giggled and chased each other barefooted as I pulled the wagon over the yard. I stopped to get my camera out of the bike basket before heading down Zooks' bumpy lane to the main road.

"Don't you go hurting your arms pulling me around," Rachel said.

"It's no problem." I turned off SummerHill Lane and headed down the well-worn path to the thickest part of the willow grove.

Under the graceful covering of branches and leaves, I spread out the quilt from the wagon and helped Rachel sit down. "How's that?"

"Look at this view we have," she said as I sat beside her on the quilt. She was right—the view was perfect. We could see everything from here.

The men crawled over the beams like ants, working at a feverish pace while Rachel and I talked leisurely about the summer coming up. "My aunt Teri's expecting twins this summer," I said. "In June, I think."

"Twins?" Rachel looked a little surprised. Maybe because she knew Faithie and I had been so close. "You're going to have two new cousins at once."

"That's right," I said. "They'll be her first children."

"Will she hafta teach the little ones how to sign?"

I hadn't thought of that. "I guess so." I reached for the plate with the angel food cake and gave a piece to Rachel. After that, we nibbled on our cookies, soaking up the sun. Feeling lazy and good.

By ten o'clock, it was time for the first break, and we could see all the activity from our vantage point. Women and girls scurried here and there serving sandwiches and doughnuts in baskets to their husbands and fathers. It was a holiday atmosphere, with plenty of laughter and lots of pranks.

After they served Abe and Levi, Nancy and Ella Mae came dashing across the pasture, climbing over the picket fence with tall glasses of cold lemonade splashing out as they came.

"Thanks," I said, taking a sip of the cold drink.

"Anything else?" Nancy curtsied to us, pulling on her black apron, pretending to be our maid.

"No, thank you, not for me," I said. "And you?" I turned to Rachel, playing along.

"I'll have a sandwich, if you please," she said, sounding like a regular English lady.

Ella Mae got the giggles and Nancy challenged her to a race to the picket fence.

I reached for the bag with my camera inside and set up a shot of the quilt and lemonade glasses. "Don't worry, I won't get you in the picture," I promised.

Rachel smiled, trusting me. She leaned over to steady her glass. "That's better."

I stepped back several feet, away from the cozy retreat. Aiming at the quilt, I made the lemonade glasses the focal point.

Click. The picture was done, but something behind Rachel caught my eye. Something red and blue. Something plaid.

I hurried to investigate. When I knelt down, I discovered it was Elton's backpack!

"What did ya find, Merry?" Rachel asked.

Almost reverently, I carried the small plaid backpack over to our quilt. "This belongs to the boy who saved my life," I said softly.

The zipper was open, so I peeked inside. "Oh, look at this." I pulled out my Polaroid camera. "It wasn't burned up after all." A truly happy feeling swept over me.

Rachel peered over my shoulder as I felt around inside the backpack. "What else?"

"Oh, just some pictures he took for an art project," I said, pulling out the developed shots he'd taken.

We looked at Elton's pictures together, and Rachel seemed to enjoy them. "There's our old barn," she said, pointing to the silo.

I looked at the next one. It was the same barn. Same silo. Cows grazing peacefully. Martins flying overhead. A car parked in front of the house . . .

"Wait a minute!" I showed Rachel this one. "Look at that!"

Rachel gasped. "Ach, no! That's Ben Fisher's car. What is it doing out in front of our house?"

Quickly, I looked at the next picture. "Who's that walking toward the barn?" My heart was pounding so hard I couldn't see straight.

"Oh, Merry," Rachel said, holding her chest. "It's Ben!" She stared at the picture, squinting. *"Himmel,"* she whispered. "That's a gasoline can."

Our eyes locked.

"Ben Fisher *did* burn down our barn!" she said.

Trembling with relief, I placed my Polaroid camera and Elton's pictures inside the blue-and-red backpack. I'd found proof. The proof Officer Vyner needed to clear my friend!

Rachel assured me she'd be okay there in the secret place until I got back. She grinned at me, clapping her hands as I carefully threaded first one bandaged arm, then the next, through the camera strap and Elton's backpack. The scene was something out of my early morning dream.

"Thank you, Lord!" I shouted through the willows. I ran like the wind down the narrow dirt path toward SummerHill Lane. "Thank yo-o-u!"

Nineteen *Secret in the Willows*

Elton didn't nod or shake his head or anything when I asked him later that evening to go to Spring Spree with me.

"It's tomorrow at the church, in case you forgot."

He stared straight ahead.

"I'm paying. It's the least I can do."

His eyes blinked.

Grandma Winnie came out on the porch of their home and sat down, smiling. "Elton's been mighty excited about your gift." She leaned next to him, adjusting his head bandage.

"Really? How do you know?" I asked.

She picked up his pen and handed it to her grandson. "He's wanted to 'talk' about Bible stories since yesterday."

"That's good," I said. "What's he saying?"

"Just watch," she said as Elton's pen began flying over the sketch pad. A drawing of Adam and Eve began to take shape. They were situated in a beautiful garden. A garden with dense trees, some shaped like willows. And there was something else. I watched curiously as he sketched.

Then I saw it. Way in the very back of the garden. "It's a covered bridge!"

Elton's face remained unchanged, but the windows of his soul were shining.

"You've got a great sense of humor," I said, looking right at him. "Maybe you could team up with Anthony, the artist from Vermont."

Suddenly, Elton reached over and began thumping on his Bible. I was sure it was his way of saying thank you. Maybe much more.

All the pieces didn't quite fit yet, but I knew the encounter in the hallway at school hadn't been an accident after all. Besides that, there was a photo that had yet to be printed. One featuring a very special person.

Ben Fisher was tracked down somewhere in Ohio and brought back, though the Zooks refused to press charges against him. Last I heard, Levi had been going to visit Ben nearly every day. Like I said, Levi was a loyal, true friend.

And Ben repented, escaping the shunning. Thank goodness!

Lissa talked her mother into letting her go to Spring Spree with my brother, saying it was only a one-time thing. In fact, Lissa and Skip and Elton and I doubled up in Skip's car for the evening. I must admit it wasn't easy pulling Elton into the conversation, but, oh well . . . sometimes silence is golden.

Jon Klein and Ashley Horton experienced a somewhat golden evening, as well. In fact, every time I happened to glance over at their table, they were silent.

At the end of the banquet, Elton and I posed for pictures, showing off our matching white bandages. Well, Elton didn't ham it up that much, but at least he got his nodding ritual going again.

I can't decide exactly where his picture—the people picture—will fit on my wall gallery just yet. But it's going up there—no matter what!

Who knows, I might start a new gallery, one featuring windows of the soul. I think it's about time.

Catch a Falling Star

To Dave,
with thanks for the simple gifts—
long walks and quiet talks . . .
and stargazing.

'Tis the gift to be simple.
'Tis the gift to be free.

—Old American Hymn

Catch a Falling Star **One**

I probably would have ignored Lissa Vyner the rest of the school year and all summer, too, for doing what she did. In fact, I was one-hundred-percent-amen sure if Lissa hadn't been my friend I would have refused to have anything whatsoever to do with her.

Outrageous. That's what it was. How dare she ask Jonathan Klein to be her project partner! But she had. And I could still see her waiting outside social studies, all pert and confident with her wavy blond hair pulled back, her blue eyes shining.

It wasn't as if Lissa was totally tuned out with no idea of how I felt. Last month she'd even asked me point-blank if I liked Jon. Silly me, I'd changed the subject. The truth was, I truly admired Jon, maybe even the L word, but I'd tried desperately to keep all traces of such things hidden. Aside from the fact that he considered me his equal when it came to playing his alliteration game, I doubted Jonathan Klein even knew I existed—as a potential girlfriend, anyway.

"Who're you teaming up with?" I asked Chelsea Davis in the cafeteria line the next day.

She puffed out her cheeks and rolled her eyes as though the assignment were something out of grade school. "You kidding? Why do we have to have partners to do a family history?"

"Well"—I wondered why she was so upset—"doesn't sound like such a bad idea to me. Might be kinda fun."

"I'd rather go bungee jumping over a pool of hungry sharks," she protested.

I reached for the soy sauce and sprinkled some on my chicken chow mein. "Maybe you'll uncover some never-before-discovered secrets. Don't *all* families have skeletons in their closets?" I rubbed my hands together.

She snickered.

"So . . . wanna be my partner?" I asked.

Chelsea gathered her super-thick auburn hair away from her face and flung it over her shoulder before picking up her tray. "I can see this is gonna be a kickin' good time."

"Truly?" I followed her to our table.

She laughed. "You're crazy, Merry Hanson."

"Good, then it's set." I dropped my schoolbag on the chair across from her. "We're a team."

Chelsea nodded nonchalantly.

Honestly, I was relieved. Last I checked, there were only a couple of kids unclaimed as partners. One was Ashley Horton, our new pastor's daughter. Since Lissa had snatched up my number-one choice, I was more than happy to settle for Chelsea. I don't mean that Ashley was all that bad. Actually, the girl had a lot going for her. Great smile, nice hair, and truly sweet—she wasn't the stereotypical preacher's kid. In fact, she was the kind of girl most guys would easily fall for. Fall in love with, and then not be able to engage in decent conversation. At least that's how she struck me.

For that one reason I didn't want to link up with Ashley for the end-of-the-year project. Well, there was one other minuscule reason. Unfortunately, it had to do with Ashley's making a not-so-subtle attempt last month at getting Jon's attention.

Sigh. Why did it seem as though every girl in Lancaster County was attracted to the Alliteration Wizard?

After lunch, I was opening my locker when I heard the familiar greeting, "Mistress Merry." I turned to see Jon hurrying down the hall toward me.

"Soon school'll be squat," he said, starting up our alliteration game as he stood beside my locker.

"Three more weeks and ninth grade's history." I looked up just in time to catch his heart-stopping smile.

"Say that with all *g*'s," he teased.

I could see Ashley at the end of the hall, fussing around in her locker. She primped in her mirror as though she didn't know what to do with herself. But I knew she was spying. Several lockers away from Ashley's, Lissa peered over her shoulder, glaring in my direction, no doubt longing to know what Jon and I were talking about.

Not wanting to clue in either girl as to Jon's and my word-game connection—after all, it was all we really had, so it was precious to me—I turned away from their surveillance and lowered my voice. I couldn't pass up an opportunity to show Jon my amazing intellectual stuff. "All *g*'s, you say?"

He nodded. "Oh, you know, give or take a few."

"Good-bye, grand and glorious grade of nine. Gimme ghastly halls of high school," I said.

He grinned at me—really grinned. Then he reached up and leaned on my locker door. "I take it you're not looking forward to sophomore year?"

"Did I say that?" I shrugged, staring down at my tennies. His hand was touching my locker door! His arm was so close to me. So close . . .

I wondered if Lissa and Ashley were still gawking. Shrugging the thought away, I felt embarrassed admitting to my fellow classmate and word-game equal that the thought of high school sent me into jitterland.

"High school is just one step up from here, right?" he said. "No problem."

Maybe not for him.

I forced a smile. "I guess change is good."

He stepped back slightly and ran his free hand through his light brown hair. "Well, I guess it's all in how you look at it."

"Say that with all *y*'s," I said, eager for this conversation to last forever. But the hallway was becoming crammed with students, growing more noisy by the second. "Oh well, skip it."

"Later?" His brown eyes twinkled.

"Okay." But I had a feeling our wonderful word game was over, at least for today. And I was right.

By the end of the day, Lissa showed up at Jon's locker with a spiral notebook. Probably with talk of their social studies project. I was pretty sure she would monopolize him for the next three weeks. And after that, school would be out for the summer.

I hated the thought of summer vacation. For one thing, I liked school, really and truly; it had nothing to do with seeing Jon every day. Fortunately, he attended the same church I did, and there were lots of youth services and special activities all summer long.

I peeked around my locker door the way Lissa and Ashley had done earlier. I made sure Lissa didn't catch me, though. As for Jon, it was impossible for him to spot my envious eyes—he was facing her.

Reaching for my math and social studies books, I was dying for one more glance. But it was a mistake—I never should've taken another look. Jon reached up and held on to her locker door exactly the way he had mine while Lissa gazed up at him all dreamy-eyed.

Swiftly, I stuffed my books into my schoolbag and closed my locker. I needed some fresh air. Fast!

Catch a Falling Star *Two*

A bunch of kids were already waiting for the bus at the bottom of the steps of Mifflin Junior High—hallowed ground, in my opinion. With only a few weeks left as a ninth grader, I was entitled to feel this way about my school. Three solid years of memories—some good, some not. I consoled myself with the thought that I'd have all summer to get used to the idea of high school.

I turned around and scanned the steps, wondering when Lissa would show up. Usually, I sat with Chelsea on the bus, sometimes Lissa.

Today, I wanted to be alone. But I didn't plan to budge before I saw with my own eyes that Lissa's conversation with Jon was over.

The bus made the turn at the end of the drive, and the crowd of kids jammed up, moving toward the bold yellow lines. That's when I heard Jon's voice.

I turned to see him hold the door for Lissa, and she stepped out of the school like a princess. A golden glow graced her face, and I stared, trying to decide if the lustrous shine came from the sun illuminating her wheat-colored hair—or was it because of Jon's attentive smile?

A kid behind me yelled, "Keep it moving."

"Chill," I shot back and headed toward the bus.

Instead of sitting in the front as usual, I felt like going to the back of the bus and crawling under one of the seats. Especially now that it looked as though Jon and Lissa were going to keep talking. Through the smeared-up bus windows, I spotted them and felt my throat turn to cotton.

On my way to the rear of the bus, I passed Ashley Horton and several church friends sharing a bag of chips. Miss Preacher's Kid hardly noticed me. At least she didn't bother to say anything or glance my way.

Suddenly, I was hungry. Stress did that to me. Sliding into the last seat, I took refuge by leaning against the hard window. I watched Jon and Lissa as they stood side by side outside, still talking.

My stomach growled, and I reached into my schoolbag, pulled out an apple, and bit down hard. From my vantage point, I noticed Jon's hands gesturing rapidly as they often did when he talked. Lissa's eyes were incredibly bright. My guess was she was falling hard and fast. For *my* guy.

I chomped down on the next bite of apple, trying to compose myself. *Get it together, Merry. He's only being nice.*

"Whatcha doin' all the way back here?" Chelsea asked, plopping herself down next to me.

I forced my eyes away from the window. "Don't ask."

She glanced out the window. "Oh, *I* get it."

"Get what?"

"Not what, Mer—*who*?" And with that remark, she pointed toward the window.

I shoved her arm down. "Chelsea, please!"

"Oh, don't tell me . . ." She scrunched down, putting her knees up against the seat in front of us. "This is one of those truly horrible days of your life, right?" She'd used my own words to mimic me!

It was bad enough being secretly in love with Jon, but having to observe him with someone else—especially a good friend—knowing they'd probably be going to each other's houses for the social studies project . . . well, it was truly horrible.

Then, to top things off, when the two of them finally did board the bus, Jon slid in next to Lissa—the seat where she and I usually sat. Not once did she check to see where I was sitting.

Friday afternoons weren't supposed to be like this. A girl ought to be able to go home from school feeling good for having done her best work all week long.

Do everything for the honor and glory of God, Mom always said. Dad, too, only he wasn't given to hammering away at his philosophies. For as long as I could remember, the concept had been drilled into my head. My brother's, too. And it must've worked for Skip, because my brainy brother was going to graduate from high school with honors!

The bus jolted forward, and I tried my best not to look at Jon and Lissa even though they were smack-dab in my line of vision. I took another slurpy bite of my apple and slumped down in my seat, pushing my knees up against the seat in front of me, copying Chelsea.

She smirked. "Now you're getting the hang of things. And just think, you won't have to ride this rotten bus again till Monday morning."

"Oh, terrific," I mumbled. But she was right. One good thing about today's being Friday, I wouldn't have to suffer through another Lissa-and-Jon day till Monday. I could use a weekend about now.

Then I remembered. Sunday—church!

Surely Lissa wouldn't carry her newfound link with Jon through the weekend, drag it right into church, and parade it in front of me.

I must've gasped or something because Chelsea said, "What's wrong?"

"What?"

"Your face is all white, Mer."

"I'm fine, really." Then I changed the subject. "When do you want to start working on the family history assignment?"

"Never." Her sea-green eyes looked sly.

"So, what about tomorrow?" I laughed.

"My house?" She pulled out her schoolbag and found her daily planner. "What time?"

"After lunch?" She wrote my name in the Saturday, May 13 box. "About one-thirty?"

Chelsea elbowed me. "Hey, maybe you'll get so absorbed in your past, you'll forget about your future." She jerked her head toward Jon.

"What a truly horrible thing to say!"

"Uh, there you go again," she teased. "Where do you get this, Mer? Truly this and truly that. C'mon!"

I sat up, mostly to create some distance between us. Thumbing through my social studies book, I found the scribbled notes I'd made for the Hanson family tree project.

"Hey, don't take it seriously," Chelsea said, her voice softer now. "I was just kidding."

"Whatever." I shuffled the papers, frustrated with the world.

"Mind if I take a look?" she asked.

I relinquished my notes, not caring whether Chelsea read the details of my father's Swiss ancestors. Some of them had survived hideous treatment for their beliefs; other Anabaptists had been murdered.

Chelsea was suddenly quiet as she read through my pages of notes. "This is unreal," she said, referring to the martyrs, I guess. "How could they do it—I mean, just let someone torture them to death?"

"My dad says God gives people martyrs' grace."

"What's that?" She studied me with intense eyes.

"I think it means God softens the pain of dying somehow."

She scoffed. "Whoever heard of that!"

"Don't laugh," I said. "It's true."

"How would *you* know?"

I couldn't believe it. Just when I thought I was actually getting somewhere with her. In fact, every time I thought I was making spiritual headway with Chelsea, she'd pull out a response like this.

I refused to display my exasperation. "There are many examples recorded in the *Martyrs Mirror*."

"Martyrs what?"

"It's a German book about a thousand pages long," I explained. "It's nearly sacred to the Amish. I've seen it lots of times at Rachel Zook's house."

"Your neighbors?"

I nodded. "Rachel says the book is really sad. It tells about men and women being murdered—their little children, even babies, being orphaned—all sorts of horrible things because of what they believed."

"Sounds awful."

She turned back to my notes, poring over them as her thick, shoulder-length hair inched forward and dropped, hiding her face from view.

I stared out the window at lilac bushes in full bloom along SummerHill Lane. Leaning up, I opened the window and breathed in their sweet aroma. Then I settled down to finish off my apple.

Acres of meticulously plowed fields stretched away from the road for miles. Yards of neatly mown grass and elaborate flower beds with deep red and bright pink peonies were evident at one Amish farmhouse after another.

I began to relax as we rode toward the old house on the corner of SummerHill and Strawberry Lanes. There was something peaceful about this three-mile stretch. And after a day like today, I needed *something* soothing.

I glimpsed Rachel Zook, my Amish friend, and her younger sister Nancy working two mules in the field closest to the road. The mules were hitched to a cultivator, weeding the alfalfa—the preferred hay in Lancaster. I'd heard that in one growing season, it was possible for an Amish farmer to get as many as three or four cuttings—something to do with the land's having a limestone base. I smiled as I watched

Rachel handle the mules. She held the reins loosely and, like the mules, could probably perform this job blindfolded.

I wondered how Rachel felt about her younger siblings completing another year of school. Like me, Rachel was fifteen, but the Amish only attended school through eighth grade. After that, girls helped with making and canning grape juice, "putting up" a variety of vegetables, bread-making, quilting, and keeping house. And waiting for marriage.

Rachel and a group of her Amish friends had started a "charity" garden on a one-acre plot on their land. They were in charge of planting and caring for the garden until harvest time, when they'd harvest the vegetables and freeze or can them. Later they would label the fruits of their labor and distribute the vegetables to several "English"—non-Amish—shelters nearby. It was a garden of love.

Rachel and her mother were a team in the female domain of getting garden produce from the soil to the kitchen table. And, at sixteen, like most Plain girls that age, Rachel would begin "running around" with a supper crowd on weekends and attending Sunday night singings, where she could meet eligible young Amishmen.

On the north side of the house, Levi, Rachel's sixteen-going-on-seventeen-year-old brother, worked the potato field with his younger brother, Aaron. Levi, tall and slender and the cutest Amish boy ever, was well into in his *Rumschpringe*—the Amish term for the running-around years. Amish parents loosened their grip on their teens long enough for them to experience the modern, English world. Most teens eventually returned to their Amish roots, got baptized, and settled down to marry and raise a family of seven or eight children.

Levi took off his straw hat and wiped his forehead on his arm. He must've spotted the school bus at that moment, because he began to wave his hat. A wide, sweeping wave.

Surprised, I turned away. Amish boys weren't supposed to flirt with English girls. But Levi didn't seem to care about such things. He was *always* flirting with me—he'd even asked me to ride in his open courting buggy last month. He didn't know it, but I'd secretly nicknamed him Zap 'em Zook because of his wild and reckless buggy driving.

Living on adjacent properties had had its advantages during our growing-up years. All the Zook kids, except Curly John who was much older and married now, had been my playmates. In fact, once when all of us were swimming in the pond behind our houses, Levi got his foot stuck in a willow root under the water. None of the other kids seemed to notice he'd disappeared, but I had. Being a truly brave eight-year-old, I dove down and untangled his foot—seconds before his lungs would've given out.

I'd saved Levi's life. From that time on, he'd said he was going to "get hitched up" with me someday. Silly boy. Cute as he was, Levi Zook had beans for brains!

Three *Catch a Falling Star*

I wrapped my apple core in a tissue and stuffed it down into the corner of my schoolbag as the bus approached my house.

Chelsea straightened my family history notes. "Here you go," she said, handing them to me. "I can't imagine letting someone set me on fire for believing in God. Too bad your ancestors didn't know they were dying for nothing."

She had that unyielding look on her face.

"God is real, Chelsea, whether you say so or not."

She gave me a half smile. "You're not gonna preach now, are you?"

It was her standard line. But I wasn't giving up on my self-proclaimed atheist friend. Not today, not ever!

"Well, here's my house. I'll see you tomorrow at one-thirty." I crawled over her to get to the aisle.

"See ya," Chelsea called.

I held on to the seat, waiting for the bus to stop. Even though I had to walk past Jon and Lissa, I didn't let their "Bye, Merry, have a great weekend" comments get to me.

Waiting for the bus doors to open, I realized something amazing. This research project was just what I needed to get my mind off less important things—present parties included! Talking about my ancestors had done the trick.

I hurried down out of the bus and ran up SummerHill to our sloping front lawn, around the side yard to the white gazebo, and collapsed on the steps.

My cats, Shadrach and his brother Meshach, followed by my beautiful white kitten, Lily White, made their appearance from under the gazebo, looking plump and sleepy.

"Where's Abednego?" I inspected the dark, cool area beneath the gazebo.

My cats were not only beautiful, they were extremely intelligent. Their choice of a cool and carefree place to snooze was just one more indication of that.

I called for Abednego, who was always the last one to show up. Slowly, grandly, he emerged into the sunlight, squinting his eyes as he made his debut.

"Take your time, why don'tcha?" I teased him. But he wasn't moved by my words and came nuzzling up against my leg. "You think that's all it takes for an apology, huh?" I scooped him up and carried him to the house in my schoolbag.

Lily White scampered ahead of me, meowing for equal time. She and I didn't go back as far as the three Hebrew cat children, but beautiful Lily was extraspecial. I had saved her life in Zooks' barn fire last month—risking mine to do it.

"Come on, little boys," I called over my shoulder. They did as they were told, obeying their mistress Merry to a tee. I choked down the thought of referring to myself that way—it only reminded me of my jovial Jon, who was probably still sitting next to the light and lovely Lissa.

"Mom, I'm home!"

The kitchen smelled like rhubarb pie mingled with the aroma of roast beef. Clean and free of clutter, the kitchen sparkled as though the cleaning lady had just been here. But it was Friday, and Mrs. Gibson came on Tuesdays.

Something was up.

I dumped my schoolbag on a chair. Carefully, I lifted Abednego out of his hiding place and carried him to the counter. "Check this out," I said as we sniffed two big pies cooling near the window.

Mom came sailing through the room. "How was school, honey?" She kissed the air near my cheek, then scurried off to the dining room.

Lily White let out an irritated, whiny *meow*. Even though she loved me, she was still adjusting to the rest of the Hanson family.

"School? Oh, it was there." I couldn't tell Mom how school had really been. It involved talking about Jon, and no one needed to know that secret part of my life. "We're doing a cool assignment in social studies," I mentioned, opening the fridge.

"Oh?"

"Yeah, it's a good way to close out the school year." I poured some milk and crept into the spacious formal dining room to observe Mom—busy as usual.

"Why's that, honey?" She glanced up momentarily as though she was interested in a reply, but I could tell her mind was on other things. Like polishing silverware and wiping off her good china.

"Someone coming for dinner?" I asked.

She smiled, completely forgetting about my social studies project. "Some of your father's relatives are in town. They're staying at a bed and breakfast in Strasburg but called to see if they could take us out to eat." She sighed, counting the salad forks. "I thought it would be just as well to invite them here. You know how your father likes to unwind after a long day at the hospital."

I smiled to myself. Mom sometimes liked to use Dad as an excuse to do things her way. Sure Dad would be tired from making rounds and treating patients, but it was really Mom who preferred to dine at home. Besides, this would be another opportunity for her to be the perfect hostess.

I wandered back into the kitchen, pouring fresh milk for the cat quartet. Eagerly, they crowded around the wide, flat dish, their pink tongues lapping up the raw milk straight from moo to you from the Zooks' dairy farm next door.

"Oh, Merry," Mom called from the dining room as though she'd forgotten something. "Someone else called—for you."

I hurried through the kitchen again. "Who? Someone from school?"

She straightened up, holding a fistful of spoons. "You know, it almost sounded like Levi Zook," she said, a curious look in her deep brown eyes. "There was background noise, though, like he was calling from town."

I frowned. "Didn't he say who he was?"

She shook her head. "I asked if he'd like to leave a message, but he seemed to be in a hurry."

"That's weird." If it was Levi, I wondered what he was up to.

I asked for more details. "What kind of background noise did you hear?"

"Come to think of it, he may have been down at the Yoders'— they have that new carpentry shop over in Leola." She carried the silverware into the kitchen.

I followed.

"But the Yoders are Amish, too," I reminded her. "They don't have a phone, do they?"

"Well, maybe they do," she said, searching for some silver polish under the sink. "More and more Amish are having phones installed in their businesses, but the way I understand it, they aren't allowed to use them for personal calls."

"So you really think it was Levi?"

"Almost positive."

"Hmm . . . okay, Mom. Thanks." Hurrying out of the kitchen, I headed down the long hall to the front staircase, carrying my book bag and a second glass of milk, this one spiked with a touch of chocolate syrup.

What does Levi want? I wondered.

Inside my room, I emptied my schoolbag, taking time to organize my books and notebooks on my massive white antique pine desk. Mom had found it at an estate auction years ago in disrepair. After stripping and repainting it white to match my corner bookcase, the old piece added charm to my room like nothing else. Except for my wall gallery, of course, on the opposite side of the room.

I'd framed and displayed my best photography there, starting with pictures taken in first grade with my little camera. Cheap as the camera had been, the colors had turned out clear and bright.

Thoughts of Levi and Jon twirled in my head as I surveyed the entire wall. Recounting the pictures of my life was a kind of ritual. I drank in the tranquil scenes of Amish farmhouses, the willow grove, and a covered bridge not far from here. There were before-and-after pictures, too. Like the one of a fresh apple pie made by Miss Spindler, another neighbor, before and after it had been sliced into six pieces.

Last month I'd had a change of heart and decided to include pictures of people in my wall gallery. The decision was triggered by an incredible event that happened right after the Zooks' barn fire. Anyway, I now had enlargements of my favorite people displayed on the wall. People like Mom, Dad, and Skip posing in front of our ivy-strewn gazebo, Lissa and Chelsea hamming it up on the school bus.

But the best picture of all was one I'd taken as a little girl. It featured Faithie, my twin, before she got sick and went home to Jesus.

Mom had helped frame some of the pictures with bonafide antique frames, but she couldn't stand to have old relics around unless they were immaculate.

I wondered as I looked at Faithie's picture if my twin might have inherited Mom's interest in antique treasures had she lived past her seventh birthday. One thing was certain, Mom had not passed on her obsession with old things to me. It wasn't that I didn't appreciate them. I guess it had more to do with growing up with so many Amish neighbors—not to mention the ones way back in my family tree—and wanting to be my own person. A *very* modern girl.

I changed into white shorts and a red top, with red shoes to match. Then I headed into the bathroom adjoining my room and washed my face, careful not to smudge my mascara. A quick look in the mirror, and I grabbed a hairbrush. When my hair was smooth, I stepped back to scrutinize myself.

"Ready or not, here I come," I said out loud, eager to get over to the Amish farm next door.

It was time to set my friend Levi Zook straight. Once and for all.

Mom was still busying herself with preparations for the evening meal when I darted through the kitchen. "Merry," she called just as I reached the screen door.

"Yes?" I turned around.

"Come tell me what you think," she said from the dining room. "I need your expert opinion."

In a hurry to see Levi, I rushed back through the kitchen and found my mom holding a matching set of white candle holders. "Which looks better?" She held them up dramatically, eyeing the floral centerpiece—pink and white roses scattered with babies' breath and greenery. "Do you like the table with or without the candles?"

I waited as she placed the candle holders on the table, one on either side of the white basket of flowers. "Without," I said. "Too formal with candles."

She stepped back, concentrating on the table. "Are you sure?"

"I'm sure, Mom. Why'd you ask me if—"

"Merry," she said, glancing at me. "You don't have to get upset about this."

"I'm not upset," I insisted. The phone rang, and I ran into the kitchen. "Hanson residence, Merry speaking."

"Merry, hi!" It was Lissa.

"Hi." I sounded completely unenthusiastic.

"Are you busy?" There was that certain edge to her voice as if she was dying to tell me something, yet waiting politely for me to respond.

"Not really," I said, raising the pitch of my voice to ward off more questions. "What's up?"

"You'll never guess!"

I braced myself. "Guess *what*?"

"Oh, Merry, this is just too good to be true."

"What is?" My throat was already dry. I wished I hadn't asked.

"C'mon, Mer, you have to guess."

"Look, I don't feel like playing a guessing game right now, so either you tell me or you don't." I inched around the refrigerator, checking to see if Mom seemed interested in my end of the conversation.

Good! She was squatting down in front of the buffet, reaching for some serving dishes.

"Merry," Lissa said, sounding hurt. "What's wrong?"

"Nothing's wrong."

"You sound mad or something."

"Well . . . I'm not." I took a deep breath. "So, what were you saying?"

"It's about Jon Klein . . . and me."

My heart started beating ninety miles an hour. "Jon?" I managed to squeak out.

"And *me*," she said. "We're going to the ninth-grade picnic together—you know . . . at church."

I switched the phone to my left ear, hoping maybe I hadn't heard correctly. "I . . . oh, that's nice."

"You'll never guess how he asked me," she continued.

I knew I'd probably seem like a real jerk if she kept talking and waiting for upbeat responses from me, but the truth was I wasn't happy for her. How could I be?

"Merry? You still there?"

"I've really gotta get going," I said.

"Okay, then," she said, almost giggling, "I'll talk to you later. 'Bye."

I didn't say good-bye. Just hung up the phone and stood there staring at it, refusing to cry.

"There we are," Mom said from the dining room as though I'd never even left to answer the phone. "Now for the roast and all the fixings."

She didn't even seem to notice the state I was in as she flounced through the kitchen, pulled out a drawer, and found a fancy apron to wear.

"I'm going for a walk," I said, attempting to make my voice sound normal. It cracked a little.

"Merry?" Mom turned to look at me. "What's wrong?"

"It's been a long week," I said, turning to leave.

Long wasn't the only thing the week—the day—had been. Long and lousy, both!

I thought of the Alliteration Wizard with a lump in my throat. Had Jon introduced Lissa to *our* word game? My heart sank at the thought. I hoped not. But then again, if he'd asked her out, maybe . . .

The sun beat down on me as I jogged the sloping stretch of road between our front lawn and SummerHill Lane, where the school bus always stopped. About a block away from my house, a dirt path led away from the road to a shortcut through the willow grove, to the Zook farm.

I kept running, feeling the anger rise in me.

Lissa and Jon. He'd asked her . . . not me.

My throat ached; the tears came. I ran harder, my red shoes pounding the ground. The path cut into the thick wild grass on either side as it headed into the dense, hidden part of the grove.

Faster and faster I ran. The distance from here to there seemed desperately long, not like it usually was when I came to visit Rachel. We would talk about the day, maybe have a slice of warm bread and her wonderful grape jelly. Sometimes she would show me a new pillow or doily she had made for her hope chest.

I made my legs move through the willow grove and down the pasture to the white picket fence. Through my tears, I could see Levi in the potato field, still working the mules. Levi—my childhood friend. Dear, fun-loving Levi.

I stopped crying. Catching my breath, I wiped my face on the tail of my red shirt and decided to stop in to see Rachel. This way, Levi would never have to know I'd been crying when I headed out to the field later.

"*Wilkom,* Merry." Rachel stepped out of the back door just as I came up the walk.

"Hi," I said. "I guess it's time for milking, right?"

"Jah." She wiped her hands on the long black apron covering her brown work dress. "Come help if you want."

Milking cows was one of my least favorite chores, especially the way Rachel and her family did it. Wiping down the cows' udders was the worst of it.

"I think I'll pass," I said. "Maybe I'll just take a walk and wait for you."

Rachel shielded her eyes with her hand as she looked at me. "Merry, is everything all right with you?"

"Don't mind me." I wondered if there were tearstains on my face. "Just thought I'd stop by and say hi."

She laughed. "Well, hi, then."

Abe Zook—her father—and Rachel's younger sisters, Nancy, Ella Mae, and little Susie, showed up outside the barn as if on cue. The whole family, except Levi and Mrs. Zook, was going to milk today.

"Guess you'd better get going," I told her. "I'll see you later."

"Sure you can't stay and help?" It was as if Rachel viewed the milking experience as something quite special.

"I'm sure, but thanks."

Rachel smiled her wide, energetic smile and scampered off barefoot to the barn.

Still wondering about my face, I hurried to the well pump a few feet away. I gave it a few good cranks and icy cold water poured out.

The tin bucket caught the spillage, and I hurried over to dip my hand into the water, washing my face, especially my cheeks.

Now I was set.

I walked, ambling past the expanse of yard behind the old Zook farmhouse and the smaller addition built onto it called the *Grossdawdy Haus*, where Rachel's grandparents lived. On my far left was the long, earthen ramp that led up to the second story of the new "bank barn." The hayloft was up there, and for an instant I was tempted to go and throw myself into the warm, sweet hay. But I kept going.

In spite of my day—in spite of Lissa's news—I had some truly good friends right here on SummerHill Lane. Rachel, a dear friend, full of cheer and always helpful. She'd even made a patchwork pillow for my hope chest. I guess she thought every girl had one.

And there was Levi, handsome and full of fun. As I walked through the potato field toward him, he pulled on the reins, bringing the mule team to a halt. With a wide grin he tipped his straw hat, and I almost forgot why I'd come.

"Merry!" he called from his perch. "It's good to see ya."

Maybe it was the way he stood there tall and confident with the dust and dirt of the day caked on his dark trousers and work shoes. Maybe it was the way his blue eyes twinkled when he smiled. I wasn't exactly sure why, but as I stood between the rows of potatoes, I didn't see the sense in setting Levi straight about the phone call. About anything.

"Did you call me today?"

Levi halted the mules. "I wondered if you'd like to go to the Green Dragon with me tomorrow."

"The Green Dragon?"

"They have soft pretzels and cotton candy." He paused. "It's like a carnival and—"

"I *know* what the Green Dragon is, Levi. But I'm not Amish, remember?"

His face clouded for a moment. "Well, I wish ya were Amish, Merry," he said hesitantly. "It would make things easier."

"Not for me," I insisted, laughing. "I don't have to wash down the cows' you-know-whats before I can pour milk on my cereal."

The smile returned to his tan face. "That's not what I mean."

I wasn't going to ask what he *did* mean. After all, I wasn't completely ignorant—I'd seen this moment coming for a while now. "How are you getting to the Green Dragon?" I suspected he wasn't taking his buggy.

He glanced from side to side as though he was going to share something top secret. Then he pulled his wallet out. "I just got a driver's license," he said, showing me.

"Levi, why?"

"Two of my cousins own a car," he whispered, quickly putting the card away. "We're in the same crowd together. We're called the Mule Skinners." He said it with pride.

I'd heard about the rambunctious Amish group. "Aren't they a little wild?"

He chuckled, carefree and easy. "Barn dancin' never hurt anyone."

I sighed. "Well, there's a big difference between a barn hop and going out with an English girl."

Levi's face lit up. "Are you sayin' you'll come?"

"Well, I won't go if *you're* driving!" I was serious and he knew it. "Besides, your father will tan your hide if he catches you."

"*Dat* will never know."

"Well, if I were you, I'd ask an Amish girl instead."

He took his hat off suddenly. "But, Merry, you're *not* me, so you don't understand." His eyes were more sincere than I'd ever seen them.

I felt awkward. Levi wasn't kidding. He really wanted me to go. "We have Sunday school and church early," I said, hoping to defuse his eagerness. "I'd be tired if I was out late Saturday night."

"What about Sunday night?"

"Levi," I snapped, "what do you think my parents will say?"

He wasn't going to stand for any lecture from me. The women in his life were taught to be compliant and submissive. "Please, will ya listen?" He touched my arm lightly.

"No, I won't. Just because you're not baptized yet doesn't mean you should push the rules. Your father's counting on you to follow in his footsteps."

I didn't really know that from Abe Zook directly, but it was the Amish way—passing the faith and culture from one generation to the next.

"I have plenty of time to decide about baptism," he said with conviction. "This is *my* life. Nobody else can live it for me."

In a strange sort of way, I understood.

"Well, what will your answer be?" he asked. "Will ya say 'Jah, *des kann ich du*'?"

Shielding my eyes from the afternoon sun, I looked up at him. "What's that supposed to mean—jah, des kann . . . uh, whatever?"

"Just say, 'Yes, I will.' "

Even if I had wanted to go—and I wasn't sure I did—there was no way my parents would let me. "I'm really sorry, Levi."

He placed his straw hat back on his sweaty head, then picked up the reins and slapped the mules without speaking.

I thought I'd offended him by turning him down, and probably would've worried about it if I hadn't stayed for a moment longer.

To my surprise, when he reached the end of the row, Levi turned around and waved. "Maybe some other time. Jah?"

I have to admit I was relieved to see he was cheerful again. I waved back before going to find Rachel.

All the way to the barn, I thought of Levi. It seemed so strange, his interest in me. Sure, we went back a long way—to childhood days. And yes, I'd saved him from drowning, but why wasn't he flirting with Amish girls after late-night singings like other Amish boys his age?

Why me?

Supper that night was eaten by candlelight.

Everyone except Skip was seated at the table, made lovely by Mom's attention to lace, centerpiece, and polished silver. My brother had an appointment. At least that's what he said on his way out the back door before company arrived. But if you ask me, he was probably going out with Jon Klein's older sister. Again.

The roast and potatoes were baked to perfection, and Dad's cousins, Martin and Hazel, seemed pleased. Mom too.

Dad's relatives actually showed interest in my family history assignment, although at first I thought they were only being polite.

Then Hazel mentioned something about her grandfather's journal. "You might want to include this tidbit of information in your project, Merry," she said, leaning forward and adjusting her glasses. "From what I understand, one of our ancestors, Joseph Lapp, was quite a fascinating fellow."

Dad agreed, chuckling. "One of the more interesting characters in our family tree."

I perked up my ears. "Was he the one who left the Amish?"

Dad nodded. "He's the black sheep of the family, I guess you'd say. Although—" he paused—"Hazel and I are his descendants, so I don't know where that puts us."

Mom smiled at Dad's remark.

Hazel's eyes brightened. "Weren't there some letters written by Joseph Lapp after the shunning?"

Dad nodded. "I'm not sure where they are, but it seems to me I have them packed away somewhere."

"Probably in the attic," Mom said, refolding her napkin and placing it under her dessert fork.

I had to know more about this shunning business. "Who were the letters written to?" I asked.

"I believe they were sent to Joseph's younger brother"—Dad glanced at the ceiling as though he was trying to put all this in perspective for me—"who would be your great-great uncle Samuel."

Hazel slid her glasses up her nose again. "Weren't the letters written during the six-week probation period before the actual shunning?"

"You know, now that you mention it, I think that's probably the case," Dad said.

Mom started clearing off the dinner plates. "Maybe you could locate the letters for Merry," she said.

"Oh, could you, Dad?" I pleaded.

He scratched his chin, looking rather nonchalant. "Well, I suppose so . . . if you'd like."

Like? I was delirious with the thought. "When can we do it?" I asked, ready to drop everything, candlelight dinner included.

Mom came in and filled the coffee cups, sending me a warning signal with her eyes. "I'm sure this can wait, Merry."

Cousin Hazel appeared to be as disappointed as I. But she didn't press the issue further, and all of us settled into a calm and quiet half hour of rhubarb pie, with black coffee for the adults.

I may have appeared to be calm and quiet, but I sure didn't feel that way. Dad's long-ago relative had left the Amish culture and gone through the *Bann* and *Meidung*.

Excommunication—the Bann—was bad enough, but not being allowed to eat or associate with his Amish relatives or friends in any way? Being completely disowned?

I wondered about Joseph Lapp. Who was he, really? And what had made him leave?

Later that night, Dad agreed to help me find the letters. "First thing tomorrow," he said before I headed off to bed.

Unfortunately, Saturday morning he was called away to the hospital before I got up, so I asked Mom where I should look.

"Try that old steamer trunk up in the attic." She stopped to think. "You might have to move some rugs to get to it."

"No problem," I said, scampering off to my parents' bedroom. Filled with anticipation, I opened the door leading to the attic.

Steep and solid, the attic steps were the original wood, as well built as the rest of our hundred-year-old colonial frame house. The steps creaked, and I remembered the days when Faithie and I had played up here.

Years ago, Dad had succeeded in converting the drafty old place into an enchanting secret playroom simply by adding extra insulation and Sheetrock. Later, he painted the walls and put up oak trim around the gabled window. Next came bright and thick rose carpet. Faithie loved the color. I didn't at first; it grew on me, though.

Now the space had been turned into storage, and although boxes were stacked and color-coded in the far corner, the room still held its rustic charm.

Mom had kept all of Faithie's toys, dresses, and baby things, tenderly packing them away up here. The pain of loss had prompted

Mom to save everything. She'd actually refused to part with any of it.

Two years had passed since I'd last set foot here. Staring at Faithie's childish art—drawings we'd hung on the walls—I realized once again how desperately I missed my twin.

The wind came up under the eaves, whistling a mournful tune, but there was no time for sadness now. I searched for the trunk Mom had mentioned and found it easily. Just as she had said, it was piled high with afghans and blankets wrapped in loose plastic, and Amish hook rugs by the dozen. With armloads of two or three at a time, I hauled them onto the floor, placing them carefully in a neat pile.

Then, slowly, carefully, I opened the giant lid. Peering into the enormous trunk, I saw all sorts of long-forgotten things.

One by one, I lifted small boxes out of the trunk, creating a semicircle of memories behind me on the floor. Then, almost unexpectedly, I noticed a sealed plastic bag wedged in between the wall of the trunk and another box. Taking care not to bend or disturb the contents, I pulled the plastic square out of its hiding place and into the light.

Old letters—at least five of them!

I studied the writing closely through the plastic. The name *Samuel Lapp* was visible in the center of the envelope, and although very faded, the gray ink was quite legible.

"Mom!" I sat at the top of the steep steps and scooted down like Faithie and I had always done as little girls. "I found the letters!"

"In here, Merry," she called from her bedroom.

Excited, I dashed over to the wide window seat where she sat reading a book in the sunlight.

"Well"—she peered over her book—"why don't you have a look?"

"Do you think Dad'll mind if I read them before he gets back?"

She smiled wholeheartedly. "I doubt it—go ahead."

I sat on the edge of the antique four-poster bed, unsealed the plastic, and pulled out the stack of letters. "Wow," I whispered. "Can you believe this? These are *so* old."

Mom nodded. "Over a hundred years."

"It's like a blast from the past." I shivered. "O-oh, I feel like I'm beginning to tread on—"

"Merry," she interrupted, laughing. "You're dramatizing again."

"That's what Chelsea Davis says—constantly." I fingered the ancient envelopes, wondering more than ever about the life of Joseph Lapp, cast out as he was by the Amish.

"Well, maybe it's good to have friends like Chelsea," Mom said, giving me her undivided attention for a change. "I guess all of us can use a nudge toward reality now and then."

"Sure, Mom," I said, even though I had no idea what she was talking about.

I opened the first letter, careful not to tear the near-brittle, parchmentlike stationery. I scanned the page. The writing was foreign to me. My heart sank when I realized it was written in German.

"Something wrong?" Mom set her book aside.

I held up the letter. "Joseph Lapp spoke German, right?"

She threw her arms up. "Oh, of course!"

"Well, now what?" I said, more to myself than to Mom.

"Your father doesn't speak a word of it . . . never has."

"Wait a minute." I got up and went to the wide triple window overlooking the Zook farm. "I think I know someone who can translate these."

Mom swung her legs down off the cozy, pillowed perch. "Rachel might be able to decipher it, although she speaks a Pennsylvania Dutch dialect."

"I know," I said, "but she reads the Bible and other books in German."

Mom pointed to the letters lying on the bed. "Please take care of them. Your father didn't appear to be interested in this last night, but take my word for it, he would be mighty upset if the letters got lost."

"Count on me." I gathered the letters into the plastic once again and zipped them safely inside. "All set. Now I'm off to see Rachel."

"Not without breakfast, you aren't."

"Oh, Mom," I fussed.

Her eyes meant business. "Breakfast, Merry."

There was no way out of it. My mother had a hang-up about food. She truly believed a person had to eat heartily in order to stay healthy and productive. It was also the mentality of the Plain people around us.

I sighed and went to my room with the letters, placing them safely on top of my desk. Then I hurried down the back steps leading to the kitchen.

Mom encouraged me to eat. And eat. Finally, I held up my hands. "I'm full, honest!"

Skip grinned, accepting a third helping of fried eggs and ham. "You can't be full," he teased.

"Oh yeah? Well, maybe *my* stomach hasn't stretched out as fat as yours."

He scowled. "Who said anything about fat?"

"That's what'll happen if you keep scarfing down everything in sight."

"Aw, how sweet," he said, taunting me. "Little Merry's looking out for her big brother." He reached over and tickled my elbow.

I jerked my arm away. "Quit picking on me!"

"Skip, please," Mom intervened. Then, eyeing me, she said, "Remember, Merry, your brother won't be around here next year."

"Hallelujah for college," I mumbled.

Skip laughed. "You'll miss me. You'll see."

"I can't wait to find out!" Pushing my chair back with a screech, I ran upstairs to brush my teeth.

What a relief, I thought. Starting next fall, I'd have Mom and Dad all to myself. Just like an only child . . .

Only child. That thought got me thinking about Lissa Vyner, an honest-to-goodness only child—the last person I wanted to think about!

Eager to show Rachel the German letters, I gave my hair a quick brushing. Then I emptied my largest camera case, making room for Joseph Lapp's letters. I couldn't wait to find out more about this great-great grandfather of mine. Why *had* he abandoned his Amish life so long ago?

Staring at the letters, an anxious feeling crept over me. I remembered the words I'd said to Chelsea yesterday. *Don't all families have skeletons in their closets?*

I reached into the camera case and caressed the old letters. What secrets would I discover in my own family closet?

Rachel and Nancy Zook were helping their mother make schnitz pies when I arrived at their back door. My mouth watered as I smelled the delicious tartness of dried apples. Mm-m! Maybe I wasn't as full as I thought.

"Merry, it's good to see ya!" Rachel said, dropping everything to hurry to the screen door. "Come on in and sit for a spell."

I sat at the long wooden bench behind the equally long table in the spacious kitchen, observing the bustling activity. Rachel and her sister wore long dresses with black belted aprons pinned to their waists, and a *Kapp*, a white netting head covering similar to their mother's.

"How many pies are you making?" I asked.

"Oh, seven or eight," Rachel replied. "The Yoders are having a quilting frolic. We're going over there later on to surprise them." She seemed very excited. "Sarah, my sister-in-law—you know, Curly John's wife—is expecting a baby in the fall."

"So you'll be an aunt for the first time?" I said.

Rachel noticed my camera case, but I quickly opened it, showing her it was empty except for the letters. The Amish shied away from cameras because they believed the Bible told them not to make any graven images—photographs included.

"I wonder," I said, pulling the first letter out very carefully. "When you finish with the pies, could you read this to me?" I showed her the envelope, explaining my school project.

"Jah, this is German." She jabbered something quickly in Pennsylvania Dutch to her sister and mother while washing her hands, then dried them on her long black apron. "Come with me, cousin Merry."

I always grinned when she called me that, even though I'd been hearing it from her nearly all my life. Rachel Zook viewed me as her cousin, which I was. A very distant one.

We headed for the front porch, going through the wide dining room with a built-in corner cupboard where many fancy dishes were displayed. Next came the large, open living room. The Amish liked their living rooms uncluttered, without much furniture—a hickory rocking chair, hand-painted wooden chairs, and homemade throw rugs—so it was simple to set up for church when it came their turn to host.

"The letters are very fragile." I gave the first one to Rachel. Her blue eyes were wide and she had a strangely curious expression.

"They even feel old, jah?" Rachel sat down on the old porch swing, sniffing the paper. "Smell old, too."

I leaned against the porch railing. "Very old."

She began to read under her breath as though she was trying to determine the content. "This is what Joseph Lapp wrote to his younger brother," she began, glancing at me with sincere eyes. "'My dear brother and friend, Samuel Lapp. It is with great sadness that I write these things. I can no longer live in the Amish community. I will miss you, my brother, and my sisters, too, and dear *Mam* and faithful Dat. With everything in me, I will miss all of you. It is not because of lack of love or respect for my family that I do this thing. It is for Mary . . . all for Mary, whom I plan to wed.'" Rachel stopped reading and sighed.

"Mary who?" I asked, eager for her to read on.

"Wait now," Rachel said, reading further silently. "He says something here about her being English—an outsider!" Rachel exclaimed.

"He writes this: 'I love Mary deeply. I must be true to my heart and make her my wife.'"

Rachel stared at the letter for a moment longer, not reading. Her face turned suddenly pale. "*Ach, der gleh Deihenger*—so this is the scoundrel!"

"What are you saying?"

"This man, this Joseph Lapp—your relative—is the same shunned man Grossdawdy has been telling us about for many years. He has set Joseph Lapp up as an example of wickedness for as long as I can remember."

"Because of the shunning?" I said softly.

She nodded. "And because my own brother Levi is every bit as headstrong as Joseph Lapp was." She glanced around as if it was something she shouldn't be saying.

I rushed over and sat beside Rachel, gazing at the letter, then at her. "Your grandfather has heard stories about Joseph Lapp?" I whispered. "Wow. This is heavy."

Rachel frowned. "Heavy?"

"Surprising," I restated my words.

"Surprising to you, but shameful to me."

"For you, Rachel? How?"

She nodded, solemnly. "This man"—and here she tapped the letter—"was one of *my* ancestors, too."

"So *that's* the connection between us," I said. "I always wondered how we were distant cousins." I glanced at my watch, then at the letters. "Will you read the rest to me sometime?"

"Jah, sometime."

"Thank you, Rachel." I paused, studying my friend. "I never meant to upset you."

"I'll be fine." But her eyes looked sad.

"I better get going. I've heard enough to get started on my school project. You've been a big help." I stood up to leave, eager to start working with Chelsea.

Rachel handed the letters back to me. "Just ask if you need more help," she volunteered, following me down the front porch steps.

"I hope your schnitz pies turn out extra good," I said, trying to get her mind off the sorrowful thoughts. "Please tell Curly John that Skip and I said hi. I'm sure he'll make a very good father."

She broke into a smile. "I will, Merry. And may God go with you."

I waved before leaving, feeling sorry about stirring up sad feelings in my friend. And yet I wondered about Rachel's emotional reaction to the letter. Why had this story been told so often in the Zook household? Was it really because of Levi?

I flew through the pasture, over the white picket fence, and into the willow grove. Out of breath, I stopped for a moment in the dense, thick part—Faithie's and my old secret place, now where Rachel and I often shared secrets.

Right then, standing in the middle of the trees with summer green sheltering me and sunlight twinkling around me, I remembered Levi Zook's words. *I wish ya were Amish, Merry. It would make things easier.*

Knowing that Levi had heard the story of his rebellious ancestor at the knee of his grandfather since childhood, I wondered exactly what he meant.

That's when the realization hit me. Hit me between the eyes as I stood in the wispy willows on the dividing line between the Zooks' Amish farm and my own home. I, Merry Hanson, might very well have been Amish had it not been for Joseph Lapp!

Catch a Falling Star **Eight**

Chelsea Davis was waiting for me in her backyard when I arrived.

I'd gone around the house and through the brick archway when no one answered the front door. There, amidst elaborate flower beds arranged in lovely designs, I found her sitting on a padded lawn chair under the shade of a patio umbrella. She was wearing her favorite shorts outfit from last summer.

Chelsea was sketching her family tree on a long, vertical piece of art paper, her hair pulled back in a single, thick braid.

I cleared my throat, and she looked up, somewhat surprised. "Nobody came to the front door," I said, explaining my unannounced appearance. "I thought it was okay to come around."

She stretched and smiled. "Is it one-thirty already?"

I nodded. "Actually, I'm a little late."

"Better late than never." She laughed. "Pull up a chair."

"Thanks." I pulled out the lawn chair next to her, away from the glass patio table. Taking my time, I spread out the background information on several relatives, including Joseph Lapp.

"Hey, no fair. Looks like you're half done with your project," she teased.

"How far are you?"

She held up her family tree, clearly sketched with long lines drawn straight and neat under each set of branches. "I'm not sure how far back I can go . . . or want to go," she said, glancing over her shoulder toward the house.

"How come?"

Chelsea's mind seemed to wander. "Well, from what my mom says, there've been some really weird types floating around in the branches of our family tree."

I smiled. "Really? Couldn't be any weirder than anyone else's family."

"Oh yeah?" She crossed her legs beneath her and leaned forward. "I told you I'd rather go bungee jumping over sharks."

I nodded, not believing her. "So, what could be so weird?"

"You won't freak out if I tell you?" she asked, looking serious.

"Why should I? It's *your* family."

"I take it that's a promise," she said without cracking a smile.

"Sure, whatever."

Holding up her sketch, Chelsea pointed to a double branch three lines above her own name. "Right here." She pointed. "This is my great-aunt Essie Peterson."

"Really? You're related to *her*?"

Chelsea's green eyes widened in horror. "You mean you know about her?"

"Doesn't everyone?" I said.

She scrunched up her face, looking deflated. "But Essie was so strange."

I wondered if Chelsea's great-aunt was the reason why my friend fought off all my comments about God.

"Check this out." She reached for her spiral notebook lying on the glass table across from me. "Essie was my grandfather's sister on my dad's side. She had healing meetings where sick people came from all over. People said she had some kind of power, I guess."

"From God, right?"

"Well, from something." Chelsea laughed. "She'd go without eating, sometimes for several days before her so-called healing meetings. My dad said the way he heard it, Essie was tuned in and turned on—like a charge of electricity."

"And people got well, right?"

She nodded, pushing a stray wisp of hair back over her ear. "That's the weirdest part, I guess. People showed up sick and went away just fine." She paused, that faraway look returning. "How do you figure?"

I saw my opportunity, and with a silent prayer for wisdom, I forged ahead. "Remember the martyrs we were talking about yesterday? Well, the same God who softened the last terror-filled minutes of their lives . . . that same God gave His Son power to heal people. And right before Jesus went back to heaven, He told His disciples that they'd do even greater things than He had. I know it sounds truly amazing, but it's all in the Bible."

"Well, forget it, then. I don't believe all that nonsense." She went back to her sketching.

Why does she always do that? I thought. I couldn't get a grasp of this recurring problem. It seemed as though Chelsea allowed herself to get only so close to the Gospel and then *bam!*—she'd cut herself off from it.

Disappointed, I refused to be sucked in to her little game. On again. Off again. I could only hope that every talk we had about God really was leading Chelsea slowly but surely to Him. Because as frustrating as she was, the grandniece of the late Essie Peterson was a precious soul in God's eyes.

We moved on to other topics, but the idea that she'd have to divulge her connection to this woman of God in front of the entire social studies class really seemed to bug her.

When I asked her about it, Chelsea was firm, not embarrassed. "People like me shouldn't have relatives like Essie Peterson."

"Really?" I decided to tone things down, hoping to open the door again.

She exhaled loudly. "You'd think that somewhere in my genetic makeup there oughta be someone like me . . . somewhere way back there." She waved her hand. "You know, someone who thought all this God business was for the birds."

I thought of referring to the scriptures I knew about God's care for even the smallest sparrow, but didn't. "Do your parents believe in God?" I asked.

She blew air through her mouth in disgust. "I wish I *knew* what my parents believed these days."

I didn't want to touch that remark, so I kept listening, looking at her.

"Mom's into some bizarre stuff," she said. "I don't think she even knows for sure what it is. Her assortment of crystals seems to be growing by the hour. She even has a mood ring, whatever that is."

Sounded like the occult to me. "What about your dad?" I asked in a hushed voice.

"Oh, he reads all these books on past lives and wonders what he'll come back as next. None of it makes any sense." She reached up, stretching, her fingers almost touching the edge of the patio umbrella.

"You're right, it doesn't."

"Hey, good. You're not going to preach." She looked so confident perched there on her lawn chair.

I wanted to tell her that what her parents were getting into was dangerous. Instead, I said, "No preaching, Chelsea, but I won't stop caring about you."

For a moment, I thought I saw her eyes glisten, but she looked away, and not wanting to stare, so did I.

Catch a Falling Star *Nine*

After breakfast Sunday morning, I looked in my dresser mirror, watching my shoulder-length hair flip from side to side as I tried to air dry it a little before using the blower.

Staring at my eyes, I wondered about Joseph Lapp. Was he brown-eyed, too?

I smiled into the mirror. Did he ever wish for the ability to take pictures, long before digital cameras?

Glancing at my wall gallery, I focused on the tall picture of a lone willow tree. Did Great-Great-Grandfather Joseph ever contemplate his life out among the trees and beside the river the way I often did?

It wasn't fun being left in the dark about someone so fascinating. Or as Rachel had said, a scoundrel. But was Joseph Lapp a wicked man, really?

The silence started to bug me, or I should say, the *questions* I was asking myself without any hope of answers bugged me. I turned on the blow dryer to fill the silence.

Lily White jumped off the bed and darted over to me. "You wanna go to Sunday school, huh?" I leaned down and picked her up with my free hand, nuzzling her against my damp hair, letting the blower tickle her white coat. She arched her back and let out a long hiss, so I put her down. "I suppose we'll just have to wait and see what happens with Lissa and Jon today at church," I told her, even though she seemed more interested in sulking under my bed. "They'll probably be sitting together, you know."

I braced myself against that discouraging thought.

"Merry?" Mom poked her head in the door.

I shut off the blower.

"I heard you talking." She glanced around.

"Oh, I was just having a chat with Lily White. She's not very interested, as you can see."

Mom inched her way into the room. "Is everything all right?"

"Why shouldn't it be?"

She shook her head. "Well, I don't know. I just haven't heard you sound so depressed like this."

"Like what?" I demanded. "What did you hear?"

She stood beside me, looking in the mirror at the two of us. "There was a time when you could tell me anything, remember?" She slipped her arm around my waist.

I was silent.

"I miss those days." She gave me a little squeeze.

Frustrated and upset that she'd probably overheard me mention Lissa and Jon, I felt my muscles stiffen against her. "Do you think Dad could tell me more about Joseph Lapp sometime today?"

Mom stepped back out of the mirror's reflection. "Why don't you ask him?" Her face clouded.

I hadn't responded to her plea for intimacy, and she was hurt. I'd turned the tables and requested an audience with my dad instead of her.

"Well, we'd better get moving." She turned to leave. "You know how your father is on Sundays."

Dad was a stickler for promptness, especially Sundays. He was a fanatic about leaving the house on time. I chafed under the time pressure, and to speed things up, I turned my hair dryer on the highest setting. The strong heat would make my hair frizzy, but it was better than a tongue-lashing from Dad.

I can't begin to recount the happenings of my time at church. Here it was already May 14, close to the end of the school year, and every girl in the youth class was sitting with a guy.

Honestly, I felt like an alien from another planet. It wasn't so much embarrassing as it was ridiculous. Why did everyone wait until the end of the school year to pair off?

I scanned the room. As I'd predicted, Lissa and Jon sat together across the room. I purposely chose a place where I wouldn't see them every time I looked at Mrs. Simms, our super-cool teacher.

Repeat performance for church an hour later. It seemed that Lissa had abandoned her mother to sit with Jon in the Klein family pew. Jon's older sister Nikki had her eyes on Skip, however, as I slid into the pew next to him several rows back.

I had no idea what Nikki Klein saw in my cat-queasy brother. Skip was good-looking enough, I guess—for a brother, anyway. He was tall with golden-brown hair and hazel eyes that sparkled sometimes. But if Nikki *really* knew him—the way I did—she'd probably run the other way. Fast!

I scarcely heard the pastor's sermon, even though I truly wanted to. The sight of Lissa and Jon sitting together kept distracting me. Jon Klein looked absolutely delighted sitting there with Lissa at his side. Completely crushed, I wondered if he'd introduced her to the word game yet. And if so, could she keep up with him the way I always had?

As best I could, I avoided them after the service by simply hanging around my parents. Dad seemed happy with the extra attention I gave him on the way down the aisle and out to the parking lot. To my delight, he agreed to tell me more about Joseph Lapp.

"We'll talk right after dinner," he said, holding the car door open for Mom.

After a spectacular spread of baked chicken, mashed potatoes, gravy, yellow buttered squash, peas and carrots, and a whole series of "no thank yous" when I felt too stuffed to move, Mom shooed Dad and me into the living room.

Skip helped in the kitchen at her request. I was surprised he didn't give her a hard time about it. Maybe being a senior was doing him some good. If I could just get him to accept my cats as part of the family . . .

Dad settled down in his easy chair to tell his tales. "To begin with, your grandfather Hanson, my father, was as sharp as a tack when it came to remembering passed-down details and events. So I guess you could say I have him to thank for the stories about Joseph Lapp."

I sat on the end of our green sofa, sharing the matching otto-man with Dad, intent on what he was about to say.

"Joseph Lapp, I was told, had a rebellious streak in him from the day he was born," Dad said.

I thought of Levi Zook's grandfather, who had pounded away with stories of Joseph Lapp's rebellion and consequences.

Dad continued. "Evidently, Joseph was the last to be baptized in his family, and even then, he broke his vow by marrying outside the church."

"What did he look like?" I asked.

Dad moved a tasseled throw pillow out from behind him. "As a matter of fact, he was tall and lanky, had a full head of light brown hair, and the bluest eyes this side of the Pocono Mountains."

The description matched Levi Zook perfectly.

"Sounds like someone I know," I replied.

"Well, plenty of Amishmen match that description, I suppose." He leaned back. "But not many do what Joseph Lapp did, at least not back in those days."

"What do you mean?" I was all ears.

"Being ousted from the church—that's excommunication. An Amishman's life revolves around the community of men and women who make up the church district. They fill one another's silos and plow or milk when a farmer is too sick or has no sons. They pitch in money to take care of one another during drought or hard times. They rejoice when new babies are born, and they mourn and bury their dead together." Dad paused, sighing. "The key word to remember about the Amish is *community*."

I crossed my legs on the ottoman. "If a person is kicked out of the community, how does he survive?"

Dad's eyes grew more serious. "Many Amish who leave often return because of the hardship of shunning."

"Something like being disowned, right?"

He nodded. "Not only does the person lose close ties with his family, he isn't allowed to eat or do business with *any* of his Amish relatives or friends. It must surely seem like a death to the loved ones involved. But if it weren't for the shunning, lots of young Amish teens today would leave the church for cars and electricity."

"Do you think Joseph Lapp ever repented?"

"Well, if he had, you and I might be sitting in the middle of a group of Amish folk right now, finishing up Sunday dinner," Dad said with a weak smile and then a hearty yawn.

I could see he was tired. Sunday was the one day out of the whole week he wasn't on call, and he wasn't getting any younger. In fact, this summer Dad would celebrate his fiftieth birthday.

I gave him a hug before covering him with one of Mom's many afghans. Then I giggled looking at him lying there. "Just think, by now, if we were Amish, your beard would be down to here." I pointed to my stomach.

"Very funny, Merry," he said.

Hurrying upstairs, I wrote down everything I could remember about Joseph Lapp, wondering why he'd married outside the Amish church.

After that, I went to Dad's study and was closing the door when I turned around and discovered Skip there on the phone. He gave me one of his get-lost looks.

"For how long?" I whispered.

He said, "Excuse me for one sec, Nikki," covering the phone as his eyes squinted into narrow little slits.

I stood my ground. "I need the phone."

"Wait outside," he barked. "And shut the door when you leave."

"How much longer?"

"You're really making this difficult, you know?" Skip glared at me.

"I'll give you five minutes. If you're not off the phone by then, look for me in your room raiding your desk drawer."

Skip's eyes bulged. "You wouldn't dare!"

"Five minutes." I turned and walked out, leaving the door wide open. His gasps of exasperation were obvious as I scurried down the hall, suppressing a giggle.

Precisely seven minutes passed. I headed directly for my brother's room. The door was partway open, so I barged in, heading for his desk.

Not everyone knew my brother kept a journal. It seemed like a girl thing to do, but he really enjoyed keeping a record of his life. So did I, in a more unusual way—by photographing people, places, and things.

I slid his chair away from the desk, making sure it screeched across the hardwood floor. That way Skip would know I meant business, since his bedroom was directly above Dad's study.

Listening, I smiled. The unmistakable sound of footsteps could be heard on the stairs.

Genius!

I made a mad dash out of Skip's room and down the hall to my bedroom. With my heart pounding ninety miles an hour, I locked the door.

"What were you doing in my room?" Skip bellowed through my door.

I giggled at his reaction. "I gave you fair warning."

"I'm telling Mom!"

"Go ahead."

I heard the pounding of his big feet on the back stairs that led down to the kitchen. But as fast as he left, he returned, thumping his fist against my door.

"Where's Mom?" he demanded.

"Probably out for her afternoon stroll, dear brother," I said, sprinkling my words with a British accent.

"Cut the Brit routine," he sneered. "You're dead meat for this."

"What did *I* do?"

He stomped around outside my door. "Did you snoop through anything?" There was a twinge of desperation in his voice.

Good. Maybe this would give me some leverage for later. If and when I needed it.

"So," I began snootily, "it's you and Nikki, is it?"

"When are you ever going to keep your nose out of other people's business?"

I let him rant on and on while I reclined on my bed, stroking my four cats. The door seemed to heave and sway with the noise of his threats and accusations.

When I didn't comment for a long time, he insisted that I answer. I remained silent, laughing under my breath that I'd never even touched his precious desk drawer. Or journal. Finally, he evaporated—the weirdest brother a girl could ever have.

When I knew he was back in his room, probably recounting his most recent romantic chat in his journal, I crept down the hall, past his door, to the steps.

Downstairs, I found peace and solitude in Dad's study as I talked on the phone to Chelsea. When I hung up, Lissa called.

"Hi, Mer," she said, all pert and sweet.

I curled my toes. She was the last person on earth I wanted to talk to. "How's your family tree growing?" I said.

She laughed. "Very clever."

I held my breath, afraid she'd say, *Say that with all c's.*

"Chelsea and I got most of ours done yesterday," I said.

"Jon and I are nearly finished, too," she said.

More than anything, I wished *that* were true. Finished as in kaput—over!

Lissa continued. "I can't wait for the ninth-grade picnic. It'll be really cool. You're going, aren't you?"

"Not sure." If she and Jon were going, there was no way I'd be showing up.

"Why don't you ask someone?" She sounded all excited. "Then the four of us could go together!"

Oh no! This was truly horrible.

"We'll see," I said, gritting my teeth.

"Don't wait too long," she advised. "The picnic's less than two weeks away."

"I'll remember that."

"Well, I'd better get going. See ya." We hung up.

Frustrated, I went to do math homework, trying not to think depressing thoughts. It wasn't easy. Lissa was wild about Jon; there was no getting past that. But how interested was Jon in *her*?

I finished my algebra in record time, then headed to the garage to get my bike, securing my camera case and water bottle in the bike basket before pushing off.

I wondered if I'd see Mom out walking, but I knew she usually went *up* the hill toward Strawberry Lane. I was going down Summer-Hill to the covered mill bridge several miles from here. Besides, I needed to be alone.

It was a good long distance to pedal, but the exercise wasn't the only draw. Hunsecker's Mill Bridge was beautiful any time of year, but especially in late spring. A truly peaceful place to contemplate life's disappointments . . . among other things.

The afternoon was humid, but a mild breeze rippled the grass in the ditch beside the dirt road. Birds sang heartily as I followed the banks and curves of SummerHill Lane toward the main road. I suspected an afternoon shower—the birds seemed to know these things first—although there was little indication from the sky. A perfect deep blue, and only a few thunderclouds in the distance.

Everywhere I looked, flowers were beginning to push their heads up, adding a colorful addition to my ride and a fragrant touch to the air. Summer was almost here!

I stopped by the side of the road to take a picture of Mrs. Fisher's flowers. Profuse with dark pink peonies, the lovely flower garden was framed by two lilac bushes, one on each side. Carefully, I set my camera for the proper lighting and distance, then snapped away, hoping at least one of the shots would capture the brilliance.

Just then Ben Fisher, the oldest son, came outside. "Hello, Merry!" He sat on the front step.

I smiled. "Don't worry, I didn't get you in the picture."

"That's good. I've been in enough trouble for a spell." He exchanged a somber look with his elderly father, who sat in a hickory rocking chair nearby, puffing on a pipe.

I snapped my camera case shut and waved good-bye, wondering how Ben was doing. He'd dabbled with the modern world for a while—sowed some wild oats as the Amish say—even bought a car and had an English girlfriend. But Levi Zook, his true and loyal friend, had helped bring him back into the Amish community, even after Ben was uncovered as the culprit behind the Zooks' recent barn fire.

Last I heard, Ben had given a kneeling confession in front of the local church district not long ago. All was forgiven. I wondered if Levi and Ben were still good friends—and if so, why was Levi running with a crowd like the Mule Skinners?

I hurried down the road, eager for the tranquil setting of the Conestoga River and the old covered bridge. Pedaling hard, I flew down SummerHill to the intersection at Hunsecker Mill Road.

Minutes later, I arrived at the bridge. I got off my bike and pushed it through the deep wild grass along the south side. Locating a tree, I abandoned my wheels, and with camera and water bottle in tow, headed for the quiet banks of the river.

There, in the partial shade of a giant maple, I settled down for some serious photo shooting. First, I took several shots of the bridge itself, finding the most unique angle possible for my scrapbook. Next came the river and the large, stately trees and flowering bushes. What a glorious day!

I put my camera away and sat there, listening to the sounds of springtime as the midafternoon light cast curious shadows over the water. I wondered what it would be like to have someone fall in love with me. Really and truly in love.

Oh, I'd formed some ethereal ideas about it, of course, but never anything concrete. Maybe he'd paint my name on a billboard somewhere. Maybe he'd hire a sky painter. And there was always the Goodyear blimp . . .

I daydreamed about the endless possibilities. And by so doing, forced the discouraging thoughts of Jon Klein out of my mind.

Down the road to the east, I heard hoofbeats. Fast, clippity-clopping ones. Soon the horse and buggy came into view. For a fleeting moment, I envied the young couple in the open courting buggy.

I stood up, trying to get a better look.

The buggy made the turn into the bridge. Pounding hoofbeats rattled the loose boards inside. Was it my imagination, or had the driver increased his speed? It sounded like the wild, reckless way Levi Zap 'em Zook handled his horse.

I sat back down in the grass, ducking my head, hoping Levi wouldn't see me. If it *was* Levi.

"Merry!" came his voice. "I know you're over there."

I popped up like I'd been shot out of a cannon. "Hi, Levi," I called to him. "What are you doing here?"

"I should ask you the same question, jah?" He tipped his hat flirtatiously.

My brain was definitely out of commission, but I must not have been aware of it then. I stooped to pick up my water bottle and camera case and proceeded to walk over to the road. To Levi.

"Well, now, Merry, wouldja care for a lift home?" he asked, glancing heavenward. As if on cue, a thunderclap made me jump.

"I . . . uh, better not. But thanks," I said, gazing at his beautiful black buggy.

"It's all right, Merry. Honest." He leaned forward, his foot on the rim, extending his hand to me. I had to admit he looked handsome in his Sunday best, his light brown bangs peeking out of his black wide-brimmed hat. Very handsome, now that I thought about it.

Hesitant, I asked, "What if someone sees you with me? Won't you be in trouble?"

He laughed, suddenly displaying an umbrella. "Not for being neighborly."

I smiled. He had a point.

"What about my bike?" I glanced over my shoulder.

"Easy as pie," he said. "It'll fit." And he jumped down and went with me to retrieve it.

"Well, I guess you win this time," I said.

When my bike was finally situated, Levi helped me into the front of his buggy. I sat beside him to his left and caught the scent of sweet aftershave. Had he seen me leave my house earlier? Had he planned this encounter?

Feeling shy, I looked down and noticed the slate-gray wall-to-wall carpeting on the floor. A large speedometer attached to a mini-dashboard on the right side was planted directly in front of Levi.

Quickly, he opened the umbrella. "It's starting to rain," he said, holding it over our heads with one hand.

I glanced at the dark sky from my sheltered perch, still surprised that I'd allowed myself to do this. "Thanks for the ride," I said for courtesy's sake. Yet I felt safe and protected next to Levi. Nothing like the way I thought it would be riding in an open buggy on a rainy Sunday.

Levi turned to face me under our private canopy. "I've been waiting a long time for this, Merry." The serious look in his eyes took me off guard.

Then, gallantly, he picked up the reins with his other hand and *gently* trotted his beautiful Morgan horse up the road toward SummerHill.

All the way up Hunsecker Mill Road, Levi and I talked. There was plenty of time for it. The pace of horse and buggy transportation wasn't exactly speedy at twelve miles per hour—and that was pushing it.

Under the menacing rain clouds, Levi and I talked about everything. I never realized how much we had in common. He truly loved nature. He appreciated the beauty of the earth-brown soil, the golden corn tassels, and the blue of his alfalfa field—together creating a colorful patchwork quilt.

"Have ya seen the mint leaves growing over in the meadow behind the barn?" Levi asked, full of questions. "Have ya seen the sun setting behind the Yoders' tobacco shed?"

I waited till the flow of questions stopped. "It's going to be a beautiful summer," I said at last.

"Jah," he agreed. "It could be a wonderful-*gut* summer." He slowed the horse from a trot to a leisurely walk, still holding the umbrella over our heads.

I wondered why we were slowing down.

"Merry," he said, turning to me. "I want to know something."

My hands felt clammy in my lap.

Levi didn't smile as he spoke. "I like ya, Merry. Always have."

I gave a soft little laugh, remembering our childhood pranks. The rope swing in the hayloft. The fun of growing up next to a houseful of Amish kids. "We've been good friends for a long time," I said.

"But I must know your true answer."

"To what?"

Levi pulled on the reins with his free hand, halting his horse right there in the middle of the road. He paused a second, studying me. "Merry, will ya be my girl?"

Any other time I would've been shocked by such a question. But sitting here, sharing our interests and talking freely the way we had, his question seemed like a semi-reasonable request.

His eyes were sincere and made me feel shy. I responded by looking down at my lap, speechless.

"Merry?" His voice pursued me.

I looked up slowly. "There's a lot to think about, Levi. For one thing, you're Amish. Remember what happened to your friend Ben Fisher?"

He shrugged. "Ben did some terrible, awful things, but you . . . you and me, we're friends from long past."

"Still, how could you think of dating an English girl?" It was the argument I'd brought up two days ago in the potato field.

"I'm not thinking of dating an English girl." His face broke into a broad grin. "I want to spend time with *you*."

"And I'm English." I sighed. "Besides, I'm too young to be courted."

"Merry, we'd just be getting to know each other better. And I will be busy working the farm this summer, ya know. There won't be much time for—"

"What are you saying?"

"Amish boys see their girls every other Saturday night and sometimes after Sunday night singings. They go for a long drive."

I leaned back, giving him an honest-to-goodness straightforward look. "Oh, so *that's* it." I laughed. "You intend to hide me under the stars."

He grinned. "We always keep such things secret. That's our way. But I would not hide ya purposely from the view of my parents."

I understood. All Amish dating and courtship was conducted under the covering of night. No one ever really knew whom an Amish boy was seeing until the *Schteckliman* or go-between verified an engagement of marriage with the bride-to-be and her parents. Levi and his people had been doing things the same way for three hundred years.

"But what would happen if you were seen with me?" I asked, still curious about Levi's willingness to risk being caught.

"It won't happen," he said firmly.

"And if it did?"

Levi let the reins drop over his right knee. He steadied the umbrella with both hands, leaning close to me. "I am not certain about my future as an Amishman," he said, almost in a whisper. "Baptism into the church would change everything for me, Merry. For now, I am free to decide, don'tcha see?"

This was serious talk. I felt uneasy hearing Levi discuss his uncertainties. "What about the girls in your crowd?" I asked. "Won't they wonder why you're not asking them out?"

Levi picked up the reins with his right hand, still holding the umbrella over my head. "There are no Amish girls for me, Merry." He looked away, suddenly paying more attention to the road ahead.

A car was coming in the opposite lane, and for the first time since I'd consented to ride with Levi, I felt nervous. Worried for him, I slouched a bit, hoping the driver wouldn't see me.

The red sports car sped past us, and I felt a light spray. The rain had stopped beating down on us now, but the road glistened from the afternoon shower. A gentle drizzle made the ride in Levi's buggy even more enchanting.

Suddenly, I realized who the red car belonged to. Miss Spindler—Old Hawk Eyes herself!

My throat went dry thinking about the nosy neighbor who lived behind my house. If she had spotted me with Levi just now, we were as good as published on the front page of the *Lancaster New Era*!

"I could leave the Sunday singin' early and come getcha," Levi was saying.

"Only if I agree to it."

He nodded solemnly, playing along with me.

Then I giggled, thinking about the snazzy red sports car and its owner. "That was Miss Spindler back there, in case you didn't know."

"Ach, she's harmless," he said. "What good would it do for her to tell on us?"

"Oh, you might be surprised. Old Hawk Eyes lives for the opportunity to spy on her neighbors."

A chuckle escaped Levi's lips. "Well, then, our problem is solved, isn't it?"

I was totally confused. "What problem?"

"If she saw us, then everything's already out in the open." His eyes were shining. "No more worries, jah?"

"Maybe not for you." I shook my head, thinking about Mom and Dad. What would *they* think if I consented to go out with an Amish boy?

When we approached the dirt lane leading to the Zook farm, I asked Levi to let me out. "Thanks for the ride," I said, eyeing the speedometer on his makeshift dashboard. There was no question in my mind that he would've zipped down SummerHill if I hadn't accepted the ride.

"I hope I'll see ya again soon," he said, bringing the horse to a stop.

"If the rains keep coming, maybe you will," I joked, glancing at the sky. "I would've been soaked if you hadn't come."

He leaped into the back of the buggy to unload my bike. "Will ya give me your answer soon, Merry?"

"I'll think about it," I said, even though I had no idea what on earth there was to consider.

"Okay, then," he said, smiling to beat the band. "I'll say good-bye."

"Bye, Levi. And thanks again."

He sprang up into his buggy, lifted the reins, and sped toward his house. I giggled as I hopped on my bike. Zap 'em Zook was showing off again.

After I arrived home, I finished the remaining work required for my family history by making several phone calls to local relatives. It was actually fun doing the phone interviews, and since it was Sunday, most everyone was home and eager to chat about their life, reciting dates and details.

I was surprised that nearly all my Hanson relatives had heard about Joseph Lapp and his shunning.

Later, Mom gave me permission to call her sister long distance. Because Aunt Teri was deaf, I knew I'd be talking to Uncle Pete. He would sign the questions to his wife and she'd sign her responses back to him.

"Hello?" he answered the phone.

"Hi, Uncle Pete. This is your niece in Pennsylvania."

"Well, how's merry Merry doing these days?" He always said my name twice.

"I'm fine, thanks." I explained that I was working on an assignment for school.

"Family trees, eh?" he said. "Well, we're adding two more branches to *our* tree very soon." Aunt Teri was expecting twins at the end of June. Both she and Uncle Pete were counting the days.

"How's Aunt Teri feeling?" I asked.

"She has to rest a lot, but other than that, real fine."

"I was wondering if Aunt Teri could answer some questions for my school project."

"Let me check." Uncle Pete went to find her. Soon he returned. "I'm sorry, but your aunt's sleeping soundly. Why don't you give the questions to me, and I'll jot them down and call you back tomorrow evening."

"Okay, thanks," I said.

One by one, I read my list of questions. When I finished, I thanked him for taking the time. "Let us know when the babies come."

"We certainly will."

I felt awkward, unsure of what to say next. Then I blurted, "Have you picked out names yet?"

The idea of having twin cousins seemed strange to me. Actually, I felt a total reluctance toward another set of twins in the family. Maybe I was hesitant for other reasons. Maybe I was afraid the advent of twin baby cousins would stir up suppressed memories of Faithie, neatly tucked away like her dresses and toys and things in the attic playroom.

Uncle Pete laughed, robust and jolly. "Oh, we're still throwing names around. Any suggestions?"

Honestly, I hadn't given it a single thought and didn't really care to—but I would never let that on. My lack of enthusiasm might hurt Uncle Pete. "Maybe you should wait till after they're born to see what names fit them."

"That's a terrific idea." He continued to chuckle in the midst of our good-byes.

I hung up the phone and sat there in Dad's study, staring into space. *Lord, help me accept Aunt Teri's twin babies,* I prayed silently. *Maybe it would help if you'd let them turn out to be boys.*

As for Levi Zook, I had no idea what to pray. I'd promised to give him an answer. What on earth was I thinking, accepting a ride in his buggy? I'd probably never live it down. He would take it as a good sign—that maybe I was actually thinking of accepting his invitation.

I thought back to the afternoon I'd spent with Levi. We'd discussed many things. And surprise, surprise, I had more in common with him than I'd ever dreamed.

Sitting back against the comforting fabric of Dad's desk chair, I daydreamed about my bike ride to the covered bridge, the quiet moments on the riverbank, the pictures I'd taken . . . and the more I relived the day, the more I realized something. Something quite disturbing, actually. I *liked* Levi Zook.

I liked his rambunctious, carefree way. The way he could go from driving his buggy recklessly through the covered bridge, to gently trotting his horse in a spring shower with a modern girl at his side.

The boy was truly unconventional. He seemed to know what he wanted and went after it. And he was stubborn. Persistent, too. Joseph Lapp must've had some of the same personality traits.

Dad came into the room, and I popped out of my daydreaming. He looked refreshed after a long nap.

"Feeling better?" I asked.

"Forty winks can make a big difference." He ran his fingers through his graying hair and yawned.

I almost brought up the subject of Levi Zook but chickened out and showed him my phone interviews instead.

"Come to think of it, we might have a book of family crests around here." He surveyed his book shelf.

"That'd be great."

He searched for the book, then located it. "Here we are." He thumbed through the pages to the 1918 Hanson coat of arms. On the page was a full-color picture of the crest; a lion holding an antler in its forepaw was the focal point.

"Looks like the name Hanson spells courage," Dad said proudly.

"Mind if I borrow this to make my sketch?"

"Help yourself."

"Thanks, Dad." I skedaddled off to my room to work on the artistic part of my project.

Lily White rubbed against my leg as I sat at my desk trying to concentrate. Finally, after persistent meowing from my cuddly kitten, I picked her up. "What do you want, baby?" She began to purr as I nuzzled her face with my hand.

"How's this for attention?" I propped a small pillow under her and she curled up contentedly on my desk. "Wanta know a secret?" I whispered, putting my face down close to hers.

She closed her eyes halfway.

"Well, *do* you?"

I crossed my arms and leaned my chin on my hands. "I think someone might be in love with me. Or at least he thinks he is." I sighed, smiling. "And to think, just today I was wondering what it would be like. Well, now I know . . . and it feels warm and weird all at the same time."

Lily White opened her drowsy eyes for a moment, and I stared at the distinct golden flecks in them as we sat facing each other nose to nose.

"Maybe the weird part comes from not knowing if you could love someone back."

Lily White offered no help, so I went back to my sketching as she napped away our heart-to-heart talk.

"Knock, knock."

I turned to see Mom standing in the doorway. "Got a minute?"

"Sure."

She came in, leaving the door ajar. "I wondered if we could talk." I recognized the hesitation in her voice and steeled myself.

"Have a seat." I offered my bed, where the three Hebrew felines were sacked out in various states of consciousness.

"I was thinking," Mom began. "If your aunt Teri has twin girls, would you mind if I give her the baby outfits you and Faith wore?" Her deep brown eyes registered concern. Why was she asking my permission?

"It's really up to you," I replied. "I don't care either way." It was the truth. What Mom did with Faithie's and my baby things was her business.

"Are you sure?" she probed.

I nodded. "One hundred percent, amen."

Mom smiled. "That's cute, Merry."

At first, I thought she was going to come rushing over and hug me or something, but she sat there looking like a helpless child. I swallowed the lump in my throat. No sense crying over any of this. Twins were a *doubly* special gift from God. What could I say to make Mom feel better about losing one of her own little gifts?

"What if she has boys?" I offered cheerfully.

Mom smiled. Good. That's all it took to bring her out of the doldrums. Boys . . . twin boys. Now *that* I could handle.

At church that night, I ran into Jon Klein downstairs at the water fountain. He seemed preoccupied as usual, but when I started to say something in alliteration-eze, Lissa came floating down the hall in her new springtime-blue dress, eyes shining.

"Oh, there you are," she called to him as though they'd planned to meet.

His face lit up when he saw her, and quickly I discarded the notion of speaking to him. Emotionally, I slinked back into my shell. Next to listening to Lissa's plans with Jon on the phone this afternoon, witnessing his obvious interest in her was the worst thing ever.

The two of them walked down the hall and turned to go upstairs without ever acknowledging my presence. Was I really that invisible?

I darted into the ladies' room and stared in the mirror. What incredible thing did Lissa have that I didn't? Or was it just me?

Lifting my hair up away from my face, I turned sideways. Was it my shape? I certainly wasn't as flat-chested as some girls my age. I smiled broadly at the mirror. Was it my teeth? My face? Did I smile enough?

I shrugged at the reflection in the long mirror. Wasn't Merry as merry as everyone said? Second thought—maybe Jon wanted something more than words these days. Maybe Lissa was a better choice for him, after all.

No. I had a difficult time accepting that. Bottom line: Jon had simply forgotten what we had together. The intellectual bond, the lighthearted fun of putting words together.

I wanted to cry. The Alliteration Wizard was truly out to lunch. And out of reach.

After church, Mom made sandwiches for everyone. Skip snatched up four halves and hurried off to his room. I was surprised that he wasn't out with Nikki Klein again but assumed he probably had tons of homework. After all, he was graduating.

I took half a sandwich and wrapped it in a napkin, heading outdoors. The evening was warm and muggy from the afternoon shower. I sat under the white-latticed roof of the old gazebo in our backyard. Nibbling on my roast beef sandwich, I contemplated my sad state of affairs.

My longtime crush liked someone else. Jon and Lissa together? Somehow their names didn't roll off my tongue the way Jon and Merry did. It was actually an effort to shape my lips to say Lissa's name after Jon's.

I whispered their names into the dim light of dusk. Over and over I spoke the words, as though saying them would help soften the pain of disappointment. But the truth was, I never wanted to see them again.

I bit into my sandwich and decided it might be best to change churches. It was the only solution. But then there was another problem—school. Tomorrow!

The grass glistened in the light of a half moon, and I pushed the back of my tennies against the gazebo step, leaning both elbows on my knees. Thinking . . . remembering.

Levi had said something today that made sense. *I am not certain about my future. . . .* He'd said it in reference to his baptism into the Amish church—a sobering thought. His hesitancy had surprised me then, but his words clicked with me now and made me aware of my own uncertainties. Especially about Jon Klein.

Why *had* Jon pursued me all through ninth grade with one word game after another? Didn't he realize that seeking a girl out like that—hanging out at her locker and having a good time—meant something?

I ate the last bite of my sandwich and stood up, brushing the crumbs off my jeans. The heavy smell of lilac hung in the air, and I breathed its perfume deep, longing for its sweetness to wash away my despair.

Sadder than sad, I walked toward the road in the shadow of a deep May moon. Planning for the future was overrated. Maybe it was better to simply live one day at a time. Maybe Levi was right. I *did* have time to decide things.

Shadrach, Meshach, and Abednego came running after me as I headed down SummerHill Lane. Lily White meowed at us, scolding because we hadn't waited for her. I retraced my steps and went back to pick her up.

"You're getting to be a demanding little so-and-so," I said, giggling into her kitty ear. When I got to the turnoff to the willow grove—the shortcut to the Zooks' farmhouse—I purposely ignored it. The light breeze felt good against my face and hair, and I slowed my walk to a stroll, enjoying the spring night.

In the distance, I heard the clip-clopping of horses and the clatter of buggy wheels heading down SummerHill. Happy Amish teenagers wending their way to the various singings around Lancaster. The familiar sound made me think of Levi again, and I glanced toward the dirt lane leading to the Zooks'.

Levi's courting buggy was nowhere to be seen. Would he really come home alone after the singing? The fact that I'd given it another thought startled me. Where did Levi fit into my life? Should I even be thinking about him this way? After all, the Zook family members were dear friends. I didn't want to hurt them.

I snuggled Lily White next to me, then put my head down close to her, listening to the rumble of her purring. "What should I do about Levi?" I whispered. "This summer could be awfully boring with Lissa spending time with Jon."

I dreaded that thought. Not only was I losing the hope of having Jon as my boyfriend, I knew my friendship with Lissa would suffer, too.

A tiny shiver flew up my back and I pushed the painful thought out of my mind. "Maybe I *should* be Levi's girl, just for the summer," I said to my cat quartet. "What do you think?" Abednego arched his fat black body.

I laughed out loud. "I should've known you'd be the one to protest. Come here, you!" I put Lily White down and chased after Abednego until I ran out of breath. Then, realizing it was getting late, I called the cats. Abednego didn't come at first, but what else was new.

With only three of my cats trailing behind me, I turned and headed back up the hill toward home.

The next day at school, I busied myself with as many things as possible. That's what I always did when I was upset.

I tried not to notice Lissa waiting at Jon's locker. She hadn't come in on the bus this morning. Maybe she was running late and missed it. I forced away the thought that she'd gone out after church last night. Feeling a twinge of guilt, I didn't attempt to catch her eye, or wave as usual.

I was thrilled to see Chelsea, though. She rushed down the hall toward me, calling "Merry!" as she balanced a pile of books in her arms. "You have to see these cool family crests." She opened one of the fattest books. "Check it out."

The Davis crest displayed a spear thrust through a sphere with two black-and-silver dragon's wings decorating the sides.

"These *are* cool," I said. "Are you going to do yours in full color like this?"

She nodded without looking at me. "Might help my grade, don'tcha think?"

"What could go wrong with your grade?"

Chelsea glanced around for a second. "Well, you know the faith-healer aunt I was telling you about?"

"Yeah, so?"

"You don't think the teacher'll mark me down for having a weirdo in the family, do you?" She snickered.

"Get a life, Chelsea." I closed my locker. "You won't get a bad grade because of an ancestor. Count on it."

She wiped her forehead and pretended to shake the perspiration off her hand. "What a relief."

"Silly you." I felt more confident about things as I passed Lissa and Jon at his locker and slipped into the bustling hallway to first period—art class.

Halfway through art, I asked Mrs. Hawkins, our expert teacher and artist-in-residence, for ideas on doing a watercolor rendition of my family's crest. She suggested I first do a pencil sketch on a large piece of construction paper.

"When you've added the paints, you might want to mount it on tagboard," she said.

"Good idea, thanks." I went to the art supply closet and found the paints I needed but decided to wait for the tagboard till later. There was no room to store it in my locker anyway.

While I was returning to my seat, I had a peculiar idea. I could make a coat of arms for the Zooks. Even though their family name originated in Switzerland, I could create one for fun. It would be a friendly gesture, nothing more.

After supper, Uncle Pete called to fill me in on Aunt Teri's answers for the family tree. It was good of him to help me this way, and I thanked him.

"Remember to pray for your auntie," he reminded me before we said good-bye.

"Oh, we are."

"She needs all the prayers she can get."

I didn't have the courage to tell him I'd asked God for *boy* cousins. But it probably didn't matter to them. This being the first pregnancy for Aunt Teri, they would be thrilled with whatever children God gave them.

All week long I was able to avoid Lissa and Jon, even though it wasn't easy. Sometimes it actually seemed as though they wanted to be isolated from the rest of us.

Chelsea noticed, too. But I was the one who brought it up. "What's with Lissa and Jon?" I asked on Friday while we waited in the cafeteria line. "They're together all the time."

"They're trying to get perfect scores on their family history projects," she said. "That's probably all it is."

I took a deep breath, clinging to my book bag for dear life.

"You're not jealous, are you?" She inched closer.

"Who, me?"

Chelsea grinned. "I *know* you, Merry. You're not the martyr type."

"I need martyr's grace," I muttered, letting the first words of truth escape my lips. "But don't you dare tell a soul."

"So . . . you *do* like him!"

"Treat the truth with care," I warned her, straight-faced.

She pushed her hair away from her face, laughing. "Merry, you're such a kick. I love it when you get dramatic."

I groaned. "Let's drop it."

"Whoa, Merry, don't take it out on me." Chelsea looked dumbfounded. "Relax, Mer. It's just a little crush, right?"

"No comment."

"It'll go away eventually. Besides, you can do better than Jon Klein." She put a carton of chocolate milk on her tray.

I glanced at the brown carton. "You'll get zits from that."

"That was an amazing leap of logic." She laughed and so did I, and together we found a table off to the side, away from the noisy meanderings of students. My mind was stuck on what she'd said about doing better than Jon. What did she mean?

Things started to settle down as we ate. We talked leisurely about our family crests and Chelsea's latest find at the library. I was even digesting my lasagna fairly well when Lissa and Jon came in together.

Instantly, my stomach lurched. I reached for my lemon-lime soda and mistakenly breathed in the sparkling spray off the top. It made me cough into my glass, nearly choking. Everyone around me stared. Jon too.

I could hardly wait for the weekend. Ninth grade had never been so traumatic!

Catch a Falling Star Fourteen

After school, I hurried next door to see Rachel. She invited me to help with the milking. I accepted the invitation cheerfully for a change.

"Des gut," she said, obviously excited.

I hurried behind her to the barn. As I helped wash down the cows for the milking, I thought of my great-great grandfather. If Joseph Lapp hadn't left the Amish way back when, I might be doing this chore twice every day.

As it turned out, I spent nearly the whole weekend with Rachel, helping her bake bread early Saturday morning. Before lunch, we weeded and watered string beans in her charity garden.

Sunday was the Lord's Day, but not a church day this week for the Zook family. The Amish attended church in one another's homes every other Sunday. On the "off" Sundays they rested, did only necessary chores, and read from their German Bibles.

As soon as I arrived home from church and ate dinner, I carefully placed the next two letters from Joseph Lapp into the wide pocket of my backpack. I hoped Rachel and I might have a private moment together so she could translate them for me.

When I arrived next door, Rachel was getting ready for a walk and was delighted that I had come. Together, we headed for the woods behind the barn.

"Simple things are best," I said as we walked into the deepest part of the woods together.

She understood fully and lifted her rosy cheeks to the sun as its warm rays filtered down through the branches overhead.

"Would you mind reading some more of my great-great grandfather's letters?" I asked later when we stopped to catch our breath.

"Did ya bring 'em?"

"They're right here." I took them out of my pocket, plastic and all. We sat on the ground with the forest animals, squirrels and birds, skittering around us.

Rachel began to translate. " 'My dear Samuel, brother and friend. I have thought to change my given Christian name. I wish not to bring sadness and shame to my family. I will not legally change my surname, but I have chosen to be called Levi Lapp. You will address me as Levi from this day forward.' "

"Levi?" I asked, confused. "Why a biblical name if he was leaving the Amish?"

Rachel scanned the next lines. "It says here that Mary Smith picked out the name for him. Maybe she was a Mennonite."

"That's strange," I said.

She hung her head sadly. "I had almost forgotten about his changing names."

"Maybe he needed a clean slate to start over."

"Maybe so."

We talked about other possible reasons, but the discussion eventually led to Levi, her brother.

"Grossdawdy wants Levi to be baptized this fall," she said.

I wondered about that. Did her elderly grandfather feel he could die in peace if Levi was safely baptized into the church?

"Grossdawdy is afeared for Levi," she went on, looking into my eyes. "He suspects that Levi is running with a rough crowd. Maybe even the Mule Skinners."

I didn't dare tell her that what she said was true.

"Such things could give Grossdawdy heart failure," she said softly. "Me too."

Was she worried that history might repeat itself? That her own brother might become as rebellious as Joseph Lapp from so long ago?

We stood up and began walking again. Then, coming to a patch of wild clover, we bent low and filled our pockets. I thought of Joseph changing his name to Levi for Mary, his bride-to-be. It seemed strange that their names matched Levi's and mine.

Monday after school, Rachel showed me how to make a cross-stitch design without a pattern. On Tuesday, we worked on quilted pillow coverings for her hope chest. And mine.

Of course, Rachel didn't know that I owned no such thing as a hope chest. And as I sat beside her at the kitchen table hand sewing the quilted pillows, it struck me that if I were Amish, I would be steadily filling my hope chest, just as she was. In fact, if I were Amish, I'd probably be engaged to be married a few years from now. A startling thought.

Spending time at the Zooks' helped me keep my mind off Lissa and Jon. They were showing up everywhere together. At school, at church. It was unbearable.

Because stress always made me hungry, I was exactly where I needed to be. Esther Zook *always* had warm, fresh bread and homemade jellies on hand, not to mention oodles of pies. After all, food was an Amishman's middle name!

All the time I was spending with Rachel unfortunately posed an unforeseen problem. I hadn't realized it at first, but Levi was beginning to mistake my reason for being there. He kept coming around, paying more attention to me than ever. It was one thing for him to flirt with me out in his potato field, but right under his parents' noses?

I had to admit, Levi was making me nervous. Because, friends or not, I certainly didn't want Abe and Esther Zook to think I was contributing to their son's reluctance toward Amish baptism. Not now, not ever!

On Thursday after school, two days before the ninth-grade church picnic, Rachel and I moved all the furniture off her front porch—three rocking chairs and several plant tables. Both of us were sweeping, stirring up a cloud of dust, when the subject of Joseph Lapp came up.

Rachel got it started. She stopped sweeping and leaned on her broom for a moment. "I asked Grossdawdy more about Joseph Lapp."

I perked up my ears. "You did?"

"Jah." She tucked a strand of light brown hair into the bun at the back of her head. "Joseph Lapp refused to return and repent to his family and the church. He must've loved his Mary a lot to give everything up for her." She sighed. "He even lost the farmland his father had planned to give him."

I was silent. *Has Levi heard this part of the story?*

"It doesn't make sense," Rachel observed. "Why would Joseph Lapp bother kneeling for baptism if he was just gonna turn around and leave?"

"It would've been better for him in the end if he hadn't taken the baptismal vow, right?"

She nodded solemnly and slowly began to sweep again. "Baptism is sacred and permanent. If you don't take it, you never have to worry about the Meidung . . . the shunning."

"So right now you're not really in or out of the church."

"Jah. But most Amish teens who don't take the baptism pledge end up leaving. Usually they end up Mennonites."

"Why, because Mennonites allow cars and have electricity?"

"Jah."

I swept my pile of leaves and debris under the porch railing and watched it fall to the ground. "Do you think Levi will be baptized this fall?"

Rachel shrugged her shoulders and her blue eyes grew sad again. "I doubt Levi will do it. I heard him tell Dat that he wants to get his hair cut."

That got my attention. I wanted to ask her if she'd told Levi about the letters from my great-great grandfather, but instead, swept another clump of dried leaves away from the house.

All day Levi had been cultivating the cornfield, and I wanted to see him, especially after Rachel's remark about his hair. It was hard to think of Levi with a contemporary haircut. Harder still to think of being his girl. As I headed for home that evening, I went out of my way to say hi.

Instead of stopping everything and greeting me like he usually did, Levi waved. "Hullo, Merry! Come ride with me."

"I better get going," I replied. "Mom'll have supper waiting."

He grinned, looking cuter than ever. "Come back after," he said, pushing his straw hat forward, hiding his eyes.

I snickered at the cockeyed hat and walked along the row of corn to keep up with the mules and the cultivator. "What for?"

"Ach, just come, Merry. Will ya?" He said it playfully, but there was that underlying take-charge tone indicative of the Amish male. He took his hat off and shook the dust out of his hair. "Well?"

"I might," I teased, turning to go. Why was my heart beating like this?

"Will you have your answer for me tonight?"

I turned around. This boy wasn't giving up. *What should I do?*

He was grinning again. "You can come back, Merry," he urged, putting his straw hat back on. "No one'll mind."

"Your grandfather might."

He frowned suddenly.

"I know he wants you to be baptized soon."

"*Himmel,*" Levi said. "Rachel's been talkin' out of turn." And by my silent response I was acknowledging the truth.

I felt like a traitor. Rachel had confided in me, and here I was spilling the beans.

He waved as I stepped gingerly between the rows of corn, heading for home. Obviously, there were no hard feelings between us for what I'd said. Levi had always been one to forgive and forget. It was the Amish way.

Scurrying over the field to SummerHill Lane, I could hardly wait for supper. Not so much from hunger, but from mere curiosity. This was the night I would discuss Levi with my parents. I could only hope my brother wouldn't make things difficult for me. Wishful thinking. Ridiculing his "little Merry" was one of the things Skip did best.

"You're right on time," Mom said as I breezed into the kitchen. "Hurry and wash up for supper."

It bothered me that she was still saying the same things she'd said to me all my life. At fifteen and a half, I wasn't a kid anymore. Why didn't she realize that?

I glanced around the kitchen. Usually my brother was stuffing his face nonstop with junk food before *and* after each meal. "Where's Skip?"

Dad strolled in from the living room carrying the newspaper under his arm. "He's busy at church. The senior banquet's tomorrow night."

I breathed a tremendous sigh of relief. So obvious was it that Mom frowned and glanced at Dad. "Your brother will be involved in many senior activities between now and graduation day," she said. "He's excited, and I hope you're happy for him, too."

"Sure, Mom, I'm happy."

I'm happier for me, though. I headed down the hall to the powder room to wash up. Come next fall, I'd have the run of the house.

"I always knew that boy had it in him," Dad remarked as I came back into the kitchen. "Skip sure had us fooled in junior high, though."

Mom said, "High school seemed to make the big difference for him. I guess change is good sometimes."

Her comment reminded me of Jon Klein. That's exactly what I'd said to him—*change is good*—the day I worried out loud about going to high school next year. It was also the last day we'd played our alliteration word game together. Thirteen depressing days ago!

Dad refolded the newspaper and slid it into a large wicker basket under Mom's square antique plant table in the corner of the kitchen. She had succeeded in coaxing a multitude of African violets to life in that corner; now they were thriving to beat the band.

Dad offered to carry the platter of fried chicken to the table and sat down, waiting as Mom filled our glasses with iced tea. He looked at me from the head of the table. "You're awfully quiet, Mer. Something on your mind?"

I wondered whether to spring Levi Zook on them now or later. Opting for later, I reached for my napkin and shrugged. "We can talk about it during dessert."

"Which reminds me," Mom said, observing me, "I made chocolate chip cookies this morning."

I sniffed the air. "Can't wait. Smells great!"

Mom smiled and bowed her head.

Dad said a prayer of thanks for the food, and I ate while the two of them chatted about his day at the hospital. Evidently, a woman in labor had come to the emergency room. "She looked large enough for twins," Dad said, grinning at me, "but it turned out she gave birth to one very hefty baby boy."

"I wonder how everything's going with Aunt Teri," Mom said. "Haven't talked to her for over a week."

"She's certainly no spring chicken," Dad said, chuckling. "You have to hand it to her, wanting to start a family at her age."

I could hardly wait for the chocolate chip cookies. My parents were simply rambling, enjoying their conversation about absolutely nothing while I sat here stewing, thinking through my plan of attack.

Mom started to clear the table, and I hopped up to help. Anything to get things rolling.

At last, the ice cream was dished up and the heaping plate of cookies placed on the table. Dad smiled almost sweetly at me, leaned back in his chair, and waited. Waited silently with his arms folded across his chest.

The silence wiped me out, and I took a deep breath, hoping I could pull this off. "Mom, Dad"—I looked at both of them—"what would you say if I went out with Levi Zook?"

Silence followed. Absolute, complete silence.

Hilarious laughter would've been welcomed at this point. Anything.

But Dad's face was as blank as Mom's.

"Well?" I ventured, still waiting for some kind of response from them. "Levi is a good friend, and we've known each other since childhood."

Dad took another cookie, held it in midair, and turned it around in his hand as if it were a buggy wheel. "So it *was* you in Levi's buggy two Sundays ago."

I gasped. "What?"

His face broke into a broad grin. "Miss Spindler just happened to mention it to me the other day when I was mowing the lawn."

"I should've known," I muttered.

"Don't be upset, Mer," Dad said, surprising me. "You know how the old lady is. She makes mountains out of molehills."

I nodded. "It's her livelihood."

Mom hadn't commented on the matter yet, and her aloofness made me nervous.

Dad continued. "Where did Levi ask you to go with him?"

"He talked about the Green Dragon." I shrugged my shoulders.

Mom spoke at last. "I hope you won't go out on the highway in that buggy of his." She stared at me, her eyes penetrating. Then she cut loose with her real concern. "Merry . . . what could you possibly have in common with an Amish boy?"

Now *I* was the one leaning back in my chair. I needed space all of a sudden, and Mom wasn't helping things by inching her face closer and closer to mine. I slid my chair away from the table.

"Merry, I—"

Dad interrupted her. "Look, I don't see any harm in Merry's spending some time with her friend. Levi's a great kid. Good manners, as far as I can tell."

Mom argued. "But Merry's only fifteen."

Dad reached for her hand. "Darling, our daughter will be sixteen soon. It's not like she'd be going out with some stranger. The two of them have literally grown up together. Besides, Levi's only a year older, and he's family, in a very distant way."

That wasn't good enough for Mom. "But he's Amish. Next thing, he'll be looking for a wife."

Dad nodded, sneaking a wink at me. "You're absolutely right. You've gotta watch those Amish boys. They ride around in those noisy courting buggies all hours of the night, snatching up pretty young things, going off to the bishop, and getting married."

I stood up. "Marriage is the last thing on my mind!"

Mom smiled sympathetically. "You have many more years ahead of you to decide such important things."

"So . . . you don't mind, then?" I asked, looking first at Dad, then at Mom.

With true reluctance, Mom managed to utter, "I guess one time won't hurt."

"Promise not to tell Skip?" I said. "That is *if* I decide to go."

Dad put his fingers together like a boy scout. "I promise." He was such a tease sometimes.

I loaded the dishwasher for Mom, insisting that she relax with Dad in the living room. The Levi discussion was behind me!

Now there was only one thing left to do.

Suddenly unsure of myself, I pictured Levi working the cornfield with his mule team and cultivator, loosening the soil. Waiting for my answer.

When the kitchen was spotless, I headed outside to the gazebo. I sat on the railing, dangling my legs over the edge, facing the willow grove. I stared at the graceful trees that blocked my view of Zooks' farm. The willows were like a barrier between the Amish world and my own.

I closed my eyes and imagined what life would've been like if Faithie, my twin, were still alive. She would be sitting here on the railing beside me, encouraging me not to shut Mom out the way I had . . . to hang on to my feelings for Jon Klein even though he'd hurt me. She would tell me to pray about going out with Levi. And she would hug me and tell me I was her best friend.

Best friend. How I missed her!

A half hour later, the back door opened and Dad called to me, "Merry, someone's on the phone for you."

I leaped off the gazebo and ran into the house to the kitchen. "Hello?"

"Hi, Mer. It's Chelsea."

"What's up?"

"Just thought I'd check something out." She paused. "Look, I can't believe this could be true, knowing you, Mer, but my mom ran into your nosy neighbor at the post office today."

Gulp!

"Old Hawk Eyes said you and Levi were out riding in his courting buggy."

I laughed. "That lady gets around." Then I explained about the rain. "It was just a neighborly gesture. Really."

"C'mon, Merry," she persisted. "You were always so . . . so, uh . . . attracted to the guy."

"Attracted?"

"You know how you always watch him when we ride past his house on the school bus."

"But it's not what you think—I mean, I'm not ready to join the Amish or anything."

"You're sure?"

I took a deep breath. To tell the truth, I *had* been toying with the thought. "Look, Chelsea," I said. "If I tell you something, will you promise not to tell a single soul?"

"*Now* what?"

"Levi asked me to be his girlfriend."

She gasped—and kept doing it. Finally, when she caught her breath, she said, "Are you kidding?"

I felt an overwhelming sense of confidence. Even more so than when I'd shared the news with my parents.

"What did you tell him?" She sounded dramatically serious. The way I usually sounded under similar circumstances.

"I haven't told him anything yet," I replied. "I was just on my way over there."

"Oh, Merry, please don't do anything stupid."

"Stupid?"

"Merry, don't be weird about this. Please." She sounded desperate.

"You've never met Levi Zook, have you?"

"What's that got to do with anything?"

"Absolutely everything! You have no idea what you're saying, so if you don't mind, I think we better end this conversation now before—"

"Merry, listen to me!"

I clammed up. She was making me mad.

Her voice grew softer. "Don't do anything, Mer. Okay? I'll be right over."

"Don't you dare!" Now I was furious. "And don't treat me like a kid," I blurted. "I'm old enough to decide things like this. Besides, you said I could do better than Jon, remember?"

She exhaled into the phone. "Why do you take everything so literally? I didn't mean you should go off and *marry* some Amish guy."

"Excuse me? Who said anything about that?"

"But have you thought this through? Have you considered the consequences?" she asked.

If I hadn't known better, I would've thought she'd been playing Jon's alliteration game!

"Trust me, Chelsea. Levi's just a good friend. I like spending time with him," I said.

"Well, you can bet on this, I'm going to do whatever it takes to bring you to your senses!"

And with that, she hung up. Before I could even say good-bye.

Seventeen *Catch a Falling Star*

Levi was long gone from the cornfield when I finally wandered over to the Zook farm. From his side of the willow grove, I could see the gas lamp burning in the kitchen and assumed they were having supper. Amish farmers worked outdoors as long as there was light, then ate a hearty meal as dusk approached.

Lily White's soft little head and paws hung out of the pocket of my light jacket. She purred loudly as she rode there—next to my heart.

I strolled past the new white barn and out to the pond and the spacious meadow where the willow grove ended. Wide and very deep, the pond stretched across a large area, embracing both the Zooks' property and ours.

Sitting down on the cool grass, I freed Lily White, letting her roam as she pleased. It was almost nighttime, but it wasn't dark. The sky was filled with tiny lights, as if someone had flicked a paintbrush across the universe. And the longer I sat there, the brighter the dots of lights became.

I found the broad, luminous band of the Milky Way and the moon—a fat sliver. Its light cast a splendid ribbon across the pond.

Relaxing there in the grass just yards from the placid water, I began to pray as I faced the sky. "Lord, you know how things are with Levi and me. I don't have to tell you that he's my friend . . . and I like him. But honestly, I don't know whether to say yes or no." I sighed. "I've never gone out with anyone before. This is all so new to me."

I breathed in the fragrance of lilacs and continued. "Dad didn't give me such a horrible time about Levi. I really thought he would. And Mom? Well, you know how moms are."

I stopped. Someone was walking toward me.

Squinting into the dim light of dusk, I recognized the long strides and the tall, lean silhouette as Levi. My heart sank. Not because I didn't want to see him, but because he'd probably ask for my answer. Again.

Quickly, I prayed some more, having a difficult time finishing. Levi could *not* be in on what I was saying about him to God. Not that it was bad or anything. Actually, it was just the opposite.

"Hi, Levi," I said as he came swishing barefoot through the grassy meadow.

"Merry." He said it softly. "I thoughtcha weren't gonna come."

"Something came up." I didn't mention Chelsea's phone call. What she'd said didn't matter anyway.

"Well, you're here now." He sat beside me, a long piece of straw hanging out of his mouth.

Lily White came over and sniffed his bare feet. I laughed and reached for her. I cradled her furry body in my arms. "You remember Lily, don't you?"

"How can I forget?" Levi grinned at me.

Side by side, we listened to the sounds of night. Loud, chirping crickets, and the flutter of wings as purple martins flew home to roost in the Zooks' multileveled birdhouse.

"Remember the day you saved my life?" Levi asked unexpectedly.

"As clear as yesterday."

He laughed softly. "I was nine and you were only eight." He took the straw out of his mouth and tossed it on the ground. "I knew it then, Merry."

My heart pounded. *What* had he known?

Levi turned his face to the sky. "Have you ever seen a more beautiful sky?" He seemed to like asking questions that didn't require answers. I smiled, appreciating his love for God's creation. Wishing the question about being his girl could go unanswered, too.

We sat very still, gazing at the twinkling lights overhead. I don't know how long we sat there, but it was long enough for the moon to climb halfway up the silo.

Suddenly, Levi stood up. "Look there!"

I saw it, too. A dazzling stream of light falling across the sky.

"Quick! Make a wish," he said, and our eyes followed the star's journey as it topped the barn and fell over the horizon.

"Come, let's walk," he said, and I settled Lily White inside my pocket once again. Levi laughed as I got Lily situated. "Aren'tcha supposed to catch a falling star and put *that* in your pocket?"

I looked at him and smiled. "She's as white as any star up there." Then I turned my gaze to the sky. "What a truly beautiful sight," I said, referring to the falling star. "I don't know when I've seen such a thing."

"It means something, jah?"

I knew some Amish were a little superstitious. For instance, a bride and groom wouldn't think of singing on their wedding day because they believed that singing today meant weeping tomorrow.

"What on earth could it mean?" I asked, not realizing how naïve I sounded until the words were out.

Levi stopped walking. "Think of it, Merry. We sat there by the pond just now where my life nearly ended. I would've drowned that day without you." He looked up at the sky, making a sweeping motion with his hand. "And then the star falls right before our eyes. It surely must be providence, Merry. Nature's telling us something."

I almost laughed at the way he was making such a big deal of this. "You made a wish, right?"

"Did you?" he asked.

I shook my head. "I don't believe in falling stars. I'd rather pray about my dreams and wishes."

He touched my arm. "*You* can make my wish come true."

The air was filled with sweetness, and I thought this was as perfect a night as any I'd ever experienced.

"Levi Lapp loved Mary Smith," Levi was saying as we began to walk again. "Levi and Mary. Don't you see? History repeats itself."

"Are you saying that we belong together just because our ancestors had the same names?" I couldn't see the logic in this.

"Oh, it's much more than that, Merry," he said emphatically. "It's providence."

"Well, I'm not as sure about this as you are."

"I know," he said softly, "but maybe you will be someday."

The moon was high in the sky now. It was late, and Mom would worry. "Guess I'd better head for home."

"I'll walk ya," he offered.

"That's okay, I know the way."

I was surprised, but he let me go. And all the way home, his words echoed in my brain. *Levi and Mary.*

Levi and Merry.

Eighteen *Catch a Falling Star*

So this is how it's going to be, I thought as I stared into my locker the next morning. *Chelsea's going to snub me because of Levi.*

She'd made things instantly clear on the bus this morning. "In case you didn't know it, Merry, you're making a major mistake if you go out with that Levi boy," she said flat out.

"It's none of your business." I could be just as stubborn.

Chelsea had turned away, acting offended. In fact, she ignored me the rest of the ride, but I didn't let it bother me.

Later, after English, I was rushing to change books at my locker when I noticed her talking to Jon in the hallway near the principal's office. Lissa was hovering nearby, too, obviously interested in what was being said.

It struck me as strange. Why would the three of them be hanging out together? It didn't add up. Besides that, Ashley Horton hurried over to join them as though she was expected to show up, too.

I found my social studies notebook on the top shelf of my locker. It was bursting with information for the Hanson family history. Quickly, I deposited my English books and, without another glance at the foursome, slammed my locker door and hurried off to class.

Moments before the bell rang, the four of them rushed into class, and when I caught Chelsea's eye she looked rather sheepish. I pretended not to notice and gathered my outline and family reports as I waited for the teacher to begin.

"All family histories are due on Tuesday," she said, reminding us that this Monday was Memorial Day. As if we needed reminding! "Please be prepared to give an oral report, as well."

No problem. My work was basically done. All I had left to do was enter my data on Dad's computer over the weekend and print it out.

During the last half of class, we were allowed to work together with our partners. I motioned for Chelsea to come to my side of the room so we could confer on things. Reluctantly, she came.

"Are you done with your interviews?" I asked as she sat in the desk across the aisle from me.

"All but two." She leaned over to look at my sketch. "Hey, what a cool coat of arms."

"Oh, that," I said, pushing the sketch behind some other papers. "It's the family crest for a friend of mine." I didn't tell her it was a gift for the Zooks.

"So where's yours?" she asked.

I shuffled through my papers. "Here." I held it up. "I plan on painting a larger version and putting it on tagboard. What do you think?"

She took the sketch and studied it for a moment. "This is really good. You could be a commercial artist someday."

"It's not *that* good, but thanks."

She found her family interviews and had me proofread them for spelling errors. Grammar, too. I liked the format she'd used to set up the questions and answers on her computer.

"This looks really professional," I told her.

She slumped down in her chair. "If only I didn't have to mention my great-aunt Essie."

"Lots of kids would probably like to have someone as colorful and fascinating in their family tree."

She pushed her hair back from her face. "What? Like Amish *traitors*?"

I didn't like the way she emphasized traitors, as though I might be one myself. "My great-great grandfather made a choice for love," I explained in a whisper. "It wasn't easy for him to leave the Amish."

She nodded her head, patronizing me. "Right. And what about you and Levi? Did you see him last night?"

I nodded, egging her on. "It was enchanting, really. You should've seen the stars."

"Spare me the dramatics."

I felt frustrated. "Nothing you can say or do will make a difference. It's my choice."

"Well," she said slyly, "I guess we'll just have to see about that."

I had no idea what she meant, and to tell the truth, I really didn't care.

Mom was waiting for me on the front porch as I came up the side yard. "Merry," she called. "You have new baby cousins. Uncle Pete just called from the hospital."

I hurried up to the white-columned porch and sat on the step. "The babies came early," I said, hesitating to ask about the sex of the twins.

"They're four weeks premature," Mom said. "Not too bad for twins."

"Are the babies healthy?"

She nodded, smiling. "Benjamin and Rebekah are doing just fine. So well, in fact, they'll be released from the hospital tomorrow."

"A boy and a girl?" This was truly amazing.

"One of each," she said. "And the proud parents couldn't be happier."

"So . . . whose clothes are you gonna send them? Mine or Faithie's?"

She leaned forward suddenly. "Which do you prefer, Merry?"

I thought we'd already had this conversation. "It really doesn't matter, Mom. Do what you want." She'd never dressed us alike as babies. The look-alike thing came later in grade school, and then only on special occasions like birthdays and Easter.

I could see it was going to be a tough decision for Mom, choosing whose baby things—Faithie's or mine—to give away. She had that distant look in her eyes again, and it made me wonder if she would ever get over Faithie's death.

"I'm starved," I said, getting up and going inside.

Mom followed and insisted on peeling an apple for me. I sat at the kitchen table as she washed her hands, then reached for a paring knife from the wooden knife rack. Why did it always seem as though she needed to talk things out but couldn't? Every time we got the slightest bit close to whatever was bugging her, she'd clam up. It reminded me of Chelsea and the way she shut me out the minute I mentioned God or the Bible.

I ended up eating my apple quarters alone in the kitchen. Well, alone if you didn't count the cats. I guess they assumed that if someone was snacking, they should be, too.

Mom excused herself to go upstairs, and I figured it probably had something to do with choosing baby clothes for little Rebekah. Knowing the way Mom usually avoided the attic, I decided to stay out of her way. There was absolutely nothing I could do to help her now. Not unless she opened up and stopped playing these games. Nearly nine years had passed since Faithie's death. Why couldn't Mom talk with me about it?

In between bites of apple, I recited the babies' probable nicknames out loud. "Benny and Becky." Cute names, I thought. Alliterated, too.

And for the first time in two weeks, I didn't feel wiped out about the Alliteration Wizard and his recent alliance with Lissa.

Nineteen *Catch a Falling Star*

I nearly swallowed my tonsils when Jon Klein called later that evening. "Mistress Merry," he said when I answered the phone.

"Jon?"

"A bunch of us are going to help serve at the senior banquet tonight at church. Want to come?"

"Oh . . . I didn't know," I said, floundering for the right words.

"Well, I thought you might want to help."

"Uh . . . thanks."

I thought the conversation was over when he said, "Oh, Merry, what about the picnic tomorrow? You'll be there, won't you?"

"Haven't decided yet." And after I said that, I wished I hadn't. Now he knew I didn't have a date.

"You really oughta come, Mer, since we're all graduating from ninth grade together." It was very thoughtful of him to call. But why now?

All of us kids from church, and several others like Chelsea Davis, had gone through most of grade school and all of junior high together. Except Lissa. She'd moved here toward the end of eighth grade.

"So, what do you say?" he asked again.

"I'm, uh . . . I might be busy."

For a long, unbearable moment he didn't say anything. Then at last, "Well, I hope to see you."

We both said good-bye, and I placed the receiver in its cradle as though it were my only link to him.

That's when I remembered we hadn't played the Alliteration Game just now. And I felt a twinge of sadness.

———

After supper, Dad decided he wanted some soft ice cream, so the three of us hopped into the car and headed for the Dairy Queen. Since Skip was busy with Nikki Klein and his graduation banquet, it was nice to get out with Mom and Dad by myself.

When we drove past our church, I thought about Jon's invitation. There had been that same friendly ring to his voice. But I wondered why he'd called, really. Especially since he and Lissa were together.

Mom started discussing the new babies, and I eased back into the soft padding of the booth, waiting for our ice-cream orders. Dad came up with the bright idea for Mom to go to New Jersey and help Aunt Teri with the twins.

"Why don't you go tomorrow?" he suggested.

Mom protested a bit. "But it's Memorial Day weekend."

Dad glanced at me. "We can manage for a few days. Can't we, Mer?"

I nodded my consent. "Besides, it'll be fun for you to help with the babies." I caught myself before saying that it would be like old times. Even so, I couldn't help but think it would be good for Mom to be around newborn twins again.

Dad put his arm around Mom. "What do you think, hon?"

"Well, I know Teri will need an extra pair of hands."

"Then it's settled," Dad said as his hot-fudge sundae came.

Mom's eyebrows shot up when she saw her banana split. "Are you sure you're not trying to get rid of me?"

"Oh, Mom, really." I picked up a spoon and dipped into the rich, creamy goo on top of my peanut butter sundae.

She studied me for a moment. "You won't be going off and marrying Levi Zook while I'm gone, will you?"

"Right," I said. "It's not like you don't have to notify the Amish bishop ahead of time and everything. Besides, the Amish around here get married in November."

Dad grinned at Mom. "Sounds as though she's thought this through, wouldn't you say?"

"Dad!"

Mom frowned, looking far too serious. "Merry, promise me you won't go riding in his buggy again."

"Levi and I aren't going out in his buggy," I assured her. I could've saved her a lot of concern by telling her I hadn't agreed to go *anywhere* with him.

Saturday dawned long before I chose to crawl out of bed. Mom had other plans for me. She had an agenda, all right, and barged into my room to inform me of it. "You'll be the only female around here while I'm gone," she stated.

"Female?" I mumbled from under my comforter. *What is that supposed to mean?*

"You know what I'm talking about."

I was still sleepy-eyed from the sandman, and here she was rehearsing Dad's hospital schedule and telling me when Skip was supposed to be home.

"Can't you write it down?" I said. "What time is it, anyway?"

"I've been up for hours packing and arranging meals and things, Merry. The least you can do is cooperate for one minute."

"What?" I sat up.

"You heard me." She got up and flung my bathrobe at the bed. My cats didn't seem to mind the terry cloth robe next to them. In fact, they began rearranging themselves on it, which only infuriated Mom. "Honestly, you have way too many cats."

This was the first I'd heard such a thing.

"We really need to talk about this problem." She glared at my beloved babies.

"How can you say that?" I replied, now fully awake. "They're not a problem to me, or anyone else." *Except for Skip,* I thought disgustedly.

"I should've said something long ago" came her terse response.

"But, Mom."

"I really don't have time for this now," she said, standing at the foot of my bed in her traveling clothes—a yellow sweat suit and tennies to match. Her graying hair was pulled back into a clump at the back of her neck and fastened with a bright yellow organdy tie. She looked a little like a canary.

She glanced at her watch. "It's already seven o'clock," she said. "Can you be downstairs in five minutes?"

I groaned, falling back onto my pillow. "How could you do this to me?"

She didn't respond with words but turned on her heels and left the room. I could hear her doing the same thing to Skip down the hall, waking him up too early.

What was bothering her? Was it the fact her younger sister had given birth to twins?

I hated to disturb my cats, but I needed my robe. If I didn't show up in a flash, Mom would really be upset.

Wandering into my bathroom, I stretched. *Mom isn't herself these days,* I thought, reaching for a washcloth. She irritated me, yet I felt sorry for her. Her daughter Faithie was dead—nothing could ever change that. But what bothered me even more was the fact that I was alive—and being treated like this.

I knew better than to dawdle when Mom had deadlines, so I hustled downstairs. She was already writing things in her lined tablet. "There's a salmon casserole dish in the refrigerator for supper tonight," she began. "Just warm it up in the microwave for the three of you."

"That's easy," I said, noticing the suitcase beside the back door. And a duffle bag bursting with baby clothes, no doubt.

She continued to rattle on about additional dinner possibilities, when to do laundry, and would I please pick up the house for the cleaning lady? "You won't forget anything, will you?"

"The list is all I need."

She pushed it across the table. "Better put it on the refrigerator or somewhere safe."

"Relax, Mom, everything'll be fine."

"Well, I hope so." She stood up then. "I'm counting on you, Merry."

That's when I noticed how vulnerable and sad she looked. I moved toward her, wanting to hug her. "You can always count on me, Mom. You know that."

Tears sprang to her eyes, and she darted toward the table. Away from me.

Sadly, I watched her pick up the list and put it on the refrigerator, turning her back on me. Strange as it seemed, posting her list on the fridge was somehow more important than my hug.

Getting up early on a Saturday wasn't so bad, really. It meant that I could spend more time at the Zooks'.

Before I left, I finished making their family crest, outlining the watercolored sections with black marker. Then, carefully, I rolled it up, carrying it under my arm.

Mom had left in a hurry once we discussed her list, and as far as I could tell, Skip had gone back to bed. Dad would be tied up at the hospital till six tonight. Basically, I had the day to myself.

⸻

Esther Zook was delighted with my present and promptly hung the colorful drawing on the kitchen wall. I was surprised because the Amish usually didn't decorate their walls much.

"This is so kind of you, Merry," Esther said, standing back to admire it.

"I'm glad you like it," I said.

Rachel began to set the table. "Will you stay and eat the noon meal with us?"

I remembered my promise to Mom this morning. She was counting on me to make sure things ran smoothly at home. "Better not today," I said, explaining that Skip would be starved.

"Come back later, jah?"

"After lunch."

Levi seemed pleased that I was spending the day there, and later, when he and I went to the barn to round up the cows for milking, he asked, "Why didja make us the drawing?"

"I wanted to." I pulled on a pair of old rubber work boots belonging to Levi's father.

He studied me hard. "You put a five-pointed star right in the middle," he said. "Does that mean something?"

"I just made it up," I explained. "There are no real family crests for the name *Zook*. And the star seemed to fit." I chuckled, remembering the falling star that night by the pond.

"I don't think you can laugh when providence comes knocking." His eyes were serious.

"Well . . . maybe."

"Not *maybe*, Merry," he said. "Providence is something we Amish folk live by."

It was interesting to hear him say "we Amish."

"I thought you weren't sure about your future here on the farm." My words were sincere, and I saw by his face that he hadn't misunderstood.

"Providence must be attended to no matter what," he went on. "Just think what might've happened if your great-great grandfather had not married outside the Amish."

"What? You think *that* was providential?"

"You, Merry, would not be here today if Levi Lapp had not married Mary Smith." He turned to me, his expression soft and thoughtful. "That's providence. A very gut thing!"

The sweet smell of hay made the moment stand out in my mind long afterward.

Rachel and her sisters showed up for milking right on time; little Susie, too. They stared at my giant boots, caked with dried cow manure, and giggled.

"Sorry"—I glanced at their muddy bare feet—"but I'm not quite ready for squishy stuff between my toes." While we washed down the cows for milking, I enjoyed the chatter around me, feeling very at home. Rachel and Ella Mae, Nancy and little Susie, engaging in the art of conversation. Pennsylvania Dutch style.

After milking and helping Rachel tend her charity garden, I headed home. Minus the work boots, naturally. I thought of Levi's words. *You, Merry, would not be here today . . .*

I wasn't exactly sure how I felt about all this talk of providence, but I did know one thing: History didn't have to repeat itself unless the people involved allowed it. Levi Lapp and Mary Smith really and truly had nothing to do with how Levi Zook and Merry Hanson lived out their lives.

Skipping through the willows, I felt good, surprising myself that not once had I thought about the ninth-grade picnic. Or Jon Klein.

The thoughts came later, though—after supper when Chelsea called. "Hey, you'll never guess what," she said. "I went to church today."

"To the picnic?" I was thrilled; this was a good first step for an atheist. "How was it?"

"Okay, I guess, for a *church* picnic."

I overlooked her remark.

"You should've come, Mer," she said, a question in her voice. "Everyone was asking about you. I even heard that Jon called you from the church office."

"He did?"

Twice in two days!

"You mean you didn't talk to him?"

"I was gone all day," I admitted. Then I asked, "Does Lissa know Jon called?"

"How should *I* know?" She sounded vague. "You know how these boy-girl things are."

I wanted a straight answer. "Did Jon hang out with Lissa or not?"

"Why don't you find out straight from the horse's mouth?"

"Why should I call him when *you* were there?"

"Oh, Merry, you're being a stubborn mule."

"Thanks a lot."

Neither of us spoke for a moment. Then she said, "You said you were gone. Does that mean you were with Levi?"

I couldn't tell her about my long day at the Zook farm. To tell an outsider about the way I'd interacted with my Amish friends would take away some of the specialness.

Instead, I shared the news about Aunt Teri's babies, which instantly got her off the Levi subject.

"Aw, you're kidding, you have twin cousins?"

"Uh-huh, and I think my aunt and uncle are coming up next month. Maybe you can see the babies then."

"What did they name them?"

"Benjamin and Rebekah."

"How sweet. Benny and Becky."

I laughed. "I thought of that, too. But I'm not so sure my aunt's gonna want nicknames just yet."

"Why not?" She was actually in a great mood now, and I was relieved.

"Oh, you know how new mothers are," I said. "They want their offspring to start out with good, solid names. That's why my parents named me Merry, for one thing. They never dreamed I'd get pegged with a nickname."

She laughed. "And so you get Mer all the time."

"Yeah." I thought of my twin sister. "And Faith got Faithie."

"I remember," she said softly.

After we said good-bye, I set the table and warmed up the casserole dish Mom had made early this morning. Skip didn't have much to say other than that Jon had called. Old news.

Dad looked worn out from a hectic day in the emergency room. As soon as we finished with supper, I heard him shuffle down the hall to his study—probably to call Mom.

I didn't feel like a fight, so I didn't bother asking Skip for help cleaning up the kitchen. The minute things were spotless, I hurried upstairs to the attic.

I had told Mom it didn't matter which baby clothes she took along for baby Rebekah. And I truly felt then that it didn't matter. But after my conversation with Mom this morning—and the indifferent way she had treated me, getting me up early and forcing me to listen to her instructions while I was half asleep—I wanted to know whether she'd taken Faithie's clothes or mine.

I groped around for the attic light switch, encouraging Lily White to curl up somewhere. Wanting to be near me always, my little "shadow" had followed me up the steep steps.

Quickly, I located the boxes marked baby clothes. Several sat open and empty on the floor. My heart pounded as I opened first one, and then the other, of the remaining boxes. I knew it was probably ridiculous to feel this way, but I had decided while cleaning up the kitchen that if Mom had given Faithie's baby things away, it was a good sign. A sign that she was beginning to deal with her loss. A sign that I was as dear to her as the memory of her other daughter.

Lily White couldn't stay away from the action and rubbed her head against my arm. Her softness comforted me as I knelt on the thick carpet and peered into the first box. I braced myself for the worst.

Twenty-one *Catch a Falling Star*

Mom had always dressed me in baby blues and soft yellows. Faithie had worn greens and pinks.

Tears stung my eyes as I picked frilly *blue* dresses and lacy *yellow* playsuits out of the box. I held my tiny outfits near my heart, sobbing.

Lily White sensed my emotion and jumped into my lap, purring away like a mini-motor. In the quiet of the somewhat musty attic room, I laughed and cried for joy.

⁂

On Tuesday, Chelsea and I presented our family history reports to the class. She held up my family crest while I pointed to the lion, representing my courageous ancestry. When I told about Levi Lapp and Mary Smith, I noticed Jon Klein lean forward, paying close attention. Had he caught the similarity of names?

Chelsea was next. I held up her family tree while she went through her generations on both sides. No one even cracked a smile when she told about her great-aunt Essie Peterson, the faith healer. I knew all along it would be just fine.

After class, I was gathering up my books when Jon came over to my desk. "We missed you at the picnic Saturday," he said.

Who was *we*?

"Sounds like it was great." I hadn't thought I'd missed anything by not going. But maybe I had, and by the way Jon was grinning from ear to ear, it looked as though he was mighty glad we were having this talk.

Only a few kids were left in the room, including Chelsea. When she saw us together, she exited quickly. And there was Lissa, but she was busy talking to the teacher.

"Did your brother tell you I called?" Jon asked.

"Uh-huh." I was dying to ask why he'd called but didn't.

"I haven't seen you around much," he said.

I picked up my books. "You know how it is with big projects this time of year."

He looked concerned. As if there was something else on his mind. As if he didn't believe what I'd just said.

Then Lissa came over. "Hi, Merry. Long time no see." Like that was *my* problem. She handed Jon some papers. "Well, see you two," she said and left.

What is going on?

"Well, the bus'll be here any minute," I said. "I'd better get going."

Jon followed me to my locker. "Say that with all *b*'s," he said.

I grinned a bit too broadly and reached for my combination lock. Jon leaned over, looking at me comically. "So . . . does this smile say something?"

Opening my locker, I said, "Say that with all *s*'s!"

"I just did!"

The guy was good. I'd forgotten how good.

"Wait right here, Merry." He rushed off to his locker, threw his books inside, and slammed the door. What was on his mind? And where was Lissa?

"We have to talk," he said, following me out to the bus.

"What's up?" I thought this might be about Lissa. Maybe he needed some womanly advice.

On the bus, once the noise rose to a dull roar, he turned to look at me. "Merry, I hope you won't take this wrong, but some of us were talking, and . . ." He paused as though he wasn't sure what to say.

"About what?"

He took a deep breath. "It's only my opinion, but I think you're missing out on a lot."

I was confused. "What are you saying?"

He looked miserable. Absolutely miserable. As though he wished he hadn't started this. "Hanging out with that Amish guy keeps you from—"

"Excuse me?" I shouted.

Jon waved his hands. "No, no! Relax, don't get on Chelsea's case. Please! She's just concerned. All of us are."

I felt my face scrunching up. "Look, I don't interfere in *your* life. What right do you have—"

"Don't be ticked, Merry. It's only a friendly suggestion." He actually looked sincere. He sighed. "None of us think you belong with the Amish."

I turned around to look for a vacant seat toward the back. Anywhere on earth would be better than sitting next to Jon. Anywhere!

Spotting Lissa, I motioned for her to trade seats with me. "Thanks for nothing," I said to Jon. Then, sliding out of my seat, I made my way back to where Lissa had been sitting next to Chelsea.

She was wearing a mischievous grin. "*Someone* had to bring you back to your senses," Chelsea said, her green eyes flashing. "I knew Jon was the best choice."

"Well, it didn't work."

A question mark in the shape of a frown slid between her eyes. "What are you thinking, Mer?"

I refused to respond.

"Okay, go ahead and be Amish," she taunted. "Have a nice life, but don't say I didn't warn you."

The bus took an eternity to get to SummerHill, but when it stopped at the willow grove, I leaped out of my seat and dashed down the aisle.

Outside, I stood in the road, watching the bus chug up the hill. "Good riddance," I said, as much to the sputtering, coughing school bus as to my former friends. Maybe now I knew firsthand, on a small scale, what it was like to be shunned. Why were they acting this way?

I began running up the hill to my house, but something was changing in me. I was beginning to feel tall now. Tall and proud. Jon couldn't hurt me like this. I wouldn't let him. I'd . . .

It was then that I knew I didn't need to run. I could do anything I wanted to. Jon Klein or not. My life didn't revolve around the Alliteration Wizard!

Several days passed before I saw Levi again. He was hitching Apple up to the family buggy in front of the house when I walked down their lane.

"Hi, Merry." He tipped his straw hat, keeping it high off his head for a moment.

I stared at his hair. Short!

"You got a haircut?" I said.

He removed his hat completely, proudly displaying his cropped hair. "Do ya like it?"

"It's . . . it's not very Amish," I said.

"You're not sore about it, are ya, Merry?"

"Just surprised." I couldn't get over how modern he looked. Except for his white shirt, black trousers, and the tan suspenders he always wore.

He finished hitching up the horse, and before his mother and little Susie came down the steps, he put his hat back on. "Let's take a walk, jah?"

"Okay." I had a feeling it was close to being the right time to give him my answer. A long-awaited one.

We walked through the side yard and back around to the barn, then up the earthen ramp to the second level and the hayloft.

I grinned as Levi opened the double doors. He knew I loved this place. Some kids grow up playing make-believe in tree houses. We'd grown up in the Zooks' old barn. Fortunately, the new one was exactly like it.

My heart did a dance as we entered the secret world. Levi reached for the long rope and jumped on, swinging out and over the wide opening below us where the livestock were fed and stabled and where the cows were milked twice a day.

I leaned back against a bale of hay, breathing in its sweet aroma, watching him swing back and forth. This was heaven on earth!

"You want to be my girl, jah?" he said as he flew back toward the haymow on the rope. Levi's eyes caught mine, and I was thankful he'd chosen to communicate this way. Discussing your summer while swinging on a rope probably made it easier for him, too.

There was only one word I knew Levi longed to hear. And I said it with confidence, with the best Pennsylvania Dutch accent I could muster. "Jah."

Levi leaped off the rope and hurried over to me. He held out his hand. It felt warm from the rope.

We ran down the ramp, around the barn, and through the meadow. Together.

On June 3, my brainy brother graduated from high school. Nikki Klein joined us for the celebration. As much as I want to get away from Jon, if things keep going the way they are with my brother and Jon's sister, maybe he and I'll end up closer than I'd like! Yee-ikes!

But . . . college often changes things. At least, that's what Mom said when we talked the other day. "You won't be losing your brother to another girl. At least not for a long time."

That's when she told me Skip had decided to walk in Dad's footsteps and become a medical doctor.

As for Jon, I couldn't stop thinking about how he'd stuck his neck out and talked straight to me on the bus. For a quiet guy, it probably took a lot of courage. And being a Hanson, I could definitely relate to that.

Chelsea stopped freaking out about Levi soon after school was dismissed for the summer. She told me yesterday I could do whatever I wanted, even though she thought I'd truly flipped.

Lissa still seemed starry-eyed over Jon. Thank goodness, Chelsea never told her how I'd felt about him!

Last evening, Levi and I walked around our pond without Lily White tagging along. I didn't even think of teaching *him* the Alliteration Game; we had other things to talk about. Like how hard would it be for me to become Amish. Not for the purpose of marrying Levi someday, but if I should *want* to be Amish for myself—to restore my family heritage. To "redeem" my great-great grandfather Lapp, who went to his grave a shunned man.

It was all just talk, of course. And we didn't witness any falling stars, but *this* time, I let Levi walk me up SummerHill and back to my house.

Never once did we look into each other's faces, but a billion stars above us witnessed Levi's new haircut. And my enormous grin.

It was going to be a truly special summer.

Night of the Fireflies

For
Mother and Dad,
who caught lightning bugs
in Pennsylvania
and Kansas
long before they met.
Together,
they caught souls for the Kingdom
for nearly fifty years.

God, give me work
till my life shall end
and life till my work is done.

—WINIFRED HOLTBY

Night of the Fireflies One

I was staring at Penney's display window admiring a blue-striped sundress when she came walking toward me.

"Hi, Merry!" her perky voice called.

I smothered my initial response. "Not Lissa Vyner," I muttered to myself. Usually I was super polite, but courtesy didn't come easily around Lissa. Not these days. Not since she'd stolen Jon Klein out from under my nose!

She was standing beside me now, gazing at the current summer teen fashions. I caught the light scent of her perfume. "What's up?" she said.

"Oh, nothing much." I peered into the window and wished she'd go away.

"That outfit would look so cool on you," Lissa said, and I turned to see her pointing at the striped dress. "You should try it on."

And you should go jump in a lake, I thought, feeling instantly guilty for having such lousy thoughts about the girl I'd been so close to since last November.

"You know how you adore striped things," she was saying. "Especially blue and white."

"Maybe you're right." Quickly, without looking back, I headed into the store, hoping she'd leave me alone. But when I got inside, I realized she'd followed me.

In the junior department, I found the rack of casual summer dresses and searched for my size. Lissa flipped through the rack, too, only on the opposite side. In the petites.

Glancing at her, I noticed Lissa had filled out a bit—in all the right places. Her cheeks had a rosy glow to them, and her blue eyes sparkled when she smiled. In many ways, Lissa looked healthier and happier than ever.

I sighed, thinking about the part I'd played in helping to end her abusive home situation. Her father was still attending group therapy for his drinking problem, but the abuse had stopped. Thank goodness.

Lissa caught me staring at her. I glanced away, avoiding her gaze. *No wonder Jon likes her,* I thought. *She's tiny . . . and pretty. Prettier than most girls I know.*

"Merry?" She circled the clothes rack to stand beside me. "I really get the feeling something's wrong between us," she said softly, almost sadly.

I knew it would complicate things to let her know about my past friendship with Jon. And about our secret word game. "Everything's fine," I said, forcing a smile.

"You say that, Mer, but it seems to me you've been upset for a long time—since before school let out last month." She paused, fingering the price tag on one of the outfits.

"Don't worry, Liss." I held up the blue-striped dress. "I think you're right, this *is* definitely me." And I flounced off to the dressing rooms to try it on.

When I went to pay for the outfit, Lissa was gone. Part of me was relieved. Even though Lissa and I were friends, she'd become a force to be reckoned with. And I was partly to blame for the conflict between us.

I'd stuck my neck out to help her escape her father's abuse, and invited her to our church youth group. To make her feel more con- nected to the group, I'd introduced her to my friends—Jon Klein included. Losing *him* was my reward for being a good friend!

I waited in the cashier line while shoppers snatched up bargains around me. Typical for a Fourth-of-July weekend madness sale. To make matters worse, only one register was working. The other wore a handwritten sign that read *Out of Order.*

I stared at the sign and thought back to last night and the way my mom had laid into me at supper. *She* was out of order mentioning Levi Zook the way she had. Weeks ago, the next-to-oldest son of our Amish neighbors had asked me out, and against all my friends' wishes—at church and at school—I had accepted. No one seemed to understand why I'd want to hang out with an Amish boy. But they'd never met Levi. Not only was he drop-dead cute, he was responsible and solid. And a true gentleman.

But Mom didn't seem to care about any of that. "Honestly, Merry," she'd said, "you talk about the Amish as though they're somehow better. Dressing plainly and driving buggies doesn't make people closer to God." There was a twinge of resentment in her voice.

I frowned, thinking back to the stressful kitchen scene. Dad had kept stirring his coffee—I knew by his movements that he was upset about the conflict, but he didn't interfere. He also didn't join Mom in commenting about me not using my head. That was Dad. Always cool and mostly collected when it came to his daughter. Not that he was partial to me, but I had a feeling that Dad was thinking ahead to next fall when I'd be the only kid left in the house. Skip, my older brother, was headed for college. And Faithie, my twin, had died of leukemia when she was seven.

I wanted to spout off—to tell Mom that just because she didn't understand my Amish friends didn't mean she should talk about them that way. After all, they were peace-loving, hardworking, obedient people. So what if they wanted to do without fancy clothes, cars, and electricity. Personally, I admired their lifestyle.

But I kept my mouth shut and stirred my iced tea. Like my dad, I believed that a soft answer—or none at all—dispelled anger. Especially in this case. It was plain to see that Mom was wound up, so there was no dealing with anything now.

The more I thought about Mom's remarks, the more it seemed right for her to apologize. She was being totally unreasonable about Levi—thought I was spending too much time with a backward Amish farm boy, as she put it. Thought his philosophy of life was beginning to rub off on me.

What it added up to was this: My personal choices didn't count. And worse, she'd implied that my judgment couldn't be trusted.

The woman's voice at the cash register brought me out of my daze, and I stepped up to the counter to pay for my new clothes. That's when I realized I was starving. Stress always made me hungry.

After I put away my change, I made a beeline to the nearest fast-food place. It wasn't far—just down the escalator to the first floor and around the corner. But there was such a crowd of shoppers that it took me longer than usual, and by the time I arrived, another long line awaited me.

Undaunted, I slipped into the back of the line behind some tall guy. Standing on tiptoes, I tried to see around him to read the menu. But my shopping bag must've bumped him, because suddenly I found myself staring up—into the face of Jon Klein!

"Mistress Merry," Jon said, smiling. "What a nice surprise."

I met his gaze with enthusiasm. "Imagine meeting you here."

"Well, what's with . . ." He paused, probably trying to think of another word starting with *w*.

"What's wrong?" I smiled. It had been ages since the Alliteration Wizard and I had played our word game.

His brown eyes sparkled. "Guess I'm a little rusty."

I wanted to shout "Hallelujah," but succeeded in controlling myself. So . . . he *hadn't* introduced Lissa to our special game. This was truly amazing!

"It's been a while for me, too," I said, referring to being out of practice. Now he would know I'd been loyal. Hadn't played the Alliteration Game with Levi Zook, or anyone.

Jon caught the message. I could see the recognition in his eyes.

"I hope you're going on the river hike next weekend," he said.

"I can't. My aunt and uncle are coming. They're bringing their newborn twins."

"Twins? Really?" He seemed surprised, and then I realized how very long it had been since we'd talked. I realized something else, too. Lissa had not been conveying anything about me to Jon.

Quickly, I filled him in on my life, leaving out certain private things such as the chunks of time I was spending with my Amish neighbors. Especially Levi and his sister Rachel.

"So how long will your relatives be in Lancaster?" he asked as the line moved.

"Just next weekend, I think."

"We should get together and practice our word game sometime." His smile sent my heart sailing, and I waited for him to say that he and Lissa had called it quits. But he didn't.

The girl behind the counter said, "May I take your order, please?"

Jon stared up at the menu board. "I'll have your Number Three Super Special and a large lemonade." Then he turned to me and asked, "Can I buy you lunch?"

"No, but thanks anyway," I said. It was probably a very wise choice on my part, because just then Lissa came breezing past the line.

"Hi again," she said, spotting me.

"Oh, hi," I managed to say.

Jon turned around, obviously happy to see her. "What're you hungry for, Liss?"

"How 'bout a Number Three Super Special and a large lemonade."

I stifled a sigh. Maybe they had more in common than I thought.

Jon was still smiling, only now at me. "Sure you won't join us for lunch?"

"No, really," I replied, my heart sinking fast. "I have tons more shopping to do. I'll eat as I go."

Jon nodded. "Say that with all *g*'s."

Lissa frowned. "What's that mean—say it with all *g*'s?" She looked first at me, then at Jon.

I excused myself and got out of there fast. Worried, I could only imagine the explanation Jon must've conjured up to cover his tracks.

Almost instantly, I changed my mind about shopping. And eating. I took out my cell phone, stomach still growling, and called home.

"But, Merry," Mom argued, "it's only been a little over an hour since I dropped you off. I thought you wanted to—"

"Please come get me." I had to avoid running into Jon and Lissa again.

"Is everything okay?" she asked.

"I'm fine." I wished she wouldn't interrogate me like this. "Just come, okay?"

"I'll drop everything." She sounded upset, as if I'd ruined her plans. "I'll meet you at the bus stop in front of Penney's, but it'll take me about twenty minutes."

"I know, Mom." She didn't have to remind me that we lived miles from civilization. On SummerHill Lane—a dirt road smack-dab in the middle of Pennsylvania Amish country.

Hanging up the phone, I glanced outside. I had time to grab a bite. But where? All the fast-food places were *inside* the mall.

I left through the heavy glass doors and took off walking, enjoying the hot July air. It was the clearest, brightest day of the summer so far. A great day to be outdoors. I thought of Lissa and Jon cooped up inside the mall having lunch. And I thought of Levi, probably working outside in his potato field. He would've already eaten lunch—a man-sized dinner, with fried ham, mashed potatoes and gravy, and a fat slice of his mother's strawberry pie.

Levi . . .

What fun the past month had been. Far different from any June in my entire life, but fun. Levi had actually shown me how to cultivate, letting me hold the reins for two mules at once. And there'd been evening hours spent swinging on the rope in the hayloft or hanging out with Rachel, talking in soft voices until she and I fell back into the hay, giggling. Levi didn't seem impressed with those moments of hilarity, but he put up with them. And why not? I was his girl, after all.

Levi and I were rarely ever alone, which was just as well, since I was worried his parents might think I was a bad influence.

One night Levi had hitched Apple, the family's beautiful Belgian horse, to their hay wagon. Levi's ten-year-old brother, Aaron, stayed up front with him, chewing on pieces of straw while I sat back in the hay with all four of his sisters. Rachel, almost sixteen, whispered secrets to me about one of the Yoder boys down SummerHill. Nancy, twelve, and Ella Mae, just turned nine, taught me how to sing "Amazing Grace" in German. And six-year-old Susie, the youngest Zook, showed me how to catch fireflies without smashing them.

We were like one big happy family. Distant cousins, really, because my great-great grandfather also had been Amish.

I pressed the red pedestrian button at the busy intersection and waited for the light to change. Across the street and halfway down the block, I could see an Amish road stand. There'd be carrots, strawberries, ripe melons, and much more. My mouth didn't exactly water at the prospect of raw vegetables, but a handful of red-ripe strawberries might stop the grumbling in my stomach.

One by one, tourists drove by slowly, most of them gawking. Some had cameras poking out of their car windows. Others milled around, chatting with the girls running the stand.

When I arrived, I noticed a group of people hovering over a child lying in the grass behind the stand. I hurried to investigate.

That's when I spotted Rachel Zook. She was holding something up to the little girl's forehead. I moved in closer, trying to see over the group wearing white prayer caps and long black aprons atop even longer dresses. Then I caught a glimpse of the petite girl. Susie Zook!

I rushed to Rachel's side. "What happened?"

Rachel looked surprised to see me. "Hello, Merry." She didn't answer my question, and there was a noticeable edge to her voice. Was she upset at me?

I brushed the thought aside. "Did Susie fall?" I persisted, kneeling beside Rachel's sister.

Rachel threw up her hands. "*Ach, Der Herr sie gedankt*—thank the Lord she wasn't killed! Susie was climbing that tree"—she pointed to a huge elm—"and, ach, if she didn't up and fall out!"

"Knocked me silly," Susie said, her voice trembling as she sat up.

Rachel nodded. "And now she's all *stroovlich*."

I could see what she meant. Susie's blond braids had come loose, and her long rose-colored dress was ripped at the seam.

"Poor thing," I whispered. "Can I help?"

Sad faced, Susie removed the ice to show me her bump. "It's a goose egg, *jah*?" she said.

It was big all right. "Does it hurt?" I asked.

She nodded, tears welling up.

I leaned closer, inspecting her latest battle scar. "Better put the ice back on," I said to Rachel.

Susie reached her hand up to me. "*Ich will mit dir Hehm geh,*" she said.

I held her hand in both of mine. "What's she saying?"

Rachel looked worried but avoided my eyes at first. "She wants to go home with you."

The Amish girl to my left leaned over and whispered, "I think she's conked out of her head."

A concussion? I hoped not.

Then I remembered my mom was on her way to meet me. Might even be waiting in front of Penney's by now. "I could take Susie home," I offered, "if there was some way to get her over to the mall." I explained to Rachel that my mother was coming for me.

Rachel eyed the horse and buggy parked off the street. "Too bad you can't take our buggy."

I shook my head. "I'm not taking that through traffic." Truth was, I'd never taken a horse and buggy anywhere. Sure, I'd ridden in one, but that was much different from actually driving one.

"I can take her," said a familiar voice.

I turned around and there was Levi—eager to help, as always. Rachel explained about Susie's fall and that she should be taken home, out of the heat. "It'll be much quicker if she goes with Merry's mother," Rachel said.

"Jah, good idea." Levi leaned down and gathered his little sister into his arms. With long, careful strides he carried her to the family buggy and gently laid her in the backseat.

Rachel and I followed close behind without talking. The silence between us was deafening.

I spotted Apple and the Zooks' market wagon piled up with fresh produce Levi had brought to replenish the road stand. It struck me as curious that Old Order Amish were allowed to ride in a car but couldn't own or drive one themselves.

"Come along, Merry," Levi said, putting on his wide-brimmed straw hat. "You can show me where to meet your mother." He glanced at the market wagon and at Rachel, who promptly left without saying good-bye, scurrying back to help at the road stand. Levi called to her, "I'll come and unload the wagon after a bit."

She nodded to him, avoiding my wave. It bugged me, this obvious problem between us. But what was it?

Night of the Fireflies Three

I got into the buggy on the street side, then scooted across to the left, where Amishwomen always sat. Levi got in, picked up the reins, and deftly drove Susie and me through the heavy weekend traffic. It seemed strange riding on a modern highway in the Zook carriage. We were somewhat enclosed inside the gray, boxlike buggy, and it helped take away some of the uneasy feeling.

After one long red light, we arrived safely at the main entrance to the mall. And there we sat in front of Penney's, waiting for my mom to show up.

I tried desperately not to think about Mom's initial reaction to my being here in the Zooks' buggy. Knowing her, she'd be silently freaking out about it all the way home. Little Susie's presence would keep the conversation at a low ebb . . . until we got home.

Levi turned to glance at Susie, resting in the backseat. "How are ya doin' there, sister?"

She groaned. "I'll be better when I get to Merry's house."

He glanced at me. "Why's she wanna go home with you?"

I whispered, "I think the fall might've made her kind of confused."

"Oh," Levi said, nodding. "Susie's real spunky—she's always getting herself into scrapes."

I remembered hearing about several of those incidents. "What else?"

Levi let the reins drop over his knees. "Well, once she fell off the hay wagon, and we nearly ran her over."

A tiny giggle escaped from the backseat. I turned around. "Did *you* do that, Susie?"

Her eyes looked brighter now. "Tell about the time when that *alte Kuh* kicked over the milk bucket and stepped on my foot," she said.

"That wasn't funny, Susie," he said. "Ol' Bossy nearly broke your toe!"

Susie discarded the ice bag, letting it drop onto the floor of the buggy. "My head's near froze," she said.

The bump was still protruding. "Better keep the ice handy," I suggested, feeling a bit motherly toward her. "When your head warms up, you should put the ice back on. It'll make the swelling go down."

She nodded, then sat up slowly. "I still wanna go to your house."

"What's so special about my house?" I asked.

"I wanna see your twin. Faithie—the little girl you told me about."

"Oh, you want to see *pictures* of Faithie?"

She smiled, pushing long, loose strands of hair away from her face. "Jah." I spied a deep dimple in her left cheek.

I studied Levi then. "Will your mother mind if she comes?"

He shook his head. "I'll head on home and tell her after I unload the market wagon. It'll be about an hour and a half."

Mom pulled into the parking lot just then. Susie waved to her from the back of the buggy. As I'd predicted, Mom looked startled. Quickly, she composed herself and turned the car into the first available spot.

She was getting out of the car when I noticed Jon Klein—with Lissa—coming out of the mall entrance. They were headed right for us!

I grabbed my shopping bag and hopped out of the buggy, turning my back to them. Maybe, just maybe, they wouldn't see me.

Levi reached into the backseat, lifting Susie out of the buggy. Her bare feet dangled out from under her long dress. She was holding the ice bag on her head again.

That's when Mom came over.

Please, Lord, don't let her say anything, I prayed silently. And before she could speak, Levi started explaining things.

"Wouldja mind taking Susie home?" he asked. "She needs to lie down . . . get out of this heat."

"Certainly," Mom said, reaching for the little girl's hand. "Come along, honey." No one had to explain that travel by horse and buggy took much longer than by car. Besides, anyone could see by the size of Susie's bump that she would feel better at home.

I stayed for a moment to thank Levi. That's when I realized Jon and Lissa were standing on the opposite side of the buggy and witnessing the exchange between us.

"Merry?" Lissa said, looking completely aghast. "What's going on?"

Jon looked equally surprised but wasn't asking questions. Not now, at least. He had been quite verbal in the past, asking lots of questions about my interest in the Amish—even wondering why I wanted to spend so much time at the Zooks'. But that had been before school let out for the summer.

I had no choice but to entertain a round of introductions. So while Mom was getting Susie settled in the car, I introduced the Alliteration Wizard to the Amish farm boy. The moment would probably go down in history as the most awkward one of my life.

Both boys handled themselves well—Jon reaching out politely for Levi's hand, and Levi accepting the handshake with genuine courtesy. It was Lissa who seemed the most bothered by the encounter. I knew by the way her eyebrows knit together, she was completely bewildered.

Glancing over at our car, I wished now that Mom had come back to make small talk. But she seemed to be waiting for me patiently in the driver's seat. "Guess Mom's ready to go," I said, noting Lissa's eyes growing wide as she surveyed the Amish buggy. I didn't know why she was making such a big deal about this. After all, she'd seen Amish buggies before. Lots of times.

"I'll see ya soon, Merry," said Levi, wearing an enormous grin. "After supper, maybe?"

"Okay" was all I said.

It was next to impossible to ignore the curious look on Jon's face as he began to piece the puzzle together. It was all I could do to keep from blurting out, "Say it with all p's!" before I turned to go.

On the drive home, I showed Mom the outfit I'd purchased.

"Cute," she said. And that was the end of that.

I could see she wasn't in the mood for discussion. Evidently, I'd interrupted something important at home by calling her back too soon to get me. Or maybe she was upset at seeing me with Levi in his family buggy. *That* was probably the reason.

I tried not to make too much of it and thought instead of the moment when Jon extended his hand to Levi. It seemed so bizarre for the two of them to meet like that. And with Lissa observing the whole situation!

Thank goodness Mom didn't pound me with questions about it. That is, not until Susie asked, "Didja know my brother is gonna get hitched up with ya, Merry?"

I wanted to melt into the dashboard.

"Then you won't just be my far-off cousin, you'll be my sister, too," she explained from the backseat.

That's when Mom cut loose with questions. She did it quite creatively, asking me leading questions in such a way as not to clue in little Miss Susie with the bump on her head. And the big mouth!

We made a pit stop at the nearest Burger King because by now I was famished. Susie insisted she wasn't hungry, and Mom decided it was wise for her to wait. "A bad fall like that can knock the appetite right out of you," she said, straight-faced.

I laughed a little. "Sounds like some wise old saying."

She didn't seem to find the humor in my remark. Then I knew I was *really* in for it—sooner or later.

When we arrived home, I steadied Susie as we climbed the long staircase to my bedroom. She seemed to be feeling better, and when I checked her forehead, the bump looked smaller.

Mom disappeared to her sewing room without saying much. Eventually, the dam would break, and she'd spill out her concerns about Levi. Again.

In my room, I made Susie relax on my bed. "How do you feel now?" I asked, anxious to know why she'd said Levi was going "to get hitched up" with me.

She grinned that adorable smile, creating a dimple . . . reminding me of Faithie. "I'm better, *Denki*."

"Well, that's good, because I was really worried about you." I sat beside her on the edge of my bed, touching her long blond hair. Most of it had fallen out of the braids. I got up to find a brush, wondering how on earth to bring her back to the subject of her brother's comment.

Susie didn't seem too interested in having her hair put back in its usual little-girl Amish style. "Can I see the pictures now?" she asked.

"What if I fix your hair while you look at my scrapbook?"

She nodded enthusiastically. "Jah!"

I tossed a hairbrush onto the bed and went to my walk-in closet to locate the powder-blue, silver-lined scrapbook—the one that recorded the first seven years of my life with Faithie.

"This is my all-time favorite scrapbook," I said, handing it to her carefully.

She scooted up against the bed pillows and peered at the first page. "Ach, you two are so little here." She stared at the first baby portrait. "Faithie looks smaller than you," she said, her blue eyes filled with curiosity.

I nodded, continuing to braid Susie's near waist–length hair. "Faithie was always small-boned. Everyone said she was tiny for her age. I never thought of her that way, though. Not until after she died."

Slowly, Susie turned to the next page, making endearing comments about the baby twins—my sister and me—as she tiptoed, page by page, through Faithie's short life.

I finished winding her braids around her head long before she finished with the scrapbook. Silently, I sat there, trying to forget what she'd said about Levi and me, letting her take her time gazing into my past.

Suddenly, she leaned forward. "Look, Merry, I see a dimple. Faithie had a dimple just like mine!" She smiled, searching with her pointer finger for the indentation on her own face. "Faithie and I match."

"You're right," I said, realizing there were other similarities between them. Faithie had always been delicate like Susie. And she had fit the role and temperament of the baby of the family even though she was really the *older* twin—by about twenty minutes.

There was something else, too. Faithie had always looked up to me. The way Susie seemed to today.

She closed the scrapbook. "I loved seeing this, Merry," she said softly. "We Amish don't make pictures of ourselves, ya know. But aren'tcha glad ya have these?" Glints of tears sparkled in the corner of her eyes.

"Yes, I'm *very* glad." Lovingly, I held Susie as she cried soft, sad tears for my sister.

After a long, tender moment, the girl sat up and wiped her eyes. "*Dat* and *Mam* don't ever cry out loud for dead folk," she said.

I understood something about what she was saying. The Amish believed that God allowed people to live just until their work on earth was done. Death was accepted as simply an aspect of life. The patchwork quilt of Amish life consisted of birth, maturity, baptism, marriage, children—lots of them—and death.

"It's like the crops," Susie remarked, sounding older than her six and a half years. "We plant and water, then the weeding comes, and then the harvest. After that, the dried-up plant goes back into the soil. When someone dies, they get put back in the ground, too."

I knew that Susie's remarks were a result of her Amish training, yet I marveled at her perception of life. I must admit, I didn't agree with it, though. How could I possibly believe that Faithie's work on earth had been finished? She was only seven when she died, for pete's sake!

Carefully, I put my scrapbook away, but now Susie wanted to look at my pictures on the wall opposite my antique dresser and desk.

"You're looking at what I consider to be my best photography," I said.

She liked the scenery best. That's what she was used to seeing on calendars and wall-hangings at her house. Since the Amish didn't believe in being photographed, only farmscapes and nature were acceptable.

After she had surveyed each one of my framed pictures, I offered her something to drink.

"Jah, some milk," she said, and we went downstairs to the kitchen together. My cats—all four of them—were having their afternoon snack. Compliments of Mom, who'd made herself quite scarce.

"Do ya like Bible names?" Susie asked, watching the cats lap up the cream from the Zooks' dairy.

I wondered if she was thinking about Shadrach, Meshach, and Abednego—three of my cats. "You mean my three Hebrew felines?"

She giggled. "Ach, such funny names for cats, don'tcha think?"

I nodded, opening the strawberry-shaped cookie jar. "Want a cookie?"

"Denki," she said politely.

I took a handful of Mom's chocolate chip cookies out of the cookie jar, placed them on a small plate, and carried it to the kitchen table.

"Do you feel well enough to walk home?" I asked while pouring milk for her. "I can walk over with you if you like."

She looked up at me with her milky white mustache. "Oh, will ya?" she pleaded as though it meant the world to her. "And can we take the shortcut—through the willows?"

I chuckled. "Okay."

"Then will ya come tonight after supper?" Her cheery, round dollface burst into a wide grin. Leaning close, she whispered, "We can catch lightning bugs."

"Only if you feel up to it," I said, inspecting her forehead. "How's your bump now?"

"Much better." She blinked her saucer eyes.

I felt surprisingly warm and comfortable playing this big-sisterly role to Susie Zook, the youngest of our Amish neighbors.

After supper, I started cleaning up the kitchen, coaxing my brother to help. Having Skip around was a surefire safeguard. For one thing, I was pretty sure Mom wouldn't launch off on something about Levi and me with Skip hanging around. Besides, even if she did, Skip would probably turn the conversation away from Levi to someone else. Like maybe *his* current romantic interest, none other than Jon Klein's older sister Nikki.

Since Dad was working late at the hospital, I couldn't count on him as my ally. It was interesting the way Dad viewed this thing with Levi and me. I remembered the first time I'd asked Mom and Dad about going out with Levi Zook. A really weird, blank expression landed on Dad's face, and I thought for sure all hope was gone. Mom too. Only *her* facial statement remained the same. Later, after Dad discussed the subject in such a lighthearted, casual manner, Mom started to come around. Just a little. I can't actually say she'd given

me the green light, but after I assured her I had no plans to turn
Amish, she seemed to relax.

It was true about my not turning Amish. Even though I'd toyed
with the idea, spending days on end over at the Zooks' place and
"trying on" their beliefs and customs, I really had no idea how being
Plain could possibly fit into *my* life. Especially now, during the beastly
hot dog days of July. Those heavy, long Amish dresses and aprons
would wipe me out!

Give me good old shorts and T-shirts and striped sundresses, I
thought as I rinsed the plates and silverware and Skip loaded the
dishwasher.

"Hey, Mer, I heard your friend Levi's got big plans for you," he
blurted out. Right in front of Mom!

This is truly horrible, I thought, glaring at him. I'd totally over-
estimated his worth.

"You're joking, right?"

"Guess again." Skip leaned over to stuff a handful of utensils
into one of the square-shaped compartments. "The word's out all
over SummerHill."

"What are you talking about?"

"I think you already know." He glanced knowingly at Mom.

"Get a grip," I snapped. "Don't you know Levi's been teasing
me about marrying him ever since I pulled him half dead out of
the pond?"

Skip nodded. "Say what you want, little girl, but Levi Zook's no
fool. He thinks you're gonna marry him when you grow up."

Mom inched closer. "Which means he's probably trying to convert you."

"Really?" I said sarcastically. "Isn't that funny—*I* never noticed
any of this."

"Love is blind," Mom stated.

"And the neighbors ain't!" Skip teased.

I turned off the faucet. "Who said anything about love? Levi and
I are just . . . friends." I refused to cry in front of my interrogators.

Skip harrumphed. "That's what everyone says."

"So . . . is that what you and Nikki are, too? Just friends?" It was a low blow, but Skip had it coming.

He snickered. "Wouldn't *you* like to know?"

"Save your breath." And with that, I tromped out of the kitchen.

I was thrilled to have an excuse to leave the house. Anything to get away from Skip's weird comments . . . and Mom's insinuations.

Little Susie waited barefoot on the front porch step as I came down the Zooks' long dirt lane. Her grandfather was relaxing in one of the old hickory rockers and smoking his pipe. His untrimmed beard was long and white, and chubby bare feet stuck out of his black trousers.

"Hullo-o, Merry!" called Susie, getting up and running across the well-manicured lawn. "Come look what Mam gave us to catch the lightning bugs in." She reached for my hand, and we headed back toward the old farmhouse.

I hurried to keep up with her, and when she settled down on the porch step, I noticed only a slight reddish spot on her forehead where the goose egg had been earlier.

Grandfather Zook smiled and nodded as I sat on the porch step. "*Wilkom.* How's our girl?" The way he said it made me wonder if he was in on Levi's plan to convert me. If there even was such a thing.

"Fine, thanks," I said. "And how are you?"

"Oh, fair to middlin'." He took his pipe out for a moment. "It's a fine summer's eve—a fine night for fireflies." He glanced at Susie, who picked up a small canning jar with blades of grass inside.

She peeked at the holes poked through the top. "These are so the lightning bugs can breathe," she explained in her husky little-girl voice. She handed a glass jar to me. "Are ya ready?"

"Wait now," Grandfather Zook said, as though he were expecting dusk to descend on us any minute. "They'll be comin' out by the thousands in a bit."

And he was right. A few minutes later, hundreds of fireflies began twinkling their bright, intermittent lights, sending their courting signals all the way across the field and up and down SummerHill Lane.

"Let's go!" Susie said.

"Be careful now," Grandfather said. "Don't smash 'em." We knew he was teasing.

Susie's eyes grew wide. "My brother Aaron catches 'em and pulls their tails off."

"Must be a guy thing," I said, remembering that my own father had admitted to pulling their tails off when he was a boy. He'd also stuck the tails on his fingers to make it look as if he were wearing glowing rings.

"But *we* hafta be careful not to hurt 'em," she said.

She was so precocious—carefully reminding me how to capture these twinkly bugs without smashing them. To her, it was very important not to kill her exquisite fireflies.

We spent a half hour chasing and catching, turning our canning jars into miniature lanterns. Off and on the fireflies blinked their luminescent lights, like twinkling stars.

"Look!" Susie cried, staring down at the ground. "We've got 'nough bugs to light up the path."

"Hey, I have an idea. Let's experiment with our lanterns in the willow grove. It's darker there."

"Jah!" she squealed with delight.

Off we ran through the side yard, climbing over the white picket fence. Then, carefully dodging fresh cow pies, we rushed into the pasture. Levi and Aaron waved to us as they unhitched the mules out back, taking them to the barn to feed and water and to rest from the long, hot day. Nancy and Ella Mae ran toward the house barefoot, carrying buckets of vegetables from Rachel's "charity garden."

Carrying our firefly lanterns, Susie and I kept running toward the willow grove. At last, we came to the densest, darkest spot, where the willow branches created a most secret place. A woodland alcove away from the world.

"O-o-oh, this is fun!" Susie held her jar down close to the grassy area beneath her bare feet. The soft, pulsating lights made the willow-sheltered haven seem mysterious as we stood there in the dusk.

"See how much brighter our jars look here," I said. "The darker the night, the brighter the candle."

Susie looked up at me. "Where did ya hear of that?"

I laughed. "Oh, it's something I read in English class last year."

"It's like the beginning of a poem." She brought the jar of fireflies up next to her face. "You should hear *Grossdawdy*'s poem."

"Your grandfather writes poetry?"

She nodded. "He's workin' on it every night after supper—till his poem is all done."

This was a surprise. I'd heard that some Amish thought displays of individuality led to high-mindedness and pride. As far as I was concerned, Grandfather Zook didn't have a prideful bone in his seventy-year-old body.

"Do you like your grandfather's poem?" I asked.

She raised the jar of twinkling fireflies high over her head. "Jah, it's beautiful." Her eyes were full of wonder and excitement. "It's called 'Night of the Fireflies,' " she said in a hushed voice.

"That has a poetic ring to it," I whispered. "Sounds like a truly good poem title."

"Or maybe a book, jah?" she said. "Do ya think you'd ever wanna write one?"

"Write a book?" I had never thought of such a thing.

"I like books. Lots of them." Susie looked around as though her words were secrets. "Levi does, too. Only Mam and Dat don't know."

"What do you mean, they don't know?"

"Promise not to tell?" she said. I had no idea what she was talking about.

I sat down in the soft wild grass. "Why can't we tell?"

"Levi, he's miserable," she confided, sitting down beside me. "Growing up Amish is real hard for him. Alls he's got to read is the Bible and the *Sugarcreek Budget*." The latter was a weekly newspaper published in Ohio for Amish all across America.

"What do you think he'd like to read instead?"

"Something else besides what's in the house. Maybe magazines." Susie paused, thinking. "And maybe some books from a Bible college somewheres."

This was the first I'd heard anything about Levi's interest in higher education, or Bible school. Eight grades of school were all the Amish felt necessary—higher education was considered useless. Even discouraged.

Susie stared at her bug lantern. "Rachel's mad at him for it."

I wasn't surprised. "I hope she doesn't think I'm to blame."

Susie shook her head. "It's not yer fault, Merry." She sighed. "Levi's always been *anner Satt Leit*."

I knew she meant her brother was more English, or modern, than Amish. But I wasn't convinced. "Well, he sure looks Plain to me . . . except for his new haircut."

She frowned. "Oh, that."

"Does it bother you—Levi's haircut?"

She shrugged her shoulders. "I think he wants ta go English."

I gasped. "Who told you that?"

"Levi did! He said not to tell Mam and Dat . . . and 'specially not Grossdawdy and *Grossmutter*."

"Does Rachel know?"

"She's madder'n a hornet 'bout it," she said. "And about you."

So *that's* what was bothering Rachel today in town. It hurt me that she thought I was putting Levi up to such things. "Does Rachel think I'm causing trouble?"

"Jah . . . I think so. She doesn't want Levi to go off and get hitched up with you, like he's always saying."

I was shocked. "He actually talks like that?"

She nodded. "All the time."

"In front of your parents, too?"

"Levi's a *Deihenger*—a little scoundrel."

"He's not so little, really," I said. "He's nearly seventeen now." Levi's birthday was coming up at the end of the summer, in August.

"Grossdawdy wanted him to get baptized this fall, but he won't. He's bein' stubborn."

It was unsettling hearing this news about Levi—and Rachel— from their youngest sister. But Susie had a daring streak in her, and it wouldn't surprise me if someday she started talking about leaving the Amish, too.

I remembered what Mom and Skip had said about Levi's making plans to convert me. Were they ever wrong!

Susie started counting her fireflies, first in English, then in German. And when she finished, she began to hum a familiar tune— "What a Friend We Have in Jesus."

I joined in, trying to remember the German words. When I forgot, Susie helped me on the second verse.

It was truly enchanting here, singing softly like this in the middle of the willow trees. Spending time with a little girl so much like Faithie—my long-ago twin. I leaned back in the grass listening to the sounds around us as we sang our song. It seemed as though all of nature wanted to join in on the last stanza, and one by one, tiny creatures of the night began to emerge from their hollows.

"Listen! I hear something," Susie whispered.

I stopped singing. "What?"

She put her jar down and kneeled up, cupping her hand around her ear. "Ach, there it is again!"

I peered into the darkness on all sides of us. I really didn't think there was anything to be afraid of, but I wanted Susie to know I could take care of her . . . in case there was.

"We're safe here, jah?" she asked.

"Don't worry." I glanced around the familiar area. I'd grown up playing in this thick strip of trees. The willows grew in long rows, dividing our property from the far edge of the Zooks' pasture to the west of their farmhouse. I knew every inch of this grove.

Rachel and I had spent many hours here. Faithie too. It was a splendid place to conduct secret meetings, make mystery-solving plans, and . . .

Susie jumped. "Didja hear that?"

"I hear it now."

She clung to her glass jar.

A sound, almost like a horse whinny but not quite, rippled through the stillness. It sounded close. Maybe a few yards away.

"Let's get out of here!" I grabbed her hand and we ran through the trees, pushing tendrils of long weeping willow branches away from our faces. At last, we reached the open pasture.

"Are we safe now?" Susie asked.

"Looks like it to me," I said, noticing her fireflies were gone. "Oh no, did you drop your jar?"

She looked down. "Ach, where could it be?"

"Stay here. I'll go search for it."

"No, Merry! Don't go back."

I knelt down, looking into her angel face. "Don't worry, I'll find it. Here, hold my jar—keep it safe, okay?"

She nodded, her lower lip protruding. "I'll stand right here till ya come."

I hurried back toward the willows and was out of breath by the time I found the spot where Susie and I had sat in the grass.

It was dark now, no moon to speak of. *The jar of fireflies should be easy to spot,* I thought as I searched the area.

That's when I heard the strange sound again. My ears tingled. The sound was definitely a horse, but a horse in desperate need.

I envisioned a colt caught in the thicket. Should I call for Levi's help?

Walking in the direction of the neighing, I felt truly courageous—at first. Then, as it started up again, I heard rustling behind the thick, wide trunk of a willow tree.

My throat turned to cotton. Even if I had wanted to call for help, I—

Suddenly, whatever was behind the tree began to thrash around. I was close enough to touch it!

My heart pounded in my throat.

Legs cramped, I inched backward, unsure of my next move. The thought crossed my mind that I should run for my life. I paused, trying to think rationally. What could possibly cause so much commotion?

Part of me wanted to forge ahead—find out what was lurking in the darkness. But another part of me—my legs—absolutely refused to move.

I backed away from the tree and the strange sounds. It was a cowardly act, but I'd promised to rescue Susie's lightning bugs.

In the distance, I spotted a glowing object. Off and on it flickered, a few yards from where Susie and I had whispered our secrets just minutes before.

I made my legs move toward the radiant jar.

"Stop!" a voice rang out.

I froze. "Who's there?"

The scratchy-throated voice of someone pretending to be a horse broke the stillness.

"Rachel? Is that you?"

Slowly, hesitantly, she emerged from behind the tree. Rachel's *Kapp*, her white prayer bonnet, had slipped halfway off, and her apron looked mussed. "Ach, I can't fool ya," she said, wrestling with a stray willow branch. She tossed it aside.

"Rachel, what on earth are you doing? You nearly scared the wits out of your little sister—and me." I looked to see if Susie was still standing in the side yard where I'd left her. The blinking fireflies in the jar she held for me told me she was.

Rachel's voice sounded edgy. "Guess I oughta be sorry, but . . ." Her voice trailed off.

I knew why she'd scared us. Rachel was mad.

We walked all the way down the slope to Susie's jar of fireflies, then out of the willows and through the pasture in silence.

When Rachel spoke, her voice trembled. "I should be awful ashamed, cousin Merry."

I wanted to say *you're right,* but I didn't. "Look," I snapped, "I'm not putting ideas into Levi's head, if that's what you think."

"Well, I think ya must be."

"Well, I'm not."

"Maybe ya oughta leave him be," she huffed.

Now I was mad! I stopped in front of the picket fence. "In case you didn't know it, Rachel, it wasn't my idea to be Levi's girlfriend, and if you think it was, maybe you'd better go talk to him!"

It was the first time we'd ever exchanged harsh words.

"Let him find an Amish girl," she said. It was a desperate plea.

"If that's what he wants, fine with me," I retorted. But I knew better. Levi liked me better than all the girls in his Amish crowd. He'd said so!

I glanced over my shoulder at the willows. "I know you were listening in on Susie and me before, so don't say you weren't."

"I wouldn't lie to ya." She picked up her long skirt and climbed over the fence.

Of course she wouldn't lie. After all, Rachel was Amish, through and through.

When we reached Susie, I handed over the second jar of fireflies. "You scared me," Susie told Rachel.

"I'm sorry," Rachel said, touching her sister's head. "It was foolish."

I wasn't in the mood to hang around, not the way Rachel had been acting, so I started to tell Susie good-bye.

"Please don't leave yet, Merry," she pleaded. "It's still early. Maybe Grossdawdy will read ya his poem."

Rachel brushed off her apron, then turned and headed for the back door without saying good-bye—so foreign to the way she usually treated me. Susie didn't seem to notice the friction between her big sister and me, though. She reached for my hand, leading me around to the front porch, where both Zook grandparents were sitting and chatting in their matching hickory rockers.

The two of them looked sweet relaxing there, and I began to forget about the trick Rachel had pulled in the willows.

"Grossdawdy, how's your poem comin'?" Susie asked, going up the porch steps to lean on his shoulder.

"Jah, *well* Ich *bins zufreide*," he said softly with a smile. "All right. I'm satisfied."

"Could ya read it for Merry?" she pleaded.

Grandmother Zook shook her head. "He still has a ways to go yet."

"That's okay. I can wait," I said, leaning on the railing. "Susie told me the title—it sounds beautiful."

"Jah," Grandma Zook said, nodding her head up and down as she rocked. "Wonderful-*gut* title."

"Where did you get the idea for it?" I asked.

He stroked his white beard. "From my youngest granddaughter here." He looked at Susie, grinning. "She loves them fireflies," he said. "And she's a lot like 'em, too. Shining her little light for the world to see."

"*I'm* not a lightning bug!" Susie exclaimed, then burst into a stream of giggles.

"Hush, child," Grandma said. "It's eventide. Time to reflect on the day . . . time to read the Bible some."

"And pray," Grandfather added. "Practice saying 'The Lord's Prayer.'"

Susie bowed her head and folded her hands. "'Our father, which art in heaven,'" she began, reciting the entire prayer.

When we opened our eyes, Grandfather whispered, "Now in German," with a grand twinkle in his eyes. And Susie started over again.

Afterward, the screen door opened and Levi came out. "Time for evening prayers." His face broke into a broad smile when he spotted me.

"I better say good-night," I told Susie.

She came over to me, putting her bare foot between the slats in the white porch railing. "Will ya come tomorrow?"

I smiled at her, warmed by her attention. "If you want me to."

"I do, I do!" she sang.

"Susie!" Grandmother Zook said as she got up off the rocker and headed into the house. "Come along."

Susie picked up the jars of fireflies. "Quick," she whispered. "We hafta let 'em go."

"Better not keep your family waiting," I warned, remembering her grandmother's tone of voice.

Opening the lid on her jar, Susie looked at me, expecting me to do the same. "Ready, set—now!" When I opened mine, a wispy spray of light floated out.

"Truly beautiful," I whispered.

Susie turned to go inside, and I noticed Levi still waiting at the screen door. "Merry," he called to me. "I hafta talk to ya."

I was curious about the urgency in his voice. "Something wrong?"

He shook his head. "Tomorrow night I'll pick you up in my buggy."

"I . . . I don't know if I should," I said, thinking about the things Rachel had said before. "Maybe we should talk about it."

He frowned. "Well, then, can ya meet me in the barn after last milking?"

"Okay."

So it was set. I would meet with Levi in the barn, probably the hayloft, so we could discuss getting together later—to talk about something else. This was truly bizarre!

When I arrived home, Dad was enjoying a bowl of chocolate ice cream. His Bible was open on the table. I pulled out a kitchen chair and sat down.

"How was *your* day?" he asked, looking up.

I told him about spending the day with Susie Zook. "She's real spunky, that girl," I said, explaining about her fall from the tree. "Susie's fearless—I don't think she's afraid of anything."

Dad nodded. "Maybe she knows this verse in the Old Testament." He moved the Bible closer to me.

"Which one?" I leaned over the table.

"Here—Second Chronicles, thirty-two, seven. 'Be strong and courageous. Do not be afraid or discouraged.'"

"Maybe you're right." I laughed. "But I never hear Susie quoting Bible verses. Not Rachel, either. Some Amish don't teach their children to memorize scriptures."

"But they *do* get their children outside and working, doing chores, and learning new things real young. That toughens them up." He glanced at the ceiling as though he was thinking back. "I remember when Levi was about six. Old Abe had him out plowing the field by himself."

"That young?"

Dad scooped up more ice cream. "Come to think of it, Levi was out driving a pony cart up and down SummerHill Lane around the same age."

No wonder Levi's so comfortable driving a buggy, I thought, remembering how he'd steered us through congested traffic today.

"Well, little Susie's just like him," I said. "But catching fireflies is her big interest now." I described how she and I had run around putting them in canning jars.

"I did the same thing as a kid. We'd catch them and pull their tails off. The light would keep shining for a long time afterward."

"So you've told me. I still think that's gross." I glanced around the kitchen, even leaned my chair back and peered into the dark dining room. "Where is everyone?"

"Skip's out on a date, and your mother's visiting Miss Spindler. Took a plate of cookies over to her."

"Old Hawk Eyes," I said, referring to the neighbor behind us on Strawberry Lane. "Usually by this late in the summer, she has the neighborhood news posted on every street corner."

Dad chuckled. "What would it be like, living for the sheer pleasure of gossiping?"

"It's gotta be mighty boring—I mean, it sorta tells you something about *her* life, right?"

"Can you imagine how hot her phone lines must be?" He dug into more ice cream. "Speaking of phones, Lissa Vyner called about thirty minutes ago."

I didn't have to guess why she was calling. She was probably still recuperating from seeing me with Levi today.

Reluctantly, I scooted my chair out from the table. "Mind if I use your phone?"

Glancing up, he mumbled something and nodded. I headed down the hall to Dad's private study and closed the door.

Lissa answered the phone on the first ring.

"Hi," I said. "You called?"

"Merry, have you lost your mind?" I should've known this wasn't going to be friendly.

"That's it, cut right to the chase," I muttered.

"Look, Mer, I know you're mad about something."

"What're you talking about?"

She breathed into the phone. "Well, if you won't level with me, at least maybe you can clear up something else."

Here it comes, I thought.

"I couldn't believe it when I saw you in that . . . that . . ."

"Amish buggy," I stated matter-of-factly. "Repeat after me: b-u-g-g-y."

"Merry! What's wrong with you?"

"Maybe I should ask *you* that question."

"I'm just worried," she said. "What's wrong with that?"

"You're worried because I happen to have some very nice Amish friends?"

"C'mon, you know what I'm talking about," she said.

"Oh, *do* I?"

Lissa sighed into the phone. "You're making this hard."

"Well, I'm sorry," I said, ready to cut this discussion short. "Why don't you just spell it out?"

"Okay. Why are you still hanging out with that Amish guy?"

"And why not?"

She was obviously past the boiling point. "We . . . I . . . thought it was only a crush, that you'd be over Levi Zook by now."

"Well . . . welcome to the real world!"

"What's *that* supposed to mean?" She sounded completely baffled. "You're not actually going out with him, are you?"

"Why should I change my mind now?"

"It's just that I hoped you'd get tired of being with those Amish farmers and . . . and come back—you know, to us."

"Who's us?"

"Your *real* friends."

I almost choked. "Real friends don't do this."

"Merry, you're turning the whole thing around. I called to tell you that I miss you. So does everyone else."

Jon too? I wondered.

"I got a postcard from Chelsea today," she continued. "She's in California at Disneyland."

"I know . . . so?"

"She asked how you were doing, like she was concerned."

Chelsea Davis and I had known each other since grade school. Recently, we'd gotten better acquainted when we teamed up on a social studies project at the end of the school year.

"Chelsea doesn't have to worry," I said. "And neither do you. I'm having the time of my life. And if you can't understand that, then I guess we have no reason to be talking right now."

"But, Merry—"

I hung up. Just like that—hung up the phone.

***

The next morning I slept in. Saturdays were made for sleeping late, especially when it was so warm and humid outside. Two more days before the sizzling Fourth.

Halfway between consciousness and drowsiness, while curling up with my pillow, I thought of Lissa. I'd done the wrong thing by hanging up on her, even though I felt she had it coming. Doing the right thing wasn't always easy, especially for an impulsive person like me, but the fact that I'd led Lissa to the Lord made me feel irresponsible.

The whole thing had gotten out of hand, starting with the way she'd accused me of losing my mind just because I was friends with Levi. After breakfast, I thought of calling her to apologize, but Dad was involved with some computer work in his study, and I didn't want to risk being overheard on another phone in the house.

Mom was busy baking for the Fourth of July. She had the idea that a holiday—*any* special day—was an automatic excuse to cook up a storm. And company or not, we always had oodles of food around. Even for incidental days like April Fool's Day and Mother-in-Law Day.

I hurried upstairs to my room, hoping I wouldn't be asked to divide egg whites or measure sugar for Mom's pies. The truth was,

I felt betrayed. She'd sided last night with my brother on the Levi issue, accepting what Skip had said—that Levi was out to convert me—as fact. After all, I was her daughter, her own flesh and blood. She ought to know me better than that!

I'd tried to block last night's conversation out of my mind, but her words rang in my memory: *Love is blind.*

How could Mom jump to such a conclusion? Why did she have such a hard time remembering what it was like being fifteen, nearly sixteen?

A brief, yet intensely satisfying feeling stirred through me as I reveled in my secret knowledge. Levi had no intention to convert me to Amish. But he *did* have plans . . . for himself. Now, if I could just hear them straight from Levi's lips.

I set to work organizing my room, sorting through scenic photos I'd taken last month, arranging them according to subject matter: flowers, trees, the banks of the Conestoga River, and an old covered bridge. My plan was to purchase another scrapbook with next week's allowance.

That finished, I played with my cats, forgetting about calling Lissa. Then I really lost track of time while going through my bookcase. Looking through my poetry collection, I found some great stuff to show Susie's grandfather.

After lunch, Mom asked me to take a lemon meringue pie over to Miss Spindler. I watched as she placed it carefully inside her cloth-lined pie basket. "What's the occasion?" I asked.

"It's almost the Fourth, you know. Just wanted to do something nice for Ruby Spindler."

I headed out the back door and past the white gazebo in our yard. Old Hawk Eyes was sitting on her patio thumbing through a craft magazine when I arrived.

"Well, hello there, dearie." She got up from her chaise lounge. "How's every little thing?"

"Fine, thanks." I held out the pie. "Mom made this for you."

She peeked inside the basket. "Ah . . . my very favorite." Turning back to me, she said, "Well, now, Miss Merry, you tell that mama of yours a big thank you. Ya hear?"

I nodded. "I will. And you have a nice Fourth of July."

"Well, I certainly hope to," she replied. "And you . . . you will, too, won'tcha, dear?" A curious expression crossed her wrinkled face. "But of course, the Amish don't celebrate *that* holiday, do they?"

Now I was the one with the curious look.

"Honey-girl, don't look so surprised," she went on. "Everyone round here knows 'bout you and that Zook boy. Personally, I think it's kinda sweet—if I say so myself."

"Excuse me, Miss Spindler," I said. "What is it everyone knows?"

Her mouth drooped. "Well, I'll be . . ." She paused. "You really don't know what you're getting yourself into, do you, darlin'?"

I could see this had the potential for turning into a long, drawn-out conversation, and I certainly didn't want to feed her gossip column with my personal views and opinions. It was flat-out none of her beeswax about Levi and me!

She tilted her head to one side. "Are you all right?"

"Just fine, thanks. Now, if you don't mind, I better go."

My heart pounded heavily as I ran across her backyard and down the slope to ours. I could never be sure, but I was almost positive Miss Spindler was watching my every move. I could feel her eyes boring into me. That's what the old lady was all about. That's why Skip and I, and Rachel and Levi—all of us—called her Old Hawk Eyes.

Knowing how she was, I should've dismissed her outrageous comments for what they were. Outrageous and absolutely false. But for some reason, I let her words sink into me long into the afternoon, on until it was time to meet Levi after milking.

⌒⌒⌒

"Wilkom, Merry," he said as I came into the barn.

"Hi." I spied the long rope in the hayloft. It was the same rope Levi had been swinging on when I said I'd be his girl.

"*Was ist letz?*" he asked. "What is wrong?"

I looked around to see if we were alone. "Is it safe to talk here?"

He took off his straw hat and wiped his forehead. "Dat will be comin' in soon, so best hurry."

I didn't waste any time. "I'm sorry, Levi, but I'm not going anywhere with you in your buggy tonight."

His eyebrows shot up.

"Your family's concerned . . . they don't want me to be your girlfriend."

He put his hat back on. "I hear in your voice that there's more to it, jah?"

I sighed. "Everyone's talking, Levi. People who don't even know you—and others—are saying things."

"Ach, what things?"

I moved closer to him. "That you're thinking of leaving the Amish." I studied him closely, tracing with my eyes every familiar angle of his tan face. This fantastically handsome face I'd known since I was a kid. "Is it true?"

"You will be the first to know," he said confidently, as though he'd already made up his mind. He reached for my hand. "There's so much I wanna tell ya."

Gently, I pulled my hand away, and it was a good thing, too, because just then Abe Zook came into the barn the back way, through the cow door.

"We hafta talk more," he said with serious eyes, and I knew by the tone of his voice it couldn't wait.

No matter what, I would meet Levi later tonight. With or without the buggy ride.

Eight *Night of the Fireflies*

At dusk, I took my poetry books over to Grandfather Zook. He was sitting with his wife in the front yard when I came. For more than an hour, they watched Susie and me catch fireflies. This time we filled nearly three-fourths of each jar. When we returned, we showed our bug-lanterns to Grandfather Zook.

"*Des* gut," he said, holding the jars in his calloused hands. "God has put His light in these here critters."

"Jah!" Susie said, grinning at me. "Now we hafta let 'em go."

"So soon?" I stared at the twinkling lights in my glass jar. "We just caught them."

"Maybe it's time for me to read ya my poem," Grandfather said. He grunted a bit as he got out of his lawn chair. Grandma Zook followed him up to the porch and waited along with us.

Soon, he was back carrying a pad of yellow-lined paper. "Here we are." And he sat down in his old hickory rocker.

Susie crept in closer and sat at her grandfather's feet. She pulled her knees up under her chin, her long dress and pinafore apron billowing out over her bare feet.

Grandfather peered over the top of his glasses. "Now, when I do this"—and here he pointed to us—"both of you let your fireflies go."

"Okay!" Susie cried, obviously enjoying the dramatic prospect. "We're going to act out Grossdawdy's poem." She giggled.

Her grandfather waited without speaking, and Susie settled down. Then he began to read:

"Night of the Fireflies"
by Jacob Zook

'Tis the night when martins sing,
'Tis the night for crows to caw,
And dusk comes soft on tiptoes,
In time for the firefly ball.
Come one, come all,
To the firefly ball.
Dance with 'em, laugh with 'em,
Run straight and tall.
'Tis the night when fireflies blink,
'Tis the night for stars to fall,
And dusk comes wearing red satin,
To await the firefly ball.
Come one, come all,
To the firefly ball.
Dance with 'em, laugh with 'em,
Run straight and tall.

Grandfather pointed to us and we knew it was the cue to set our fireflies free. We opened our canning jars, releasing a spray of dazzling light as he read the third verse.

'Tis the night of the fireflies,
'Tis the night of grand light,
And dusk wears honeysuckle,
To dance at the firefly ball.
Come one, come all,
To the firefly ball.

> Fly with 'em, flit with 'em,
> Run straight and tall.

He stopped reading and set his pad down in his lap. "It seems to me there oughta be one more verse." He looked a little dreamy eyed.

"Wow," I whispered. "I think it's great just the way it is!"

"I told ya," Susie said, jumping up. "Grandfather's a real poet."

I was curious. "How did you learn to write poetry?"

"Oh, every now and again I'll scribble some things down," Grandfather said. "Sometimes the words just seem to fit together." He sighed audibly.

It was getting late, and Levi would soon be coming for me. I hated to disturb the serene moment but said my good-byes to Susie and her grandfather. "Keep my poetry books as long as you like," I said before leaving.

"Denki," Grandfather said, waving. "Come again, jah?"

"I will," I promised, hurrying down the Zooks' lane to Summer-Hill. I thought of Susie and the fun we'd had. And Grandfather Zook's lovely poem. Now, what on earth was Levi going to discuss with me?

An hour later, a light splashed on my bedroom window. When I stuck my head out to investigate, I saw Levi below with a flashlight. "Can ya talk now?" he asked.

"Meet me in the gazebo," I said and hurried downstairs.

Mom and Dad were relaxing, watching TV in the family room when I headed for the kitchen for some matches.

"Where're you off to?" Mom called.

"I'll be in the backyard," I said, taking the matches along to light the citronella candles that kept the mosquitoes away. I didn't say why I was going or who I was going to meet. But Mom was smart about things—she'd probably already figured it out.

I heard Skip snicker. "Be sure and take your dumb cats with you. Maybe they'll scare your boyfriend away."

"Whatever." I closed the screen door behind me. They had no idea what they were saying. Levi was the sweetest, kindest boy I'd ever known.

He sat on the gazebo step, waiting. Shadows from the giant maples surrounding the white latticework played around him. I couldn't see him clearly at first. Then, when I was within a few feet, I caught a clear glimpse. Levi was wearing contemporary clothes!

"What on earth?" I said.

His hair had been cut and styled weeks ago, so that was nothing new, but the blue jeans and button-down short-sleeve shirt . . . well, this new look was completely unsettling. Levi Zook could've passed for any other modern kid around!

"Whaddaya think?" he asked.

I avoided his question. "What does this mean?"

"It only means that I'm trying on English ways."

My throat felt dry. Was this what he meant earlier today? Was this the way I would be the first to know?

"I hope this doesn't have anything to do with me." I didn't want to sound presumptuous.

"Don'tcha worry, Merry. I've been thinkin' about this for as long as I can remember."

"Going English—really?"

"Jah," he said, moving over to make room for me to go into the gazebo and light the bug-repellent candles. "I'm not happy farmin', and I wanna know what's in books. I'm hungry for learnin'. Do ya understand?"

I was relieved about his reasons. "You're following your heart, then, right?"

He nodded, looking at me as I motioned for him to sit on a padded lawn chair. "In another way, too." He came and pulled the chair up next to mine, then reached for my hand. I could feel the coolness of his hand against my knuckles. My heart did a little dance.

Yee-ikes! What was he going to say now?

"I know we're real young and all, Merry," he began. "But I've been waitin' a long time to ask you this."

"Wait, Levi—don't say anything! Please!" I had to stall him. There was no way I was ready to be proposed to—not two months away from turning sixteen. Sure, if I were Amish, maybe a guy might soon ask me such a question, but I'd made it clear to Levi that I was years away from that. Or so I'd thought.

"There's nothin' to worry about, Merry," he said, his voice mellow and sweet. "I would never wanna hurt you. You see, I love ya, Merry. Plain and simple. Always have."

He sounded terribly convincing, even without a full moon to enhance the setting. Sincerity and honesty were two of Levi's many good traits. And the way he looked, wearing modern clothes— dressed like my own brother or any other boy in town—made me more inclined to want to believe him.

I started to speak, but his finger gently touched my lips. "You don't have to say it back. We have lots of time ahead of us."

"Time?"

"I want some more book learning. Maybe I'll go to a Bible college somewheres. But I will *not* be a farmer."

"What will your parents say? How long can you live at home?" I worried that he was deciding things too quickly.

"Mam and Dat already know some of this," he explained.

"Rachel too?"

"Jah, Rachel . . . and my other sisters and brothers."

"You know, Rachel thinks I'm to blame for this. Can't you explain the reasons why you want to leave? It would help things between Rachel and me if you did."

"I can if she'll believe me."

"Please don't quit trying," I pleaded. "It's important for me to have her as my friend. Little Susie, too."

He smiled, his eyes twinkling in the candlelight. "Susie loves ya, Merry," he said. "She thinks you're her special playmate—her firefly friend."

I remembered the dimple in her left cheek and the similarities between her and my twin, Faithie. "I love her, too."

He leaned back against the lattice frame. "I s'pose she'll wanna read lots more books than Mam and Dat can offer. Just like her big brother."

I told him what she'd already said about wishing there were more books in the house.

"I think maybe Susie and I are cut from the same cloth." We talked awhile longer, then he pulled some keys out of his pocket. "Wanna go for a little spin?"

I gasped. "You have a car?"

"A couple of my cousins and I went together and bought a real nice one."

My heart sank. "Won't this bring more trouble for you?"

He didn't respond to my question, jingling his car keys instead. The sound brought Abednego, my fat black cat, out from under the gazebo. "Here, kitty, kitty," Levi called.

Abednego arched his back, showing instant dislike.

"Don't mind him," I said. "Abednego has an obvious disdain for most all of the human male species."

He chuckled, then changed the subject. "Shouldn't ya ask your parents' permission to go for a ride?"

I knew he'd gotten his driver's license, but I was also familiar with the way he handled a horse and buggy. "I don't call you Zap 'em Zook for nothing," I said, laughing.

He didn't seem to mind the joke. "We won't go too far up SummerHill," he coaxed.

"I better not, Levi." Then I asked, "Are you still running around with that wild bunch of boys?"

"I've sowed my wild oats, Merry. More and more I go to Bible studies at my Mennonite friends' house."

I knew some of the Amish didn't allow independent study of the Bible. They viewed the bishop as the dispenser of spiritual wisdom and truth. And certain Scriptures were used as examples over and over in the preaching services, often to the exclusion of others.

"I wanna know more. I . . ." He paused. "I wanna be a preacher, Merry, a minister of the Gospel."

Levi, a preacher? I thought. *How truly exciting!*

I wanted to hug Levi, but I only squeezed his hand. "That's wonderful," I said.

"The Bible, it's so plain about showin' the way," he said with shining eyes. "I wanna share the Good News with everyone I meet!"

I leaped up out of my chair. "Go into all the world and tell the good news. You're following the Lord's command, 'Reverend' Levi Zook!"

He chuckled. "Merry Hanson, you'll make a fine preacher's wife someday."

"That's what you think," I said, laughing.

Night of the Fireflies *Nine*

The next day was Sunday.

Lissa and Jon sat together during Sunday school and church as if they were a regular couple. It was becoming less difficult for me to see them together, maybe because they were *always* together. Still, sometimes I missed Jon—and our secret alliteration game.

During the singing, I thought about Levi and the long talk we'd had last night. He seemed determined to follow God's plan for his life.

I remembered the verse in Second Chronicles that Dad had read to me: "Be strong and courageous. Do not be afraid or discouraged."

Now that Levi had a goal in mind, he seemed stronger than ever. I liked unwavering strength in a guy. But . . . I also liked Jon Klein and the way we'd hit it off during our junior-high years together. Why did things have to be so complicated?

After church, Jon and Lissa came up to me in the parking lot. Lissa was all ears—eyes, too—when Jon asked if I was ready for the Alliteration Challenge.

I gulped, trying to hide my delight and surprise. "Are you serious?"

"When's a good time for you?" he asked.

"I'm out of practice," I told him, nearly dying of embarrassment as Lissa's eyes started to bulge. "Maybe we should wait."

"What're you talking about?" Lissa demanded.

He still hadn't told her!

"It's, uh . . ." Jon glanced at me, his eyes begging for assistance.

"It's just a thing," I blurted.

Lissa's eyes widened. "A thing? Like *what* thing?"

I had no intention of filling her in on Jon's and my private word game. But it was Jon's problem now—he'd gotten it started. I stared at him, hoping he'd take my lead and say something amazing to appease his girlfriend.

He tried to explain. "You know how some friends have inside jokes?" He sounded terribly patronizing. "Well"—and here he glanced at me with the most endearing look—"Merry and I have an inside game, I guess you could call it."

"Merry and you?" she echoed.

Jon nodded. "It's just something we—Merry and I—do."

I could see this vague explanation wasn't going to suit Lissa at all. She whirled around and stormed across the parking lot, not looking back.

"Uh, maybe that wasn't the best approach," I said, slightly concerned. "She's obviously upset."

The corner of his mouth wrinkled up, and I suspected that he'd set this up on purpose. "Lissa doesn't understand that people can have more than one good friend at a time," he said.

I noted that he'd almost said *girlfriend!*

"Well, I hope she gets over it," I said.

"Say that with all *e*'s!" he teased.

"Okay, I will." I paused to think, feeling lousy about Lissa leaving like that. Seconds passed, then it came to me. "Eventually, endurance evolves to an end."

Jon wore a quizzical expression. "Huh?"

"I told you I was out of practice!"

"That wasn't so bad, really." He flashed his wonderful smile. "Just didn't make any sense."

"I'm sorry about what happened just now with Lissa."

He shrugged as though it wasn't something to worry about. "She gets overpossessive sometimes."

I struggled with mixed emotions. It was exciting being with Jon again—like old times. The passion for words was still strong between us. But Lissa was also my friend, and I'd played a big role in making her very upset.

⸻

After dinner, Lissa called. "Why were you flirting with Jon like that?" She sounded more accusing than interested in a genuine answer.

"Well, I don't know what to tell you," I said, making an attempt at courtesy. "I didn't think I was flirting."

"C'mon, Merry, you were!"

I sighed. "Well, I guess if you say so, then I was."

"So . . . you're admitting it?"

"Isn't that what you want to hear?" Frustration was a way of life with this girl!

She exhaled into the phone. "What I want is for you to stay away from Jon. He's my guy, and that's the way it's gonna stay."

"Well, I understand how you feel, Lissa. I'm really sorry you misunderstood. And I'm sorry about hanging up on you yesterday. Honest." I must've sounded a tad too sweet, even though I meant to be sincere.

Anyway, my words obviously backfired on me—now it was *her* turn to hang up on *me*. Except Lissa didn't simply hang up. She slammed down the phone.

What was going on? Was Lissa really and truly afraid of losing Jon? And if so, why?

Ten *Night of the Fireflies*

The Sunday evening service was canceled so people could spend time with their families since it was the night before the Fourth.

Dad knew he would probably be busy in the ER tomorrow. More accidents happened on a big holiday than at any other time, he often said. Kids mishandling firecrackers, people drinking and driving. He'd be working all day tomorrow. That's how it was when your dad was the head honcho—the best—on a city hospital trauma team.

Dad was stretched out on his chaise lounge in the shade of the gazebo. He was taking it real easy this afternoon. Two bluebirds and three sparrows sparred over who got dibs on the birdbath in our side yard.

Things were quiet. Peaceful. Skip was out on a date with Nikki Klein, playing badminton at her house. Made me wonder if Lissa and Jon were making it a foursome. I tried not to think about them, though. Lissa's response to my apology was troubling. I wondered how I could patch things up with her.

Mom was taking her usual Sunday afternoon walk. She liked to walk briskly several times a week. Did it like clockwork—especially on Sundays after dinner. The steep jaunt up Strawberry Lane, the road behind our house, was a workout for anyone, fit or not.

"It's good for her," Dad said, reaching for his iced tea. "Gets her heart rate up."

"What about you, Dad?" I sipped on a tall glass of lemonade. "Shouldn't you be exercising, too?"

He agreed with me. "Guess I'm getting old and worn out, though. Sometimes it's easier to take a nap, especially on a hot afternoon."

I poked him playfully. "Oh, Daddy, you're not *that* old."

"The big five-o is coming up fast," he said, looking serious. Too serious.

"Oh, so what. Fifty's just another number." I hoped that would cheer him up. Lately, it seemed every time he mentioned his age, a cautious look crossed his face. It made me feel uneasy.

Later, we talked about Amish doctrine and how it was different from our beliefs. When Dad was close to dozing off, I mentioned Levi's interest in becoming a preacher.

His eyes popped open. "Levi Zook?"

"Yep."

"Well, if that doesn't take the cake!"

"Will it be tough for him—leaving the Amish eventually?"

"Not nearly as hard as if he'd gone along with baptism and then left. This way, he'll always have the fellowship of his family and friends. He won't have to suffer the shunning."

I was relieved. Levi didn't need the stress of abandonment along with everything else. We talked more about Amish life and their tradition. Then, during a lull in the conversation, I glanced at Dad and noticed he'd given in to an afternoon nap.

That's when *I* went for a walk. I decided my heart needed stimulation, too. Even though I was only pushing sixteen!

Many more cars were driving up and down SummerHill today than usual. Tons of tourists were in Lancaster County for the Fourth. And by the looks of the traffic, lots of them had discovered the best views of Amish farmland were out here off the beaten tracks.

Halfway down the road, past the willow grove and near the Zooks' lane, two cars pulled over. Several people got out carrying pocket cameras. I could spot out-of-state tourists almost instantly by their throw-away cameras and the way they dressed. Especially the middle-aged men—floral-patterned Bermuda-length shorts and knee socks with sandals were a dead giveaway.

One tourist had a video camera. I watched out of the corner of my eye as I walked along the opposite side of the road. The man with the camcorder started moving slowly across the road, zeroing in on the large wagon-wheel mailbox at the end of Zooks' lane. The closer I got to him, the more upset I became.

Then I heard Susie Zook calling my name. "Merry!" Somehow she had sneaked up on me and was running toward me. She came barefoot, the narrow white tie strings on her Kapp flying.

I shouted to her, "Quick, cover your face!"

It was too late—the heartless tourist aimed his camera right at my friend.

I ran over and stood in front of her. "Take *my* picture if you have to."

"Move away there, missy," he said, motioning me aside. "Just one more quick shot of the little Amish girl won't hurt anything."

I felt Susie's arms slip around my waist. And for one fleeting moment I remembered another day, another time, when Faithie had put her arms around me this way.

We had been posing for pictures while riding a white pony. It was our seventh birthday, and Faithie was terribly frightened. She'd clung to me, with her arms around my waist. . . .

"Go away!" I yelled at the tourist. "These people are not zoo animals. They're human beings!"

The man lowered his camera, staring at me. He reached into the pocket of his floral-patterned Bermudas and pulled out a wad of dollar bills. "Well, here, maybe this'll change your mind."

Susie's arms tightened around me.

"Go away, please!" I said. But the man kept coming toward us. Closer . . . and closer.

Be strong and courageous. Do not be afraid.

Susie and I inched backward a few steps at a time, but there was no convincing this guy. He wasn't simply a rude tourist—he was downright mean!

Just then, I saw a jazzy red sports car flying down SummerHill, headed right for the cameraman. The way the car zigzagged on the road was enough to scare tourists out of the county—and right out of their Bermuda shorts!

"Yee-ikes!" I cried, pointing. "That's our neighbor. She can't drive worth beans!"

The man jumped the ditch and dashed to the other side of the road, wearing a look of terror. Not to be defeated, Old Hawk Eyes bore down on him.

It was clear as anything—Ruby Spindler was up to her old spying tricks. Somehow she'd seen exactly what was going on out here. She had come to rescue us!

Abruptly, she braked her car, sending billowy clouds of dust into the air. Then, jumping out of the driver's seat, the old lady—with cell phone in hand—ran over to the guy with the camcorder. "Lookee here, mister," she squawked. "I don't know what yer business is, but as far as I can tell, you've been trespassing on private property." She glanced over at me, still hiding Susie. "Now I'm tellin' you—git!"

She backed up her words by dialing 9-1-1, reporting a harassment inches away from the tourist. It was as in-your-face as you get! And by the time she started to give pertinent information, the intruders had sped off down SummerHill.

Susie crept out from behind me. "You saved us," she cried. "Oh, Old Hawk—"

"Uh . . . Miss Spindler, you were amazing," I interrupted.

"How's every little thing here now?" she asked Susie, leaning over to shake her hand. "Are you gonna be all right, darlin'?"

Susie nodded. "They were making *Schpott* of me, jah?"

"Not anymore, they won't make fun," Ruby Spindler said. "Not anymore, no indeedy!"

I stared in amazement at Old Hawk Eyes. Everyone knew she was a full-fledged busybody, but there was clearly another side to her. A very caring, almost parental side. I could hardly wait to report this aspect of her personality to Dad.

Much later, after the tourist ordeal was behind us, Mom decided to serve a light supper outside in the gazebo. Dad had slept the afternoon away, and Mom, fresh from her long walk and a shower, carried out a huge tray of chicken-salad sandwiches. There was potato salad made my favorite way with diced dill pickles, and a strawberry Jell-O mold with peaches hiding inside. Dad had to have his iced tea in a giant-sized tumbler, so I ran indoors for more ice and a pitcherful of tea.

I told my family about the adventure—about hiding Susie from the tourists and discovering the nurturing side to Miss Spindler. "It was actually scary there for a while," I said. "Old Hawk Eyes saved the day."

Skip snickered. "Man, what a snoop!"

"I have no idea how she does it—how she sees so far."

"It's gotta be some high-powered telescope set up in her bedroom," Skip said, pointing at her house in the distance. "Hey, we should all wave at her right now and freak her out."

"Skip Hanson, don't you dare!" Mom reprimanded.

"Don't worry," he said, reaching for three sandwich halves. "But I bet anything she's watching us."

I stole a glance at the old house. Wondering . . .

We bowed our heads for prayer. And while Dad blessed the food, I prayed silently for Lissa.

Later, during dessert, Susie Zook showed up at the gazebo. "Can Merry play?" she asked my mom.

"Of course," Mom said, winking at me. "As soon as she's finished cleaning up the kitchen."

"I'll do the dishes," Dad volunteered. "You two run along."

I spied the canning jars in Susie's hands. "Are we going to catch fireflies again tonight?"

"Lightning bugs," she insisted, grinning. One of her front teeth was missing.

Skip must've noticed, too. "Hey, looks like the tooth fairy's coming to your house tonight!"

Susie looked puzzled. "Tooth fairy?"

"Oh yeah," Skip said, scrunching up his face at me, trying to get me to bail him out.

"Tooth fairies aren't real," I began. "They're only pretend, like . . ." I paused, trying to think who on earth might make the connection in her Amish mind.

"Ever hear of Santa Claus?" Skip chimed in, getting himself in even deeper.

Susie frowned. "Ach, Santa Claus is worldly. Is the tooth fairy his dentist?"

Not one of us laughed, although I could tell by the way Dad looked down quickly, stirring his iced tea, that he was mighty close to it.

"Maybe we oughta just go catch some fireflies," I said, heading for the side yard with her.

"You mean lightning bugs, jah?"

"Jah." The word slipped out, and I smiled to myself without turning around to see Mom's expression. She was probably worried sick that the Zooks were getting their hooks into me.

Eleven Night of the Fireflies

We hurried down SummerHill Lane, and then Susie had the idea to walk in the ditch that ran along the road. "We can hide in there and jump up and catch 'em," she announced, referring to her beloved bugs.

"Good idea." I crouched down in the grassy ditch, playing her little girl games—the kind of games Faithie and I had played so long ago. Kneeling down in the grassy area where wild strawberry vines grew thick and beautiful, I pretended to be as young as my friend.

One after another, the fireflies twinkled and came within catching distance. Occasionally, I caught one. Other times, they'd blink at me and disappear.

"Fourteen . . . fifteen . . . sixteen . . ." I heard Susie counting as she put the bugs inside her glass jar.

I thought of her grandfather's poem and stared at the fire-red sky. *Dusk comes wearing red satin.*

The tourists were out like flies tonight. Cars everywhere. Some of them pulled off to watch the Pennsylvania sunset. Others drove by slowly. Most of them never even noticed Susie and me creeping along in the ditch beside the road. *Dusk comes soft on tiptoes.*

Susie darted out onto the road to run after one hard-to-catch bug. She jumped into the air with her glass jar. A look of delight danced across her face. "I caught it, Merry! I caught it!"

I began to chant the firefly poem. "Come one, come all, to the firefly ball. Dance with 'em, laugh with 'em, run straight and tall."

Susie joined in, reciting the poem with me. "Come one, come all, to the firefly ball," she repeated in a sing-songy voice. "Dance with 'em . . ." She ran across the road without looking.

"Susie!" I called to her as a car *whoosh*ed past. "Didn't you see that car? Please, be careful." I hurried across the road and hugged her.

That's when I saw the tears. Big, round tears rolled down her angel face. "I smashed one by accident," she said. "I musta not caught it right."

I looked down at her hand. The firefly lay still in her palm, its light still glowing steadily.

"Don't worry," I said, comforting her.

"Did it feel the pain?" she asked.

"Probably not too much."

"I hope not." Still holding the dead firefly, she sat down and stared at the mass of twinkles in her jar.

I thought of Faithie as I watched my little friend. At six and a half, *she* had been full of questions, too. Always trying to understand nature and how things worked in God's scheme of things.

"We could go to my house and have lemonade." I sat down in the grass next to her, trying to get her mind off the smashed firefly. "Would you like that?"

"I wanna get a whole jarful tonight," she insisted, wiping tears off her cheeks.

I knew she needed time to calm down. So we admired our gleaming jars and said Grandfather Zook's poem again. "Come one, come all, to the firefly ball. Dance with 'em, laugh with 'em, run straight and tall."

We tried to remember the verses but got all mixed up. Susie remembered the part about dusk wearing honeysuckle, and we leaned our heads back and breathed in the sweetness around us.

"Why do ya think God made lightning bugs, Merry?"

"Why do *you* think He did?"

"I'm gonna find out," she whispered, leaning close. "Levi snuck me some library books. He read some of the pages to me and told me it's good to be a thinker."

"Levi's right," I said. "It's good to think and ask questions."

"Mam and Dat say not."

I was silent, amazed at her understanding of things.

"I ask the Lord questions sometimes," she said. "When I pray."

"You do?"

"Jah, every day when I'm doin' chores. Levi's the one who taught me how to pray to Jesus."

I felt warm and good hearing Levi's name linked with the Lord's. My Amish boyfriend was turning into a regular missionary!

Dusk had descended and the area was thick with dancing lights—more than I'd ever remembered seeing. With the darkness came less traffic, and I was glad to reclaim our peaceful strip of road.

"How's Rachel doing?" I asked. "Is she still mad at me?"

Susie took a deep breath. "Levi was talkin' to her out in the barn early. Somethin' 'bout you and her still bein' friends."

"That's good."

Susie stood up. "Rachel's real stubborn sometimes. I asked her, but she wouldn't even come one, come all, to the firefly ball."

"Did she know I would be coming, too?"

"Maybe."

So, Rachel was still holding a grudge. If only I could make her see that Levi's interest in the Bible and other things was his own doing. Not mine.

I followed Susie to a honeysuckle bush off the road. She picked some blossoms and put them inside her canning jar. "Lightning bugs like nectar."

I laughed. "Your firefly books say that, right?"

"I can't read yet, but Levi's teachin' me how."

"You'll be in the first grade soon," I said.

She nodded enthusiastically. "Come fall." She wandered back onto the road and squatted there, ready to catch another firefly.

Two of them flew past me—right in front of my nose—lighting up simultaneously. A duet. Maybe they were twins!

I ran after them, determined to have the twin fireflies together inside my canning jar. Safely together. I followed them as they flitted and fluttered toward the willow grove, alluring me with their matching lights.

"I'll be right back!" I called over my shoulder to Susie.

"Hurry," her voice floated back to me.

I raced after the twosome.

Dance with 'em, laugh with 'em. Run straight and tall.

I reached up, stretching with all my might . . . and captured them. A triumph!

Quickly, I headed back through the grove of graceful trees. I couldn't wait to tell Susie.

How truly terrific it was having someone like her in my life. She'd come along just when I needed her. And even though it was hard to admit to myself, she was actually beginning to fill Faithie's shoes in her own unique way. Well, not exactly, but very, very close.

I quickened my pace. A car's headlights shone beyond the crest of the hill. I called to Susie, "Get off the road!"

A cold fear gripped me as I realized she was facing away from the car. She hadn't heard my warning.

"Su-sie!"

Dust was flying from the tires as the car sped down the narrow road.

I cupped my hands over my mouth and screamed, "Susie! A car's coming!"

Everything happened so fast. Loud, squealing brakes. The crash of a glass jar against the hood. And the sickening thud . . .

The air had a strange smell to it. Like the way it smells right after a lightning strike.

My heart pounded as I flew to her. My young friend . . . my adorable playmate. Susie lay as still as death in the soft, grassy ditch beside SummerHill Lane.

I knelt over her, sobbing. "Susie . . . Susie . . . oh please, please don't die!" My jarful of fireflies rolled out of my hand and into the grass.

The driver came running over. "Is she alive?" I heard a low, choked sound and knew he was weeping. "I didn't see her! I didn't—"

"Run, get help!" I shouted. "My father's a doctor." I pointed to our house up the lane. "Go to that house and call an ambulance! Quick!"

He left his car parked in the road with its flashers going. I could hear his desperate footsteps as I put my face down next to Susie's, listening for her breathing. "Can you hear me?" I whispered.

No response.

I touched her wrist gently, searching for a pulse. But my own heart was pounding so hard, I couldn't be sure. With trembling fingers, I picked up her white prayer cap. It had fallen onto the grass beside her. Something in me longed to place it back on her head where it belonged. But I held it close to my heart instead, fearful of moving her.

Be strong and courageous. Do not be afraid.

"Oh, help us, dear Jesus. Please help us!" I prayed.

Then I heard anxious footsteps pounding down the Zooks' lane. "Merry! What's happened?"

It was Levi. He knelt beside me and touched his sister's hand tenderly.

"A car hit her," I managed to say. "I can't tell if she's—"

"I . . . I'll call an ambulance," he stammered.

"Someone already has."

"Then I must tell Dat and Mam," he said. And he dashed off toward the Zook farmhouse.

Up the road, my father and Skip were running toward us. "Susie, hang on . . . don't give up. Help is coming," I said into her ear.

Then I touched her left wrist again, and when I did, her fingers opened, revealing the dead firefly in her cool palm. Its steady light was still shining.

In the dark I began to cry silently. For Susie, and for myself.

Still clutching Susie's prayer cap, I stepped back to make room for Dad and his medical bag. Skip brought a blanket and covered Susie's tiny body.

Within minutes, Abe and Esther Zook came running with Levi and the rest of the children. Rachel came over to where I was standing. She was crying. "Didja see it happen?" she asked.

"I tried to warn her ... it happened so fast." I reached for Rachel's hand. I was shaking. "I would've done anything ... anything ... to stop this from happening." I could hardly talk, my teeth chattered so hard.

"I know, Merry. I don't blame you." She turned to me and we clung to each other.

Then I gave Susie's white Kapp to her. "It fell off. . . ." I tried, but I couldn't say more.

Rachel seemed to understand and held her sister's prayer covering almost reverently in both hands.

The Zook grandparents arrived on the scene using their canes to steady themselves. I shivered even more when I saw them. As I inched backward, farther and farther away, I covered my face with my hands, shutting out the horror.

The frantic wail of an ambulance rang out in the distance. I knew it wouldn't be long till Susie would be speeding off to the hospital.

Abe and Esther hovered over their daughter, looking solemn and sober in the light of an eerie set of headlights. I could hear Dad's calm, professional voice explaining that he had begun to treat Susie for shock symptoms, but that her pulse was very faint. I shuddered to think of my firefly friend—so energetic, alive, and spunky just minutes ago—now so lifeless.

Esther dropped to her knees, leaning over the still form of her baby daughter. She rocked back and forth as though travailing, but not a sound escaped her lips.

Mom came running down SummerHill, along with the driver of the car. The man was around Dad's age, and he looked thoroughly shaken. Once he almost fell as he made his way to the scene of the accident.

The closer he got, the more I wanted to lash out at him. Let him know I hoped he had to pay, and pay dearly, for this truly horrible thing.

Mom came over to me and held me close. "Oh, honey," she whispered. "Honey."

My knees felt weak and I nearly collapsed. Dad rushed over and had me lie down in the grass, my head cradled in Mom's lap.

And then the ambulance arrived. Lights swirled round and round, casting reddish shadows on the trees surrounding us.

In the darkness, I thought how it would be to take Susie's place. For me to be the one dying instead. For me to be going to heaven ... to Faithie.

Tears rolled down my face and slid into my ears. But I let them fall, wishing something would block out the sound of Susie's body being lifted onto a stretcher and into the ambulance, its doors closing heavily. I trembled uncontrollably and was only vaguely aware of someone covering me with a blanket.

Mom's gentle voice was somewhere above me. "I'm here, Merry," she said. And then came Dad's strong arms, lifting me up and carrying me home.

———

I tossed and turned between my sheets, reliving the accident, calling out to Susie in the night. I even dreamed the whole thing—except in my dream, she'd heard my warning. And was safe.

Close to midnight, I fell into a deep, sorrowful sleep.

The next morning, I couldn't remember the details of my dream. I knew I'd been catching fireflies with Susie and calling . . . calling. But nothing else was clear. And try as I might, I couldn't recall the outcome.

The longer I lay there, the more restless I became. I checked the time on my blue-striped wall clock. Already ten o'clock!

I got out of bed, eager for news of Susie. Was she alive? Had she survived the first critical hours?

I grabbed my robe and stumbled into the hallway, calling for Mom.

"Downstairs," she answered, meeting me at the bottom of the back stairs leading to the kitchen.

"How's Susie?" I stood there stiff as a soldier, bracing myself for the worst.

"Come, sit down." Mom guided me over to the table.

I felt suddenly guilty for sleeping while my friend was shut away in the hospital. Maybe dying.

"Your dad went to the hospital last night after we got you settled. He stayed through the night with Susie and her parents." Her voice was thick with concern. "Honey, it doesn't look good."

My throat felt cottony, and I wished I could go back to bed, to sleep and have all this be just a bad dream.

She reached over and touched my hand. "Susie's in a coma."

My heart sank. "A coma?"

She nodded, a hint of tears in her eyes.

"I want to see her," I whispered.

"I knew you would, so I fixed some pancakes. I can warm them up right away for you."

I shook my head. "I'm not hungry, Mom."

"But you nearly fainted last night," she said, getting up. "You ought to try and eat something. For nourishment."

"Okay, but just a little."

I watched her slip into hostess mode and hurry to the fridge, where she located a pitcher of orange juice. She poured it thoughtfully into a small juice glass and brought it over to me.

"Thanks," I said in a daze.

"The Zooks were so kind to your father last night," she offered. "They never questioned anything in the ER. Their only concern was for Susie."

"I'm not surprised," I said. "They trust Dad. And most of all, the providence of God."

She set the microwave on reheat and put a plate of pancakes inside. "Your dad said Levi was a big help, filling out forms for the nurses and in general handling the whole situation amazingly well."

There was so much she wasn't saying. I knew it by the look in her eyes. She desperately wanted to have the Amish conversion conversation now.

"Mom, the Zooks aren't trying to convert me, I promise you. There *are* some things going on with Levi, though." I sighed. "I just don't want to talk now."

She put the orange juice back in the fridge. "It can wait." She forced a smile.

I could feel the tension between us.

I got up and looked out the back window. The gazebo reminded me of Levi. He was so mature, much more settled than I'd ever dreamed. Settled and now tremendously strong. He wasn't nearly the flirt, either. That change in him was actually refreshing. I had to admit, the new Levi was more intense. God-directed, too.

I wondered how God looks at our lives, knowing the end from the beginning the way He does. Knowing whether or not Levi would wait for me. And whether or not I'd want him to.

I turned away from the window. Now wasn't the time to be thinking about Levi. So much was at stake. Susie's life was on the line.

One pancake was all I could eat. Thank goodness, Mom didn't coax for more. It was clear she wasn't herself. I wondered if Susie's accident had jolted her—forcing her to reevaluate her relationship with me.

***

We stopped in at the Zooks' before heading to Lancaster General Hospital. I got out of the car and went inside, asking if anyone wanted to ride along.

Grandfather Zook stood up and took his cane, looking relieved. "I'll go in with ya. Denki for thinking of us."

Levi and Aaron were covering the chores for their father. Rachel, Nancy, and Ella Mae were helping, too. By the looks of things, Grandma Zook had taken over all kitchen duties.

Poor Grandfather. He'd been twiddling his thumbs, not knowing what to do with himself. "Yous are a Godsend," he said, getting into the backseat of our car.

"Glad to help," Mom said. She had an uncanny ability to pull herself together. Mom talked softly with him, filling him in on the latest hospital information from Dad as she drove us toward Lancaster.

I shut out their talk, remembering back to Faithie's cancer diagnosis. The outlook had been bleak right from the start. The cancer had crept up on all of us—taking a head start on everything medically possible. In eight short months she was gone.

Gone!

I trembled at the thought. Would we have to go through the same trauma and grief again? Wasn't it enough to lose Faithie? Wasn't it?

I felt hot—caged in—sitting here in the front seat of Mom's expensive car. At the red light, I put my hand on the door handle and, in my mind, jumped out. I imagined running down Lime Street—all the way to the hospital.

The weather was beastly hot and sultry, as though a thunder-shower was imminent. A sizzling Fourth.

Even though Mom had the air-conditioner going full blast, I was perspiring to beat the band. The sheer thought of seeing Susie in a hospital bed frightened me.

As it turned out, Abe Zook had to do some fast talking to let Mom and me in to see Susie at all. He called us cousins, which we were, only very distant ones. The nurse in charge eyed us suspiciously, probably because we didn't look one bit Plain.

Abe and Esther Zook had been taking turns in the intensive care unit off and on since last night. Abe looked washed out, exhausted. Esther too. Someone at the hospital had taken Levi home in the wee hours.

Tears came to Esther's eyes when she saw Grandfather Zook shuffling down the hall, his cane in hand. The three of them stood in a huddle, speaking in Pennsylvania Dutch quietly as they shared their grief, felt one another's pain and, by their faces, the hopeless-ness of it all.

That's when Mom encouraged me to go inside to see Susie. I felt a lump in my throat. It choked me so that I could hardly breathe as I stood at the foot of her bed.

Do not be afraid or discouraged. . . .

White sheets draped the bed, matching Susie's pale face. Her braids had been wound around her head in the typical little-girl style, and her white net bonnet covered her small, round head.

I studied her eyelids, hoping they might flutter open. "Oh, Susie," I spoke to her, trying my best not to cry. "I know you can't see me, but I'm here. I miss you." I took a deep breath for courage. "I know you'd rather be anywhere else but here. And believe me, I wish you weren't here, either."

I longed for some kind of signal. Something to let me know she could hear—that she was listening. But there was nothing at all. Not the slightest movement of her fingers or her eyelids.

Nothing.

Slowly, I walked around to the side of her bed. I touched her left hand gently. The hand that had held the smashed firefly last night.

"I'm going out tonight . . . to catch fireflies. Hurry and get well so you can come with me," I said with absolutely no hope that she would ever come to another firefly ball.

I stared at the monitors everywhere and at the curtains, pulled shut. This place was like a morgue. Except for one thing. There was a *live* body in this room. A living, breathing person!

Dad had always said, "Where there's life, there's hope," and I clung to that. Susie might've died last night, but she was alive, her heart beating. Breathing on her own!

So much to be thankful for.

I thought of the firefly poem Grandfather Zook had written. "'Night of the Fireflies,'" I said out loud. "Come one, come all, to the firefly ball. Dance with 'em, laugh with 'em. Run straight and tall."

I looked at Susie—really looked at her. She was somewhere inside that seemingly lifeless body; I knew it. Her light was still shining. Same as the firefly she'd accidentally smashed. Shining steadily . . . telling us not to give up. To keep believing that she would run and laugh again. That she would chase fireflies again.

But no one else, not her family and not the nurses, seemed quite as hopeful. Dad came up on one of his breaks. He checked her chart and reaffirmed the grim outlook. Susie was in a deep coma.

"Can she hear anything?" I asked.

"Sometimes comatose patients have keen hearing; they're aware of their surroundings. My guess is that Susie can probably hear the voices of those she loves."

"My voice, too?"

Dad kissed my cheek. "Perhaps."

I stayed all day, rotating turns with Susie's mother, father, and grandfather. I used the Gideon Bible from the drawer in Susie's hospital room to read passages from the Psalms out loud.

Grandfather Zook had his firefly poem with him, and while he waited for his visits, he worked on creating the last verse. When the words didn't fit just right, we would talk, sharing special memories of Susie.

We weren't being morbid or anything. Actually, our time together was very sweet . . . and touching. Fond memories of Susie kept us going. Kept us hoping.

Thirteen Night of the Fireflies

A Fourth of July without fireworks. No hot dogs or corn on the cob. No root beer floats.

I was content to sit at Susie's bedside a few minutes at a time, reading Psalms to her and praying out loud—making sure the light inside her kept shining.

"Here's a good one—Psalm ninety-one," I said, settling down for another Bible-reading session. "It's one of my favorites. 'He who dwells in the shelter of the Most High will rest in the shadow of the Almighty.'"

I paused, thinking about the sheltering willows in our secret place—the willow grove. "Remember how bright our jars of fireflies were in the willow trees? Well, I guess you could say the willows are like the shelter in this psalm. Can you picture yourself being sheltered there, Susie—safe in Jesus? He is the Almighty."

I looked at her as I spoke, hoping, praying for a response. Anything.

Undaunted, I picked up the Bible again and continued to read. " 'I will say of the Lord, "He is my refuge and my fortress, my God, in whom I trust." ' "

Then, as I did after every short session, I repeated her grandfather's poem, "Night of the Fireflies."

"Come one, come all, to the firefly ball. Dance with 'em, laugh with 'em. Run straight and tall."

Mom left the hospital around noon, taking Abe Zook home en route to our house. He'd gone to catch forty winks, planning to return to the hospital with the rest of the Zook children after the last milking. They came into Lancaster together, piled up in the usual way in their horse and buggy.

Levi, Rachel, Nancy, Ella Mae, and Aaron all gathered around their sister. They were allowed to stay as long as they were quiet.

Curly John, the oldest Zook boy, and Sarah, his young bride, also came to visit. Sarah was starting to look as though she was expecting a baby. The new little Zook was scheduled to arrive in mid-November.

When the young couple came out of Susie's room, they had tears in their eyes but no other display of emotion. Quietly, they stood talking with Abe and Esther in the hall, and then there was a long period of silence.

It was difficult for everyone to see the young girl, once so lively and vibrant, in this languishing, dismal state—hanging somewhere between life and death.

My dad had agreed to take me home when he got off work later. I felt truly blessed to have spent this day—off and on, of course—with my friend. Our time together had been nothing like our jaunts around the farm chasing fireflies, but it had been special. Special beyond words.

The scriptures and the prayers had touched the very heart of me. I could only hope they had reached Susie, too.

After a while, Levi talked his parents and grandfather into going home for some rest. "Try and get a good night's sleep," he urged them. Then, to put their minds at ease, "The doctor will call Merry's house if Susie takes a turn for the worse."

"Or if there's good news," I added cheerfully.

Esther and Abe finally agreed and took Grandfather and their brood home for the night—in a mighty cramped buggy.

Much later, when the only sounds to be heard in Susie's room were the distant pops and explosions of shooting fireworks, Levi and I had another private talk.

"I've read nearly ten psalms to her today." I showed Levi the Bible I'd found.

He cast a tender look at his sister. "Susie loves the Bible, jah," he said, returning his gaze to me. "Do ya think God's Word will heal her?"

"One-hundred-percent-amen sure!" I said. "In fact, there's a verse in the Psalms about it."

"Ach, let's find it." Levi went to the drawer and pulled out the black Gideon Bible. "Which psalm do ya think it is?"

"Check in the back—there's a small concordance."

I peeked over his shoulder as he searched under the word *healed*. And, sure enough, there it was.

"Psalm one hundred seven, verse twenty," I said.

Levi's face lit up when he found it. "Here's the whole verse. 'He sent forth his word and healed them; he rescued them from the grave.'"

Levi looked at me, his face shining. "Oh, Merry, it's a wonderful-gut verse! We gotta keep on reading God's Word to her!"

It was a startling remark, especially because it seemed to indicate that he thought Susie could hear us.

"My dad says unconscious people are aware of loved ones surrounding them—that what we say should be positive and uplifting," I told him.

I went to sit in the soft chair near the window across the room. Levi kept standing, though, leaning against the windowsill—the Bible still open in his hands. He began to read several more verses from the psalm.

From my chair, I surveyed Susie's tiny form covered with hospital-white sheets and a lightweight blanket. When Levi stopped reading, I asked, "Do you think she knows we're here together, you and I?"

"Betcha she does." He smiled, closing the Bible. "Ya know, Susie's wanted you for a sister of sorts ever since I can remember."

I grinned, enjoying the idea of being someone's big sister. Actually, Susie and I *had* been like sisters for the past several days.

"I'm going to come see her every day till she wakes up," I announced. "And I don't care how long it takes!"

Levi was silent, and by the look on his face, troubled.

"What's wrong?" I asked. "Don't you believe she'll—"

"Merry, *please*. This has nothin' to do with believin'. Sometimes God's plans are different than ours. Sometimes . . ." His voice trailed off.

"Well, I won't give up hope."

"But ya hafta prepare yourself for the other possibility, ya know."

"But I thought—"

"I believe God heals the sick, jah—but *you* know as well as I do that sometimes the healing comes by lettin' a person die."

I squinted my eyes nearly shut. "What are you saying?"

"It's just that . . ." He paused, having trouble getting the words out. "Susie . . . uh, might not make it."

"Better not be saying that in *this* room!" I insisted. "If Susie's listening, which I'm sure she is, you oughta be saying good, truthful, powerful things. Things that'll stimulate her mind. Things to make her want to wake up."

Levi frowned. "Don't hide your head in the sand, Merry. I would be so sorry for ya to be disappointed."

"I won't be, you'll see!" And I leaped out of my chair and left the room without saying good-bye to him.

Or to Susie.

⌒

On the ride home, Levi asked my dad many questions about comatose states. He seemed hungry to know as much about Susie's condition as possible. Still, I was upset at the abrupt change in his attitude. Did he believe the Psalm or not?

Dad was kind enough to answer Levi's medical questions, even though I could see he was fairly wiped out from having been up all last night. On top of that, he'd worked the ER all day.

Finally, when we made the turn onto SummerHill, all of us grew quiet. I turned my attention to the scenery outside.

Susie's lightning bugs were out in droves—almost as thick as I'd seen them last night. The night of the accident . . . the night of the fireflies.

I thought of Grandfather Zook's poem—the references to dusk wearing red satin and honeysuckle. My mind drifted back. How uncanny that there had been a fire-red sunset like a red satin gown. And the night air had been heavily sprinkled with the sweet smell of honeysuckle. Susie had even stopped to pick several blossoms!

I closed my eyes, refusing to look at the scene of the accident as we came near it. When we passed it, I caught Levi's sad eyes staring at me. He wasn't just sad—Levi was ticked. We'd had our first fight, and over a life-and-death issue. Over Susie's life, and whether she would come out of the coma, or die and go on to heaven.

As I looked at Levi's grim face, I couldn't tell whether the pain he was feeling was stronger for Susie, or for me.

Night of the Fireflies Fourteen

I told Dad I wanted to sit outside for a while after we arrived home. "I need some time alone."

"You sure, kiddo?" he asked.

I nodded, trying to ignore the sweet fragrance around me. "I'm sure."

"Well, then, take your time." He left me sitting outside on the gazebo steps.

As I looked up into the evening sky, I wondered where Susie really was. Oh, I knew where her *body* was. But she was unconscious, so where was her mind? And what about her soul—the spirit of her?

Susie's most essential natural reflexes were working without artificial means—her heart beating, her lungs breathing. It was her mind that was shut off. And the more I thought about it, the more determined I was to find a way to awaken her. To bring her back—all of her!

I decided not to catch fireflies after all. There was thunder in the distance, and it was getting late. Besides that, I was tired from the events of the past two days.

I called for my cats, wondering if they were hiding in their usual spot under the gazebo steps. "Lily White? Are you under there?"

Abednego, the cat who was usually missing, showed up first. He padded up to me, his persistent meowing getting to be a bit much.

"Okay, okay. I know you're glad to see me, little boy." Abednego wasn't so little anymore. In fact, he was downright fat. Probably due to the rich, raw cow's milk from Zooks' dairy. "I should put you on a diet!"

He didn't appreciate that comment and arched his back in disgust. My tone of voice had probably offended him. He was terribly sensitive and *very* smart. In fact, all four of my cats were super intelligent. They just didn't understand English.

Minutes later, I was joined by the rest of the feline delegation of the Hanson household. Lily White, the youngest, led the pack. She was petite and wore a regal coat of white. Shadrach and Meshach were golden-haired brothers, younger siblings to Abednego. I'd noticed recently that Lily and Abednego had been viciously vying for my attention.

Lily was the new cat on the block, still attempting to establish her worth, while the three Hebrew felines had been around for years.

A gust of wind took me by surprise. Quickly, I gestured to my cat quartet, informing them of the impending storm. "Let's get inside before it pours," I said, gathering Lily White in my arms. Abednego took notice and ran under the gazebo, having a temper tantrum.

Thunder rolled overhead.

"Aw, c'mon, little boy," I called to him. "You don't want to get caught in a thunderstorm. Please come."

I squatted down, peering under the gazebo, still holding Lily White.

Abednego was stubborn and going to play his game. I was pretty sure if I put Lily down and *then* coaxed him, he'd come out in a flash. But I was too tired emotionally and physically to plead with the spoiled old feline, so I scrambled into the house as lightning lit up the sky.

"Merry," Mom said, looking concerned as she glanced out the back-door window. "I was just coming to get you. There's a severe thunderstorm warning out for Lancaster County. We just heard it on the radio."

I put Lily White down. "Abednego's still out there!"

Skip looked up from his plate of pie and ice cream. "What's *his* problem?"

"Probably jealous." I turned around, staring out the window with Mom, upset at the way Abednego had ignored me. Didn't he know by now that I wanted the best for him? That I only wanted him to be safe?

I went to the fridge in search of sandwich fixings.

"Jealousy is as cruel as the grave," Mom stated.

Her words stung my heart. "What?" I said, even though I'd heard her just fine.

"Abednego's competing for all he's worth," she said. "Lily White makes him mad because she moved in on his territory."

I knew all that. But it was the "cruel as the grave" part that I couldn't get out of my mind.

Mom insisted on warming up something for Dad and me to eat, even though I was content with making a sandwich. "You've had a long, stressful day," she said, coming over to the counter. "You have to keep up your strength."

Dad sighed, running his hand over his prickly chin. "I could use a good hot shower and shave."

It was obvious Dad had already filled Mom in on Susie's condition, yet neither of them offered a word about her recovery. That bothered me. Was I the only one holding out hope?

After Dad and I had eaten, Mom said she and Skip would clean up the kitchen. I was relieved. There was no way I'd survive even a half hour of chitchat with them. Everyday living seemed so mundane and unimportant when faced with eternal questions about life and death.

⌒

The next day I got up early and rode into town with Dad. I was going to spend the whole day with Susie.

Mom had made an enormous sack lunch for me, and when the nurse saw me brown-bagging it, she let me use their staff refrigerator. I was all set.

Rachel and her mother arrived soon after I did, and we traded off visits the way we had yesterday. I read all of Psalm one hundred seven to Susie without interruption from nurses or other visitors, emphasizing the part about being rescued from the grave. Then, as my five minutes drew to a close, I recited "Night of the Fireflies," ending again with the refrain.

"Come one, come all, to the firefly ball. Dance with 'em, laugh with 'em. Run straight and tall."

When the doctor came in for morning rounds, he solemnly indicated to Esther that Susie seemed to be drifting deeper into the coma. Truly horrible news!

However, because of that fact, Esther, Rachel, and I were allowed to stay in the room for longer periods of time.

There was only one problem with that—I couldn't conduct my visit with Susie the way I had been. That worried me because I was sure my interaction with Susie was helping. Not that I had anything solid to go on—no flutters of movement or deeper breathing—it was just a strong feeling.

Esther Zook scooted her chair up close to her daughter's hospital bed, which had been slightly elevated for the doctor's examination. She wore a black dress with a gray apron and the white prayer bonnet. Holding Susie's hand in hers, she closed her eyes in silent prayer. For nearly an hour she sat there without moving or speaking.

I was frustrated. She needed to be talking to Susie! How could I tactfully tell her?

After lunch, more and more Amish and Mennonite relatives began showing up, filing in and out of Susie's room, some staying as long as fifteen minutes at a time. Others came in briefly to greet Esther and Rachel. Several of Susie's aunts and uncles recognized me and kindly came over to the window where I sat. They were warm and sincere in their hellos and thank-yous, but I was one-hundred-percent-amen sure they could've done miraculous things if they had simply gone over to Susie's bed and spoken to *her.*

Word had spread through the Amish community about the accident, and by late afternoon the trickle of Plain visitors had become a steady stream.

I needed a break from the funeral-like atmosphere and the "silent treatment" they were giving Susie. It seemed as though they were coming to pay their respects!

There was only one good thing about my being here today, I decided. Rachel and I might have an opportunity to work out our problems over Levi. Maybe . . .

Like the longtime friends we were, she and I settled down into the soft green leather sofa in the private waiting room down the hall. People with family members in ICU could use the room as a place to relax or wait for word from a doctor or surgeon. Rachel and I used the cozy place, surrounded by fake greenery, to begin our peace talks.

"I think I understand why ya wanted Levi to talk to me," she began hesitantly.

"You do?"

"I never meant for Levi's decision to make us enemies." She folded her hands in her lap. "He's always been interested in finding out answers to things. Never content to take no for an answer."

I nodded. "Levi can be stubborn sometimes, but maybe this is a good thing."

Rachel looked a bit surprised. "I don't see how that can be."

I covered my mouth with my hand, thinking, choosing my words carefully. "Levi says that the name of a church or religion doesn't count for much. It's the way a person lives, the way he walks with God that matters."

Rachel's blue eyes grew wide. But she didn't respond.

I sighed. How could I explain to her what Levi had confided in me? How much did she know about his plans to attend Bible school?

"Well, I know ya didn't have anything to do with Levi's decision to become a preacher," she said softly. "He has lotsa Mennonite friends. They feel called to evangelize."

"How do your parents feel?"

She turned to face me for the first time, and I saw tears well up in her eyes. "Levi's not rebellious like he was. We've seen a change in him. It's for the better, jah."

"So he won't get kicked out or anything?"

"Dat says he can stay and farm as long as he likes."

I was glad to hear it, and even happier to know that Rachel and I were back on good terms.

Suddenly, Esther Zook came into the room, surrounded by her older sisters. She was leaning on them as though she was about to faint.

"Mam!" Rachel hurried over to help her. "Was ist letz?"

"Ach, she's exhausted," one of Rachel's aunts explained, looking mighty worried as she fanned a handkerchief.

"She's plain worn out from all this," said the other aunt. "And I'm afraid there's more bad news."

I cringed. I couldn't bear to hear it. Quietly, I excused myself.

I hurried down the hall to Susie's room and tiptoed inside. My eyes scanned the room. Excepting Susie, it was empty!

My heart stood still. What if Susie had already gone to heaven?

I rushed to her bedside—forcing my eyes to focus on the heart monitor, relieved to see the IV still attached to her arm. Confused, I stood there surveying the situation. What *was* the bad news?

"Susie," I spoke to her. "I'm here to give you some good news. I believe God is going to make you well, and I have just the words to prove it."

I reached for the Bible in the small table beside her bed. "Listen to this." And I began to read out loud again from Psalm one hundred seven, verse twenty. " 'He sent forth his word and healed them; he rescued them from the grave.' "

I read it again and again, feeling the intensity, the power of the words. Then I read the next psalm, and the next. I talked to her, recounting the many adventures we'd had together. I talked of the lovely poem her grandfather was writing and all the unfinished things in her life.

"Curly John and Sarah are expecting a baby sometime before Thanksgiving. You're going to be an aunt, Susie. An aunt at age seven! That's amazing, don't you think? I'm sure you'll want to hold your little niece or nephew—rock the baby to sleep sometimes. Show him . . . or her . . . how to catch lightning bugs." Tears stung my eyes.

I stopped to catch my breath, stroking her hand. I remembered the dead firefly with its shimmering tail. "Long before Curly John and Sarah's baby comes, you and I will be out catching lightning bugs again. As soon as you're up and out of here, we'll start. Is it a deal?"

I looked in the back of the Bible and found oodles of verses about light. Susie loved light. Especially her bugs.

I looked up every verse dealing with light. One after another I read them to her, sometimes adding my own two cents' worth about the particular verse. Not embellishing it, just simply explaining it.

My voice was starting to wear out from all the reading, but I refused to stop.

Once, I actually thought her hand twitched. I couldn't be sure, though. I didn't want to stop and tell the others. I knew I was making progress here, and time was too precious to waste.

When it came time for supper, I didn't bother to eat, even though my dad had ordered food for me.

Rachel, with some strong assistance from her aunts, was able to talk her mother into going home for a nourishing meal and some much-needed rest. Levi and his grandfather would return later.

I was overjoyed about having more time with Susie. Now I could stimulate her brain to my heart's content—with long chapters from the Bible. With heartfelt prayers for her recovery. With long, intimate talks about everything under the sun. And more.

The nurse came frequently to check monitors and Susie's temperature. The nurse was friendly, and I was encouraged that she didn't act as though I were in the way. She seemed to welcome my presence. Hours later, though, she looked surprised to see me still there.

"You must be a good friend of our little miss," she said while taking Susie's blood pressure.

"We're very close, almost like sisters."

The nurse smiled, then checked the amount of fluid left in the IV. "Susie is very lucky to have you."

"She's very special, and I'm not giving up," I told her. "I want to be right here when she wakes up!"

"Wouldn't that be wonderful?" she said.

Around eight o'clock, Levi and Grandfather Zook arrived. I was glad to see them and asked Levi to read the Bible or talk to Susie in Pennsylvania Dutch, hoping the familiar language might trigger something in her.

"Jah, I will," Levi said. "Good idea."

I was glad to hear the friendly ring in his voice. But I wondered how he felt about our former disagreement.

I sat in the chair next to the window while Levi spoke to his sister in their first language.

Next, Grandfather Zook took a turn. "Susie, my little one," he began. "I'm done writing your poem. Jah"—and here he nodded his head slowly—"my work is done."

He reached into his pocket and pulled out a folded page. "I have it right here if ya wanna give a listen."

I sat up, eager to hear the final verse, wondering if Susie was excited about it, too—inside herself somewhere.

"First, I brought somethin' for ya." He held up a glass canning jar filled with fireflies. With a slow sweep of his hand, he motioned for Levi to turn off the lights.

Gently, using the covers to prop it up, he placed the jar of Susie's beloved lightning bugs in front of her face. "There, child," I heard him whisper.

A lump caught in my throat as he stood there in the silence of the dim room, the shimmering glow of the fireflies reflected on Susie's angel-white face.

Then Grandfather Zook began to read his newly completed poem. "'Tis the night of the fireflies, 'Tis the night of God's call. Dusk comes and is gone, and now . . ."

I held my breath listening to the poetic phrases.

"True light shines on us all."

My face was wet with tears as he began the familiar refrain. Quietly, I went to stand beside the old man, saying the rest of the poem with him.

"Come one, come all, to the firefly ball. Dance with 'em, laugh with 'em. Run straight and tall."

And again . . .

"Come one, come all, to the firefly ball. Fly with 'em, flit with 'em. Run straight and tall."

Levi's eyes appeared misty. But it was Grandfather's eyes that spilled over with tears. He shook his head slowly when I looked up at him, reassuring me that I shouldn't worry.

I reached up to touch his cheek, then put my arms around him. His weeping came softly, without sobs. And I let my own tears fall unchecked.

As nine o'clock neared, Levi suggested to his grandfather that they
head home before it got late. But before they left, I asked Levi if we
could talk in the hall. With Susie's door safely closed behind us, I
whispered my secret to him about the slight twitch in Susie's hand.

"Ach! Are ya sure?" His eyes searched mine.

I shook my head. "I wish I could say for sure." I waited. "But I
do have this strong feeling. . . ."

"I know whatcha mean." He looked at me thoughtfully. "I feel
it, too."

"Oh, Levi, I'm so glad!" His blue eyes twinkled under the fluo-
rescent lights, and for a second I honestly thought he was going to
hug me.

Curious glances from the nurses' station told us we were drawing an audience. Levi pointed to the more private waiting area,
where we went to talk things over. Our conversation centered around
yesterday's tiff.

"I went home and read my Bible most all night," Levi began. "I
found lotsa verses about healing." He paused reflectively.

"It's so strange and new to me, Merry. All my life, I was taught
that whatever happens is divinely ordered—our fate. When our
barn burned down, it was just supposed to be—we were suffering
the wrath of God for the whole community."

He took a deep breath. "When someone dies, we say, 'The Lord giveth and the Lord taketh away'—but I wanna know that God hears the cries of His people. That He is touched by our grief. That by our prayers we can move the hand of the heavenly Father."

I looked at him, astounded. "Levi Zook, you sound like a preacher!"

His eyes were shining like the fireflies Grandfather had brought for Susie. "I'm believin' with ya for Susie," he said softly. "And I'm sorry about getting in a huff about it before."

"Things are hard for all of us," I said. "No need to apologize."

After Levi left with his grandfather, I went back to Susie's room. I started telling her the things Levi and I had discussed.

"There are *two* of us now, Susie." I pushed the big, comfortable chair over next to her bed. "Levi and I both believe God's going to heal you . . . one of these days."

That's when I decided I wanted to sleep right there in the enormous chair beside her bed. I wanted to fall asleep talking to my friend.

Dad didn't put up much of a fuss when he came to take me home, but I guess Mom thought it was ridiculous when he called to tell her. "Your mother's concerned that you're overdoing it," he said after hanging up.

"Tell her I'm fine. Honest." I went over to hug him.

"I can see that." He kissed my forehead. "The hospital only makes exceptions for spouses or close family members of patients."

"Aw, Daddy. Can't you clear it with the nurses?" I pleaded. "Please? I *have* to do this!"

"Don't get your hopes up about staying. I can't promise anything." He left me alone with Susie as he went to try to push his weight around.

I sat twiddling my thumbs, not sure what to do with my nervous energy. Praying silently, I hurried to the windows and peered out at the ink black sky. An array of twinkling lights mingled against the backdrop of darkness.

The moonless sky reminded me of Susie's coma—black and hopeless. But the city lights were like the fireflies still shining intermittently beside her in the canning jar. The light meant hope. Hope . . . and courage.

When Dad didn't return right away, I became nervous. What if the hospital wouldn't let me stay?

I went to Susie's bedside. I looked at the still, limp form that was her body. It was difficult seeing her like this. The Susie Zook *I* knew would've wanted to leap out of bed by now. She'd be chattering, too—about everything under the sun. That was the girl I was waiting for.

The door opened.

Dad was wearing a big, almost mischievous grin. "What do you need for the night?" he asked. "A pillow, maybe?"

"I can stay?" I ran to him. "Oh, thank you, thank you!"

"You're doing the patient a lot of good," he said. "The nurses said so."

"What's that mean?" My heart was pounding with excitement. "Is something new happening?"

He shook his head. "There's nothing new to report on Susie's condition, but look, see that color in her cheeks?" He went over to the bed and touched her face gently. "Just a hint of color."

We stood side by side, looking at her.

"You're right," I said, picking up the small jar of fireflies. "Do you believe in miracles, Daddy?"

"Sure do."

"They happened in the Bible all the time." I kept staring at the lights inside the jar.

"Miracles can happen any time. Sometimes when we least expect them."

Dad made sure I was comfortable—I had several pillows and a lightweight blanket—before he left. "I'll see you in the morning." He hugged me close. "You're a very courageous young lady."

I sighed. "I sure hope Mom's not too upset."

"Don't worry," he said with a wink. "She'll be fine." Then he was gone.

I turned to Susie, still holding the jar filled with fireflies. "I'll be right back. I have to set your lightning bugs free."

I told the nurse at the nurses' station where I was going, then hurried to the elevators and down to the main level. Outside, I opened the lid.

"Come one, come all, to the firefly ball," I quoted Grandfather Zook's poem as the twinkly bugs flew out of the jar. "Dance with 'em, laugh with 'em. Run straight and tall."

Then I raced back inside. That's when I bumped into Lissa Vyner.

"Merry, hi!" She sounded excited to see me.

What is she doing here?

I had just pressed the elevator button. "Oh . . . hi." I remembered that I'd thought of calling her several times this week. Now I felt worse than ever because I hadn't.

"I . . . uh . . . really wanted to clear things up between us," I began, faltering a bit. "I wanted to talk to you about last Sunday—"

"Don't worry about it," she said. "Jon and I aren't going out anymore."

"You're *not?*"

She studied me for a moment. "Oh, Merry, I'm so sorry about your Amish friend. When I heard about Susie and everything, I wished I hadn't said all those things about you and . . . and them."

She stared at the numbers above the elevator door. When the door opened, we got on together. "That's why I'm here. We've been such good friends, until . . ." Her voice trailed off.

"Guys can get in the way sometimes," I said, still wondering if she suspected anything between Jon and me. "You'll have to come help me talk to Susie."

She looked at me with a blank expression. "I really didn't come to see her." She stepped off the elevator when the doors opened, and we walked together down the hallway to the waiting area.

I explained my ideas, strange as they sounded. "Susie's in a coma, but I've been talking to her anyway. I'm trying to stimulate her brain."

"You have to do this?"

"I don't have to, really. I guess you could say it's more of a faith thing—something Levi and I are doing because we found this really great verse in the Psalms."

"Levi? I thought he was Amish."

"That's another story," I interrupted, not wanting to share Levi's plans just yet.

"So you're saying Levi's not into powwowing—that folk-healing thing some of the Amish farmers do?"

I'd heard about it, too. But most of the Amish I knew frowned on the practice. They viewed the use of charms, amulets, and silent incantations as questionable. Possibly evil.

I took Lissa into Susie's room. "Here she is," I said, introducing Lissa to my friend. "And, Susie, this is my girl friend from school, Lissa Vyner."

"This is so weird, Mer. You're talking to Susie like she hears you." Lissa stared at me.

I nodded. "I honestly think she does."

"Really?"

"It's a strong feeling I have."

Lissa and I stood at the foot of Susie's bed and talked about all sorts of things. I couldn't believe how far behind I'd gotten on the activities at our church youth group.

"Don't forget we're having that river hike Saturday," she reminded me. "Maybe you and I can team up."

"I'm sorry, but I can't go. My aunt and uncle are coming with their new twin babies."

"Lucky for you," she said pensively. Then, "I've really missed you, Mer. It seems like ages since we've really talked."

"I know what you mean." I was curious about what had happened between her and Jon, but I didn't dare ask.

After she left, I pulled a chair of equal height up to the big, comfortable chair, making a little bed for myself. When I had both chairs situated so I could stretch my legs out slightly, I positioned the pillows, then reached for the Bible.

Susie and I were going to have a Bible study. She was going to know what God's Word said about miracles.

I propped my pillows up so I could see her from my chair-bed. My plan was to talk until I fell asleep. Maybe I'd even talk *in* my sleep!

Long after midnight, the super-friendly nurse came in for a routine check. "Everyone ought to have a friend like you, Merry." Her words were the very last thing I remembered as I fell, exhausted, into a deep sleep.

Sometime before dawn, I awoke with a start. The Bible had slid off my lap, inching its way down against Susie's bed. The hard edge poked into my legs.

Drowsily, I reached for it, putting it on the table. Then I began the flow of words to Susie's brain. "It's almost morning, and can you believe it—I've been here all night! This is my very first hospital sleepover." I chuckled to myself. "Sleepovers are supposed to be full of excitement. People aren't *really* supposed to sleep at these things, you know. So, c'mon, Susie, won'tcha ple-ease wake up?" I stretched a bit, trying to get the kink out of my neck.

Then I felt it. Something powerful. My heart beat a little too fast, and I looked over my shoulder, wondering if an angel had come to call.

Rubbing my eyes, I heard a tiny sound. It came from Susie's bed. My arms froze in place as I turned around.

Slowly, I opened my eyes, half expecting to see her guardian angel.

"*Wo bin* ich?" came her husky voice. "Where am I?"

I sat up, nearly falling out of my makeshift bed of chairs.

"Susie! You're back!"

I was afraid to hug her, but I leaned over the bed, smiling, not sure what to do.

"What happened?" she asked, sounding groggy.

"There was an accident. But you're going to be fine now."

"Come one, come all . . ." Her voice was weak.

I grinned down at her blue, blue eyes. "Susie . . . could you hear me reading to you? Did you—"

The door opened and the morning nurse breezed in. Her face burst into a surprised but delighted expression. "Well, what do you know!" She grinned from ear to ear, looking first at Susie, then at me.

"This is my friend Susie Zook," I said.

From that moment on, there was a flurry of activity. Almost more than when Susie had been in the coma. Her Amish friends and relatives came from miles around to witness the truly amazing change in her.

"Jah, it's a miracle," Grandfather Zook said later, stroking his beard. He touched Susie's forehead lightly.

I noticed his hand tremble as he did.

"Well," he continued, "you shoulda seen them fireflies last night."

I explained to Susie that he'd brought a jarful to keep her company.

"Jah?" she said, eyes bright. "Ya brought 'em here? To the hospital?"

Grandfather nodded. "Right here, child." He showed her where the jar had sat on her chest, nearly touching her chin.

"Ya didn't let 'em die, didja?" she asked me.

I spoke up. "I set them free—right out in front of the hospital."

A smile spread across her thin face.

"And I read ya the last verse of my poem," Grandfather said. He didn't exactly sound proud, as in arrogant, but there *was* a hint of pleasure in his voice. "My work is done now, little one. My work is done."

His words gripped me. What did he mean?

"I wanna hear what you wrote, Grossdawdy," Susie said. "Can ya say it by heart?"

Grandfather reached into his black coat. "My mind's not what it used to be." He unfolded the paper, and I saw it shake as he began to read. "'Tis the night of the fireflies, 'Tis the night of God's call. Dusk comes and is gone, and now . . . true light shines on us all."

Susie's face shone. "It's so-o pretty!"

He smiled. "It's *your* poem, child. 'Tis for you."

A soft, distant look crept into her eyes. "I had a dream about beautiful lights. Lights . . . everywhere."

I thought of the many Bible verses I'd read about God's light. Maybe Susie *had* heard my words.

Be strong and take courage. The words buzzed in my head as I left Susie's room. Filled with absolute delight, I headed down the hall to call my mother. In spite of the excitement, I knew I was worn out. My adrenaline was depleted; it was time to go home.

Susie would be coming home, too. Sooner than anyone ever expected.

"What a wonderful thing for you to witness firsthand," Mom said as she drove away from the hospital. She was cheerful and full of questions.

"I don't know how to explain it," I said. "Somehow I knew that I was supposed to be with Susie last night. And when she woke up . . . it was so-o incredible. It was the most wonderful thing that's ever happened to me."

"In your whole life?" Mom was smiling.

"In my whole, entire life!"

Mom was dressed up—her best white summer suit and pumps. I wondered if she was headed somewhere important. But when I asked her about it, she said she was celebrating life.

"Me too!" Actually, I couldn't wait to get home to SummerHill Lane. I needed a shower and a change of clothes. I'd been wearing the same ones way too long.

Mom came into my bedroom to chat after I was dressed. Honestly, it was like old times. The tension between us had disappeared. She was relaxed about everything. Even when I told her Levi's plans to attend a Bible school. She didn't second-guess me the way she'd been doing the past few months.

"Guess we've all seen it coming," she said about Levi.

I cuddled both Abednego and Lily White. "For as long as I remember, he's been pushing the rules over there." I glanced out my bedroom window.

It was truly good to be home. The smell of the country and the sounds—it sure beat the hospital all to pieces!

"It's good to have you here, Merry," Mom said. The way she said it made me wonder. Had Susie's accident changed things for *everyone*?

───

Susie came home on Friday, and the next day my aunt and uncle arrived with their six-week-old twins, my new cousins, Benjamin and Rebekah.

Miss Spindler showed up for the occasion. Her blue-gray kink of hair was done up all prissylike. "Oh, aren't they the most adorable little precious things ever!" she exclaimed when she saw the babies.

They were precious all right. Baby Benjamin wore the tiniest blue suit I'd ever seen. Petite Rebekah was dressed in one of Faithie's fanciest pink lace dresses—looking like a real live doll.

Mom took Rebekah from Aunt Teri, and Uncle Pete placed Benjamin in Miss Spindler's skinny arms. I stood back, observing Uncle Pete as he began signing rapidly for my deaf aunt's benefit. She broke into a big smile as Mom and Miss Spindler oohed and ahhed over her darling babies.

I don't know why, but it took me several hours before I could get it together enough to hold them. I'd heard it was important to feel truly confident when holding an infant, and I certainly didn't feel that way now. Their teensy bodies, so fragile and delicate, could fall right through my fingers.

So for my first encounter with Ben and Becky, I sat on the living room sofa and held them. One at a time.

I half expected my new baby cousins to cut loose crying when they sensed my uncertainty, but thank goodness, both of them slept right through their initial visit with me.

After lunch, I called Chelsea Davis to see if she was back from her Disneyland vacation. When Lissa Vyner answered, I was completely thrown off.

"Uh . . . is Chelsea there?"

"Oh, hi, Merry," Lissa said, recognizing my voice. "Just a sec."

Chelsea got right on the phone. "What's up, Mer?"

"How was California?" I asked.

"Hot, hot, and guess what?"

"You met a guy," I replied.

"How'd you know?"

"I have my ways," I said secretively.

"Well, how are you and Levi?" she asked.

"You won't believe everything that's happened." I filled her in on Susie's accident and miraculous recovery.

"Really? She pulled out of it, just like that?"

"Well, it wasn't really all that fast. I mean, she was out for almost *three* days."

"Man, I'd hate to think what I'd be missin' being stuck in the hospital that long," Chelsea said.

"Wouldn't we all," I whispered.

"By the way," she continued, "what's the deal with Jon Klein?"

"Better ask Lissa."

"She's not saying much. Are they—"

"Uh-huh."

"So does that mean you and—"

"Don't say anything! Promise me?" I said.

"Yeah, okay. But you better hurry and snag that boy before Ashley Horton does. I saw her eyeing him at the river hike today."

"*You* went on our church hike?" This was unbelievable!

"Now, don't go getting all excited," she said.

It's a beginning, I thought, thrilled that my atheist friend had found her way to a church activity.

"Well, so what do you think?" she asked.

"About what?"

"About Ashley, your pastor's daughter? Does she have a chance with Jon or not?"

I honestly thought Ashley was a thing of the past. At least for Jon. "Probably not," I said.

Chelsea started laughing. "So . . . sounds to me like you're still interested in you-know-who?"

"Aw, Chelsea, for pete's sake." I groaned. "Is Lissa hearing all this?"

"She's in the kitchen raiding our cookie jar. Mom made brownies this morning."

"Bring some over," I teased.

"Maybe I will."

"Hey, you've gotta see my baby cousins," I said.

"Oh, so *now* you tell me!"

I peeked around the corner at the portable bassinets in the dining room. "They're sound asleep, but they'll be waking up soon to nurse. You should come see them before my aunt and uncle leave."

"Lissa too?"

"Sure, that'd be great." I went on to explain that Lissa and I had made up at the hospital.

Chelsea was confused. "What was *she* doing there?"

"Trust me, it's fine."

I happened to glance out the window as I hung up the phone. Looked like a parade of buggies parked next door. Was there a work frolic going on?

Stepping out on the back steps, I strained my neck to see, but the willows blocked the Zook house from view. Still, the lineup of buggies and all the people made me wonder.

Surely, Rachel would've invited me if they were having something special for Susie. But it wasn't like the Amish to throw parties. Unless . . .

Fear clutched my throat. "Mom!" I raced inside.

Mom was sipping iced tea at the kitchen table with Uncle Pete. "Mom," I said softly. "Can you come outside a sec?"

I guided her out to the backyard.

"Look." I pointed to the Zooks' front yard and their long dirt lane. "Have you ever seen so many buggies?"

Mom frowned. "I hope Susie's all right."

"Me too!"

We both heard the phone ring, and Mom rushed inside to get it. In a few minutes, she was back outside, standing in the grass beside me. "Honey, that was Miss Spindler calling. She just saw the Amish funeral director drive away."

My hand flew to my mouth. "No! Not Susie!"

I ran faster than ever before down SummerHill Lane and through the willow grove. Over the picket fence and into the meadow.

My heart pounded ninety miles an hour. *Susie . . . Susie . . . Susie.*

The Amish expected visitors to enter the house without knocking at a time like this. I caught my breath as I stepped through the front door and surveyed the large gathering of Plain folk. The partition between the large living room and the kitchen had been removed, and relatives and friends were seated in a wide circle of somber faces.

Women scurried around in the kitchen, all of them dressed in black—washing dishes and busy with food preparations. Men were seated, silent and resigned. Only an occasional word was spoken by Abe Zook, who invited me to join the others.

Soon, Rachel came in and sat beside me on the wooden bench, briefly touching my hand. Her face was solemn and pale.

My throat was dry, too dry to speak. I coughed down the tears. "What happened?" I whispered. "What went wrong?"

"He died in his sleep."

"*He?*"

"Grossdawdy," she said softly. "He sat down in his rocking chair after lunch and . . . was . . . gone."

I was overcome with emotion. Grandfather Zook? How could it be? I thought back to how he had come to the hospital Tuesday night . . . read his poem to Susie and . . . and . . .

Then I remembered his trembling hands. The way he'd said that his work was done.

My heart ached, remembering how I'd embraced the old gentleman. Overwhelmed, I let the news slowly soak in. Little Susie was alive . . . Jacob Zook was dead.

"He wanted to die at home," Rachel whispered. "If it was to be, it's best this way."

I nodded, my brain hazy. "How's Susie?"

"She's resting upstairs. Wanna see her?"

I nodded, and we tiptoed through the sitting room to the steep wooden stairs. When we arrived in Susie's room, she glanced up from her bed.

A smile swept across her rosy-cheeked face. "When are we gonna catch fireflies again, Merry?"

I hurried to her and smoothed the handmade quilt at the foot of the maple bed. "As soon as you feel better."

"I'm gut, really I am," she insisted. "Mam wants me to rest up so I can go to Grossdawdy's funeral."

I looked at Rachel. "When will it be?"

"Monday." She folded her hands and stared at the floor.

Susie pleaded, "Oh, Merry, you must come."

"Sh-h!" Rachel warned. "Keep your voice down."

Susie nodded her head slowly, looking repentant.

Rachel moved across the uneven floor to a framed piece on the wall above the bed. Carefully, she took it off the nail and showed it to me.

It was the firefly poem, beautifully framed in solid pine. "Your grandfather made this?" I stroked the wood, feeling its silklike smoothness.

Rachel nodded. "After breakfast Grossdawdy was out in the barn hand-rubbing the wood."

I studied the poem, written in Jacob Zook's own hand. "'Night of the Fireflies,'" I said thoughtfully. "He finished it just in time."

"Read the last verse to me," Susie said, leaning forward slightly.

I turned the framed poem so she could see it. Pointing to each word, I began, "'Tis the night of the fireflies, 'Tis the night of God's call. Dusk comes and is gone, and now . . . True light shines on us all."

Tears filled Susie's eyes as she chanted the refrain. "Come one, come all, to the firefly ball . . ."

Suddenly, Rachel's face grew serious. "Ach! Grossdawdy must've known." She peered over my shoulder. "Look, it says, 'Tis the night of God's call.'"

It was hard to put into words, but looking at the last verse, it almost seemed that Grandfather Zook *had* known—that he was preparing us.

After a silent moment, Susie spoke. "I like this line best." She pointed to the last line. "'True light shines on us all.'"

"Jah," Rachel whispered. "Jah."

Three different clocks chimed nine times in the Zooks' house on Monday morning. When the last clock stopped, the Amish bishop removed his hat. At once, all the other Amishmen took off their straw hats in a swift, precise motion.

Benches had been placed parallel to the length of each of the three large rooms. The kitchen, dining room, and living room were packed with nearly two hundred fifty people, as many as had attended Curly John and Sarah's wedding last November. They, along with the other Zook family members, sat facing the unpainted pine coffin at the end of the living room with their backs to the ministers.

I noticed Esther glance at Susie once during the thirty-minute *first* sermon. The speaker made reference to the fact that God had spoken to us through the death of a brother.

"We do not wish our brother Jacob back, but rather we shall prepare to follow after this departed one. His voice no longer is heard amongst us. His hand is absent at the plow; his presence—'tis no longer felt. His bed is empty, his chair . . ."

I tuned the minister out. Hearing the way these people solemnly accepted the death of this dear, dear man made me even sadder than his passing. Where were the words of comfort, the words describing his beautiful, joyous life? The joy, the love he'd passed to others? The way he loved God?

Fidgeting slightly, I wondered how Levi felt about all this now. Was he feeling the pain, too?

A second minister stood to his feet and began to say that a call from heaven, a loud call, had come to this very assembly. "The holy Scriptures admonish each one of us to be ready to meet our death. We do not know when it is that our own time will come, but most important—we *must* be ready!"

I studied the steady rising and falling of Susie's, Aaron's, Ella Mae's, and Nancy's shoulders as they sat next to one another, looking like stairsteps. Rachel and Levi sat at the end of the bench row. Their bereaved grandmother sat between Abe and Esther, and occasionally, she slumped in her chair. I held my breath, hoping she wouldn't pass out or maybe even pass away in front of our eyes.

Amish funerals usually lasted about two and a half hours. I felt truly sorry for Grandma Zook. Then, when the minister began to direct his comments toward the teenagers gathered there, I began to feel sorry for Levi.

"My dear young people," he said, "when you reach the age to think of joining the church, please do not put it off." The words were accented with strong emotion, and I wondered if they would have an impact on Levi and his plans for the future.

Two long passages were read from the Bible. But no one said anything about Jacob Zook's life. The thrust of the sermons was an appeal to the people to live godly, righteous lives. To prepare for death, as well.

Next, the first minister stood up and read a brief obituary. "Jacob's memory is a keepsake—with that we cannot part. His soul is in God's keeping. We have him in our hearts."

There were no flowers at this funeral. No music, either. Someone read an Amish hymn, then all of us sitting in the living room went outside while the ministers arranged for the coffin to be placed on the front porch—the most convenient area for the final viewing.

Abe, Esther, Grandma Zook, and all the Zook children stood behind the open coffin as the long line of friends and relatives filed past. Some shed tears, but I didn't hear any weeping. Not even from Jacob's widow. It was surprising how matter-of-fact these dear friends were about embracing death.

I wondered if things would've been different if Susie had been the one lying in the pine box today. But it was Jacob's time, the minister had said. *Jacob's.*

When I stood in front of the coffin to say good-bye to Grandfather Zook, Susie left her family and tiptoed silently to stand beside me.

Gently, she slipped her small hand into mine and whispered, "Come one, come all, to the firefly ball. Dance with 'em, laugh with 'em. Run straight and tall."

Through my tears, I saw Grandfather Zook's body dressed in the traditional white—a special white burial vest and trousers. His white dress shirt was neatly pressed for the occasion.

I held in the sobs that threatened to burst out, remembering the feel of his cheek against my hand in the hospital, then my arms around him. I remembered the exuberant way he'd first read his poem to me, here on the front porch while he sat in his hickory rocker. And the way he'd brought the jar of fireflies to the hospital for his unconscious granddaughter.

" 'True light shines on us all,' " I whispered. "I'll miss you, Grandfather."

Susie let go of my hand and slipped back into line with her family. I walked to the driveway to stand with the rest of the mourners, waiting for the horse and buggy processional to the graveyard. I glanced over at a group of Amish teen boys preparing the hearse—a one-horse spring wagon with the seat pushed forward.

At last, the viewing line ended. The horses were hitched up to the many buggies parked in the side yard and along the Zooks' lane. Levi was going to drive one of them since there wasn't room in the family buggy for all the Zooks. So Rachel, Nancy, and Susie rode with Levi and me.

What a long procession it was. Susie sat close to me up front, sometimes leaning her head against my shoulder.

"How are you feeling?" I asked her.

"Not sick, just lonely."

For Grandfather, I thought as I watched the stately line of horses and carriages slowly making their way down SummerHill Lane. A sobering sight.

"There're about two hundred buggies in the caravan today," Levi remarked, glancing at me. "It'll take us about an hour. Hope you won't be too tired."

It was a thoughtful thing for him to say. After all, I was used to getting places fast in fancy cars. But today, the slowed pace allowed time for reflection. A nice change from the hustle-bustle of the modern world.

By the time we arrived at the Amish cemetery, the sun was high overhead. Susie and Rachel stood on either side of me as four pallbearers carried the coffin to the appointed sight. The hole in the earth was ready, and Susie reached for my hand, squeezing it hard as her grandfather's coffin was lowered into the ground.

The pallbearers dug their shovels into the rich Pennsylvania soil. *Clump.* The sound of the dirt hitting the top of the coffin brought tears again to my eyes. Susie sniffled, and Rachel kept her hands tightly folded as she stared at the ground.

When the hole was half filled, one of the ministers read a hymn. Then another recited, " 'The Lord giveth; the Lord taketh away. . . .' "

I glanced down at Susie, surprised to see an endearing smile on her angelic face. *The Lord giveth.*

How glad I was that the Lord had given her back—had answered my prayers. I wanted to sing for joy. I wanted to run around and shout God's mercies to the mourners. But I didn't want to embarrass Levi or Rachel, and I certainly didn't want to give my spunky little friend any ideas. However, I must admit, I was mighty thankful. God was good!

Nineteen Night of the Fireflies

Susie and I eventually did go chasing fireflies again. Levi and Rachel got in on the fun, too. We even taught them to say the poem by heart.

Word of Jacob Zook's poem spread up and down SummerHill. Everyone was saying it, and those who hadn't learned it wanted to.

I got the bright idea to self-publish it—even took some time-exposed shots with my camera at dusk one night. The sky was hazy red and the fireflies were dancing and twinkling everywhere you looked. One picture turned out better than the rest, so I made a bunch of copies to go along with the poem.

Rachel, Susie, and I had a regular assembly line going. Rachel copied the poem in her own handwriting, I glued the photo in place, and all three of us started distributing them.

Before long, every neighbor on SummerHill had a hand-printed copy of the poem with the picture glued to the bottom.

As for Lissa, she and I started spending more time together. Lots more. We secretly teamed up to pray for Chelsea. When I told Levi, he wanted to be in on it, too. The way I see it, Chelsea doesn't stand a chance of continuing her atheist routine.

Jon Klein called several times, and we've actually started playing our alliteration game again. Maybe Ashley Horton *is* going to make her move, but I'm not worried. She can't alliterate worth beans!

Which brings me to Levi. My Amish friend wants to take his GED so he can go to Bible school in September. I'm excited for him, and if all goes well, he'll be a college freshman.

School—now *there's* a scary thought. Tenth grade's coming up mighty fast. Too fast. I guess if I could make a wish and have it come true, I'd want the summer to last forever.

Earlier tonight, Rachel, Susie, and I sat on their front porch sipping lemonade. In the stillness, I could almost hear Grandfather's sweet, wavering voice as though it were coming from his hickory rocker—now vacant in the fading light of dusk.

'Tis the night of the fireflies . . .

A Cry in the Dark

For
Barb Lilland,
who first shared the dream
that became
SummerHill Secrets.
And . . .
who received
a true gift from God
one Christmas Eve—
Jordan Robert.

*A joy that's shared is
a joy made double.*

—Anonymous

A Cry in the Dark One

"Don't move!" I aimed my camera lens at the blond, wispy-haired girl posing on my front porch. "This is it! A truly amazing shot. Don't breathe!"

"For how long?" Lissa Vyner asked, smiling.

"Till I say so."

Slowly, I backed away from the porch, where my friend balanced gracefully on the white banister leading to the sidewalk. Dressed in summer pink, she put on airs for the camera. She'd worn the dazzling junior bridesmaid's dress to her cousin's wedding last week, and by the dreamy look on her face, I knew she was still chock-full of romantic whimsy.

Three more shots. Each took several minutes to set up. That's how I liked to work—meticulously. Photography was my passion, and when I was working with film, like now, I had to be even more particular.

"Hurry, Merry, it's hot out here," Lissa urged.

"Can't rush a masterpiece." I carefully checked the aperture on my camera, adjusting the lens opening for appropriate light.

Out of the corner of my eye, I noticed a pickup truck coming down SummerHill Lane. The noisy muffler captured my curiosity. I wouldn't have bothered to look, except the old rattletrap swerved off the road, crept along the shoulder, and came to a shuddering stop right in front of our mailbox.

"Expecting company?" Lissa teased.

I had no idea who the driver was or what he wanted. And since my parents were in Lancaster running errands, I kept my distance.

A hefty guy in his early twenties leaned his arm on the window and hollered out, "Y'all live here?" He glanced for a moment at Lissa, who was still perched on the banister waiting for the next picture.

"Are you lost?" I asked, avoiding his question.

"Jist wonderin' about this here neck of the woods" came the reply. "Shore would call it the sticks back home. Not much activity round." His eyes were a hot blue—far different from the kind, innocent blue of Lissa's eyes. I felt uneasy.

"Are you looking for a street address?" I asked politely, careful not to display my concern.

"No, ma'am, I ain't." His accent was southern, and his answer rather blunt. He ran a chapped hand through his thick, greasy hair. "Is thar a doctor in these here parts?"

"Is someone sick?" I studied him from my vantage point. He didn't appear to be in need of medical help.

"Well, it ain't yer run-of-the-mill sickness, if that's whatcha mean. . . ." His voice trailed off.

"There's a hospital in town about twenty minutes away." Although our mailbox noted the fact that my dad was an ER doctor, I was hesitant to divulge family information, especially to a stranger.

"In town, ya say?" He craned his neck, looking around. "Alls I see is fields and barns, and . . ." He paused. "Them Plain folks . . . uh, whatcha call 'em?"

"They're Pennsylvania Amish." I said it proudly, as though I were one of them. My great-great grandfather had been Amish, and one of my dearest friends, Rachel Zook down the lane, was, too.

The stranger nodded, scratching his left eyebrow. "Well, thanks for yer help. I 'spect I best be goin'." With that, he turned on the ignition and steered his clunky pickup onto the road and down the hill.

I scurried up the lawn to Lissa. "Did you catch that?"

She nodded. "Seemed kinda strange."

"Sure did," I said, fooling with my camera. "I'm glad he's gone."

Lissa agreed. "Did you notice his license plate?"

"Nope, did you?"

"Well, I know it wasn't a Pennsylvania plate, but I couldn't see the state." She wiggled around, swinging her legs. "How much longer do I have to sit here?"

"Just keep smiling. I'm almost done—honest." *Click!* I took five more shots before calling it quits. "Okay, you can relax now," I said, walking toward her.

"Grammy will be so thrilled." She stood up and brushed herself off.

"Why'd your grandma want so many pictures?" I leaned against the porch railing.

"Grammy Vyner broke her hip last week and couldn't come to my cousin's wedding," Lissa explained. "You should meet her sometime, Merry. My grammy lives for family events. Her life revolves around them." She sighed. "Her hip surgery—the whole thing—completely devastated her."

"She probably wanted to see her granddaughter in a dress, right?" I laughed.

"Silly you." Lissa twirled around, and the fancy skirt billowed out. "It's not like I never wear one."

I put my camera in its case and set it down on the step. "Okay, when was the last time, not counting the wedding?"

Lissa stared at the cornfield across the lane. "Let's see . . ."

I waited, then—"See! You can't remember the last time you had on a dress."

"Merry Hanson, don't exaggerate!" She chased after me as I ran down the sloping front yard toward the dirt road.

"When's the last time you ran in dress shoes?" I yelled back.

But my taunting didn't stop Lissa. She kicked off her white leather sandals and ran along the road barefoot through the wild strawberry vines nestled in the grassy ditch.

"Watch out for garter snakes," I teased.

"What?" She stopped running.

I turned around, calling back to her. "Didn'tcha know? Snakes come out when city girls come to visit."

"Merry!" she hollered. "You know that's not one bit true! Besides, I'm *not* a city girl!"

I grinned at her, my good friend Lissa Vyner. Gullible. Stubborn too. Pete's sake, she'd stolen Jon Klein, my secret crush, out from under my nose last spring. But Lissa and Jon were a thing of the past.

"Thirsty?" I asked.

She wiped the perspiration off her face. "It's way too hot, running around in this heat."

"Okay, we'll go inside and cool off." I hurried up the lane, matching her stride. "The humidity's a killer."

We walked up the hill together, past the willow grove and the shortcut to the Zooks' farm. Then I heard a familiar noise. The sound of that rickety old pickup. It was coming up the lane, right behind us!

"Look who's back," Lissa said as the truck slowed down.

"Let's go!" I grabbed her arm, and we ran all the way up the hill to my house. When we were safely inside, I peeked through the living room curtains, catching my breath.

"What's he want?" Lissa whispered.

"I wish I knew."

The two of us watched as the faded pickup slowed to a crawl. The driver eyeballed the house. My heart pounded when his eyes came to rest on our mailbox. "Oh no," I whispered. "Now he knows Dad's a doctor. What if he comes to the door?"

"It's locked, right?" Lissa asked softly.

I nodded. Still, I was fearful.

Then, without warning, the faded blue truck accelerated, struggling against the steep grade. It snorted and puffed, leaving a trail of dust in its path.

"Man, he needs some new wheels," Lissa remarked, a hint of relief in her voice.

"A new muffler, too," I said, remembering what my older brother had told me about worn-out mufflers. For once, something Skip had said actually stuck in my brain.

"That guy scares me," Lissa said, still peering out the window. "What's he want?"

"I know one thing, I wasn't going to stick around to find out."

"Maybe he's a serial killer," she suggested.

"We're still alive, aren't we?" I forced a laugh, which helped lessen the tension. "There's something weird about him, though. Something about the way he kept checking the place out. And looking at our mailbox."

"What could it mean?"

"I'm not sure," I said. "I hope he's not a burglar. Maybe he's into identity theft."

Lissa and I headed up the long wooden staircase to the second story of my family's hundred-year-old farmhouse.

"I can't wait to put on some shorts," she said as we entered my room.

"See, I told you! You hate dresses." We laughed about it. I'd caught her good.

While Lissa changed clothes, I put my camera away, trying to shake off the weird feeling. But as hard as I tried, I couldn't get the stranger in the blue pickup out of my mind. I must admit—he gave me the willies!

Two A Cry in the Dark

"It's a scorcher," Dad said as he and Mom came into the kitchen loaded with grocery bags.

"You're tellin' me." I got up to help. "It was so hot, Mrs. Vyner brought ice cream over when she came to pick up Lissa. The three of us made cones and sat out in the gazebo trying to cool off."

Mom turned the lazy susan in the corner of one kitchen cabinet. "How's Lissa doing these days?"

I knew she really wanted to know how Lissa's *father* was doing. He'd had severe problems with alcohol and abuse—so bad that Lissa had run away. Thankfully, those frightening days were behind them. "Lissa says things are totally different since her dad's been going for therapy."

"So, you think the abuse has stopped?" Mom asked, searching me with all-knowing brown eyes.

"I'm one-hundred-percent-amen sure."

Mom smiled. "That's good."

I stretched on tiptoes, sliding two cans of tuna onto the top corner shelf. "Lissa says her mom's going to invite him to the church potluck next week."

"Great idea," she said. "I hope he'll come."

I smiled, watching Mom dash around the kitchen, putting things away. The old tension-filled days between us were gone. Mom was relaxed now, no longer preoccupied with the loss of Faithie—my twin sister—who had died of cancer the summer she was seven. Actually, Mom's cheerful demeanor surprised me because the anniversary of Faithie's death was coming up. Three days from now—July 31.

Dad hauled in two more grocery sacks before sitting down with a glass of iced tea. "Sure will be nice to have your brother home," he remarked to me.

My obnoxious big brother had gone to help out at a camp for handicapped kids—something he did every summer. This time would be his last before heading off to college next month. I couldn't wait for that moment. Total peace and quiet—my life could possibly be stress-free for a change. "When's Skip supposed to get back?" I asked.

"Let's see." Dad pulled a pocket calendar from his wallet. "He'll be home the weekend after next."

"Just in time for the church potluck," Mom added happily. My parents missed their one and only son; that was plain to see. Losing their firstborn to college would be tough.

"Need some sugar?" I asked Dad, bringing over the bowl and setting it near his glass.

He waved his hand. "Nah, I'm cutting back on sweets all around."

"Hey, that's a first," I teased.

"Your father's counting calories these days," Mom said, coming over to sit at the table. "He'll be fifty next month, you know."

Fifty in August, I thought. Someone else was having a birthday next month. His seventeenth. But I didn't want to clutter my brain with Levi Zook just now. Rachel Zook's brother had shocked the local Amish community and decided to go off to a Mennonite Bible school. Oh, sure, he and I were still friends—very good friends, in fact—but I hadn't exactly thought through a possible long-distance relationship. Levi hadn't, either.

Besides, now that Jon Klein was available . . . well, I wanted to wait and see what might happen.

Later, during supper, I brought up the subject of the stranger. "Have you ever seen an old blue pickup around here? The jalopy has a really bad muffler."

Mom shook her head. "Why do you ask?"

"Just wondered," I said. "The driver seems displaced, I guess."

"Homeless, perhaps?" Dad suggested.

"I don't think so. It's hard to put a finger on it," I said, "but I know there's something truly strange going on."

"Well," Dad said, rubbing his hands together, "I'll be on the lookout. In the meantime, keep the doors and windows locked at night, okay?"

I must admit I was glad our bedrooms were high up on the second floor. Without air-conditioning, it was way too hot to sleep with the bedroom windows closed. Around here, we called these sultry summer days, dog days. Even the dogs were hot. Cats too.

Mom pinched off the dead blooms on her African violets while I loaded the dishwasher. She had a knack for making them flourish—even the velvety green leaves looked plump. Her plants dazzled the corner of our country kitchen with blossoms of purple, pink, and snowy white.

"Do you think Dad has an enemy?" I said, letting the words slip out.

Mom straightened up and turned to look at me. "Honey, why would you think such a thing?"

It was the stranger. I couldn't get him out of my mind. I folded the dishcloth before responding. "It just seems weird that a guy would be asking around for a doctor, like maybe he was trying to track Dad down or something."

"It's most likely a simple coincidence," Mom offered, going back to violet pinching.

"Maybe." I left the kitchen with Mom still fussing over her plant babies.

Upstairs, I grew more and more impatient with the stifling heat. It was too hot for a shower up here, I decided. So I went to my room and found clean clothes, a bath towel, and a brush for my hair.

I dashed down the steep back steps leading to the kitchen and flicked on the light as I opened the door leading to the basement. Dad had rigged up a small shower in our cellar years before, but we rarely used it. My cats Shadrach, Meshach, and Abednego followed close behind. Lily White, my kitten, was probably outside snoozing under the gazebo.

Musty and cool, the cellar was a welcome change in temperature, and I congratulated myself on this wise move. I ran the water, making it tepid, the perfect temperature to refresh my perspiring body. While scrubbing my arms, I thought of Faithie. She'd hated this dark cellar—in fact, she had recoiled at anything related to darkness. I remembered several moonless nights long ago when she had crawled into bed with me, trembling with fear.

Poor little Faithie, I thought.

I missed her terribly. In all my nearly sixteen years, no one had come along to truly soothe the pain of loss. No one. And yet I longed for it. Prayed for it.

It wasn't like I didn't have good friends. I had plenty of them at school and at church. And there was always Rachel, my Amish girl friend in the farmhouse beyond the willows. Her youngest sister, Susie, and I had become close pals, too. But something always seemed unsettled—amiss—in the soul of me. I longed for a Faithie replacement. Someone exactly like her.

I reached up and turned the cold spigot just enough to cool the water, letting it beat on my back. Then I began to pray. "Dear Lord, it's been such a long time since I mentioned this, but maybe you could find it in your will to help me. I feel sad, like I haven't in a long time. Maybe it's because of July 31 . . . it's coming so soon. Faithie's gone-to-heaven day."

The memory made my heart heavy, and tears spilled down my face. Purposefully, I turned and raised my face toward the splashing stream, letting the water bounce off my cheeks. In that moment, I comforted myself with the knowledge that Faithie was surrounded by light. By Jesus himself! Never again to experience darkness or the fear of it.

"Oh, Lord," I cried. "Let some of that same light pour into my own heart."

I lingered in the shower stall long after I wrapped myself in a heavy towel, hoping for an answer.

Hours later, as dusk approached, I sat outside in the gazebo. Wearing a T-shirt and gray shorts, I relished the evening breeze. My cats, all four of them, surrounded me with their purring, cuddly selves.

"You guys weren't even born back when my twin sister was alive," I told them.

Abednego, the oldest, lifted his head nonchalantly as if to say, *I've heard this story before, thank you kindly.*

"Don't give me that look," I reprimanded. "You should be thankful I took you and your brothers in. Homeless strays, that's what you were."

Lily White shook her head and a dainty little sneeze flew out. Shadrach pounced on her, and off they went, down the white gazebo steps, rolling and playing. Meshach eventually got in on the action, but it was Abednego who stayed closest to me. Usually, *he* was the one off somewhere else.

"What's the matter, little boy?" I touched his soft black head. "Too tired to play?"

He twitched his whiskers.

"Are you protecting your mistress Merry?" I chuckled, thinking of Jon Klein. He'd often referred to me as Mistress Merry, a direct result of our private alliteration word game.

Jon and his family were off on a camping trip in the Poconos. The Alliteration Wizard had actually called to say good-bye. The old spark was definitely alive between us.

Lissa, of course, knew nothing of it. She'd had her chance with Jon, and although they seemed to get along fine, I knew she wasn't a candidate for alliteration competition. Not to boast, but for as long as I'd known Jon, he and I had had this amazing attraction to word play. Because of it, we were drawn to each other.

Merry, Mistress of Mirth was Jon's favorite way to address me. He was an intelligent, jovial guy, but totally spacey when it came to girls. I often wondered if he had any idea how I felt about him. Jon head-in-the-clouds Klein was special in more ways than one. He was one of the few friends I had who'd actually known Faithie—besides Rachel and Levi Zook and their family, of course, and a friend from school named Chelsea Davis.

"Merry!" My mom's voice jolted me back. "Someone's on the phone for you."

"Coming." I got up and hurried toward the back door. Abednego followed close behind. I held the screen door for him, then hurried to the phone. "Hello?"

"Hullo, Merry. It's Levi. I'm calling from town."

"Hi. What's up?"

He paused, probably getting up the nerve to ask me out. "Uh . . . Merry, how would ya like to go to a concert with me a week from this Saturday night?"

"Saturday?"

"*Jah,* in Ephrata at a Mennonite church."

It sounded like fun, but we were planning to attend our church potluck that same afternoon, and family church events often spilled over into the evening. Besides, Jon Klein would be back from camping, and I wanted to see him. "I hope you didn't buy the tickets yet," I said.

"Jah, I did. Just hopin'—ya know." There was an eager, almost impatient tone to his voice.

"Well, I can't go," I said. "I'm sorry."

"*Ach,* Merry, won'tcha think about it?" Now I knew he was perturbed.

"Please don't push me," I responded.

"Merry? Is something wrong?"

I sighed. "I'm having a rough day."

His voice grew softer. "I could come over and we could talk." His gentle words tugged at me.

"Thanks, but I'm really tired."

"Oh." He sounded dejected. "Maybe if—"

"Not tonight," I said, wishing things hadn't been left hanging between Levi and me.

"Okay, then. I'll talk to ya soon, Merry."

"Good-bye." I must've been in a fog standing there holding the phone because Mom waved her hand in front of my face. "Mer? Everything okay?" she whispered.

I exhaled and hung up the phone. I needed to talk to someone. Was Mom a good choice? Would she understand my frustration— being caught between *two* guys?

I pulled my hair back into a ponytail and then freed it, studying her. "Mom? Can we go somewhere private?"

Her face broke into a full smile. "You name the place."

"Ever been to the willow grove?" I asked sheepishly.

"Oh . . . the secret place?"

I grinned. "How do you know about that?"

We were already walking toward the back door. "Faithie took me there once," she confessed.

"Faithie?" I was baffled. The secret place had always been off limits to adults. It was one of those special spots that often existed in the heart or the imagination—but this one had the benefit of being *real.*

"She took me there several weeks before she died," Mom admitted, her eyes still shining.

Once again, Faithie had beaten me to the punch. She had always been an expert at it—loved being the first to show Mom things. Schoolwork, her drawings . . . everything. Maybe her need to do that came from having been the firstborn twin by about twenty minutes. I felt a twinge of resentment.

"Are you sure you want to go to the willows?" Mom asked.

"I'm sure." I led the way outside through the backyard and around the long side yard, to the dirt road that was SummerHill Lane. Reaching up, I caught a firefly. "It's been a long time since we really talked," I began.

"And I take all the blame for that," she said.

"You?"

She nodded. "Up until a few weeks ago, I couldn't bring myself to this point. But now . . ." She stopped. "Of course, that has nothing to do with you. Anyway, I'm very sorry."

Mom turned at the shortcut to the willows as though she'd been here more than once. I wondered but followed in silence. The path was only wide enough for walking single file, worn from constant use. Rachel and I met often in the secret place. Six-year-old Susie, too. It was a leafy green haven for the kid in you.

At last we found it, the secluded place—encircled by wispy willow tendrils, some thicker than others, and cushioned by the soft grassy floor beneath the arms of graceful branches. The air was thick with firefly light, creating a magical atmosphere.

"Just coming here helps sometimes," I said.

"I know." Mom brushed the hair away from her face.

"You've been here since coming with Faithie the first time, haven't you, Mom?"

She nodded. "You're a perceptive girl, Merry. Much like your father."

"And Faithie was like you." It was a statement, not a question.

"I guess you could say there was a similarity."

"She even looked like you," I added.

Mom was quiet now. I studied her in the dim light of dusk, wishing she'd talk more freely.

"Did you ever think you were in love with two guys at once?" The question leaped off my lips before I could reconsider my choice of words.

She leaned back, looking at the sky. "There were two boys in my life when I was in high school. I can't say that I *loved* them both."

"What did you do?" I asked. "How did you decide?"

"I prayed about it."

Her spiritual approach didn't surprise me. "Tell me more," I said, sitting on my knees.

"Well, my mother—your grandmother—told me once that she'd started praying for the man I would marry when I was just a toddler."

"Wow." This was truly amazing.

"And God arranged everything, right down to the fact that one of those boys started dating another girl his senior year. Of course, I felt that I'd lost a friend, but not my *best* friend—the other boy—who turned out to be your father."

"Really? Dad was one of the two guys?"

"Are you surprised?"

"So you're saying you might've ended up with someone other than Dad if you hadn't prayed?"

She looked at me as she spoke. "All three of us were Christians; we all wanted God's will for our lives. Both boys were perfectly suitable mates." She smiled. "You get to know that by being good friends, by not being in a hurry. The Lord has a way of making things very clear."

I thought about what she'd said. Jon, Levi, and I were good friends, too. None of us was in a hurry. But perfectly suitable mates? I had no idea about either one. Besides, I was too young to think about settling down with anyone yet.

I wondered if Mom would start her you're-too-young-to-be-thinking-this-way-about-boys speech, or if she'd actually trust me to make wise judgments on my own. She said nothing, though, and we sat there enjoying the early evening together. Mother and daughter.

A gentle wind whispered through the willows, and I had a strange feeling. A feeling that the secret place would never be quite the same.

Four *A Cry in the Dark*

It was nearly eight when Mom and I returned to the house. She went into the family room, where Dad had closed things up and turned on the only air-conditioner in the house. I said good-night and headed upstairs with my cats.

The second floor was sweltering. First thing, I opened all the windows in my room. Then I stood looking out across the expanse of field and sky. I hugged myself for a moment, thinking. The chat with Mom had warmed my heart. Was it a new beginning for us?

With July 31 so near, I knew I shouldn't hold my breath about it. Faithie's death had muddled things up for nearly the last nine years. Especially between Mom and me. I could only hope that we'd made a breakthrough today in the willow grove. I decided to pray about it.

While I stared out the window, telling God my concerns, I heard a sound. In the distance, but coming closer. The cats raised their heads, cocking their ears. "It's the jalopy again," I whispered. "I'd recognize that bad muffler anywhere."

I waited behind the window curtains, watching. Then I saw it—the old blue pickup. It stopped in front of the house. My heart pounded.

I could see the stranger sitting in the driver's seat. This time someone was with him. A young woman. No . . . a young girl not much older than I was.

Then I heard voices. Angry voices.

Shouting. Arguing.

I listened intently, trying to sort out what was being said.

"Go on—do it!" the man ordered.

The girl began to cry. Sad, horrible sobs. She got out of the truck and began to wring her hands in despair, looking into the cab of the truck every so often as though she were checking on something.

The man held up a bundle of laundry. "Do what I told ya!" he demanded.

The girl's voice was muffled with tears. "Please . . . no!"

"We haven't any choice, ya hear?" came the harsh reply.

"But I cain't . . . I cain't." More heart-wrenching sobs.

The man put down the dirty clothes and leaped out of the truck. He ran around the front of the pickup and grabbed hold of the girl, shaking her. "Now, ya listen here, and ya listen good!"

I'd had enough. I couldn't stand by and watch this guy get brutal. I ran out of my room and down the front steps. Hesitating in the entryway, I wondered if I should get Dad to come out with me.

"Dad!" I called. "Come here!" Then I remembered. The air-conditioner was going full blast in the family room. No way could he hear me.

I dashed down the hall to the kitchen and out to the family room addition. I opened the door and peeked in. Dad was resting against the back of the recliner, sawing logs. Mom was nowhere in sight. She was probably in the shower upstairs, getting ready for bed.

I reached out to touch Dad. Lightly, I tapped his arm. He moved in his sleep slightly. I realized he was out and probably would be too hazy to help even if he did wake up.

Then and there, I decided I couldn't waste another minute. I turned and ran all the way down the front hallway. The screen door was locked, and I fumbled with the latch for several frantic seconds. Finally, when I got it open, I burst out of the house.

Standing on the porch, I scanned the road where minutes before there'd been a battle raging. I couldn't believe my eyes. The pickup was gone. Vanished!

"Where'd they go?" Undaunted, I walked around the side yard facing Strawberry Lane.

No pickup and no girl.

Then I hurried around the front to the opposite side yard, facing the willow grove.

Nothing!

I leaned on a giant split log on the woodpile, puzzled. Hadn't I just witnessed a major fight? And what had that horrible guy been saying? I thought back to the frightening conversation. *Do what I told you!*

What did it mean? Was the girl the sick one? Was she too shy to ring our doorbell—to talk to a doctor? Was that it?

I ran out to SummerHill Lane where the pickup truck had been parked, scouring the area. I searched the side of the road, in the grass, and near the mailbox. There was nothing to be found.

I looked in both directions, up the hill toward Strawberry Lane as far as I could see in the early moonlight, and all the way down, toward the Zooks' farm. Way in the distance, there might have been a tuft of smoke on the road, but I couldn't be sure in the growing dimness.

How'd they get away so fast? I wondered. *And why?*

I was heading back around the side yard toward the gazebo when I heard another sound. The sound of a kitten fussing.

"Lily White, is that you?" I called. "Here, kitty kitty." I waited for Lily to come strutting her regal white self, but seconds passed and she didn't come.

Then I heard it again. This time louder. It didn't exactly sound like a kitten now, although with all that had just happened, maybe I was too shaken to sort it out.

I searched the area around me, listening, following the sound. "Lily?" I called again, beginning to worry that she'd gotten herself caught somewhere. I turned to look toward the willow grove, but it was getting too dark to determine anything without a flashlight. "Lily, are you stuck?"

The cry came again. And I began to realize it was not coming from the willows. The sound was coming from the backyard. From the gazebo.

I rushed to the white-latticed outdoor room. Inside, I noticed a pile of clothes. My throat turned dry. *Aren't these the same ones I saw in the pickup—in the stranger's hands?*

Now they were all bunched up in the corner. Yet the sound came from inside the heap of clothes. Cautiously, I approached the mass of laundry, or what I thought to be clothes, and when I focused my eyes in the darkness, I realized these were blankets.

Then I heard a distinct cry and curiously lifted the blankets. "What on earth?" I whispered into the night.

There, in a wicker laundry basket, was a baby!

I reached out in amazement and touched the thin, pink blanket. The small bundle moved slightly under my touch and began to whimper. "Oh, don't cry," I said, finding my voice. "It's okay." But I knew it wasn't.

I looked around, wondering if someone was hiding out in the darkness. Was this some kind of crazy joke?

Wait a minute, I thought. *Those people . . . those horrible people. Did they do this? Did they abandon this beautiful baby girl?*

I stood up and found the tin filled with matches and lit a citronella candle. "There. Now we can see better, can't we?" I said as much to the little one as to the dusk.

The baby cooed a sweet response, and the sound broke my heart. As I came back to kneel at the foot of the wicker basket, I noticed something. Something I'd missed before. A note pinned to the blanket.

Quickly, I removed the safety pin. And holding the note up to the candle, I began to read.

Five A Cry in the Dark

To the finder: I am two months old. My bottle is in the basket. Please take care of me and love me as your own.

I smoothed the paper and read the words again. *Love me as your own. . . .*

I hid the note in the basket and leaned close to the infant girl snuggled inside. Her eyes were closed, and her tiny face was wrapped in an angelic glow.

"You're beautiful," I whispered, stroking the satiny cheek. "I will take good care of you. I promise."

Gently, I searched the basket for a bottle. Babies needed to be fed every few hours. I knew that because my twin cousins seemed to be hungry all the time.

Deep in the basket, I found an eight-ounce bottle filled with milk. The nipple had a plastic cap, and there were several bottles of ready-made formula and some disposable diapers, too.

"Well, looks like someone planned ahead," I mumbled. But I was worried. Had the baby's parents truly abandoned her? And if so, why?

The idea of leaving a baby outside alone, even on a warm summer night, angered me. What were they thinking? I sat next to the wicker basket, never taking my eyes off the pink cheeks and the rosebud lips. "You're the most beautiful baby I've ever seen,"

I whispered. The lump in my throat grew bigger, and I thought I would cry. "How could they leave you?"

Tears sprang up and I let them fall. Silently, I cried for the baby nobody wanted. And I prayed. "Dear Lord, please help me take care of her. This darling little gift."

I stopped praying and clutched my aching throat. *A gift! Is the baby truly a gift from God . . . to me?*

My prayer!

Suddenly, I remembered. I'd prayed a prayer this very day—in the dank, dark cellar where I'd taken a shower to cool off. What exactly had I said to God?

I pondered my words. *What* had I prayed? Something about finding it in His will to help me. I hadn't specifically asked for a person—certainly not a baby—to fill the hole that Faithie's death had left in me. But now that this incredibly marvelous baby was here, I was beginning to wonder.

The light from the candle on the table cast a soft pink glow on the sleeping infant. She stirred peacefully, and as I watched, something in me longed to hold her. Strong feelings of responsibility and of love sprang up in me. I'd never felt like this about a baby. Typically, babies scared me to pieces, made me uncomfortable. When they first had come for a visit, even my baby cousins, Ben and Becky, made me nervous.

I gazed at the baby in her wicker bed. She was different somehow. "Let's make sure you're all right," I said, reaching into the basket.

I brought her up into my arms. She lifted her tiny fist and waved it in the air. I put my finger next to the plump little hand, and she grabbed hold with a mighty grip. Slowly, I carried her to the table, where the citronella candle sent out its rosy glow. I wanted to get a better look at the sleepy bundle.

There in the candlelight, I pulled back her limp blanket and saw only the lightweight cotton undershirt and diaper she wore. I placed my hand on the soft chest and tummy.

"I think it's time to give you a name," I said. "I'll name you Charity. Baby Charity."

My words, the loudest I'd spoken, must've startled her because she opened her eyes. I looked down into the bluest eyes I'd ever seen—as blue as the heavens. Charity squinted at the candlelight as if to say: *I'm trying to say hello, but it's too bright.*

I wrapped the pink blanket around her again and picked her up, moving back into the shadows of the gazebo, away from the light. "Do you like your name?" I whispered, almost cooing as I spoke to her. "It fits you." I sighed. "You don't know it, but I had a twin sister named Faith. I think she would be very happy to know that you've come to me." Again the tears fell, dripping off my chin onto Charity's baby blanket.

Now that she was here—this amazing gift from God—what was I going to do with her? I was sure Mom and Dad had already retired for the night. A quick glance at the house confirmed that. Mom probably thought I'd already gone to bed. And Dad? Well, he'd been zonked out earlier. I envisioned him stumbling up the back steps to bed, exhausted as usual.

For years now, I'd gone to bed on my own without the old childhood tucking-in ritual. I think it was Mom's way of letting me grow up, spread my wings. Although, if I'd been honest, I would've told her I missed it—being covered up and kissed good-night.

I leaned down and kissed Charity's soft forehead. "I know what we'll do. We'll sleep outside together, right here. It's a nice, warm night, and this way, you won't wake up my parents. They don't need to know about you just yet." I wanted to savor this precious moment—my special time with Charity—just the two of us. Before anyone else found out. At least for tonight, she belonged to me.

I kept talking softly to her, the way I did to my cats, who by now were probably sacked out on my bed. "We'll sleep together here in the gazebo, over in the corner just like Faithie and I did once." I caught myself before I said more. But I couldn't stop the memory.

That splendid night was as clear as though it were yesterday. It had been one short month before Faithie died. She'd begged to sleep out under the stars in the gazebo. We were really young—seven, going on eight, but surprisingly, Mom and Dad had agreed. They'd left their windows wide open. Just in case we needed something.

Thinking back, I was sure it was a granting of a "last wish." My parents knew Faithie was dying, and she could be mighty determined sometimes.

Rachel Zook had joined us that night. Rachel's mother had insisted that she bring along her pony and tie him to the gazebo railing—to alert us if there were strangers lurking. But we never feared. Barely slept, either. We were three kids having a good time. One of the last good times before . . .

All of it came rushing back. The sweet, fresh smell of honeysuckle filling the air. And the fireflies. Trillions of them.

I cuddled Charity next to me and felt the steady rising and falling of her breathing. She felt good in my arms. I wanted to hold her forever.

All around were blinking fireflies. And the fragrant aroma of honeysuckle. The air was thick with summer sounds and smells. Charity sighed in her sleep the way Faithie often did.

It was as though time had flip-flopped.

Six A Cry in the Dark

Baby Charity soon became restless. Instead of waiting for her to cut loose with the demanding cries of a hungry baby, I offered her the lukewarm milk in the bottle. She was more than willing to take it and made the gurgling, contented sounds of eager sucking.

When the milk was half gone and she was slowing down a bit, I put her up on my shoulder the way I'd seen Aunt Teri do it. Charity let out a few resounding burps and cooed a bit, then seemed fussy again.

"You're still hungry, aren't you, sweetie?" I turned her around and placed her in my arms, offering her the bottle once more. While she drank, I pretended she was my own baby, singing softly the way a real mother would.

My thoughts drifted to Charity's mother, wherever she was. Had she been the teenager I'd seen in front of the house? Was she being forced to give up her baby?

Shivering, I remembered the frightening incident that had brought me outside in the first place. The girl had needed help, that was evident. She'd pleaded with the man in the driver's seat. Sobbed pitifully. But the man in the blue pickup was relentless. Who *was* he? Certainly not the father of this baby. This wonderful baby!

I glanced down at Charity, now sound asleep. She was so helpless—no parents. No mother to care for her. I touched the top of her head, where her light brown hair formed tiny ringlets. *I* was the one Charity needed. A girl like me would never let her down. Never!

Yet two sides were arguing inside my head.

I found her! She's mine! the selfish, dreamy side insisted.

You're just a kid yourself, the opposite side reasoned. *You can't take care of a baby!*

My heart pounded ninety miles an hour, and eventually the selfish side of me won out. I put Charity back into her basket. Certain that she was in a deep sleep, I hurried to get the pad off the new chaise lounge in the yard. It would be my bed for the night. As for a cover, the night was still warm, but I borrowed one of the lightweight blankets left behind with Charity.

Peacefully, we settled down in our enchanting gazebo house. I situated her in the most well-protected corner and lay beside her, watching her in the moonlight. Minutes later, I gave in to droopy eyes.

My sleep was sweet, filled with a glorious dream. A wonderful voice said, "Your prayer has been answered, Merry Hanson."

In the recesses of my mind, I knew God had given this new baby sister to me. Dream or no dream!

I awakened with a start. The sun was just peeking over the horizon as I leaned up to look at Charity. Her little fist was moving as she peeped her eyes open.

There were sounds of *clip-clopp*ing as a horse and buggy made its way down SummerHill Lane. I wondered if Rachel would be going to market with her mother. It was Friday, and lots of Plain folk would be in downtown Lancaster at Central Market, tending their fruit stands and selling quilts and other handmade things to tourists.

"We've got to have a talk," I said to the baby. "You need some clothes—and that's not all. This basket bed you're sleeping in is going to get very small pretty soon."

She gurgled and smiled in response. Such a happy, contented baby! I continued our chat, locating a disposable diaper in the basket, careful not to lose the note from Charity's mother, or whoever had written it.

Suddenly, I realized someone was watching us!

I spun around. Rachel Zook peered into the gazebo. "Ach, Merry. Who're ya talkin' to?"

I noticed her brown work dress and long, black apron. She'd already been out milking. "What are you doing over here at the crack of dawn?"

Rachel spied the baby. "What a perty baby. Whose is it?"

"It's too long a story for now," I said. "Just promise me something."

She smoothed the hair under her prayer *Kapp* before she spoke again. "Promise ya what?"

"That you won't tell a single soul about this." Desperation seized me.

Rachel's blue eyes widened, and she crept closer. "I don't know . . ." She paused, frowning. "Where'd the baby come from?"

I didn't dare tell Rachel the whole story—not even one smidgen of it. She'd go running off to tell her mother, and before I'd know it, my secret would be out. And my plan ruined.

"Who is she, then?" Rachel asked.

"Her name is Charity." I hoped that was enough to quiet my friend.

"Charity what?"

"I don't need an interrogation," I said.

Her jaw dropped. "I didn't mean to upset ya. I just came over to see if you was up yet."

"What for?"

"Levi wants to talk to ya." She tried to keep a straight face, but a tiny smirk crossed her lips.

"Well, I can't leave Charity alone, so tell him maybe later."

Rachel put her hand on my shoulder. "What's goin' on, really? This baby . . . uh, Merry, why don't ya just tell me about it?"

"Tell you what?" She'd known me too long. Close friends could pick up on unspoken things easily.

"You're bein' too secretive for this not to be what I'm a-thinkin'." Rachel knelt down beside me. "Let's take her over to the farm. *Mam* will know what to do."

I bristled. "This is something *I* have to do."

"*Mam*'s raisin' seven of us children, Merry." My friend wasn't usually this determined. Amish girls were taught to be yielding and compliant.

"Just because your mom's got a bunch of kids doesn't mean I should give her my baby!"

"*Your* baby?" Rachel covered her mouth, looking horrified.

"No, no, silly," I explained. "She's not mine as in my own flesh and blood. She's mine for another reason."

Now Rachel was totally baffled. I could see it in the way her eyes penetrated mine. "Ya still haven't answered my question," she said. "Where'd this baby come from?"

I was about to tell her everything when Charity started to fuss. I knew she was probably hungry. Only one problem with that, though. I had to figure out a way to get inside the house without running into Mom or Dad. Baby Charity needed a clean bottle and nipple.

"Stay here for a second?" I pleaded.

Rachel nodded, still kneeling.

"If she cries, pick her up," I said. "But whatever you do, stay inside the gazebo. You won't be seen here!" I grabbed the empty baby bottle and ran to the house. Inside, I slipped into the kitchen without making a sound, then ran some hot water at the sink.

Yee-ikes! Dad was up—I could hear him walking around upstairs. My pulse raced as I poured a few drops of dish soap into the bottle, creating lots of suds.

Then I heard footsteps on the steps. Someone was coming! My fingers locked in a frenzy as I poured more water over the bottle, hiding my secret in the sink.

"Morning, hon," Mom said, wearing her bathrobe. Then she did a double take. "Merry? Up so soon?"

Actually, my being up this early wasn't highly unusual. There'd been several days this summer that I'd gotten up to have breakfast with Dad before he left for the hospital. "Morning," I replied, avoiding the question.

She pulled her hair back against her neck and yawned. "It's sweet of you to spend time with your father like this." She headed for the fridge, looking at me for a moment. "Are you washing dishes?"

I was stuck—trapped!

"Uh . . . not really. Just cleaning something I found." It was true.

Worried, I glanced out the window and scanned the gazebo. Good. Everything was still under control. But I realized that if I didn't get some formula into that baby mighty soon, there'd be a major racket going on outside!

"What would you like for breakfast today?" Mom asked, still sounding a bit dazed.

"Scrambled eggs and waffles would be nice," I said, choosing something that would take much longer than cold cereal and toast.

Mom sighed. "Waffles and eggs coming up."

I tried not to be too conspicuous and pushed the bottle down under the soapy water, holding it there. My cat quartet padded across the floor to me. Lily White *meow*ed as if to scold me for staying out all night. Shadrach and Meshach did the same. Abednego eyed me with disdain—the powerful silent treatment.

"I'll get your breakfast in a minute," I said. "Just be patient."

Mom closed the refrigerator door and asked, "Are you almost done there, Merry?" She was coming my way!

"Almost." I panicked.

What can I do now?

I prayed that something would keep Mom from finding out about the baby bottle. Anything to distract her would be fine.

Bri-i-ing! The phone rang and she went to get it.

"Thank you, Lord," I whispered and quickly rinsed the bottle and nipple. Casting a furtive glance in Mom's direction, I dashed out the back door, leaving the cats behind.

Swiftly, I hurried into the gazebo, out of sight. Rachel was doing a good job of keeping Charity quiet—letting her suck on one of her knuckles.

"I hope your hands are clean," I reprimanded her.

"Ya didn't want her hollerin', didja?" Rachel was right. A baby wailing in the backyard was sure to draw unwelcome attention.

I opened the bottle of premixed formula and poured it into the clean bottle, still warm from washing. A flick of the wrist, and the nipple was in place. "There we are," I said, reaching for Charity.

Rachel backed away, holding Charity close. "Aw, let me feed her."

Resentment gripped me. "But she's . . ."

"She's not yours, any more than I'm yours." Rachel was grinning. "C'mon, just this once?"

I relinquished the bottle and sat down on the floor, close enough to stroke Charity's silky-soft arm. "We've gotta figure out a way to hide her."

"Ach, so now it's we?"

"You want to help, right?" I said, noticing how cuddly and contented Charity looked in my friend's arms.

"First, tell me where she came from."

It was only fair to let Rachel in on my secret. Since she was going to be involved, she deserved to know something. "Okay, you win." And I told her enough to satisfy her curiosity.

A bewildered look crossed her face. "Did the truck happen to be noisy?" she asked.

"Yeah. Why?"

Rachel looked down at the baby in her arms. "'Cause I heard it goin' up and down SummerHill all last week."

"That's weird. Come to think of it, the guy in the truck wanted to know where there was a doctor," I said, remembering.

"How come, do ya think?"

"It's hard to say. Unless . . ."

"What?"

"Unless he's heard that some doctors arrange adoptions for infertile couples."

Rachel's eyes grew sad. "Jah."

"What's wrong?" I asked.

"That would be a terrible heartache, infertility—especially for Amish wives. Most families in our church district have at least eight children." She sighed. "My second cousin in Ohio could never have babies, though."

"That's too bad," I said. "But your sister-in-law, Sarah, is expecting one this fall, right?"

Rachel brightened. "Jah, come November."

"Won't that be great?" I said. "You'll get to baby-sit your own nephew or niece."

Suddenly, I felt the time pressure, but we talked softly for a few more minutes. I knew I needed to cut this short and go inside to have breakfast with Dad. Otherwise, Mom would suspect something for sure. "Can you hold Charity till I get back?" I asked.

"Where're ya goin' *now*?"

I explained about Mom making eggs and waffles and how I'd sneaked out while she was on the phone. "So will you stay here in the gazebo awhile?"

She shook her head. "I really hafta get back home."

"Rachel! You can't leave yet!"

She stood up, still holding the baby. "I'm sorry, Merry, but I can't stay."

Once again, I felt trapped. "Well, what can I do?" I said, glancing at the house. "Charity can't be left out here alone, and if I don't go in now—"

"I could take Charity with me," Rachel interrupted.

"With you?" I repeated. "That'll never work. How can I keep Charity a secret if you're gonna go show her off at your house?"

"It wouldn't hafta be that way."

"Really? Well, you better talk fast." I listened as she explained.

"I'll keep her wrapped up so no one'll see inside the basket. She can sleep upstairs in my room for a bit."

Her plan wasn't even remotely close to the way I wanted to handle things, but it seemed to be the only option. "As soon as I can, I'll come over and get her," I said, not knowing what I'd do once I got her home again. "Just please don't tell anyone what I've told you."

Rachel nodded and turned to put Charity in the wicker basket. "I think she needs another change," she said, holding her nose.

"Oh, good idea. *You* do it," I said, digging around in the bottom of the basket for the note. When I found it, Rachel's eyes bugged out.

"What's that?" she asked.

"I'll show you later." I tucked the note into my shorts pocket. "Thanks for helping, Rachel," I said. "You're a lifesaver."

She kept pinching her nose and made a face. Quickly, I left to go to the house.

"What are *your* plans today?" Dad asked as I spread soft butter on my waffles.

"Oh, I'll probably hang out with Rachel for a while. Maybe clean my room."

Mom sat down for the prayer, and when Dad finished the blessing, she looked up at me suddenly. "Miss Spindler called a little while ago."

"Oh?" My voice squeaked. "Why so early?"

"She wondered what you were doing out in the gazebo with Rachel Zook," Mom said, chuckling. "If she doesn't take the cake!"

"Old Hawk Eyes is up to her old tricks," I said, passing it off in jest. "She lives to spy on people."

Dad glanced at me. The gray hairs around his temples crinkled as he grinned. "Wouldn't it be fun to investigate the old lady—I mean, literally invite ourselves into her house and search it? She must have some high-powered telescope stashed somewhere."

"I think Dad's right." I wanted to pay Old Hawk Eyes a visit in the worst way. What had she seen? I reached for some milk, my throat horribly dry.

"Merry," Mom scolded, "don't wash your food down."

"Sorry," I sputtered, hoping Mom wasn't as curious about my early morning whereabouts as our nosy neighbor.

Dad stirred his herbal tea. "Don't you have a pie or something to take over to Ruby Spindler?" he asked Mom, then winked at me.

"I . . . uh, don't think I have time to probe into Miss Spindler's spying techniques today." I hoped I wasn't reacting too nervously. The last thing I wanted was to stir up suspicion in my parents. A baby's life and future were at stake, and I needed to handle things delicately. I wanted to get Mom and Dad to see their need for another child. And my need for a new sister. Namely, Charity.

Fortunately, the subject of Miss Spindler and her phone call was dropped. Dad kissed Mom's cheek as he excused himself and headed to his study down the hall. Mom hopped up and began clearing the table. "Why don't you run along," she said. "I know you'd probably like to visit with Rachel some more. She might be going to a quilting bee or something. If you don't hurry, you won't catch her."

"Thanks, Mom," I said, giving her a squeeze. She'd played right into my hands. And I was truly grateful!

I ran upstairs and showered and shampooed my hair. It felt good to clean up after having spent the night outside. All the while, I thought of baby Charity. She needed a bath, too, I was certain. And what fun it would be. But where? Where could I take care of her the way I wanted to?

Sweet thoughts of having a baby in the house—in *this* house— made me speed up my morning routine. I brushed my damp hair and pulled it back in a single flat barrette. Opting to skip putting on makeup, I gathered up my dirty T-shirt and shorts. Noticing the full hamper, I smashed them in before I left.

The kitchen was spotless as I breezed through. Mom had already gone upstairs to dress for the day, and Dad was still talking on the phone in his study. I pranced out the back screen door and ran. Already, I missed my baby sister!

I took the shortcut through the willows, praying all the way. If I handled things correctly, Charity could grow up on SummerHill Lane and be my adopted baby sister. God had sent her here—now it was up to me to make the situation work.

Six gray buggies were parked in the side yard at the Zooks'. Concern gripped me as I ran to the back door.

"Merry, *wilkom!*" called Esther Zook through the screen. "Come on in."

I pushed open the door, and Esther came in her gray skirt and apron to greet me. But what I saw disturbed me so much I nearly cried. There, in the center of the long, wooden kitchen table, a familiar wicker basket was on display—with Charity the center of attention!

Inwardly, I groaned. What had Rachel done?

My friend caught my eye, appearing rather distraught. She shrugged her shoulders, and I knew something had gone terribly wrong.

I made my way across the enormous kitchen. At least ten Amish-women sat around gazing at Charity, talking excitedly in their Pennsylvania Dutch dialect.

"What's going on?" I whispered to Rachel.

She guided me into the dining room. We stood in the corner near a hand-carved cabinet displaying brightly colored china pieces. "Ach, Merry, I would've stopped this from happening if I could've."

"Exactly what happened?"

"Well, it's like this. I took the babe up to my room as ya said to"—her eyes were filled with regret—"but when I left her there to go and help Mam, she started crying. Mam heard Charity hollerin' and came running. The women were already comin' for the quiltin' and, well . . . that's the way it was."

"*Now* what can we do?" I pleaded.

"Don't worry, I didn't tell them she was abandoned," Rachel said. "I knew that would be the wrong thing to say. I said she was visiting you."

I agreed. "Good thinking. But we've got to get her out of here before someone starts asking personal questions."

"Above all, Merry, we mustn't lie," Rachel said, looking even more serious. "T'would not be pleasin' to the Lord."

"You're right. We have to trust God," I said. "He started all this." Given the circumstances surrounding Charity's arrival, it felt strange appearing to blame it on the Lord. As soon as the words flew out of my mouth, I was sorry for how they sounded.

"I can't go back with ya," Rachel said. "Mam needs me here to help stew chickens for dinner."

"That's fine. Thanks." I gave her a hug. "You did your best, Rachel. Just pray, okay?"

She nodded. "There might be a bit of a problem, though, if Mam finds out about the baby."

"What do you mean?" I felt my heart pound.

"Mam's wantin' another little one. She loves babies, ya see. And she's reached her life change—she can't have more children."

My hopes plunged to the depths. "I knew something like this might happen."

Rachel held my hand. "Don't let envy rob your peace. Remember the scriptures about coveting. You hafta have a clear head to think, Cousin Merry." She liked to call me *cousin*. We had a common ancestor several generations back that made us bonafide distant relatives.

I sighed, growing more frustrated by the second. Rachel was right about the envy. Only she was forgetting one important piece of information: Charity was not up for grabs. She was mine!

With my heart in my throat, I followed Rachel back into the kitchen. The Amishwomen were closing in on poor little Charity. One of them reached over and snatched her out of the basket.

Instantly, I remembered the note—the one that had been pinned to Charity's blanket. My head felt dizzy, and I groped for a chair. *Oh no,* I thought. The note was in the pocket of my shorts—in my hamper. And at this moment, Mom was probably sorting the laundry. Discovering my secret!

Tears came to my eyes. I didn't mean to, but I stared at the Amishwomen talking in a language Charity had never heard. Esther Zook was leaning over their shoulders, touching Charity's face, her hands. What Rachel had said seemed true enough. Her mother would want Charity for her own if she knew the baby girl had been abandoned.

For the third time today, I felt trapped. This time, with absolutely no way out!

Eight *A Cry in the Dark*

"Ach! What a perty little thing," Rachel's mom was saying. "Whose didja say the baby was?" She was looking at *me* now.

I was tongue-tied. If I told the truth, I might lose Charity. If I lied, I'd lose Rachel's friendship. She was a stickler for honesty.

The whole group of Plain women was looking my way, waiting for my answer. I took a deep breath and . . .

Rachel spoke up. "Merry's needin' to get the baby back home now." She went over and took Charity from the plump Amishwoman and snuggled her back into the basket.

"I don't think she'll need the blankets today," Esther advised. "The sun's awful hot."

I went over and helped Rachel get Charity settled in. "*Denki* for lettin' me show the baby off," she said to me.

"Thank *you*," I said, and I was sure she knew what I meant by it.

"I'll walk ya to the end of the lane." Rachel held the back kitchen door for me. With a sigh of relief, I escaped down the steps to the sidewalk, carrying Charity.

"Too close for comfort," I muttered.

"You can say that again!" We walked to the end of the sidewalk. Then Rachel touched my arm. "Look who's comin'."

I glanced in the direction of the ramp leading up to the second story of their barn. Levi was heading in our direction. "Merry, s'nice to see ya again," he called.

I glanced at Rachel, wondering what do about Charity. She was already getting fussy being outside in the heat. And what on earth would I tell Levi about her?

"Looks like you've been working hard," I said as Levi approached.

He leaned down and brushed off his jeans. He'd stopped wearing the typical Old Order Amish clothes since his announcement to his family last month about wanting to attend a Bible school. "Well, what do we have here?" He gazed into the wicker basket, obviously interested.

"Uh . . . this is baby Charity," I said, giving Rachel a look that meant *help!*

"Charity?" He smiled that winning smile I'd known all these years. "That's a right good name. Means love, ya know."

I hoped he wouldn't start mentioning his "love" for me in front of his younger sister. Rachel had no idea about Levi's serious words to me one night weeks ago.

"Well, I better get the baby out of this sun." I turned to go.

Levi, however, didn't let me off the hook so easily. "We need to have a talk sometime 'fore too long," he said, following Rachel and me as we headed for the Zooks' dirt lane.

I knew what he was getting at. He'd be wanting some kind of understanding between us before he left for school, but I wasn't exactly ready to settle down. I wasn't quite sixteen. Even though Amish girls began the courting process at that age, *I* wasn't even close to being ready for such things.

"When can I call on ya, Merry?" he persisted.

"We still have plenty of time." I smiled.

That seemed to satisfy him, and he quit following us and turned and hurried back to the barn.

"Levi's bent on makin' you his wife," Rachel blurted as we headed for the road.

I gasped. "How do you know?"

"I can see it in his eyes," she said. "And the way he talks about ya. He loves ya, Cousin Merry. Honest, he does."

Levi had declared his love last month—in the gazebo, of all places. But I hadn't made any long-term commitment, even though I had to admit I liked him.

"There's a lot of deciding to do, I guess." I looked down at Charity. "But between this little gift from God and your brother's persistence, things have become mighty chaotic!"

Rachel laughed heartily. "Well, then, why don'tcha tell your mother about the baby right away?"

"Because I need time to prepare her—get her thinking about adopting a baby. *Any* baby. Then, when I reveal Charity, she'll be ready. Dad too. It's the only way it'll work," I said, worried that the note from Charity's mother had already been discovered in the hamper.

"Seems to me you've figured it all out," Rachel said.

"Not really," I admitted. "It's just that I know how my parents react to things. If I were to go home with a baby . . . well, first off, Dad would contact the Social Services or the police."

"Police?" She frowned. "What for?"

"To report a missing person or possibly a kidnapping. They would jump to conclusions." In my heart, I hoped baby Charity wasn't either of those.

"Oh, Merry, think of it!" Rachel grabbed my arm, making the basket sway. "What if Charity was kidnapped like you said? What about *that?*"

Guess now was as good a time as any to fill her in on the note. "There was a note left with Charity. Pinned to her blanket."

Rachel tugged on her prayer Kapp. "You mean to tell me someone deliberately left this baby at your house?"

I shrugged. "Looks like it. I mean, when you put all the pieces together it kinda fits—the noisy pickup checking out the neighborhood all last week, like you said. And then the way the driver insisted on the girl getting out—telling her she had no choice. Oh, and when he pulled up at my house yesterday afternoon, he asked if there was a doctor around!"

"You talked to him? Merry, you never said anything about that."

I described everything quickly—how a man in his early twenties had stopped by to ask questions while I was taking pictures of Lissa.

"You're right," she said after hearing it all. "It sounds like an abandonment. Why don'tcha tell your parents? I don't see why they'd hafta get the police to come."

I sighed and we kept walking. When we came close to my front yard, I covered Charity with a lightweight blanket, hiding her from view. Just in case. "Run ahead and see if anyone's around back," I told Rachel.

"Jah, just real quick. Then I hafta go back home and help with the quilting."

I waited in the bushes for Rachel to signal.

Seconds passed. What was she doing? Had she encountered someone?

Thoughts of the note being discovered haunted me. I wished Rachel would hurry.

At last, she came—running. Out of breath. "Hurry! All's clear."

"What? You mean it wasn't before?"

"Your mom—she was out hanging up the wash."

"You're kidding? She *never* does that. We have a dryer, for pete's sake!"

Rachel's eyes grew round as saucers. "Ya don't think she's waitin' for us—suspects somethin', do ya?"

"What are you saying? My mom has no idea about any of this. And I want to keep it that way!" I was completely flustered. Rachel was smack-dab in the middle of things, and now I wished I'd overseen all this myself.

"Are ya comin' or not?" she asked.

I shook my head. "We can't risk it. If Mom's hanging out laundry, then she's already found the note."

"Oh, Merry." Her voice was filled with dread.

"There's only one way out," I said, glancing up the hill—way up Strawberry Lane—to Miss Spindler's house.

"Not Old Hawk Eyes," whispered Rachel.

"We have no choice," I replied. "Besides, she already must've seen something going on in the gazebo early this morning. She called my mother to tell her so!"

"*Himmel*," Rachel muttered.

We crouched low and ran across the front yard on the count of three. Baby Charity slept through it, thank goodness. I reminded Rachel of her quilting frolic back home, but she was more interested in the matter at hand. Anyway, we made it around the opposite side of the house without being seen, running from bush to bush, then up . . . up the steep hill behind our house, arriving at last on Miss Spindler's front porch.

We caught our breath for a second, glancing at each other with frightened expressions. "Lord, help us," I pleaded.

I reached up to pull the heavy gold knocker on the bright red door.

Ruby Spindler took her sweet time answering the doorbell. We stood waiting a good thirty seconds before she finally came—whistling.

"My, oh my. Look who's come to call!" She was all made up—lipstick, eyeliner, the works.

"Oh, you're going out," I found myself saying.

"Nonsense!" She opened the door, showing us in as though she'd been expecting us. I wondered about that but dismissed the thought. Miss Spindler was known all over SummerHill for being a bit eccentric. Today was no exception.

"How's every little thing?" she asked, motioning for us to sit down on her sofa, which was covered with a fresh white sheet. "What brings you dears over to visit this old lady?" She eyed the basket, then Rachel and me.

"It's . . . uh, something very important," I said. "Something top secret."

Rachel nodded but let me do the talking.

"I want to show you something." I leaned over and uncovered Charity.

Miss Spindler was up and out of her chair in a flash. "Why, in all my born days . . . I never . . ." Her voice trailed off. She reached down and picked Charity right up.

I held my breath, worried that Charity might start to fuss. But I was wrong. Ruby Spindler had a real knack. She cooed at Charity as though she'd been doing it all her life. "Isn't she the most bee-a-u-ti-ful thing you ever did see?" Her eyes were focused on the baby as she spoke.

"Yes, she's beautiful," I agreed, "but . . ." I paused, hoping my words wouldn't sound harsh. "She's been abandoned."

Miss Spindler's gaze shot up to meet mine. "Abandoned, you say? How could anyone in their right mind do such a thing? Why, she's gorgeous. Simply gorgeous."

I secretly congratulated myself on this surprising turn of events. Miss Spindler was actually very good with Charity, whose tiny eyes were starting to open as the old lady rocked her and talked in a sing-song way.

"Miss Spindler, I . . . uh . . . *we*," I looked at Rachel, suddenly feeling it was wise to include her in this. "Rachel and I wondered if you might be able to keep Charity for a little while."

Her head jerked up. "Keep her? Here?"

"Just for a short time," I said. "While I talk to my parents about some things," I went on, careful not to explain too much about my plan to convince my parents.

"Heavens to Betsy, you don't have to hem and haw about something like this, Merry Hanson. Just out with it! You need someplace to hide this here little one, ain't so?"

"Hide?"

She smiled a peculiar, almost uncanny smile. "Ah yes, I saw you last evening. And again this morning. Hiding in the gazebo, you were." She cackled a bit.

I shot a concerned look at Rachel. "You didn't tell anyone, did you?"

Miss Spindler waved her bony hand. "Never you mind 'bout that."

I had to know. "But you didn't tell my mother about the baby when you called, did you?"

"Not on your life," she replied. "I saw what happened. That there feller in the pickup—my lands, what a sad state of affairs!"

I stood up. "You saw? But how?" Our house blocked her view—it was virtually impossible for her to have seen him. I was sure of it.

She shook her head. "There, there. Don't go worryin' yourself over such trivia. The fact remains, the babe's been left behind. Now, you two run along. I'll take good care of my little dumplin' here." And she rocked away, calling the baby her precious angel over and over.

I went to say good-bye to Charity—the gift God had most obviously sent to *me*. She gripped my finger in her tiny fist. But her blue eyes were fixed on Miss Spindler.

I was torn between relief and worry. Now I was free to work on my original plan with Mom and Dad, but what about Miss Spindler? What if she got wrapped up in Charity while I set things in motion with my family?

"You don't mind, do you?" I asked, almost wishing she'd hand the baby back to me.

"Scoot!" she said, shooing us out the door. "Just let me know when you want her back. In the meantime, I'll bathe her and buy her some new clothes."

Bathe her? Old Hawk Eyes was going to give my future sister a bath? Buy her clothes? Spoil her the way I'd wanted to? I could see this was already way out of control.

Rachel and I scarcely spoke as we headed down Strawberry Lane to the corner and turned left toward my house.

"I guess you have a quilting to attend," I said softly.

"Jah, I do."

We hugged, and tears came to my eyes as she left. For the first time since I'd carried the baby basket into Miss Spindler's house, my arm ached. And now so did my heart.

It was next to impossible getting Mom's and Dad's attention later at supper. Mom kept talking about how lovely it had been today. "Not hot and muggy—just nice," she said. "I even decided to hang the laundry out for a change. Oh, and it smelled so fresh when I brought it in."

I was afraid she was secretly trying to tell me about the note she'd found in my shorts, but nothing came of it. I even fished around, asking leading questions, but she didn't volunteer a thing.

Soon, something else was on her mind—the church potluck a week from tomorrow. And Dad? He began recounting several hectic experiences from his day at the hospital.

More than anything, I was dying to know if Mom had found the note in my shorts. I'd checked the hamper first thing when I returned from Miss Spindler's, but the clothes had already gone through Mom's super-systematized sorting process. In fact, all my dirty shorts from the entire week were flapping in the breeze when I hurried outside later. Unfortunately, the pockets of the gray shorts were one-hundred-percent-amen empty.

Since the table conversation seemed to be going in several different directions, I decided to postpone my discussion about the baby until dessert. From past experience, I knew it would be futile to work up to something this controversial. And I certainly didn't want my parents to become suspicious at that type of approach, so I barreled full steam ahead. Skip, my brother, had paved the way with this sort of tactic. Being younger, I'd learned more from him than I cared to admit.

Mom set a piece of black raspberry pie in front of each of us. Dad reached for his fork and took the first bite while Mom and I watched. It was a kind of game. Mom waited eagerly for his response, and Dad, being the ham he was, dragged out the suspense, rolling his eyes, licking his lips. Finally, he said, "It's absolutely delicious."

Mom grinned and picked up her fork. *Now* it was time for the baby discussion. . . .

"I think we need another kid around here," I announced. "A baby, maybe?"

I could hear the grandfather clock ticking in the hallway. I took a breath and kept going. "I mean, don't you think we ought to have another sister for me? Not to replace Faithie or anything, but it would be nice."

Dad looked straight at Mom. "What did you put in Merry's pie? I certainly didn't get any of it."

I sat up. "Dad! I'm serious."

His jawline was firm. "That's what I'm talking about. You had something very strange to eat. Or was it the iced tea?" He looked around, inspecting Mom's tea glass, then reaching for mine.

"It's not a joke!" I insisted.

"Merry, please," Mom said. "You seem all worked up about this. Does this have anything to do with Faithie's . . . anniversary?"

I got up from the table, tears coming fast. "I just wish people would take me seriously once in a while."

Dad reached out as I ran past him and into the hallway. "Merry?" he called. "I didn't mean to . . ."

I couldn't hear the rest of what he said. But I knew he'd had fun at my expense. And it hurt.

Upstairs, I found refuge in my room. The cats followed me to my bed, where I collapsed, feeling sorry for myself. "You guys never have any problems, do you?" I said as they came to comfort me with their sweet, furry heads and whiskers. "You sleep, eat, and sleep again. Must be nice."

Abednego didn't appreciate what I'd said. He whined his best retaliatory *meow*. Twice.

I pouted, staring at the wall on the opposite side of the room. The wall where my best photography had been framed and hung. My wall gallery, I'd always called it.

Sadly, I tried to imagine a picture of Charity up there—holding my finger with her viselike grip as I held her in my arms. I'd have to set up my tripod for a shot like that.

The thought was appealing, but I knew a photo of the abandoned baby would only end up haunting me. *If only my parents were more understanding,* I thought, blaming the negative events of the day on them. I turned on the radio and listened for a while—until Dad knocked on my door.

"Honeybunch," he said, using the nickname he used when I was in trouble or upset. "Mind if I come in?"

I minded, but I wasn't rude. I sat up and held Abednego next to my face—a defense against whatever Dad was going to say. "The door's open," I called, still wishing . . . hoping things might turn out in my favor.

Dad sat at the end of the bed. "I'm sorry about teasing you," he began. "It was uncalled for."

His subdued expression gave me courage, and I nodded. "Maybe you and Mom didn't understand what I was saying earlier." I wanted to give him the benefit of the doubt.

"Having a baby would be terribly rough on your mother at her age," he explained.

I shook my head. "That's *not* what I meant. You jumped to conclusions."

"Then I'm totally in the dark here. Why don't you tell me what's on your mind, Mer?"

I thought about Charity—hidden away at Miss Spindler's—and how she belonged here. "What if we *adopted* a baby?"

Mom was standing in the doorway now. I knew by her dubious look that she'd heard what I said. "Don't you think your father and I ought to be the ones deciding something like that?"

"I know," I replied. "It's something that has to be thought through. People just don't jump into embracing someone else's child as their own." I'd read that somewhere—it sounded good. Besides, I needed to make some points with my parents, who by now looked too shocked for words.

"Merry, is something bothering you?" Dad asked, frowning. "Do we need to talk about Faithie?"

"This is about *me*, not Faithie," I said, but deep inside, I knew the arrival of baby Charity was linked to Faithie—at least in my mind. Desperately, I wanted to share with them the dream I'd had last night in the gazebo. To make them see the truth about little Charity. That she was God's gift—my second chance for a sister.

Dad patted the bed beside him, and Mom sat down. The two of them, along with my four cats, studied me. I tried various approaches in my head, but none of them worked. Honestly, I couldn't think of anything to say without giving away my secret.

At last, Dad spoke. "Would it help if we didn't visit Faithie's graveside this year?"

I couldn't believe he'd said that! "I told you this has nothing to do with Faithie. It's something I really want—for us to adopt a baby. Couldn't you and Mom at least *think* about it?"

It was my best shot.

Dad looked at Mom and reached for her hand. "As far as I'm concerned, this isn't the best time for either of us to be starting over," he stated. "Babies take an incredible amount of time and energy."

Mom interjected, "Your father's nearly fifty, and we're both very busy with our present responsibilities." Her voice grew softer. "Someday, *you'll* have babies, Merry. When you're finished with college and have a husband."

My logical approach was getting me nowhere fast. The tone of Mom's voice told me she needed an emotional push. Something to jump-start her maternal instincts.

"Okay, let's just say, for the sake of discussion, that an abandoned baby is found somewhere around SummerHill. And what if that baby is a beautiful baby girl with no one to love her and provide for her?"

Mom's eyes were transfixed, and Dad was listening intently. I had them!

I continued. "What if the baby is so precious and adorable that the person who found her wants to keep her? And what if the person knows for sure that the baby is meant to be in that person's life?"

Dad scratched his chin, trying to hide his stunned expression. "My goodness, what a hypothetical situation you've cooked up."

Mom didn't wait for me to answer. She stood up and walked over to the window. "What would *I* do if I found an abandoned baby?" she asked, redirecting the question. "Well, that's rather simple, I would think. Right, hon?" She glanced at Dad.

He nodded. "First thing—we'd have to report a missing child. After all, the police should be notified in order to locate the mother."

Dad had thrown a wrench into my setup. And worse, Mom was following his line of reasoning.

"Well, what if the person who found the baby knew the baby had been purposely abandoned?" I said. "What then?"

Dad mentioned the possibility of kidnapping, completely ignoring my comment. "Unfortunately, babies are taken out from under their parents' noses every year in this country. Some are sold into the black market. Others are left to die or simply abandoned on someone's doorstep. How would the person who'd found such a baby know the child hadn't been kidnapped?" He leaned back on the bed, his hands supporting his head.

I sighed. Why were they making this so difficult? "To begin with, I just said 'what if' the person knew somehow that the baby was *not* kidnapped, but abandoned."

Dad's eyes closed as he spoke. "Merry, why don't you just level with us? Do you know someone who has found such a baby?"

I was frantic! He'd seen through it. I should've known Dad would read between the lines. Mom too.

"Guess neither of you was born yesterday." I started to explain. "Yes, a baby has been found. She's an adorable baby girl . . . and she's ours—God showed me that." I left out the part about the dream.

I told them the truth. "I was the one who found her—in a wicker laundry basket last night—in the gazebo."

Mom turned and stared. Dad was sitting upright now, the lines in his forehead creased into a deep frown. "Someone left a baby in our gazebo?"

"Merry, why didn't you tell us?" Mom asked.

"It's a long story," I whispered. But I proceeded to tell them everything, even about the note in my shorts.

Mom gasped. "There was a note, too?"

"I put it in my gray shorts and then forgot and tossed them in the laundry," I explained. "Silly me."

Mom put both hands on top of her head. "Oh dear. I found several things in your pockets, but I don't think I threw them away. I believe they're still on the counter in the—"

Before she finished, I left the room to find the note. It was exactly the proof I needed. As I rushed through the kitchen toward the cellar steps, I stopped to look out the window. The lights in Miss Spindler's house were beginning to come on. It was dusk, close to the hour when baby Charity had come to me yesterday. I stared at the tall two-story house an acre away. How I missed my sweet little Charity!

Quickly, I turned and ran downstairs to retrieve the note.

⌒

By the end of the evening—after pleading with Dad not to call the police (he did anyway) and giving a complete description of the old pickup and the people in it—I knew there was only the faintest hope for Charity's future with us. But I hung on to the hope tenaciously, prayerfully. When it came right down to it, the baby's future rested with the police's ability to track down a clanking blue pickup with an abusive driver and a tearful young woman. The rest was up to God.

Which brings me to Miss Spindler and the disturbing evening visit with the baby of my dreams.

Miss Spindler seemed quite distracted when I showed up on her doorstep. "Come in," she said, treating me more like a stranger than the close neighbor I was.

"Where's Charity?" I asked, looking around.

"Ah, you came to see my baby."

The preoccupied expression on her wrinkled face had me downright worried. "I've come to get Charity. My father has just talked to the police."

"Police?"

I nodded. It seemed as hard for her to accept as it had been for me. "It's procedure," I explained. "They'll take her to Social Services until they can determine where her parents are." The lump in my throat made it hard to talk. "If she's declared an orphan or abandoned, Dad'll talk to his administrative friends on the Social Services board about putting her in temporary foster care—with us, if all goes well." *And if I can talk my parents into it*, I thought.

"My, oh my," she muttered, fluttering around in a daze. "Going and reporting Charity missing? Why, the little darlin's been right here all the time."

She was crazy-out-of-her-mind distressed. "Miss Spindler . . . I'm so sorry. I never should've—"

"Nonsense! That youngster has been exactly what the doctor ordered. A godsend . . . yes indeedy," she said. "This lonely old woman has missed so much in life, and now . . ." Her words floated away.

She'd mentioned God, and I felt upset. How could she latch on to Charity as though the Lord had sent the baby to *her*? Careful not to let her see my irritation, I nodded, trying to think of something soothing to say. "If we pray," I said, "and if it's God's will—which I believe it is—then Charity will be right back here."

Miss Spindler's blue-gray hair was curled up in bobby pins all over her head, and she wore an ankle-length white duster. She sat down in an overstuffed chair, and for a moment I thought she was going to cry. Her voice wavered as she told about going to town to buy an infant car seat, disposable diapers, and blankets. "Aw, you should see her dressed up in her new things. She looks right fine—like an angel, if I must say so myself."

"You spent money on the baby?" I was truly amazed at her confession.

"Spent the entire afternoon rounding up all sorts of baby things," she said proudly. "I even stopped to see one of my dear old friends at the nursing home and showed Charity off." She grinned, showing her gums. "And don'tcha know—I loved every single second of it!"

Poor Old Hawk Eyes. She's gotten too attached.

"Whatcha lookin' at, dear?" she asked.

Sadness for the older lady nearly got the best of me as I stood there in her old-fashioned parlor. Quickly, I looked away so as not to embarrass her. "So," I said in almost a whisper, "that's where we stand with Charity."

Without another word, Miss Spindler pulled herself up out of the easy chair and went upstairs. I thought of Dad's comment earlier this morning about someone coming into Miss Spindler's house and searching it for spy equipment. The thought helped to lighten my tension.

Miss Spindler was gone only a few minutes before bringing Charity down.

Half asleep, the baby opened her eyes. *Blue as blue can be,* I thought.

"Hello again," I said, reaching out for her chubby fist. "I missed you so much, but I know Auntie Ruby here took extra-good care of you."

Miss Spindler was nodding and beaming. "That she did."

It nearly broke my heart to remove Charity from the old woman's arms. She helped me wrap Charity in several blankets before we headed out. Then she went about filling the wicker basket full of large cans of formula, diapers, and other baby things, saying she would drop by with the car seat tomorrow.

"There's a dear," she whispered as I stepped onto her front porch weighed down with everything. "Good-bye, angel." She touched the baby's head lightly. "God be with you."

I wanted to reach out and hug Old Hawk Eyes. She'd surprised me with her kind, nurturing ways, and I was grateful. "Thanks for your help," I said before walking out into the night sweetly fragranced with honeysuckle.

"I'll leave the yard light on for you, dear." Miss Spindler stood on the porch and watched as I headed down the hill toward my house.

"Thanks again!" I called, knowing full well the people from Social Services would be showing up any minute.

Arriving home, I hurried into the house. Mom was waiting at the kitchen door for me. For *Charity* and me.

In a few seconds, Mom was talking baby talk and making over Charity as if she'd never laid eyes on such a pretty baby.

"Will you look at those blue eyes," Mom said as Dad came into the room.

"Now, remember what I said," he admonished. "Don't fall head over heels for a baby that most likely won't be . . ."

Mom held the baby out to him. Reluctantly, he took Charity and held her up to his face. "Lookee here," he said, sounding something like Miss Spindler. "Well, what do we have here?"

"So . . . what do you say?" I said, pushing for an instant decision. "Can we adopt her?"

Mom and Dad were shoulder to shoulder, peering into the face of baby Charity—my gift from God. I tried to make conversation several more times to no avail. It was amazing—a transformation was taking place before my eyes. For people who'd just said they were much too old and had way too many responsibilities to add to their family at this late date, well . . . the way things looked from my perspective, the Social Services people could wait and show up tomorrow or the next day. Or never.

Suddenly, Dad pushed Charity into my arms. "Here, hold her for a minute." He dashed off to his study, and I heard him close the door. My heart was in my throat.

"What's Dad doing?" I asked.

Mom leaned her head close to Charity's. "Oh, you might just be surprised."

"What?" I pleaded. "Is he calling someone important?"

"Your father, as you know, is easily swayed when it comes to people with terminal illnesses, emergency situations, and . . . *babies*," she reminded me.

"I was counting on that." I grinned down at Charity. This time she was gazing up at me. "Oh, you're so pwecious."

Abednego and his brothers wandered into the kitchen just then. Abednego gave me the evil eye as if to say: *Put that human baby down this instant!*

I scolded him. "You get plenty of love and attention. Now, go find your adopted sister!" And I shooed them outside to look for Lily White.

Mom pulled out a kitchen chair for me. "I'd better give Miss Spindler a quick call," she said. "It would be nice to know when Charity had her last bottle."

Her words were music to my ears. And as I waited for her to chat with our nosy neighbor, I prayed that the person Dad was talking to on the phone would bend the rules and let us keep Charity until she was free to be adopted. "And if not, Lord," I whispered, "at least let us keep her tonight."

It was a long shot, but from what I knew of my heavenly Father, the God of the universe took great delight in performing miraculous feats.

Twelve A Cry in the Dark

The phone rang just as Dad was coming out of his study. He hurried back to answer it. I waited for him to return, hugging Charity close. Then he called to me. "The phone's for you, Merry."

I picked up the kitchen phone, holding Charity in one arm. "Hello?" I said, looking down at the darling baby.

"Hi, Merry." It was Lissa Vyner. "Just wondered if you got the film developed that you took of me yesterday."

I'd completely spaced it out. "Not yet. But I'll get Mom to take it down to the one-hour place tomorrow," I promised. "It's just that so much has been happening since you were here. You'll never believe what—"

Dad was waving at me, signaling to me.

"Uh . . . just a minute, Lissa." I handed Charity to Mom.

Dad hurried over and covered the phone with his hand. "Don't mention anything about the baby just yet," he advised. "Lissa doesn't know it, but her dad just did me a big favor at the police department."

I knew Officer Vyner was on the Lancaster police force. He and Dad had become acquaintances because of Lissa's and her mother's attendance at our church. More recently, Dad had teamed up with Lissa and me to persuade him to come to the church potluck next weekend.

"Okay, I won't say anything," I said as he handed the phone back to me. I hesitated when I got on the phone again. "So, Lissa, how's everything?"

"Merry? You were starting to tell me something," she urged, not letting me change the subject. "You were saying something about all that's been happening. Did that weird guy in the pickup show up again?"

"That's not exactly what I was talking about." I was hedging, not knowing what to say next.

Dad must've sensed my distress. "Tell her you'll call back," he whispered, moving his hand in a circular motion in midair.

"My dad's waiting to talk to me. Can I call you later?"

"Sure. But—"

"Okay, then," I said and hung up.

Dad and Mom looked like Siamese twins as they stood together in the kitchen hovering over Charity, who was obviously soaking up their attention.

"What did Lissa's dad say about the baby?" I asked. I had to walk over and stand in front of them, waving my arms. "Yoo-hoo! Remember me?"

At last, Dad tore his gaze away from Charity's face. "Oh, I'm sorry, Merry. What is it?"

I asked him again about the arrangement. "Did Officer Vyner say we could keep Charity overnight?"

He nodded. "We've got her for the night—" and here he turned and kissed Mom—"possibly several days."

"Really?" I squealed with delight. "That long?"

"Until the in-state tracking is done," he said. "By the way, Merry, hang on to that note from the mother. A handwriting analyst may be called in on the case."

My heart sank. "I don't want to help them find Charity's mother," I wailed. "She doesn't deserve our baby!"

Dad's eyes clouded a bit. "According to the law, she must be punished for this act of desertion."

"But what if they don't find her or the guy she was with?"

"One step at a time," Dad said gently, glancing at Mom, who looked smitten with baby love. "Try to be patient. Remember what the proverb says: 'Be patient and you will finally win. . . .'"

I backed away from the three of them and glanced out the window at Miss Spindler's house. "Someone *else* is anxious for Charity to stay around here, too."

Mom heard me. "Miss Spindler, right?"

"And she's not the only one." I told them about the Amishwomen next door, particularly Esther Zook.

"Well, we don't have to worry about the Amish community causing us trouble," Dad said. "They don't get caught up in legal hassles."

"Must be nice," I said, contemplating the time involved in locating an abandoned baby's parents, especially if they didn't want to be found. I turned toward Mom and the baby in her arms. "It seems like everyone around here wants to claim her."

There was no arguing that point. Even Dad nodded his head in agreement. "She's a dumpling," he said. "But we have to do the right thing by her, whether she stays with us or not." Dad usually didn't speak out strongly about his beliefs, so it surprised me to hear him talk this way. But one thing was certain, he wanted Charity as much as I did. So did Mom!

My first hurdle was history. Now, if I could just get past the next few days of waiting. Would the police be able to catch up with the rattletrap pickup and its occupants? And what about Miss Spindler? Had she lost her heart to Charity, too? I felt sorry for her—and for putting her in the middle of this.

I felt even worse the next morning when Miss Spindler came over with the promised car seat and a handful of crocheted baby booties. I met her at the back door, noting that she'd done her hair up in its usual gray-blue puff. Her cheeks had a splash of color in them, and I couldn't tell if it was rouge or if she was simply excited to see the baby again.

"Hello, dear," she said. "I stayed up late making these booties for Charity."

I looked at them—four or five adorable pairs of pink, pink-and-white, and variegated colors. "These are darling!"

"Why, thank you, Merry." She looked around, and I knew I had to invite her in. "Is the little sweetie up?"

"Come with me." I led her upstairs to the project room across from my parents' bedroom. Typically it was Mom's spot for sewing or repairing neglected antiques. "We fixed up a room for her—at least for now."

Mom was diapering the baby on a makeshift changing table, actually an antique cherry dresser. She'd made it comfortable for Charity with some waterproof pads and a soft, thick towel.

"Aw, there's a love," Miss Spindler sputtered as we stood in the doorway.

"Look what Miss Spindler made." I showed Mom the booties.

"Why, Ruby," Mom said, turning toward Old Hawk Eyes, "what a thoughtful thing."

Miss Spindler bent over and kissed Charity's head. "How's every little thing with our dapple dumplin' today?" Charity kicked her feet and tried to grab Miss Spindler's long nose.

"I think she recognizes her auntie Ruby," I said, hoping to ease the awkward situation. It was clear how much the old lady adored the baby.

Mom snapped the baby outfit and held Charity up, goo-gooing close to her face. "She's really a very placid baby," Mom mentioned. "Hardly fussed all night."

"Well, I declare," Miss Spindler said. "She fits right in here, doesn't she?"

Mom handed the baby to our neighbor. "Here, she likes you, too, Ruby." That brought a broad smile to the wrinkled face.

I let the two of them chitchat alone. Quietly, I slipped out of the room and headed down the long upstairs hall to my room, where I grabbed my digital camera. As much as I liked shooting with film, I wanted to be sure to get a good photo, and babies were tricky. I spotted the roll of film with Lissa's photos on it while loading some fresh batteries. Because of all the excitement, I'd forgotten my promise to call Lissa back. Well, not really forgotten—just couldn't pull myself away from Charity and the remarkable way my parents were responding to her.

Last night, Dad had gone to the attic and lugged down two matching pine cradles—one was mine, the other Faithie's. "We'll need one upstairs and one down," he'd explained as Mom watched incredulously from the attic steps.

"While you're up there," I'd said, "could you bring down some of my old baby dresses? Charity needs a dress to wear on Sunday."

Dad was more than willing to pile up a bunch of my baby clothes and carry them down. In fact, he was so taken with Charity, he was nearly late for work this morning. And for a summer Saturday, I was up earlier than usual, too. There was only one reason, of course.

While Mom and Miss Spindler talked and cooed at the baby, I took unposed shots of the three of them and several close-ups of Charity. Miss Spindler made me promise to give her some copies when I got them printed.

"I'd be happy to," I told her. And it was true. With my parents in the picture, Miss Spindler no longer seemed like a threat.

Later, while Mom and I were fixing lunch, I experienced a twinge of sadness for my brother, Skip, away at camp. He was missing out on the new addition to the Hanson household.

"What do you think Skip would say about having Charity here?" I asked Mom.

"Oh, you know Skip. He takes things in stride."

Mom was probably right. After all, he'd survived his breakup with Nikki Klein, one of Jonathan's two older sisters, a few weeks ago. I didn't feel too badly about it, though, probably because I didn't think Nikki and Skip were right for each other. Besides, Skip had decided on a future in medicine, and he had years of schooling ahead of him.

"Do you think Skip'll miss us when he goes off to college?" I probed.

Mom sighed, as though she wasn't ready to think about losing her only son just yet. "Well, Skip has always been a very independent person, as you know."

Obnoxious too, I thought.

Mom continued. "I think he will do just fine. Now, why don't you run and check on Charity before we sit down for lunch?" I knew it was my cue to back off about Skip. Mom was super-sensitive about her kids. It had only been the day before yesterday that she and I had been able to talk openly about Faithie's death. After nine years!

I took her lead and kept quiet. Tiptoeing into the dining room, I peeked at our baby. She was snoozing peacefully in Faithie's cradle, a heavy pine piece with a honey stain that looked antique—exactly the way Mom had requested it be made. Since antiques were one of her ongoing obsessions, the cradle was ideal.

I touched it, rocking it gently as I looked into her sweet face. "Please don't ever leave us," I whispered. "I couldn't bear to lose you."

Hesitantly, I thought about tomorrow—July 31—the anniversary I'd been somewhat dreading. Would we take Charity to visit Faithie's graveside? How would my twin sister *really* feel if she knew about Charity?

"Merry?" Mom was calling.

I hurried back into the kitchen, my mind beginning to fill with troubling thoughts. My worry escalated even more when Dad called midafternoon. Mom's face turned ashen as she held the phone, listening.

"What is it?" I whispered.

Her eyes grew wide, and she shushed me. "Where?" she was saying. "In Maryland?"

I put my hand on my heart, hoping this wasn't about finding Charity's parents.

Finally, Mom got off the phone. She hurried into the dining room, staring down at Charity in the cradle. "Oh, Merry," she whispered, hugging me. "The police have located the blue pickup."

"Oh, please . . . no." I could say no more. My hands gripped into fists, and I wanted to fly away with Charity. Far, far away, where no one could take her from us!

A Cry in the Dark Fourteen

I felt mighty droopy as I sat out front on the porch waiting for Dad. Mom had taken Charity into town for her required visit to Social Services. Since Dad had arranged temporary foster care with us, I wasn't worried about losing her to the system. It was that horrible APB and the police investigation that made me frantic.

Evidently, the blue pickup had been deserted somewhere near Baltimore, Maryland. Mom had filled me in on everything Dad told her on the phone. The driver and young woman had left no trace as to their whereabouts, but they were definitely being hunted. The pickup had been registered but not insured. I shuddered to think of Charity having to grow up with irresponsible parents.

I remembered last night. Troubled, I had stayed up late praying, then insisted on holding Charity till she fell asleep. Mom seemed to understand my need to be near her. She and Dad were showing signs of the same. When I'd finally relinquished Charity to the room across the hall from them, I noticed Miss Spindler's light was on, too. I wondered if she was thinking about Charity and the new things she'd bought her. My foster sister needed much more than clothes at the moment. She needed a miracle—we all did!

Now, as I sat on the front porch stroking my cats and waiting for Dad, I talked out loud to God. "Please take care of this situation,

Lord. You know how much we love Charity . . . how much we want her to stay with us."

Soon, I heard a car coming down SummerHill. I leaned forward, straining to see if it was Dad. It wasn't. I sighed, leaning back, wishing he'd hurry. But the car pulled into the driveway. Out hopped Levi Zook!

"Hi," I said, getting up and going to meet him. "Is this your new car?"

"Jah," he said. "Do ya like it?"

"It's great." I stepped back and surveyed the shimmering white Mustang, washed and waxed—very classy. "Where do you hide it?"

"I don't hafta anymore," he said. "But don't worry, I wouldn't think of flauntin' it in my father's face."

"Oh," I said, thinking about another father out there somewhere in Maryland or beyond. Charity's father.

"Merry, are ya all right?" Levi looked concerned.

I wasn't prepared for an in-depth explanation of the past two days of my life. Not now.

"It's Faithie's home-going anniversary tomorrow, jah?"

I nodded. "I'm okay with it."

He reached for my hand. "I'd be happy to go along if it's okay with your family."

"To the cemetery?" This was a first. No one but immediate family had ever joined us. When I found my voice again, I said, "Skip's off at camp, so maybe you could take his place."

He nodded. "There's somethin' I hafta tell ya, Merry. I'm gonna be leavin' sooner than I planned." His voice was firm, resolute. "Before I go, there are some things we hafta discuss."

"When are you leaving?"

"In two weeks. August thirteenth."

"You're right," I said. "We *do* need to talk." I'd been putting this off long enough. Unfortunately, I'd been so involved with Charity and her future, I'd ignored my own.

"Can ya go for a ride with me?" he asked.

"Not now. Dad'll be home any minute."

"Will ya ask if I can take ya for a hamburger when he comes?" Levi looked so boyish and cute. I hated to think of him going off to Bible school, leaving SummerHill behind.

"I'll ask, but I probably shouldn't tonight." I didn't want to miss out on any new developments with Charity's birth parents. It would be truly horrible to go off and have a good time with Levi only to come home and find Charity was gone.

"I could give ya a call later," he said. "I'll be down at the Yoders' place for a bit. They have a phone in their woodshop, ya know."

"Okay." I could see Levi was getting a kick out of saying he'd call me. The Old Order Amish didn't believe in having telephones in the houses they owned, so Levi had grown up without one all these years. His connections with Mennonite friends had pulled him away from the old Amish ways and dress of his youth. He was a changed person now. And he was determined to win the world for Christ—another strong Mennonite influence—one that Jesus himself taught His disciples. It was the command Levi was hanging his hat on. And his future as a minister.

"I'll call ya after supper, then," he said, his eyes shining with hope.

"I really like your car." I wasn't kidding. It was really cool. The Levi of the past obviously had incorporated his passion for wheels into this modern-day form of transportation. I knew even as I stood there waving that if Charity weren't in the middle of my life, I'd be saying absolutely yes to a drive with Levi.

I watched him drive his shiny car down SummerHill and park it quite a ways past his father's farm. What a guy! He'd had the gumption to make the break from the Amish for his own beliefs' sake, and the sake of spreading the Gospel. Yet he was careful to show respect to his parents by not flaunting—as he said—his modern wheels and his decision to go to Bible school. I admired him with renewed interest. I could hardly wait for our talk.

Dad showed up soon after Levi left, and I ran out to the driveway to meet him.

"When will we know if Charity can be ours?" was the first thing out of my mouth.

"Well," he chuckled, "it's nice to see you, too."

I apologized. "But I'm dying to find out something. How long do we have to wait before Charity's free to adopt?"

"Patience, Merry," he chided gently.

"It's too hard to be patient sometimes," I admitted.

"Why not enjoy Charity while we have her?"

"But what if she has to go back . . . to her family?" The thought nearly killed me.

"We'll deal with that when and if the time comes," he stated, and I knew he hoped it would never happen. We walked into the house together. "Your mother should be home any minute now. What do you say we surprise her and make supper?" It was a great idea. Only one problem: Dad didn't know the first thing about cooking.

"Guess we're talking pizza, right?" I teased.

He grinned. "You make the salad. I'll preheat the oven."

"Count on it." I went to the fridge and pulled out some salad fixings. Dad was in an interesting mood, one I hadn't seen in ages. I hoped his sparkling, fun-loving attitude would last, but I honestly wondered how he'd feel tomorrow afternoon—when we visited Faithie's grave.

A Cry in the Dark **Fifteen**

I rushed to the back door when I heard Mom coming. Eagerly, I scooped up Charity from the new car seat and hurried back into the kitchen. Dad and I had set the table, complete with candles. The mood was festive—after all, we had a lot to be festive about.

"Charity needs to be in on our celebration," I said.

"What celebration?" Mom asked.

"The let's-enjoy-having-Charity-around-for-no-matter-how-long celebration," I replied.

Mom looked puzzled at first. Then she glanced at Dad, whose contented expression must've helped her understand.

"Bring the little munchkin to me," Dad said, holding out his arms. While he held her, I scrambled into the dining room to get the cradle. It was heavy—well constructed, too. Handmade by one of the Yoder boys' Amish uncles before Faithie and I were born.

I carried it into the kitchen, setting it down in the middle of the room. "There," I said, "now we can all see Charity while we eat."

Mom went to wash her hands at the sink. "I'm afraid she won't make it much longer. We'd better get started."

"You mean she's hungry?" I asked.

Mom dried her hands. "She certainly didn't seem interested in eating while we waited our turn at Social Services. I ended up putting a blanket down on the floor and letting her kick her feet. She cooed and gurgled at everyone. Quite a social butterfly."

I could visualize the scene. "I'll bet you had tons of visitors swooning over her, right?"

Mom nodded. "You should've seen the people coming up and asking about her—how old she was, what was her name. Standard baby questions." Mom smiled and went over to take Charity from Dad. "But, you know, I felt wonderful. Really wonderful." Her eyes were moist as she looked at Dad. "Better than I have in years."

I wondered exactly what Mom was thinking. The tender glances exchanged between my parents were apparently not meant to include me. But even though I was the outsider for the moment, something in me rejoiced as I stood in our familiar country kitchen in our old colonial house—the place my twin sister and I had come home to. The lines in my mother's face had softened. Had Charity's coming soothed her pain, too?

Once Charity was settled in her cradle perch, Dad prayed and we ate supper. He recounted the emergency room events of his day for Mom and me. Soon, Mom was going over every inch of her day spent with Charity and me, telling about Miss Spindler's visit—and all the handmade booties—as well as every baby-related happening in the last nearly ten hours Dad had been gone.

I grinned, listening, and wondered how it had been in this grand old house when Faithie and I were babies. Before I could even bring it up, Mom started talking about the days of double everything.

"Goodness, I don't know how I kept up with things." She reached over and let her hand rest on top of mine. "Merry was the happiest baby. She could entertain herself for hours at a time." Mom smiled, reliving the days.

"That's why you named me Merry, right?"

"You never cried when you were born," she explained. "At least, it didn't sound like crying."

Dad agreed. "You laughed . . . chortled, I guess you'd say."

"Chortled?" This was the first I'd heard my birth described *that* way.

Dad rubbed his chin. "You're not going to argue with me, are you? After all, I was there—I know what I heard." Dad was laughing now, and Mom, too. Charity started to join in, at least that's how it sounded at first, but her fussy cooings gave way to hearty cries.

"Uh-oh," Mom said, turning around. "Another country heard from." She warmed up the baby's formula while Dad and I argued over who would get to feed her. Dad won out, but only because I let him. I knew it wouldn't be long before he'd be sound asleep in his easy chair. Then it would be my turn!

"I can't wait till Charity's finally ours," I said, watching Dad hold the baby with bottle tilted up.

Mom didn't say anything, but in a few seconds, Dad did. Again, his words were measured and directed toward Mom. "Have you decided what you want to do if Charity becomes available for adoption?"

A wistful look played around Mom's lips. "Well, hon, I've been praying about it, but I think we should talk—"

The phone rang.

"I'll get it," I said, jumping up. "Hello?"

"Hullo, Merry. This is Levi."

I laughed, stretching the phone cord around the corner into the dining room. "I know who you are."

"Well, didja have a chance to ask?"

Ask? Once again, I'd forgotten. Charity was taking over my entire life!

"Merry, I wanna see ya." His voice was mellow and sweet.

"Uh . . . just a minute." I covered up the phone and went back into the kitchen. However, I had to wait to ask until Dad quit kissing Mom—on the lips. "Excuse me," I said when they looked up. "Is it okay if I go for a ride in Levi's new car?"

Mom's head jerked back. "Not *this* again."

Dad wasn't going to get in the middle of anything. I could tell by the way his eyes darted away from mine and back to the business at hand—feeding Charity.

"But, Mom," I retorted. "He's a very good driver."

She grimaced. "Since when?"

"Since he . . . well, you know," I sputtered, trying to quickly remind them that Levi's wild horse-and-buggy days were over.

"Where is it you want to go?" she asked.

"Oh, down to the Dairy Queen or to get a soda somewhere." I sighed. "Levi and I *have* to talk, Mom. He's leaving for school in two weeks."

"Two weeks?" She stood up, beginning to clear the table.

"Please? We won't be gone long."

"Well, it's Saturday night, and you have plenty to do here at home to get ready for church tomorrow."

"So, can I go?"

She glanced at her watch. "Be home by nine-thirty."

"Yes!" I turned back to the phone. "Levi? I'll be ready in fifteen minutes," I said, trying not to let the excitement creep into my voice.

"*Gut*, Merry. I'll be by to pick you up at eight."

We said good-bye and hung up.

"Levi seems awfully persistent," Mom said, glancing up while loading the dishwasher.

"He goes after what he wants, but he knows when to back off, too," I said, sticking up for my friend. "That's what true love's all about, right? Knowing when to back off—to let go."

My remark was not well taken. But it got Dad's attention. "Sounds like you've been reading poetry again," he said, smiling. "But you're right. True love is patient and slow to act or react. Levi's been trained in the Scriptures all his life. He's seen love in action in the Amish community, that's for certain."

It struck me that Dad was taking Levi's side!

"Then you wouldn't mind if I agreed to wait for Levi while he goes to Bible school?" It was a test. I had to know what Dad would say.

Mom gasped in the background, but she remained silent while Dad burped the baby, talking to me. "Wait for Levi, you say? Well, how do you feel about waiting around for him when you're only sixteen—"

"*Fifteen*," Mom interrupted. "She won't be sixteen until September."

Dad jumped right in and began painting a picture of high school and the many activities looming on the horizon of my sophmore year. "Now, think of this, Mer. How would it be staying home and writing letters to Levi while your girl friends are out with guy friends at football games and homecoming parades?"

Dad had a point. He *always* did.

"I guess I'll just have to see if Levi wants to be tied down to a *fifteen*-year-old"—here I glanced at Mom, who caught the emphasis—"while he's off having a great time getting a taste of college life in the modern world."

"Levi's almost seventeen now," Mom offered. "Even though you're only a year apart, there's a big difference between high school and college. Levi will be living as an adult."

Once again, Mom was overexplaining. She was the commentator of the family and probably would've continued, but Charity let out a loud burp. Dad congratulated Charity, and Mom came rushing over to make sure she hadn't spit up on Dad's shirt.

"Have fun, baby," I called to her, blowing a kiss. "I love you." And without offering to help with dishes, I headed upstairs to get my hair and face ready for the all-important chat with Levi.

When the doorbell rang, I waited for Dad to get it. He liked to play host. He and Levi would sit in the living room and shoot the breeze for a while. Then in a few minutes, I'd come down. We'd had the same scenario twice before when Levi had come to take me for a walk.

I was standing at the top of the long main staircase, thinking it was about time to go down and make my appearance. The sun winked on the brass top of the banister, and I counted to ten.

The phone rang; someone picked it up downstairs. Then I heard Mom's voice floating up the back steps. "Merry, the phone's for you."

Not wanting to keep Levi waiting, I dashed down the hall to my parents' bedroom. "Hello?"

"Merry, Mistress of Mirth! I've missed many, many merry moments with you." It was Jon Klein, the Alliteration Wizard!

"Hi," I said. "You must be back from your vacation."

"Say that with all *b*'s," he said, laughing.

"I'd love to, but I really can't talk right now." What lousy timing!

"Let's see . . . likely not—Levi?"

How'd he know? I wondered.

"Well, actually, you're right. Levi's waiting downstairs." I wanted to be honest with him. "He and I have some things to discuss."

"Super-serious stuff?"

I paused to think. Jon's alliterating was bugging me—for the first time ever! "Could you stop talking that way and . . . and . . ."

"And what? What's wrong, Mer?" His voice was filled with question marks.

"I can't talk now, honest I can't," I said again. "Maybe I'll see you tomorrow."

"*Maybe?* You mean you're not coming to church?"

"I didn't mean that," I said. "I just meant—oh, never mind. Just forget it."

"Merry, wait." He sounded worried that I might hang up. "Can't we talk for a minute?"

"I'd like that," I said. "But I can't now. See ya."

His voice was still coming through the receiver as I held the phone in my hand, deciding whether or not to hang up. Then, feeling guilty, I brought the phone back up to my ear and listened.

"Merry? Are you still there?" he was asking.

"I'm here. Sorry."

"Hey, I called to invite you to the church potluck next weekend." His voice wavered a bit.

I was in shock. This was the first time Jon had formally asked me to anything. How long I had waited for this moment?

"So, what's it gonna be, Mistress Merry?"

My life was being ripped into pieces. Into thirds, actually. Jovial Jon, for one. And there was Levi—waiting downstairs to discuss our "future." Last, but certainly not least, a big chunk of my life was already wrapped up in Charity, my precious sister-gift from God.

As I held the phone, I felt a distinct tugging in my heart. I couldn't even begin to respond. Jon was waiting for my answer. Levi was downstairs.

The next move was mine. Help!

Sixteen A Cry in the Dark

Mom was upstairs now. I could hear her across the hall, talking to Charity. Next thing I knew, she was waving Lissa's photos in front of me.

I whispered, "Thanks," and put the photo-lab envelope on the bed. Mom left the room to attend to Charity.

"Uh . . . Jon," I said, glancing at my watch, "could I call you back later?"

"Like, how late?"

"Sometime after nine-thirty." That's when I had to be home. And that's when I would know something about my status with Levi—and whether or not I was free to go with Jon to the church potluck.

"With watchful wonder, I'll await your call," he said.

I giggled. Jon was a real nut! Why had he waited so long to show an interest in me?

———

Downstairs, Levi looked truly dashing in his new T-shirt and jeans—without the usual suspenders. I wondered if he'd given them up, too.

Dad and Levi stood as I came into the room. "We were just talking about you, Mer," Dad volunteered.

Levi nodded. "All good things." His eyes caught mine.

Suddenly, my cats showed up, sniffing at Levi's tennis shoes. "Okay, call off the cat squad," I teased, shooing the felines away. "Looks like they're still getting acquainted."

Levi grinned. "You'd think Lily White would know me by now, jah?"

I remembered the first time I'd seen Lily—in the hayloft last spring—before the Zooks' fire. Levi had called her a mouse catcher. "Maybe she's worried you'll take her back to the barn," I said.

"Never again," Levi replied. Unfortunately, Lily White hadn't heard his remark. She was already long gone.

"Well, I guess you two better be running along," Dad offered, rubbing his hands together.

"Nice chattin' with ya," Levi said to Dad, then shook his hand. I wondered if they'd come to some sort of gentlemen's agreement. It sure seemed fishy for them to be so chummy.

Levi followed me out through the wide archway and into the hall to the spacious entryway.

"Mom, I'm leaving," I called up the steps.

"Have fun," she called back.

Dad was leaning against the wide wood molding in the doorway leading to the living room. "Drive carefully" was all he said. Then with a wave, he smiled.

Outside, Levi walked around to the passenger side and opened the door for me. There was a spring in his step as he hurried to the driver's side after I was settled in. I admired the plush interior of his car. It still seemed odd to think that Levi actually owned modern wheels.

"Well, what do ya think?" he asked, jumping in behind the steering wheel.

"It's kind of strange. I'm used to seeing you with your horse, riding around in your Amish buggy."

He nodded. "I know whatcha mean." He looked at me for a second longer, then put the key into the ignition. "Are ya hungry?"

"We just ate, but thanks."

"Well, then, how 'bout a soda?" he suggested.

"Okay."

He switched on the radio to one of the local Christian stations, and we rode without talking down SummerHill Lane. At the turnoff to Hunsecker Road, Levi reached over and held my hand. My heart skipped a beat as he drove the familiar road to the old covered bridge.

"It's not gonna be easy sayin' good-bye, Merry," he said softly. "I want us to always be close like this—even when I'm gone to school."

I could hardly speak. The moment was filled with deep emotion. Levi slowed down as we approached Hunsecker Mill Bridge, and carefully he guided the car into the narrow, covered bridge. The loose planks rumbled under the wheels as we passed through.

"Do ya still wanna be my girl while I'm gone?" he asked as we headed out into the fading light of dusk. The sinking sun's red light cast a rosy glow over the road and trees as we headed for town.

I really couldn't decide. Not now . . . not with things going so well between us. "What do *you* want, Levi?"

He smiled, his lips parting slightly. "Remember our talk in the gazebo earlier this summer?"

"I remember," I said, feeling terribly shy.

"Well, I haven't changed my mind about anything. But we're still young and . . ." He paused. "And there's something else. I feel I've received a call from the Lord, ya know. A call into the ministry."

"That should come first," I replied.

By the time we got to McDonald's and went through the drive-through, Levi had pretty much come to his own conclusion about us. I was glad he was the one deciding, but very sad that he wouldn't be around SummerHill after August 13.

"I hope you'll write now and again," he said, glancing at me. "I don't wanna lose you, Merry. But it just wouldn't be fair to tie you down. Not now."

I thought back to what Dad had said at supper. If I hadn't known better, I would've thought he'd given Levi the same spiel he'd given me.

"Of course I'll write," I said, pushing the straw into the plastic lid. "And you'll be back to visit the farm, won't you?"

"Jah," he said. "Curly John and Sarah's baby will be comin' soon, don't forget. So I'll be back."

"Rachel says the baby's due in November."

He nodded. "Sarah's been busy makin' all kinds of booties and things."

His reference to booties got me sidetracked, thinking about Charity back home. "I bet Sarah's excited."

"Jah. She talks about namin' the baby after me if it's a boy." Levi was obviously delighted.

"And what if the baby's a girl—then what'll they name her?" I turned to look at his familiar face, tanned from the sun.

"My brother wants her to be named for Sarah."

"Curly John chose Sarah's name?"

Levi nodded.

"How sweet—baby Sarah Zook," I said, trying the name on for fun. "How will you tell her name apart from her mother's?"

"The Amish love nicknames," Levi chuckled. "She'll hafta have one fer sure." Then he surprised me and asked about Charity. "How's that little one ya had yesterday . . . in the basket, ya know?"

It sounded like Rachel hadn't told him about her being abandoned. "Oh, she's fine," I said.

"That's gut," he said. "Funny, though, I was sure I saw the same baby—same basket—in town with Miss Spindler yesterday afternoon."

I swallowed hard. "Really?"

"I'm certain of it." For a few moments only the radio broke the stillness. "What do ya make of it?"

"Guess she was baby-sitting," I said. Would Dad want me to tell more? I didn't think so.

"It's awful strange—Old Hawk Eyes with a baby." Levi made the left turn onto SummerHill Lane. "Who would've thought the old lady would wanna go shoppin' with a baby?"

The same question had crossed my mind. But that was before I'd come to realize how very kind, even nurturing, our neighbor lady was. "I guess when you know a person long enough . . . well, eventually the hidden secrets of their personality are revealed."

Levi looked at me. "Now ya sound like a philosopher."

We laughed together, sharing the memorable moment as honeysuckle aroma wafted through the windows of Levi's beautiful car.

"I'm glad I know ya, Merry," he said, grinning. "Do I know all the secret parts of yer personality yet?"

I kept a straight face. "I doubt it."

More laughter.

When Levi pulled into my driveway at nine-thirty on the dot, I could think of only one thing: He was leaving SummerHill. Things would never be the same between us.

"Why so glum?" he asked.

I forced a smile. "You know me, I hate change. It's always hard for me."

"Jah." He nodded. "But it's a new beginning for me. And fer ya, too, Merry. You'll be goin' to high school."

I nodded, not wild about the prospect of leaving my old junior high behind to start over in a brand-new place.

"We'll still see each other," Levi said. "I promise ya that."

Something inside me secretly wished he was making another kind of promise, even though I knew he was right about us going our separate ways.

He held tightly to the steering wheel, looking straight ahead. "Yer a wonderful girl, Merry. I've known it since the day ya saved me from drownin' in the pond behind the house."

I wasn't sure why he always had to bring that up. Was it the saving of his life that meant so much to him? Or was it me, myself?

Just then, Abednego, my fat black cat, jumped up onto the hood of the car. He arched his back and hissed.

Levi leaned back in his seat and burst out laughing.

I got out of the car. "Abednego, you crazy cat. Come here!" I tried several coaxing tactics on him, but he refused to come.

By now Levi was outside, too, still getting a kick out of the way Abednego was misbehaving. I apologized for my rude cat, and instead of continuing to persuade and coax, I left Abednego behind and walked with Levi to the front porch.

"Still coming tomorrow to Faithie's graveside?" I asked as we stood at the door. "We'll go after dinner."

"I'll be there."

"I'm glad," I said. "Thanks for the soda."

He took my hand and held it in both of his. "I'll be missin' ya, Merry."

"I'll miss you, too, Levi." We said good-night, knowing full well there were two more weeks—wonderful summer days and nights—before Levi had to go.

Yet the sadness stayed with me long after his gleaming white Mustang pulled out of the driveway and sped down SummerHill.

Seventeen A Cry in the Dark

I headed upstairs to my room. The events of the night had come as somewhat of a relief, yet I was still dealing with mixed emotions about Levi. Mostly sad ones. So sad that I completely forgot about Jon Klein and my promise to call.

Charity started to cry and I hurried to her room. "What's the matter with you, sweetie?" I asked, picking her up.

Mom came running. "I wonder why she's fussy," she remarked. "I just finished bathing her, and I was sure she was asleep."

"She just wanted to see her big sister, that's all." I walked around the makeshift nursery, hugging her close. "Isn't that right?"

Mom sat in the rocking chair and watched me. "There have been some new developments," she said.

I perked up my ears. "When? While I was gone? What?"

"Whoa, Merry, slow down." She was smiling. "There's nothing to worry about. In fact, it's very good news."

"Really?" I moved closer to Mom, eager to hear.

"The authorities have located Charity's parents somewhere in Virginia. They're in jail now. Fortunately, they have signed away—relinquished—all parental rights."

"Yes! This is truly amazing."

Charity babbled as I bent down and kissed her tiny cheek. "You're gonna be ours forever!" I danced around the room, rejoicing.

"By noon Monday, we'll have legal custody—temporarily, of course. It takes time to finalize adoptions."

"You're kidding—she's actually going to be up for adoption?" This was too good to be true.

Mom nodded. "Your dad and I agree that we want you and Skip to be involved in the final decision." She smiled, wiping a tear off her cheek. "We had a long talk about it tonight. We dearly love Charity and are willing to start over, so to speak. Things could be very lonely for all of us come fall when Skip's gone. A baby . . . a baby like Charity would be a welcome addition to our family."

"So, what's to decide?" I said. Charity was going to be ours! She was going to stay right here and grow up with doting parents and a sister who adored her. I couldn't believe God had answered my prayer so quickly.

"We want to have Charity here with us for a full week before we make our final decision," Mom said. "It's best to pray in earnest about something this important."

"I've already prayed," I said, referring to the prayer in the cellar the day she'd arrived. "God came through for me. Charity stays."

———

Jon met me at the door leading to our Sunday school class. "I waited last night for you to call," he said without the typical alliteration routine. "What happened?"

"I'm sorry. Maybe we should talk after class," I replied, heading inside, looking for an empty chair.

Jon followed, asking if he could sit with me just as Mrs. Simms, our teacher, stood up to welcome the visitors. "What about the potluck? Did you decide?" Jon whispered.

"Sure, I'll go," I answered, feeling slightly disloyal to Levi. I tried to dismiss the thought. After all, he and I were only friends now. Still, the idea of hanging out with Jon while Levi was off at the concert in Ephrata alone bothered me.

After class, I gave the package of photos to Lissa. "They turned out great," I said as she opened them.

"Wow, you're right." She looked at each picture. "Grammy will be so excited to get these. How much do I owe you?"

I gave her the receipt. "Here, you can pay me later."

"Mom'll write you a check after church, okay?" Her wavy hair was pulled back in a perky blue hair wrap. And I noticed that as we talked, she glanced at Jon several times.

"Glad you like them." I turned to go. Jon was waiting in the hallway.

"Like them? They're the best pictures I've ever had taken," Lissa said, following me out to the hall. "You're such a good photographer, Mer."

"Thanks," I said.

Lissa stood beside me while I hung out with Jon and our pastor's daughter, Ashley Horton, who just so happened to like the Alliteration Wizard, too.

"Well, who's coming to the potluck next weekend?" Ashley asked, looking around.

"Merry and I are," Jon stated, grinning at me.

Lissa acted cool, not showing her surprise. But Ashley stood there and yakked about how much fun the potluck would be. I wondered when she would stop talking.

That's when Mom came down the hall, Charity and diaper bag in tow. Apparently, she was headed for the nursery.

"Oh, Mom, let me show off my new sister," I said, taking Charity from her. "We can't put her in the nursery on her very first Sunday with us. I can hold her in church, and if she gets fussy, I'll come out and walk around with her."

Mom agreed and headed off to save a seat for me upstairs in the sanctuary.

Lissa looked shocked as she and Ashley crowded in, touching Charity's little hands and soft, chubby cheeks. "This is your *sister*?" Lissa asked.

"Well . . . she will be soon. We hope."

Lissa looked confused.

"It's what I couldn't talk about the other night on the phone. Remember?" Quickly I tried to explain. "Evidently, the stranger we saw in the pickup was looking for a place to hide a baby."

"How cruel," Ashley said. "She's so tiny. How could someone do that?"

"It's awful, that's what it is," Lissa whispered. "She's so precious."

They had lots of questions, but the music was starting and it was time for church. Jon waited around as though he wanted to sit with me. "Would it be all right with your parents?" he asked as we headed for the stairs.

"If you don't mind sitting in a pew with a two-month-old."

He smiled. "Do babies bite?"

I laughed, delighting in Jon's attention.

Surprisingly, Charity slept through most of the pastor's sermon. "Love wasn't put in your heart to stay," he quoted. "Love isn't love till you give it away." Then he read his Scripture text. "First Corinthians chapter thirteen, verses four and five. 'Love is patient, love is kind. It does not envy, it does not boast, it is not proud. It is not rude, it is not self-seeking, it is not easily angered, it keeps no record of wrongs.' Today, I want to focus on the passage, 'love is not self-seeking.' Love that is freely given is Godlike love."

I listened intently, thinking off and on of Levi, who had declared his love for me weeks ago but who refused to cling to it—releasing me for now. He'd exhibited the selfless kind of love the pastor was talking about.

After the service, Jon asked more questions about the baby. "Where did you find her?"

"It was wild, really. I thought at first I heard my kitten crying, but when I searched, I discovered this baby in our gazebo!"

He was as surprised as everyone else. My parents' friends gathered around oohing and ahhing over Charity. I gave her to Mom, who held her up for her friends to see. People just couldn't seem to get enough of our pudgy darling.

"You picked the perfect name for a pretty petite person," Jon said, beginning his irresistible word game. He smiled, egging me on. "Your turn."

"Charity? Chalk it up as a chapter in a changed heart."

Jon was clapping. "Exceptionally excellent example!"

"Thank you . . . I think." We were in glossary glory.

After dinner, Mom, Dad, and I, along with Charity, took the short ride down SummerHill to the small cemetery where grave-stones lay scattered in rows across a tree-lined meadow. Levi's car was parked nearby, and Dad mentioned how thoughtful it was that he had come.

"It was Levi's idea," I said.

"What a really terrific kid," Mom said, handing Charity to Dad. "Too bad he has to go off to school so soon."

I wondered about her statement. Just last night she seemed to be opposed to my spending time with Levi.

"Hullo, Dr. Hanson," Levi said, catching up with Dad. He spied the baby, and a shadow of surprise crept across his hand-some face.

"It's good of you to come," Dad said.

Levi stared at the baby.

"Baby Charity's going to be staying with us," I explained quietly as we fell into step together. "It's a long story."

"Ach, jah," he said, and I knew I'd have to level with him about Miss Spindler sooner or later.

Love is kind.

Solemnly, we approached Faithie's white gravestone. The roll-ing hills around us were ablaze with color. Yellow daisies bloomed everywhere. Levi went with me to gather some for Faithie's grave. It was part of our family tradition. The celebration of her life.

Finally, all of us held hands and sang "Amazing Grace." Levi's clear voice rang out, and a lump rose in my throat as I thought of him leaving. Purposely, I stared at the words etched on Faithie's gravestone. *Faith Hanson, precious daughter and dear sister, in heaven with our Lord.*

Levi had been fond of Faithie, too. Not in the same way as he loved me, but he *had* loved her. The Zook kids were Faithie's and my favorite playmates in a predominantly Amish area. Faithie and I loved spending time with our Plain friends—skating on the pond in winter, riding in the pony cart in the springtime, playing barefoot in summer . . . and then there was the hayloft. That wonderful, almost magical place high in their two-story bank barn. All this and much more, Faithie and I had shared with Levi and his brothers and sisters. We'd played nearly every day beyond the willow grove—on the Zook farm.

I choked back the tears as Dad prayed that our hearts would be tender to the love each of us shared, neighbor and family member alike. "And may we always remember that our days on this earth are numbered," he prayed. "That we ought to treasure every minute we have as a family until you call us home. Amen."

I wiped the tears from my eyes as we turned to head down the hill to the car. Dad was right. I knew in my heart that if I could do it all again—relive those seven short years with Faithie—I would be more careful to cherish every minute.

Love never fails.

When we arrived home, Rachel was waiting on the front porch. She looked pale, and as I got out of the car and ran toward her, I noticed her eyes were red and swollen.

"Rachel, what's wrong?"

"It's Sarah's baby." She put her hands to her face, covering her eyes. "Sarah's gone to the hospital."

"Why? What happened?" Fear gripped me.

Rachel shook her head, unable to speak.

Dad stopped to talk with her while Mom took Charity into the house for her nap. "Is your sister-in-law having premature labor?" he asked.

Rachel shook her head. "It can't be—it's only her fifth month."

Dad's eyes showed concern. "I'll leave for the hospital right away." He touched Rachel's shoulder.

"Thanks, Dad," I said as he hurried into the house.

Love is patient.

The wait was terribly long. Rachel stayed at our house until it was time for the afternoon milking. Before she left, I hugged her. "We'll be praying," I said. "And if we don't hear something soon, I'll ask Mom to page Dad."

She nodded. "*Da Herr sei mit du.* The Lord be with you." Off she ran down the lane toward the shortcut to the farm, through the willows.

"And with *you,* Rachel!" I called after my friend.

The phone did not ring until almost seven. When I picked it up, I detected the sadness in Dad's voice. "Sarah lost her baby."

My heart sank. "I'll run and tell Rachel. She's waiting to know . . . her parents, too."

"Tell them Sarah's resting now," Dad said. "She's being sedated."

I could not imagine what poor Sarah and Curly John were experiencing. They were young—newlyweds—barely two years older than Skip. And this was their first little one. Now Baby Zook was gone. Gone to heaven too soon.

I ran upstairs and sat on the floor beside the cradle that had been mine. Sadly, I looked down at Charity, now sound asleep. "Nothing must ever happen to you," I said out of sheer determination. "I won't let it. I won't! You're ours forever."

Love always protects.

Charity stirred sweetly in her sleep, unaware of the turmoil in my heart.

On Monday morning, Mom and Dad went to town with Charity to do the paper work for temporary custody. I stayed home and took pictures outside. The gazebo was the setting this time. With the news of Sarah's miscarriage fresh in my mind, I created several scenes using Faithie's pine cradle. I didn't mean it to be morbid, but maybe it was.

Anyway, I had my own unique way of working through my sorrow over Sarah and Curly John's loss. By combining the gazebo with the empty cradle, I was bringing three factors together: my own pain at losing Faithie, Sarah's recent loss, and the discovery of Charity—the love I was clinging to. What great joy she'd brought to me! And now to my family.

Mom had made things quite clear, however. By this time Friday, we were to make a final decision about Charity. Mom had said to pray about it. I had. There was nothing left to say. I wanted Charity—wanted her forever.

As I ran around the gazebo, taking this shot and that from various angles, I remembered Dad's words. *True love is patient and slow to act or react.*

I must admit, I'd gotten caught up in the emotion of the moment, letting baby fever run away with me. But when it came right down to it—to the everyday, day-in-day-out schedule of having a baby to care for, well . . . I could see Mom's point. I was *not* the one most involved. She was.

Was I being selfish, wanting this baby?

Love is not self-seeking.

I stopped to adjust the aperture, the lens opening, for correct lighting. Then I heard someone walking toward me and turned to see who it was. "Rachel, hi!"

"Whatcha doin'?" she asked.

I knew she'd spotted the cradle. It was the focal point of the gazebo picture—how could she miss it?

"Oh, just taking some pictures."

She was quiet for a moment, her eyes downcast. We sat on the gazebo steps while the cats came and rubbed up against our bare ankles.

Carefully, I put my camera back into its case and snapped it shut. Looking up, I saw that Rachel's eyes were bright with tears. "You're crying!"

She brushed her cheek with the back of her hand. "I'm sad for Sarah. She's brokenhearted, Merry. And there's been some very bad news."

My throat turned to cotton. "What is it?"

"The doctor says, like as not, Sarah will never be able to have children." A sad little sigh burst from her lips.

"Oh, Rachel . . . I'm so sorry." I put my arm around her, sharing her pain. Her light brown hair was wrapped up in a thick bun at the back of her head and covered by the white netting she always wore. Her shoulders shook as she wept. I'd never seen her cry so hard. Not even at her grandfather's funeral.

We sat there together under the towering leafy maples, and I comforted Rachel as best I could. At last, she dried her eyes. "Ya know, you're my best friend, Cousin Merry."

"I am?" I was startled by her words.

Her eyes widened. "Ain't I yours?"

I'd never thought of Rachel that way—only Faithie. But now that she mentioned it, I guessed she was right.

"Oh, Rachel . . ." I hugged her hard. "You're the best friend I could ever have."

She smiled through her tears, standing up suddenly. "I hafta go help Mam out with choppin' carrots and celery—we're makin' chow chow."

I sat there clinging to my cats as she dashed across the side yard and headed for SummerHill Lane. She'd called me her best friend. I shouldn't have been so surprised. Rachel and I had shared everything. Always had. And now this—the loss of her brother's baby.

In spite of the sadness, I felt consoled and heartened. It was truly amazing—even without Faithie, I'd had a best friend all these years!

Later, Shadrach and Meshach followed me as I went into the house to put away my camera equipment. I went back to the gazebo to retrieve the cradle. There on the wooden floor, I spotted the safety pin—the one that had pinned the note to Charity's pink blanket. I stopped to pick it up, turning it over in my hand.

A startling realization hit me. The note had pleaded for my help. *Please take care of me and love me as your own.* And Merry Hanson, the problem solver, had decided to do just that. That was me—Miss Fix-It.

Dad had recognized the trait in me early on, and Skip constantly teased me about taking in strays. Cats, people . . . I'd even risked my life to save Lily White—a mouse catcher, of all things. And now, my latest attempt at saving the world was a two-month-old baby!

Things were becoming clear, making sense. I understood why Mom and Dad had asked me to pray about the decision. They were absolutely right. A decision to make Charity my baby sister was far too important to simply make out of emotion.

I scooped up Lily White and held her close. "C'mon, you. We're going for a walk. Just the two of us." And down the lane I went.

Nearly four days had passed since Mom and I sat together in the willow grove talking about life and love and God's will. I wanted to go there now. To be alone. So much had happened since Thursday, and the events were beginning to overwhelm me.

Lily White must've sensed my tension. She kept meowing and trying to wrestle away. "No, no. You sit tight, little girl," I said, holding her gently yet firmly.

She fought me, trying to break free.

Frustrated, I shouted, "You're staying right here!"

The poor little fluff of white recoiled. *Mew,* she replied.

"Oh, baby, I'm sorry," I said, kneeling down on the worn, narrow path, stroking her head. "I do love you. Honest. I just want you to stay where it's safe, where I can take care of you. Don't you see?"

When I took my hands away, Lily White ran off. I hurried after her, calling for her to return. "Come back, Lily! Please! I'm sorry."

But Lily had other ideas. She skittered through the willows and down toward the meadow where the cows were grazing. Had she seen a mouse?

"Lily!" She ignored me, obviously wanting her freedom. I'd clung too tightly to her.

Crouching on the soft ground under the biggest willow in the grove, I felt as though the world was sitting on my shoulders. The secret place was nearly enclosed with green branches and tendrils, forming a canopy over my head. "Come back, Lily," I cried. "I love you too much to let you wander away. I want you with *me*."

When I stopped crying, I realized how selfish my words were. How selfish I was in other ways, too. I'd clung selfishly to Faithie's memory, blocking out close friendships and letting the obsession with it come between Mom and me. And I'd thought *she* had a problem!

Love keeps no record of wrongs.

And there was Charity. I didn't have to think twice to know the truth. I was being selfish about her, too.

A young Amish couple had heard sorrowful words yesterday upon the loss of their first baby: no birth children for them—ever!

What was it Rachel had said last week? That it would be a terrible heartache for an Amish wife to be without children.

Love is not self-seeking.

Me, me—that's all I could think about these days. *My* sister, *my* baby . . .

Leaping up, I parted some of the heavy branches, letting the hot sun beat down on my face. "Forgive me, Lord," I said simply. "Help me put the pastor's sermon into practice. Give me the kind of love that doesn't cling for dear life, because love isn't love till *I* give it away."

Though I was hot and beginning to perspire, the sun's rays encompassed me. They were like the light of God's love pouring into my soul. Shining the Father's torch of truth.

I let go of the branches and slipped into the shadowy coolness of the willow grove. A rustling came from behind, and startled, I turned to look.

"Merry, don't be frightened."

"Mom, what are you doing here?" I ran to her, careful not to awaken Charity, who was sleeping in her wicker basket. She smiled, glancing at the baby. "I thought it was time for our little one to be formally introduced to your secret place."

I nodded. "Doesn't look like she cares too much about it right now." I looked around, enjoying the moment and feeling freer than I had in years. "We have to talk," I said. "With Dad."

Mom's eyes grew serious. "Oh?"

I breathed in a deep breath, my heart pounding. "It's about keeping Charity."

We didn't stay long in the willow grove. The sparse clouds of morning had thickened and were beginning to grow dark. A clap of thunder crackled in our ears as we hurried in the back door.

"We made it just in time," Mom said, uncovering Charity, who was wide awake now and moving her little arms excitedly.

"When will Dad be home?" I asked, gazing at the baby.

"Probably late."

I was disappointed. "After supper?"

"I'm afraid so." Mom took Charity out of the basket and handed her to me. "Will you change her, please? I have some calls to make."

I wondered what Mom was up to but didn't ask. She seemed rather preoccupied. Maybe she was thinking about what I'd said in the willows. I was tempted to tiptoe down the hall and eavesdrop. One brief snatch of conversation might give me a clue.

Slowly, I inched toward the main staircase. The door to the study was partly open, and I stood there listening.

"Before you come home," Mom was saying, "can you touch base with your contacts at the Department of Social Services?"

Silence on her end. Was she talking to Dad?

Then—"I'm not sure. But check and see what must be done." It sounded as though she was about to hang up, so I scooted away from the door and carried Charity upstairs.

I wondered how Mom and Dad would feel about giving up Charity for Curly John and Sarah Zook. Of course, it was a bit premature to be thinking that way, especially since Sarah was still in the hospital and had no knowledge of our little Charity.

Torn between wanting to keep Charity and wanting to help soothe the pain for Sarah and Curly John, I played with the darling baby who'd brought us so much delight—singing and saying the nursery rhymes Faithie and I had learned. I'd grown so attached to this baby. Just thinking about taking her to live with someone else made me half sick.

And what about Mom? She loved Charity, too. How would *she* feel? And Dad? Anyone could see how charmed he was by the baby.

I changed Charity's diaper and carried her back downstairs. Mom was busily stirring something in the kitchen. She didn't even glance up as I strolled into the family room with Charity. Sometimes Mom worked out her stress in her cooking. This afternoon was one of those times, I was sure. If I was correct, it was best to steer clear.

I found the remote and scanned the TV channels while sitting in Dad's easy chair. The news was on all the major networks. A ballet was on public television. I switched it back to the local news. One of the leading stories was about couples and infertility drugs. I hoped Sarah and Curly John weren't watching. Then I remembered they didn't believe in having a television or anything else electrical in their house—probably had it turned off in the hospital, too.

I held Charity up in my arms, gazing into her eyes. "How would you like to grow up Amish? You'd never have to worry about eating junk food. Nope. You'd have fresh fruits and vegetables and lots of rich milk to drink."

She cooed a little.

"I really wish your first mama and daddy had loved you more," I surprised myself by saying. "But don't worry. You have a heavenly

Father who cared enough to send you here so we could find you a terrific home."

Mom peeked her head around the corner. "Is that you talking, Mer?"

I smiled. "Charity and I are having a sisterly chat."

"Just checking," she said and left.

"Now, where were we?" I touched her soft cheek. "Oh yes. I think I might've already found some parents for you. They don't know about it, though. When Dad comes home tonight, we'll discuss it." I stopped talking and listened to her sweet gurgling sounds.

"Merry, if the doorbell rings, will you let Miss Spindler in?" Mom called from the kitchen.

"Miss Spindler's coming over?"

"She wants to see the baby again," she answered.

"Okay."

Soon I heard Mom going upstairs. Had she called Old Hawk Eyes? I certainly hadn't heard the phone ring.

Feeling a bit gloomy, I thought back to the first night Charity and I had spent together. "You're mighty little to have already experienced your first sleepover. And outside, too . . ." I remembered Faithie's insistence on sleeping outside with me in the gazebo so long ago.

The doorbell rang, putting an end to my reverie. I peeked out through the curtains. It was Miss Spindler, all right. Dressed to the hilt.

"Come in," I said, opening the screen door. "Mom was expecting you."

"I've made some more outfits for Charity." Her voice was softer than I'd ever heard it. She looked down at the baby in my arms as though she'd just seen an angel. "My, oh my, if she hasn't grown in just two days."

I smiled, leading her into the family room, where she sat in the rocker nearest the window. I knew she was eager to hold the baby, so I relinquished Charity and went to get some iced tea for our guest. While I was in the kitchen, I poked my head into the stairwell leading upstairs. "Mom, Miss Spindler's here."

"I'll be right down," she said. "Make her some iced tea, will you?"

I congratulated myself on thinking ahead. Mom's hostess mentality was beginning to rub off, it seemed.

"Here we are," I said to Miss Spindler, the way Mom always did.

"Why, thank you, dear." She placed the glass on the windowsill, gently rocking. "I heard tell that young Sarah and Curly John had an unfortunate event happen just yesterday."

"It's very sad," I replied, pulling up a chair.

"Seems to me, they'd be needing some cheering up."

I nodded. "I'd like to visit Sarah when she gets home from the hospital."

"Well, I was thinking the very same thing. And while we're at it"—and here she lowered her voice—"why don't we take Charity along for an outing? You know, she absolutely loved riding in that little car seat I bought."

I wondered about Miss Spindler's comment. Was she thinking of the baby—getting her out for a ride—or was she thinking of Sarah? Then I wondered right out loud. "What do you think about Sarah holding a baby—you know, Charity? Do you think it would comfort her, or would it make her feel worse?"

A surprising thing happened as I looked into Ruby Spindler's face. Her eyes filled with tears, and her face ... her face began to shine with sheer joy. "Oh, Merry, you have no idea what holding this baby would do for the poor girl. Why, let me tell you something, dear."

Mom had crept in as Miss Spindler was talking, but she held her finger to her lips as the old woman continued.

"For as long as I remember, I've longed for a child. Of course, not being a married lady made it quite impossible, from my way of thinking. But when I first set eyes on this here youngster," she glanced lovingly at Charity, now wide awake, "I knew that I would be made whole if I could just hold her in my arms. I felt as Simeon of old, who longed to see the Christ child. He knew that he would not die until he held the baby Jesus in his arms and blessed Him."

I listened, truly amazed.

"Yes, my dear, this baby, abandoned and alone in the world, has brought great comfort to my heart." She sighed, touching Charity's hand. "And I do believe she'll do the same for poor, hurting Sarah."

Mom's eyes filled with tears, and when I looked up she didn't try to hide them as they spilled down her cheeks. Mom agreed with Miss Spindler. I knew it by the tender look on her face. It wouldn't be long before we'd be taking baby Charity on a very special outing—to visit Sarah Zook.

Twenty *A Cry in the Dark*

I was sound asleep when Dad arrived home from his late shift at the hospital. He was dressed and gone before dawn the next morning, so I knew our talk would have to wait several more days.

In the meantime, Mom gave her consent for Miss Spindler to take Charity and me to visit Sarah Zook. Rachel wanted to come along, too, so the four of us squeezed into the jazzy red sports car bright and early Friday morning. Rachel sat up in the bucket seat next to Old Hawk Eyes, while I sat in the back next to Charity in her infant seat.

"How's Sarah doing?" I asked Rachel.

She turned around and looked through the wide opening between the seats. "Sarah's a strong, healthy girl. She was out helping Curly John yesterday in the field."

"Really?" I was glad to hear it.

"Her body's doin' fine, but her heart, well, that's a whole 'nother story." Rachel's eyes told the truth. "She's a-hurtin' and nothin'—no one—can make the pain stop."

Miss Spindler glanced at Rachel. "She knows we're coming, though, right?"

Rachel nodded. "I told her Merry was baby-sittin' and would it be all right to bring the baby along."

"And what did she say to that?" Miss Spindler seemed too eager.

Rachel shrugged. "Oh, she didn't mind. She was glad to hear that company was comin'."

"Company, eh?" Miss Spindler cackled. And I knew she had something up her sleeve.

Sarah looked a bit pale when she answered the front door. "Wilkom," she said, noticing the baby immediately. "Come and sit."

I carried Charity inside in her infant car seat. Miss Spindler directed me to unbuckle her and take her out promptly. "How would you like to be cooped up in one of them there things?" She waved her hand at it.

Happily, I did as I was told. Being close to Charity—with her nestled in my arms—was the best place to be.

Evidently, Miss Spindler felt the same way. No sooner had I settled into one of Sarah's hickory rockers, when here came Ruby cooing and carrying on. "Let me hold the little angel," she said.

Sarah leaned forward, her eyes riveted. "Ach, what a perty baby!"

Rachel, sitting next to Sarah, nodded. "And she's gut, too, jah?" Rachel remarked.

I smiled. "I think she must be the best baby I've ever taken care of."

"Believe you me, this here little one is a gift straight from the throne of God," Miss Spindler said. I could tell she meant every word, too. Her eyes beamed as she smiled at Charity.

We chatted with Sarah, talking about the weather and asking about her quilting projects. It was hard not to notice the baby things scattered around the living room, which was as sparsely furnished as most Old Order Amish front rooms.

It broke my heart to see the large, handmade cradle in the corner of the room. I wondered why someone hadn't put it away. A cradle!

What a sad reminder to the young husband and wife. Sad and sorrowful. I had a powerful urge to get up and hide it in the attic!

Sarah stood up, motioning to Rachel. "Wouldja like a piece of pie—black raspberry? I just made it fresh before ya came."

"I'd love a piece," Miss Spindler said, glancing at me.

"Sounds good, thanks," I said.

While Sarah and Rachel were out in the kitchen, Miss Spindler turned Charity over on her stomach, laying her across her lap. "She likes the world upside-down this way," she said. "I think it helps get the gas off her tummy."

I had no idea where Miss Spindler had picked up all these tips on baby care. But it touched my heart, seeing Charity so loved by the lonely old woman. How we had misunderstood her!

Sarah carried a tray of dishes filled with large servings of raspberry pie for each of us. When she came to Miss Spindler, whose lap was plumb full with Charity, Sarah offered to hold the baby. "Ya need some space to enjoy yer pie," she said.

I grinned. It was the very thing Ruby Spindler had hoped for. Her expression gave her away, and I knew the true reason why we'd come to see Sarah today.

Dad was waiting for our talk when I arrived home with Charity. "How was your visit with Sarah?" he asked.

"She seems better, I think."

Mom took the baby from me and kissed her. "We hoped Sarah's seeing little Charity wouldn't upset her unduly."

I sat on the green paisley sofa next to Dad. "You probably won't believe it—I know *I* didn't."

"What do you mean?" Mom held Charity close. It was as though she were holding her breath, as well.

"Charity was just what the doctor ordered," I said, using Miss Spindler's expression. "Sarah literally fell in love with our baby." I realized what I'd said. "Uh . . . I mean, *the* baby."

Dad caught on and, rubbing his chin, said, "Your mother tells me you've been wanting to talk about that."

I was determined to go through with it—my change of heart. And after today, after I'd witnessed the transformation in Sarah Zook, I knew I'd have the courage to spell it out for Dad. For Mom, too.

"To begin with, I've been awfully selfish about lots of things around here. But most of all about the baby. Neither of you know it, but last week I prayed a very selfish prayer. When I found Charity in the gazebo, I just assumed she was meant for me . . . for us."

Dad folded his hands, giving me his undivided attention. "Don't be too hard on yourself, Mer. You're just a kid."

"Dad!"

"In *my* book you are." He squeezed my elbow. "Go on."

I stared at Charity, who was waving her tiny fists the way she had the night I found her. "Everyone loves this baby. And everyone who sees her wants to get their hands on her—to adopt her."

Dad nodded thoughtfully.

"You and Mom—what do you want to do about adopting Charity?"

Mom spoke up. "We've been thinking and praying all week about it."

"So have I," I said, remembering my experience in the willow grove.

"And what have you decided?" Dad asked. "We want your input, as well."

I was hesitant to just blurt it out. Mom had overheard Miss Spindler talking with me—the day she revealed how Charity had comforted her and made her feel whole somehow. Mom had cried at the old woman's sentiments.

"As hard as it would be to give Charity up, I think it's the right thing to do. There are couples waiting—women who can't have babies. Hurting people . . ." I couldn't go on. It was too hard to sit here in the same room as my little foster sister and talk about giving her away.

"We've been thinking the same thing," Mom said softly.

I was relieved.

It was Dad's turn. "The Lord's been good to your mother and me—giving us three beautiful babies—and having the blessing of seeing two of them grow up." He didn't continue, but it was what he left unsaid that spoke loudest.

Charity would be dearly loved here, but when another family was approved and ready, she would leave us. She would bring love to a couple whose waiting arms were empty.

The next day was the church potluck. We dressed Charity up in one of my old sunsuits with a lace-trimmed sun hat to match. She was the object of everyone's affection. Even Jon Klein enjoyed talking to her in alliteration-eze. In fact, he and I played our word game until the cows came home. Of course, there were no cows on the church grounds—it's one of those silly things people say around here.

And Charity? Things *did* work out for her to go live with Curly John and Sarah. Thanks to Dad's arranging it. They had to have a home study, a caseworker, and a financial statement for Social Services, but when it was finally all said and done, they were the happiest couple this side of the Conestoga River.

I was mighty happy myself. After all, there aren't many baby-sitters around who'll work for nothing. And that's just what I did. Offered my services to the sweetest baby on SummerHill.

Miss Spindler was elated. She kept making crocheted outfits and booties to match. Perhaps too many, but you couldn't stop her. She was a giver, I'd discovered. And give, she did!

Skip finally came home from camp, packed up, and left for college. He was fine with the decision to let Charity go.

Now the house is empty . . . and quiet. Sometimes too quiet. But I'm finding ways to fill it with noise. Like the sleepovers Lissa and I have planned.

As for Lissa's grammy, she's coming to Lancaster in October—wants me to take pictures of Lissa when the leaves turn. She's insisting on paying for my services, which she thought looked mighty professional. Maybe between baby-sitting and picture taking, I'll have enough experience to land a real job. In the meantime, I'm writing letters to Levi and getting good at Jon's alliteration word game.

Charity started rolling over and trying to say, "Mam," which is what the Amish call their mothers. Her name's been legally changed to Mary Zook. The first name's for me, except no Amish family would ever spell it M-e-r-r-y. But it's an honor to have the baby of my dreams with a given name that *sounds* like mine.

As for me, I'm working on the Miss Fix-It label. I'm going to try to be more content with what I have—with what God's given me. It's a new beginning.

So is being a sophomore at James Buchanan High. It's unbelievable what happened when I entered a photography contest. Who would've thought that Ashley Horton and I would go head to head over a silly contest—*and* the Alliteration Wizard—in the same month!

But that's another story. . . .

From Beverly . . . To You

I'm delighted that you're reading SUMMERHILL SECRETS. Merry Hanson is such a fascinating character—I can't begin to count the times I laughed while writing her humorous scenes. And I must admit, I always cry with her.

Not so long ago, I was Merry's age, growing up in Lancaster County, the home of the Pennsylvania Dutch—my birthplace. My grandma Buchwalter was a Mennonite, as were many of my mother's aunts, uncles, and cousins. Some of my school friends were also Mennonite, so my interest and appreciation for the Plain folk began early.

It is they, the Mennonite and Amish people—farmers, carpenters, blacksmiths, shopkeepers, quiltmakers, teachers, schoolchildren, and bed-and-breakfast owners—who best assisted me with the research for this series. Even though I have kept their identities private, I am thankful for these wonderfully honest and helpful friends.

To learn more about my writing, sign up for my e-newsletter, or contact me, visit my Web site, *www.beverlylewis.com.*

Be the first to know

Want to be the first to know
what's new from
your favorite authors?

Want to know all about
exciting new writers?

Sign up for Bethany House newsletters at
www.bethanynewsletters.com
and you'll get regular updates via e-mail.
You can sign up for specific authors or
categories so you get only
the information you really want.

Sign up today